PRAISE

Do You Take T

"Denise Williams is known for her swoon-worthy tales that celebrate love, and her latest rom-com follows suit!"

—*Woman's World*

"If, hypothetically, Denise Williams decided to establish an academy (let's call it the University of DW) and offered courses on how to write pent-up sexual tension, steamy banter, and enemies to lovers, I would burst into the classroom and yell, 'TAKE MY MONEY!!' The writing is unmatched, the chemistry is on fire, and *Do You Take This Man* has one of the steamiest, most addictive, most satisfyingly hard-earned happily ever afters I've read in ages!"

—Ali Hazelwood, *New York Times* bestselling author of *Love, Theoretically*

"Denise Williams has mastered the art of writing fun, sexy banter. Smart and witty with the perfect amount of steam, *Do You Take This Man* is a gift to romance readers."

—Farrah Rochon, *New York Times* bestselling author of *The Hookup Plan*

"Once again, Denise Williams masterfully blends humor and heart with the perfect amount of steam. *Do You Take This Man* is full of authentic characters with relatable issues, hilarious wedding hijinks, and swoony sexy times. Lear earns a place on my list of favorite heroes, and Williams cements her spot on my list of favorite writers."

—Falon Ballard, author of *Just My Type*

"This annoyances-to-lovers story is steamy like the most luxurious bubble bath! Readers are in for a beautiful ride watching the deliciously prickly RJ learn to let someone care for her body and soul. Denise Williams consistently crafts romances that are so sweetly real. Her voice shines—fullhearted and playful—through every scene."

—Rosie Danan, author of *Do Your Worst*

"Denise Williams delivers again with twice the banter, twice the heat, and the best enemies-to-lovers tension. A stellar romance!" —Jane Igharo, author of *Where We End & Begin*

PRAISE FOR
The Fastest Way to Fall

"This entertaining read will have you sweating through your next workout." —*Good Morning America*

"Warm, fuzzy, and ridiculously cute, *The Fastest Way to Fall* is the perfect feel-good read. Britta is an absolute breath of fresh air, and Wes is everything I love in a romantic lead. It's been weeks since I read this book, and I still smile every time I think about it. If you're looking for a novel that feels like a hug, this is it!"

—Emily Henry, #1 *New York Times* bestselling author of *Happy Place*

"Funny, flirtatious, and full of heart, *The Fastest Way to Fall* is an absolute winner! I loved tagging along with upbeat and utterly relatable Britta as she tries new things, gets strong, and meets her perfect match in Wes. I fell head over heels and never wanted it to end."

—Libby Hubscher, author of *Play for Me*

"An addictive romance filled with hilarious banter, sharp and engaging dialogue, heartfelt moments, and a real and empowering heroine worth cheering for. The love between Britta and Wes blooms gradually and realistically and is sure to utterly capture your heart."

—Jane Igharo, author of *Where We End & Begin*

"This charming, sexy novel pairs two people who likely would never have connected outside of an app. . . . Their slow-burn romance feels delightfully old-fashioned."

—Washington Independent Review of Books

"Williams follows *How to Fail at Flirting* with another delightfully engaging romance full of humor and surprises. Fans of Jennifer Weiner may like this one." —*Booklist*

"A body-positive, feel-good romance with highly relatable protagonists." —*Library Journal* (starred review)

"There's a lot to like in this romance with its supportive leading man, delightful heroine, and dynamic secondary cast. There's more than just romance going on, and Williams excels at juggling all the parts. . . . An emotionally resonant and thoughtful novel." —*Kirkus Reviews*

"*The Fastest Way to Fall* is not a story about weight loss, but about learning to love who you are and about falling in love with someone who helps you feel strong. Britta's triumph over her former insecurities concerning her body, her goals, and her job are transcendent moments thanks to Williams's sensitive and masterful storytelling." —*BookPage*

PRAISE FOR *How to Fail at Flirting*

"In this steamy romance, Naya Turner is an overachieving math professor blowing off work stress with a night on the town, which leads to a night with a dapper stranger. And then another, and another. She's smitten by the time she realizes there's a professional complication, and the relationship could put her job at risk. Williams blends rom-com fun with more weighty topics in her winsome debut."

—*The Washington Post*

"Denise Williams's *How to Fail at Flirting* is absolutely SPECTACULAR! Ripe with serious, real-life drama, teeming with playful banter, rich with toe-curling passion, full of heart-melting romance. . . . Her debut grabbed me on page one and held me enthralled until the end, when I promptly started rereading to enjoy the deliciousness again."

—Priscilla Oliveras, *USA Today* bestselling author of *Kiss Me, Catalina*

"*How to Fail at Flirting* is a charming and compelling debut from Denise Williams that's as moving as it is romantic. Williams brings the banter, heat, and swoons, while also giving us a character who learns that standing up for herself is as important—and terrifying—as allowing herself to fall in love. Put 'Read *How to Fail at Flirting*' at the top of your to-do list!"

—Jen DeLuca, *USA Today* bestselling author of *Well Traveled*

"Naya and Jake's relationship is both sexy and sweet as these two people, who love their work but are not skilled at socializing or romance, find their way forward. Academia is vividly portrayed, and readers will await the next book from Williams, a talented debut author and a PhD herself."

—*Booklist*

"*How to Fail at Flirting* is a powerhouse romance. Not only is it funny and charming and steamy, but it possesses an emotional depth that touched my heart. Naya is a beautiful and relatable main character who is hardworking, loyal, spirited, and determined to move on from an abusive relationship. It was thrilling to see her find her power in her personal life, her career, and through her romance with Jake. And I cheered when she claimed the happily ever after she so deserved."

—Sarah Echavarre Smith, author of *The Boy with the Bookstore*

"Williams's debut weaves a charming, romantic love story about a heroine rediscovering her voice and standing up for her passions."

—Andie J. Christopher, *USA Today* bestselling author of *Unrealistic Expectations*

"*How to Fail at Flirting* delivers on every level. It's funny, sexy, heartwarming, and emotional. With its engaging, lovable characters, fresh plot, and compelling narrative, I did not want to put it down! It's in my top reads of the year for sure!"

—Samantha Young, *New York Times* bestselling author of *The Love Plot*

"The warmth in Denise Williams's writing is unmistakable, as is her wit. She tackles difficult subjects, difficult emotions, with such empathy and thoughtfulness. Best of all: Jake is just the type of hero I love—sexy, smart, sweet, and smitten."

—Olivia Dade, national bestselling author of *Ship Wrecked*

TITLES BY DENISE WILLIAMS

How to Fail at Flirting
The Fastest Way to Fall
The Love Connection
The Missed Connection
The Sweetest Connection
Do You Take This Man
Love and Other Flight Delays
Technically Yours

0100 01001111 01001111 01001111 01001111 01001111 01001111 01001111 01001111 00111

01001111 01001111 01001111 01001111 01001111 01001111 01001111 0100111

Technically Yours

Denise Williams

Berkley Romance
New York

BERKLEY ROMANCE
Published by Berkley
An imprint of Penguin Random House LLC
penguinrandomhouse.com

Library of Congress Cataloging-in-Publication Data

Names: Williams, Denise, 1982- author.
Title: Technically yours / Denise Williams.
Description: First edition. | New York: Berkley Romance, 2023.
Identifiers: LCCN 2023013969 (print) | LCCN 2023013970 (ebook) |
ISBN 9780593437216 (trade paperback) | ISBN 9780593437223 (ebook)
Subjects: LCGFT: Romance fiction. | Novels.
Classification: LCC PS3623.I556497 T43 2023 (print) |
LCC PS3623.I556497 (ebook) | DDC 813/.6—dc23/eng/20230327
LC record available at https://lccn.loc.gov/2023013969
LC ebook record available at https://lccn.loc.gov/2023013970

First Edition: December 2023

Printed in the United States of America
1st Printing

Book design by Ashley Tucker

For T.
01101001 01110100 00100111 01110011 00100000 01100001 01101100 01110111 01100001 01111001 01110011 00100000 01100010 01100101 01100101 01101110 00100000 01111001 01101111 01110101 00001010

A NOTE FROM THE AUTHOR: This love story contains mention of pregnancy and gaslighting from a previous romantic partner that is identified. Please take care while reading.

Technically Yours

01101 01001111 01001111 01001111 0100

CHAPTER 1

Cord

Five Years Earlier

WHEN SHE WALKED OUT THE DOOR, THE SCENT OF her lingered in the air like a reminder of the what-ifs burrowing into my head, and I stared at the set of house keys on my desk. The two identical cuts sat side by side, the light reflecting on the surface of the metal. Since Pearl had made her choice, I needed to let her walk away and set off on the path she'd chosen. I needed to give up on all the nights under the stars, and the feel of her skin dusted with sand, and my pathetic heart. I knew that, but I was still on my feet and halfway to the door before the sound of her heels on the tile had faded.

"Wait," I called out. The overhead lighting against the dark sky outside the office windows was like a muted spotlight making the white of her shirt that much brighter against her skin. Her gaze had traveled back down the hall toward my door, and our eyes met for an instant. "Pearl. Wait."

At my approach, she turned, giving me her back and a view of the nape of her neck, the soft and supple skin I'd wanted to kiss a hundred times. "I don't think we have anything else to say to each other."

My instinct was to step back, to walk away and let her

go. But damnit, this was Pearl. I shifted so I was close enough to feel the warmth of her body and waited for her to pull away. I was basically asking for the pain of more rejection, but then she shifted toward me, one tiny, incremental movement, and I slid my fingertips down her biceps, the contact between us like a thousand micro shock waves on my skin. "Will you look at me?" I didn't stop the slide of my fingertips over her arms. "Please."

Her eyes met mine and held when she turned to face me, resignation in her voice. "What's left to say?"

"I just want to know one thing," I said. A crease settled between her brows and I gently wrapped my hand around her wrist, raising it so we could both see her tattoo. "Your heart." I grazed my thumb across her wrist, pausing on the third star inked there. "If it spoke louder than your head, what would it say right now?"

"Cord, what does it matter?"

I lifted her wrist higher in response, breaking eye contact with her to examine the stars I'd memorized while hoping for something more between us. "It matters to me." I spoke against the tattoo, my lips brushing over her skin, and I could feel the hitch of her breath.

"It doesn't matter what my heart would say, because . . ." Pearl brushed hair off my forehead, the contact making me close my eyes for a second. This was the moment. This was *our* moment, and I didn't want to lose it. Behind her, the doors to the elevator opened, but she didn't move as we continued to search each other's faces. The words hung between us, unfinished, while she brushed the same spot again and then slid her fingers into my hair. "Because my heart is unreliable."

Our lips were a breath apart in the empty lobby, but the

whole space felt full, full of everything I knew we both wanted, everything we could be. My voice was low when I spoke. "Nothing about you is unreliable." I drew her closer, and the soft way she leaned into me felt both familiar and brand-new.

"I should listen to my head." She stepped back, not letting go. "I need to listen to my head."

With her back against the wall, I inched closer, my hand now firmly at her waist. "But what would your *heart* say?" Pearl wore delicate diamond studs that gently scratched my lip when I spoke near her ear. "Because it should get a say."

"Cord . . ." She let my name hang there. I don't know if she moved first or I did, but then our mouths met, lips and tongues melding in the way I'd imagined for so long. The kiss deepened, and my whole body reacted to every move of her soft lips. The way she held me, fingers digging in, made me feel claimed in the best way.

"Don't go," I panted, breaking the kiss and then taking her mouth again, holding her lower back to pull her flush against me. When she rocked her hips, soft meeting hard, I groaned, needing more. "Stay with me." I trailed my lips down her jaw before finding her lips again, my palm at her neck to hold her to me.

Pearl deepened the kiss, her fingers in my hair like an answer, but then she stepped back, eyes wide and the pulse in her neck throbbing. "It's too risky." She fumbled behind her and pushed the down button as I regained my senses.

"What? No. I don't understand." My heart pounded, and I shook my head as if rebooting this moment.

When the doors opened behind her, I thought about reaching out, of pulling her back into the kiss, but she'd stepped out of reach on purpose. "If I could put heart first for anyone, Cord, it would have been you." She took two steps backward into the waiting car.

"But . . . but it *can* be me." I wished I had more practice fighting, because I wanted to fight for her, get her footsteps to move toward me and not away, but my head still spun from that kiss. "You can put your heart first with me right now."

"It's not what I need. I don't want . . . I can't want this. You know I can't." Pearl shook her head as the doors began to close. "But I wish I could."

By the time I lunged forward, my brain connecting with my body, the doors had shut and I was left in the empty lobby, with the imprint of her kiss on my lips and every muscle in my body poised to follow her and fight for this. But she didn't want to fight, and she was already gone. Still, I waited for the doors to open, holding my breath in hopes she'd change her mind.

I waited a long time, staring at my warped reflection in the elevator doors before deciding I would never wait like that again and never put myself in a situation where I wanted to.

CHAPTER 2

Pearl

Present Day

AS I FLIPPED OVER MY PHONE, THE THIN GOLD bracelet on my wrist caught the light, the chain cutting through the four small stars tattooed on my wrist.

Shea: Show me the dress.

Pearl: I'm not taking a selfie. I'm in the middle of the first big social event of my career.

Shea: I know you look bangable.

Pearl: Bangable isn't my aim. I'm working right now.

Shea: Your aim lacks creativity. This is why I'm the fun sister.

I brushed my fingers against the smooth satin of the gold floor-length gown before slipping my phone into my clutch and closing it with a gentle, satisfying snap. The wash of the cool breeze from the air-conditioning swept over the exposed skin at my back, and I straightened at the prickling sensation. The room swirled with people, and before I stepped back into the hall, I surveyed the countless donors and supporters in formal wear.

On the far side of the room, Ellie Dawson laughed with a trio of people in their seventies. The two of us had started in our new roles a few weeks earlier, and I knew in the coming years we'd compete to secure a promotion to director when the current director retired. After five years in California, I'd come back to Chicago for the right job and to leave the wrong man. Ironic, since what I thought was the right job took me to the West Coast in the first place, even though it had been impossibly hard to leave. Now I was focused on OurCode. Taking another deep breath, I reminded myself that this was *the* job. After everything I'd gone through to get to this point, this room and these new faces were an essential part of my next steps, and I couldn't afford for anything to distract me.

I stepped inside and reviewed my game plan for the evening, particularly who I was supposed to connect with based on our pre-gala preparations. OurCode, like other programs designed to encourage kids with traditionally marginalized identities to take an interest in coding and careers in tech, had support across the industry and a solid reputation. The assembled crowd had paid a thousand dollars a head to attend and would donate more to support the program's expansion to serve more kids in more ways. That expansion was a priority for the board and my boss, Kendra, and the gala was going to be the launching pad for our new plans. I scanned the room for Kendra again. It was odd that she hadn't arrived yet.

"Pearl, a minute?" The chairperson of the OurCode board touched my elbow. Kevin wore a tux, his entire look put together, except for a deep crease between his brows.

He was also the CEO of Kaleidescape, a cybersecurity company whose stock had risen fast, and he wore a harried expression on his face.

"Sure."

He waved Ellie over as well, and we walked toward a corner of the ballroom, where he waved off any pleasantries. "Kendra isn't coming tonight."

To my right, Ellie stilled, her shock seeming to register along with mine. "What?" and "Why?" came from us at the same time.

"I can't get into the details for legal reasons, but she has resigned from OurCode, effective immediately." Kevin's tone was hushed, and both of us leaned forward.

"She quit?" Ellie's voice was a hiss, and she shook her head as if trying to slot the new information into existing grooves in her brain.

The impatience that bled into his tone made it clear he wasn't planning to give us any further information. "She is no longer affiliated with the program."

I intentionally took a slow breath before speaking, the combined weight of the bodies behind us suddenly making me feel claustrophobic. "There are hundreds of people here expecting to learn about the future of the program. We arranged everything around Kendra making those announcements. What are we going to do?" In my head, I pictured the detailed plans we'd spent weeks on, the speech we'd crafted, the hours spent toiling over the right wording and how to frame the strategic goals.

"One of you will have to give the speech." He still looked like he'd rather be anywhere else.

"That will raise red flags," Ellie said. "Can you do it as chair?"

Kevin ignored her question. "Neither of you knows the speech?"

My stomach dropped, and I pulled my sweaty palms away from the fabric of my dress. "I know the speech, but . . ."

"Okay, well, Pearl, you do it. Come Monday, we'll figure the rest out. You *can* do it, right?"

I glanced to my left, expecting Ellie to step in, to take the spotlight, but she'd literally taken a step back, so I returned my gaze to Kevin. "I could, but wouldn't it be better coming from you or another board member?" *Or someone who isn't petrified by the idea of standing on a stage.*

He glanced over my shoulder, a polished expression returning to his features when he made eye contact with someone else. "I'm sure you'll be fine." He held up a hand to whoever had caught his eye. "We'll touch base afterward. Excuse me."

He left us standing in unsteady silence, and Ellie turned to me. "What the hell just happened?"

Just me volunteering to speak in front of three hundred people because our boss is mysteriously gone. I took another quick breath, knowing I didn't get to lose it, not in this space and not in this room.

Ellie's tone was doubtful, and I realized our moment of shared uncertainty was already over. "Are you sure you can give the speech?"

Even though I wasn't, her tone irked me. "I don't have a choice." *And it's not like you stepped up.* I gave her a slight smile and searched the stage for the notebook containing a printout of the speech along with reference materials. That notebook contained everything I'd need to cram before getting onstage and coming face-to-face with my fear of public speaking, and I reluctantly left Ellie to mingle with donors while I prepared.

Once I sat backstage with the binder, I let myself freak out, now that there was no one around I needed to think I was bulletproof. I'd never been one to let my guard down at work, certainly not in this new position. The only time I had was when I worked at FitMi, and even then, it was really just with one person.

Cord's face filled my mind. His sable-brown eyes and long lashes—lashes many people would kill for—and his hair that was always a little too long, falling over his face and tempting me to brush it back, the wayward strands begging for my fingers. He could have been the right man for me in a different universe. Cord told me once that he'd give me a sign if he was in the room and I had to do something hard. He'd met my eyes and told me I could speak directly to him, and he'd be smiling. I sipped from my glass of wine and grinned at the memory. He'd been so sure that if I ever had to be on a stage, he'd be there to support me. That was when the idea of us as a couple was a fantasy I only allowed myself to entertain when there was time to wrestle my heart and imagination back under control. That was before there was a real chance and then a real choice. And it was before I made that choice.

He'd been my boss, then we'd been friends, and one night, I'd given in to the urge to brush the hair off his face, and we'd almost been so much more. Now he was nothing, and we hadn't spoken in years. I let my eyes fall closed, the sounds of the hum of conversation and smatterings of laughter rising over the din of the bustling hall. They were all going to be staring at me. My neck heated, and the dress felt too small, but there was no choice—I couldn't go back to Kevin and tell him I couldn't do it or that I was scared.

I opened my eyes and read through the speech again, even though I didn't need to. I'd written it and practically had it memorized. I did not know what would happen in the organization without Kendra, but three weeks into a new job, I didn't intend to be the weak link. Ellie was hoping I'd at least stumble, giving her the upper hand.

Not today.

The lights dimmed, and the volume rose with the sounds of people moving toward seats. I imagined a sea of black tuxes spotted with colorful gowns and pastel satin moving between the tables like water, everyone full of dinner and cocktails. After a quick check-in with the student speaker I'd be introducing, I smoothed my hair, checking my edges, then rested a palm on my stomach and took another slow breath. *Okay.*

My fingers shook as I clutched the notebook, and the memory of Cord's too-long hair and baritone voice once again filled my head. *Speak to me. I'll be smiling.*

I decided I would still picture him—even though I'd made sure he would never actually be there—and I stepped out onto the stage.

CHAPTER 3

Cord

"THANKS FOR COMING WITH ME TONIGHT." ABBY smiled over one bare shoulder as we stepped into the elevator.

We'd both been focused on our phones until the play of light off their dress caught my eye. I watched the precise way Abby moved and tucked the phone away, and the movement made me think of someone else from my past. They were both smart and funny, but even though we'd been seeing each other for several months, Abby didn't invade my thoughts like Pearl had. I appreciated that. It was freeing not to be consumed by someone else. It was why I'd closed that door in my mind years earlier. Another couple joined us, and I stepped closer. "My place tonight?" I asked in a low voice.

"Maybe. I have an early yoga class." Abby started talking to someone they knew in a purple gown and linked their fingers with mine. We'd been hooking up and hanging out for months—a handhold wasn't that intimate, but it felt settled and committed, something I didn't plan to be. That was something I'd given up wanting years ago.

I caught my reflection. With my hand in my pocket and

wearing a tux, I almost didn't recognize myself. Standing there with Abby on my arm, I looked like someone who was comfortable in this kind of environment and not like someone wishing this night were already over. I glanced around the car, taking in the mirrored reflection from all angles and tuning out the conversation. I never stepped into an elevator anymore without thinking about Pearl, even after five years. And I could almost picture the way her heels would accentuate her legs and how her subtle scent would fill the small space. I'd moved on and learned my lesson about falling so hard, but elevators always brought back memories.

"Earth to Cord?" Abby nudged me, still smiling. The doors had opened, and the other two couples were ahead, moving toward the sounds from the ballroom filtering into the hall.

"Sorry."

Abby slid an arm through mine and teased me good-naturedly. "I demand you stop thinking about work. Give yourself a night off."

It was normally a good guess. Work always seemed to be taking over every thought, even when I was doing things I enjoyed. Even when I was spending time with Abby. We were the same that way, and it was why we worked well together.

"Sure. Of course. Sorry, Ab." A jazz ensemble version of "Fly Me to the Moon" was the background to the buzz of conversations as we walked into the crowded room.

Abby had volunteered for OurCode for more than a year, mentoring a high school student interested in coding. They'd tried to convince me for months to volunteer, too, and pushed me as far as signing up and going through the initial background check, but I always begged off finishing the training—I didn't have the time, and I didn't particularly like teenagers. I hadn't liked teenagers when I *was* a teenager. The least I could do was attend this fundraiser and donate.

I brushed my forehead—an old habit, only my hair was shorter now and pushed back off my face. I glanced around and stifled the urge to shove my hand in my pocket. Mingling and small talk over cocktails were part of my life now, and luckily my date was skilled at the talking part, moving from group to group, introducing me, and then leading the conversation. Screens hanging from the ceiling showed pictures of kids in the program, along with inspiring quotes. It wasn't as if the dearth of women and Black and Brown people in coding and programming was new to me. Before moving into a management role, I'd been in the trenches—usually trenches full of guys who looked like me.

"And Cord is—" Abby's voice cut into my thoughts, and I jerked my head back to the conversation. My adoring partner gave me one of their chiding looks—that was about as critical as the looks ever were. This one meant *pay attention*. "Cord heads up FitMi, the fitness app." Abby glanced from person to person, reading their faces.

I nodded, giving the expected smile. "Yep, that's me."

"I've been trying to get him involved with OurCode for ages, right, honey?"

I hated the pet name, and my tie felt too tight around my neck. The name had been used a few times lately, and it was a reminder that I needed to cut this off before things got serious. "Yeah."

The three people all pounced in a chorus of "Yes!" and "You should!" and I smiled awkwardly until they returned to their conversation, though none of them seemed to notice my discomfort.

I was subtly counting the sections in the ceiling when a tap on my shoulder pulled me out of it. "Matthews, I thought I saw you come in."

"Hey, man. How are you?" I shook hands with Kevin Corbin. We'd started in IT around the same time, two green software developers at the bottom of the hierarchy. We'd never been friends, exactly, but we shared beers every now and again and were friendly at work. Back then, it seemed unfathomable that we'd run into each other at something like this.

"Can I borrow you for a minute?"

We stepped to the side, and he held up his glass of scotch. "You want anything?"

I waved the offer away. "What's up?"

"You remember when I took the fall for the issues with the FreeWall project back in the day?"

I chuckled at the memory. There'd been four of us working together and deciding to take risks that didn't pay off. Corbin took the bullet when the project's management team came down on us for our massive mistake, born of overconfidence and misplaced dreams of glory. "You finally calling in your favor?"

He took a swig from his glass and nodded. "In a big way. I need you to join the board for this thing," he said, motioning around the room.

I followed his hand as if it would give me more information. "For . . . OurCode? Why?"

"Keep this between us, okay?"

I nodded. "Sure."

"We had to ask for the immediate resignation of the executive director this afternoon. She was screwing a board member."

"Wow. You fired her on the spot?"

"There were . . . additional factors that tipped my hand. This is going to get out, probably soon, and I need someone else I trust on the board to make sure the ship sails straight through this."

I took in his expression, the exhaustion around the eyes. I wanted to help the guy, but glancing around at the over-the-top self-congratulating happening around the room, I was pretty sure this wasn't for me. "Oh, wow. I . . . don't really have time."

Kevin scrubbed a hand over his jaw. "I know, and I'm begging." He grinned and lowered his voice. "This is PR gold. Press from that most-eligible-bachelor-in-tech thing must be wearing off, right? Though it looks like you need no help in that department." He motioned to Abby, and I wished I had a drink in my hand.

"Don't remind me about that article," I joked. That was the first and last time I ever let FitMi communications people talk me into discussing my personal life for print. Once was all it took to have people seeking me out, though. Overnight, I'd gone from a lovesick recluse stuck on Pearl to a guy committed to moving on. And on. And then on again. My elderly neighbor told me she'd looked it up, and I was a textbook serial monogamist. I'd really just been chasing a high I never quite reached, and it took me a while to realize it wasn't worth chasing. The last few years, I'd committed to the kinds of arrangements Abby and I had. Casual. Fun. No risk of upending my life or making myself spiral for someone else.

I was working out how to get out of Kevin's request

when the lights flashed and the crowd shifted toward their tables. Abby waved from our table nearby, motioning to my empty chair.

"Excuse me," Kevin said, clapping my shoulder and nodding to someone across the room. "Think about it, okay? We can talk later this week."

We went our separate ways and I strode toward the table, figuring out how to turn him down. I didn't have time to add another thing to my workload, and I definitely didn't want to volunteer to step into some organization on the brink of scandal caused by mismanagement.

Kevin stepped to the stage as the lights fell, and he introduced himself and began a brief history of the program, a series of slides scrolling behind him. I let my mind wander to possible excuses—I was in the middle of expanding programs and services. The house still needed work, and Kevin should consider asking someone other than a white man. If he was worried about appearances, that would look better, anyway, and definitely *be* better in the long run. I crafted what I'd say to let him down easy, maybe who I'd recommend in my stead.

Everyone applauded. Kevin stepped back as the speaker for the evening stepped from the wings, and I froze. I noticed the line of her calf peeking through the slit in the dress. Pearl's voice filled the room, and I nearly choked on my drink. I couldn't believe it. She was right here in front of me, and it instantly brought me back to the very first time I saw her. Even then, standing in that elevator, I had an inkling I'd never be the same, and all these years later, I knew that moment had changed something in me permanently.

CHAPTER 4

Cord

Eight Years Earlier

I RAN ACROSS THE LOBBY, SLIDING MY HAND BEtween the closing doors and hoping the sensor picked up the motion in time. I really needed that hand for coding and a lot of other things as a single guy. The Mountain Dew in my Big Gulp sloshed and my Chucks slid along the tile floor. Why anyone would willingly choose to wear a suit to work was beyond me, and I'd thrown away my khakis the minute it was official that we owned this business. My best friend and business partner told me I'd regret it, but he was wrong. Throwing away those clothes had been the best decision I'd ever made. And whether it was luck or talent or a combination of both, things had been going well since then.

Luck was on my side again, and the doors sprang back open at my wave, revealing a tall figure. The name on their badge was obscured but their pronouns and "Guest" were visible. She wore a pencil skirt that fell past her knees. It went straight down, and my vision snagged on the spot where it ended and the utter perfection of her calves. I wasn't sure I'd ever noticed a woman's calves before. It felt illicit to find them so appealing and to trace the lines of her leg up to the hem of the skirt. "Uh, sorry about that," I said, stepping inside. "Running late and didn't want to wait for the next one."

She'd glanced back down at her padfolio with a dismissive nod. "No problem."

I didn't recognize her, and I would have remembered seeing her before. She looked like an actor, with skin the color of a latte, but that comparison felt wrong—I didn't want to consume her. I wanted to learn all the colors that existed so I could describe how her skin looked warm and smooth. Her braids were pulled into a bun I immediately wanted to undo. *Who is this woman?* She looked like someone who had her life together, who never second-guessed herself.

I reached for the keypad to punch my floor, but twenty-three was already illuminated. I glanced back at her, keeping my tone casual. "Are you visiting the FitMi offices?" I sipped from my straw as the elevator inched up. From experience, I knew we'd stop on at least four floors before reaching our destination, and I'd never been so thankful for the delay.

She nodded without looking up, studying her notes closely.

"Interview?" Wes had said something about interviewing assistants today, and I wished I'd paid closer attention. Part of me hoped she bombed her interview. I might work up the courage to ask for her number on the elevator ride down if she wasn't employed by my company, but one glance at her set jaw and straight spine and I had the feeling she'd never bombed an interview in her life.

She finally looked up, meeting my eyes briefly as I stepped closer to her to make room for two people in suits entering the car. "Yes, interview." She was unimpressed by my jeans and hoodie and probably thought I was an intern or lost. "You?"

"Just a normal day for me." I'd never minded looking like an intern until that moment, when I wanted to be the guy she noticed, the guy who looked like someone who should stand next to her. I brushed my hair off my face. I was perpetually overdue for a haircut. "Can't you tell from my three-piece suit?"

"I'm not sure that counts as a suit." A ghost of a smile crossed her lips, and holy hell, I wanted to make her do that again.

"That's where you're wrong." I pointed to my jeans. "Pants. Jacket." I tugged on the sleeve of the sweatshirt before unzipping it and pointing to my T-shirt. "Shirt." I'd chosen a black one with the outline of a wagon and oxen, reading YOU HAVE DIED OF DYSENTERY.

Her eyes were back on her notes, but she smiled again, her full lips curving. "But a three-piece suit has a vest."

"Damn. You're right. Next time, I'll have a vest." I held out my hand. "I'm Cord." I was already imagining how soft the skin above her collarbone must feel.

"Pearl." She took my hand, her shake firm. Her voice had this breathy quality. It was subtle, like a whisper on top of her normal voice. "It's nice to meet you, Cord."

I immediately loved how my name sounded from her lips and wanted to hear it again and again and again. I imagined her saying it sweetly in my arms and breathlessly in my bed, and by the time the doors opened on the twenty-third floor and I watched Pearl walk toward the FitMi reception desk, I was fucked.

CHAPTER 5

Present Day

I STEPPED OFF THE STAGE AND LET OUT A SLOW breath as my nerves recalibrated. The applause had faded into the omnipresent dull hum of conversation, but awards had been given, volunteers recognized, and I'd laid out some of the strategic plans for the organization to expand and to become more inclusive. It wasn't Cord I'd been talking to, but thinking of him got me through the speech, and I'd only stumbled a few times.

Questions were surely swirling about what Kendra's departure meant for the organization, and there were at least four donors I needed to reassure directly, but Kevin called my name. "Pearl. A minute?" He waved from near the stage, his head and arms raising above the crowd. I didn't really have time—this was all scheduled out—but I smiled and walked toward him, taking a glass of wine from a passing server to have something in my hands.

As I neared, the crowd around Kevin thinned, and only one person stood with his back to me, a tall man with broad shoulders that tapered to a trim waist, his tux tailored to his frame.

Kevin smiled and motioned to the man standing next to him. "I want you to meet someone."

My breath hitched. His hair was shorter, chest broader, and he was dressed way better than when I'd known him, but those impossibly long lashes . . . "Cord."

His eyes locked on mine and his smile seemed to fill his face. "Pearl." He didn't look surprised to see me. In fact, his gaze was somewhere between assessing and remembering, and I felt my temperature rise. "You were great up there," he said, motioning to the stage without taking his eyes from mine.

I tilted my head, a hundred questions I wanted to ask flitting through my mind.

"I didn't realize you two knew each other," Kevin said with his polished smile. "That's even better."

Cord pulled his gaze from mine. Maybe it had only been a moment. It felt like hours, like a throwback to every moment in the past when we'd looked at each other for a beat too long. "Pearl used to work at FitMi." His gaze flicked back to me, and I felt like I was in the topsy-turvy version of my own life.

"A long time ago," I added, looking for a reason to break eye contact with Cord and focus on Kevin and the event around us.

Kevin patted him on the shoulder. "Cord and I go way back, and he's going to be stepping onto the board."

When I turned, Cord's eyes were on me, focused on my face like he was trying to memorize it. He said nothing—he had always taken a brief silence to figure out the right thing to say. It was something I'd appreciated at work and then slowly fallen in love with.

"The board. Wow, that's wonderful," I said, shaking off the memories of the last time he'd looked at me like that, the last time we'd ever spoken.

He gave a tentative smile, the half one where one side of his mouth tipped up. The smile made me feel something fluttery and quite the opposite of cool and collected. It made me feel like reaching to brush his hair off his face, even though it was slicked back and not at all out of place.

"It's been a while since you were at FitMi, right?" Kevin's voice interrupted my inappropriate mental swoon. "I remember Kendra saying she hired you from California."

"Five years," Cord said. He glanced at Kevin, his expression changing, shifting to something professional and cordial. We were roughly the same age, and I'd known him in his twenties, but I had the oddest feeling I was seeing Cord all grown up, all grown into himself. It was in the way he rolled back his shoulders and how he stood, looking like he'd gained all the confidence in the world in the last five years.

Kevin looked at me curiously when I didn't respond.

"It seems like yesterday," I said, holding out my hand once social graces returned to my consciousness. "It's good to see you again."

As soon as Cord's palm met mine, I was slammed with memories of the way his fingers felt against me, and my stomach fluttered again. *Damnit, Cord.*

I worried the touch would last too long, that I'd feel too much, but almost as soon as his hand was around mine, he pulled back, leaving me cold. "It's been too long," he said, stepping back and putting some distance between us.

"You'll probably work closely with Pearl." Kevin looked over my shoulder to search the ballroom, and I stole a glance at Cord, whose eyes met mine again. Kevin was oblivious, which made me hesitate and look away quickly. Maybe those long, lingering glances were in my head. Surely they were. It had been years, after all, and we hadn't ever really been anything. I dragged my eyes back to his. *Right?*

"Well, you already know how successful FitMi has been, and my man here is going to bring his expertise to the board. I'd like for you to get him caught up. I know you're pretty new, but make sure Cord has what he needs to make a difference."

I nodded. "Of course. I'd be happy to."

Kevin clapped his hands. "Great." He reached out to shake Cord's hand and then mine. "Pearl, nice work tonight. My assistant will schedule a time for us to talk first thing on Monday. Will you excuse me?"

Before either Cord or I could respond, Kevin was waving to someone in the crowd and walking off to greet them, which left us alone.

Cord slid a hand in his pocket. "I guess you got over your fear of public speaking."

"Not at all." I shook my head with a smile. "How do you remember that?"

He shrugged, the boyish expression I remembered so well crossing his face. "I just do."

I motioned to his chest, remembering how it had once felt pressed against me and wondering if he would feel different now, after so much time had gone by. "Still no vest," I said, loving the way his lips tipped up again.

"I would have worn it if I knew you'd be—"

"There you are." A blond in a periwinkle dress joined us, a hand grazing over Cord's arm. Willowy and tall, they looked at him adoringly, eyes wide with uncomplicated affection.

I took a step back, realizing we were standing too close. It had been so easy to slide back into our old comfortable rapport that it was easy to forget where we were and how much had changed.

"I'm Abby." They extended a hand with a wide smile. "I volunteer with the program as a mentor, and I'm so excited about everything you laid out." I swallowed and strove for composure but scanned my mental guest list. Abby Stiller, she/they pronouns, a software developer at Lucite Technologies. Cord was dating someone who shared his love of coding. That fit. This was the type of person I always expected him to end up with.

"It's nice to meet you," I said, returning their smile. "And thank you for volunteering."

"I love it." There was a slight gush in their voice and pinkness in their cheeks. Maybe it was the wine, or maybe they were just naturally cheery. "I've been trying to get him to volunteer forever." They elbowed him playfully, and the tone was easygoing, but the familiarity of it reminded me that I was on the outside where Cord was concerned.

"I guess you finally won him over."

The crease between his eyebrows appeared, and he shifted his own gaze, locking with mine and then looking at Abby.

"What do you mean?" They tilted their head in a way that was cute and nice. I had an unreasonable desire to befriend this person and also pull their hair. *So three cheers for maturity.*

"Kevin talked me into joining the board of directors," Cord said casually, focused on Abby, with a sweet smile. That one was new—I didn't remember it. I took another small step back, swallowing a lump of emotion because I used to know all Cord's smiles.

Abby wrapped their arms around his waist. "Honey! That's great!"

I looked away, embarrassed to watch this affection and convincing myself that was the only reason.

Cord's hand fell to Abby's back in such a familiar way that I had to remind myself I shouldn't care. "Kevin called in a favor."

"We'll be glad to have you," I said. Our eyes met again, and I bit my lip, wishing I could make a joke to cut the tension simmering between us. "Abby, it was wonderful to meet you. Cord, so good to see you again. Will you excuse me?"

I stepped away, leaving the couple to celebrate together. Abby's hand snaked around Cord's waist, and it didn't escape my notice that they looked happy, like a matching set.

"Pearl." Cord stepped forward, Abby coming with him. He wasn't calling out; his voice was casual, but the sound of my name on his lips made me feel more things I didn't have time for, like how once upon a time I had felt like we could be something. Like how once upon a time I'd turned him down and regretted it. Like how the sound of my name on his lips made me want to be the kind of woman who could put her heart before her head. "Maybe we could have lunch early in the week. It would be good to catch up."

I nodded, trying not to notice the way Abby's arm looked comfortable around him. I wondered what he felt like now—he was broader and bulkier. He looked good in a tuxedo, too, but I missed the hoodie and Converse. In some ways, I wouldn't have recognized him, but when our eyes met again, I reversed my thoughts. I would have recognized Cord's eyes anywhere. "Looking forward to it," I said.

One side of his mouth tipped up, and his eyes were bright. "Me, too."

Walking away, I heard Abby's voice and reminded myself that his smiles weren't mine to claim—they never had been. Even if he had offered them to me, I'd given them up five years earlier, and it was clear to me now that I'd have to get my body's reactions to him in check before we began to work together again.

CHAPTER 6

Cord

"WELL, CORD," LOU SAID OVER THE FENCE. "THIS is a mess." My neighbor waved one of her tiny hands in my direction, motioning to the overgrown vegetable garden. I actually wasn't sure I could call it a vegetable garden anymore. Save the memory of some overripe carrots, it was mostly a weed garden now, but the density and variety of weeds were impressive.

"Yeah," I said, giving up and standing to my full height. I brushed my hands over my thighs, trying to clean the dirt off my hands. "It's not great."

"It was that leggy one who planted it, wasn't it?"

I winced at the memory of kneeling in the dirt with Gabriela, deciding where to put the seeds she'd picked out. That breakup hadn't been pleasant. She'd thrown that year's tiny harvest at me on her way out. "Few years ago."

She nodded, still examining the patch of weeds. "That's right. That's right. She was after the one with that dog. The yappy one."

"Amber. Yeah. Excellent memory." I wiped my arm across my brow and crossed to the fence, ignoring the doghouse that was alongside my back deck. I'd meant to do something with it but never gotten around to getting rid of it.

"I thought it was Gimlet."

"The dog was Gimlet. Amber was the . . . girlfriend." I stumbled on the last word. "Anything I can do for you, Lou?" I didn't particularly want to dig into the sad attempts at real relationships that had left me with this mishmash of a backyard.

"Nah," she said, leaning against the fence. "Just checking out your lawn."

I hoped she didn't comment on the hot tub my most recent girlfriend had insisted I buy and have installed so we could entertain. Tala had had plans to make me more social and had also been the last woman I'd tried and failed to have something special with. The hot tub was a rarely used reminder of my resolution to keep my relationships casual and entanglement-free. Luckily Lou charged ahead, not giving me time to ruminate on any past regrets.

"You know, kid, your yard's like a graveyard of old loves. Anyone ever told you that?" She didn't give me time to respond, which wasn't out of the ordinary. "I mean, when you first moved in, it was a new girl every few months, and now I think I'm the only consistent woman in your life." She laughed, a full belly laugh, and added, "And you couldn't keep up with me in the bedroom, kid."

I leaned on the fence. "You know I'd try, though. Right, Lou?"

"Did you ever like gardening or dogs or hot tub parties?"

I hadn't. Something Tala pointed out when she told me I was a textbook people pleaser. It wasn't a label I'd liked or something I wanted to get into with Lou, so I attempted a subject change. "Do you want me to take your trash cans out to the curb?"

"That would be nice. Thank you," Lou said, relenting for a moment. "So, why keep all this stuff around?"

The stuff was a reminder of how easy it was to fall into things, a reminder I worried I still needed, though admitting that would lead to a longer conversation with my neighbor than I wanted right now. My ideal yard was one where I could lie out and look at the sky, something I knew deep down right after I bought the place. I didn't have a good response to Lou's question, but I'd lived next door to her long enough to know I didn't need one as she was working toward a point. I'd met her the day I moved in five years earlier, when she'd pointed out that my front steps needed replacing and that the previous owners had neglected the front lawn, and then she'd brought me a pan of the best lasagna I'd ever had. She was never short on opinions or care.

"Kid, you're one of those love-to-be-in-love people. I can spot that a mile away. My first husband was like that. Loved being in love, but he loved it so much, he just always went with what I wanted. Never put up a fight or took a stand. You were like that when I met you."

I took a step toward the gate, hoping she'd walk with me and I could escape this interrogation by taking her trash cans to the curb. She walked with me but kept talking.

"But I think one of those girls hurt you bad, 'cause now, seems to me, you're kind of scared of falling for anyone." She paused as I left my yard and crossed to her property, leading me around the house. "Are you happy with that yard?"

"Yard is a work in progress. But the rest of the house is almost done being renovated." I grabbed the handle on the molded plastic to pull the bin to the curb. "And how do you know I'm not holding out hope for you and me to give it a go?"

She laughed again. "Boy, I already had the great love of my life. No offense, but your hands are too soft to measure up." She rested a palm on my forearm, and I could feel the softness of the thin skin of her hand. Her hand weighed next to nothing, but the weight of it still made me pause. "You hear me, though, right? Despite your piss-poor gardening, I like you."

"I got it, Lou," I said, meeting her eyes. "But I'm good." The lie tasted bitter. Abby was fun company and things were uncomplicated, but I'd had my mind on someone else since Saturday. And despite how I couldn't stop thinking about Pearl, I knew she was someone I could not let myself fall for again. "And I'll work on the garden."

She laughed and let go of my arm, waving her hand as she walked beside me down the short driveway. "Oh, no. Keep it like it is. I like giving you a hard time, and I get cranky when there's nothing to complain about."

After Lou shared a few thoughts on the neighbor's dog, local politics, and another saucy new mailman—her words—I strode back into the house. Five years earlier, I'd bought the place to fix up, hoping to make it a home and give myself a project away from the office. Now it was done—well, almost done. My laptop sat on the marble kitchen counter, and I scrolled through the emails sitting in my inbox as I cast a quick look to the unfinished backyard.

One from Kevin stood out, and I opened the message faster than I thought possible. I'd not stopped thinking about the board position and the gala all weekend. I scanned Kevin's email about the paperwork to complete for the board position, but what stood out most was Pearl's phone number at the bottom, identifying her again as my point person, as if I would have forgotten. Peach, my elderly cat, sauntered by in search of food, and I scratched behind her hairless ears.

My phone buzzed beside my laptop on the counter, and I reached for it without looking, expecting Abby's voice on the other line as I read through the email again. "How was the salon?"

Without missing a beat, the voice on the other end—which definitely did not belong to Abby—volleyed back. "They never get the bikini wax quite how I like it."

I chuckled, tapping the icon to put my best friend on speaker. "I've told you more than once I don't wanna know about your bikini line."

"Yeah, but I always think you'll change your mind. Someday."

"Man, we've been friends since college and ran a business together. I think the window of time for interest in your hair-removal preferences has passed."

Wes chuckled. "Calling to see if you still needed help getting those cabinets hung in the basement."

"Yeah." I kept scrolling through the emails, but I'd opened Kevin's email with Pearl's phone number in a pop-out window, and my gaze kept drifting to the digits. "That'd be great."

"I'm thinking of planning a climbing trip to Yosemite the last weekend of April. You want in?"

I shook my head. "Can't. My dad is getting married that Saturday."

"Again?"

"Lucky number four," I said, closing my laptop. My mom had initiated their divorce, and in retrospect, I think my dad had been shocked. He'd adored her, and after that, it was like he didn't trust himself anymore. Every new woman brought on a new version of him. "The new thing is sustainable living."

"That's gotta be better than the last one. I don't know if I ever really saw your dad as a country-club sort."

"Yeah. His golf game is pretty good now, though." I glanced out the window again. After Pearl left the company and I tried to move on, I saw myself turning into my dad. Each new woman I dated was like I was trying on a new version of myself—someone who turned into whatever the person I was with wanted. A people pleaser, and I didn't like it. "Joy seems nice—maybe this one will stick."

"And if not, this wife will be better for the planet than the golf courses." Wes chuckled, and I was reminded of one reason we'd been friends for so long. If there was something we were both good at, it was using humor to deflect.

"I'll pass on all my new composting knowledge after Christmas." My dad was a good guy who deserved to be happy, but I kept that sad garden and old doghouse out there as a reminder of what happened if I let things get serious. "Did you know Pearl was back in town?"

"Yeah, she told Britt a few weeks ago."

It was good that we were on the phone and not in person, because it would have been hard to stifle the reflex to punch him in the arm for not telling me what his wife had found out. "And you didn't think to mention it?" I clicked the delete button on my laptop with too much force as I kept scrolling through my inbox.

"Oh . . ." he said with a chuckle. "You're pissed I didn't tell you?"

"You could have mentioned it," I said, settling into a

chair. He knew that, otherwise he would have texted about the cabinets.

"I meant to. I swear." Wes had been busy with work, so I could give him a pass, except I still had the powerful urge to wrestle him to the ground. "You always insisted nothing happened with you two, though."

"Nothing did happen." I glanced at the couch along the wall in my office on instinct. Wes had known I had a thing for Pearl back then, even suspected there was something romantic between us, but I'd never come clean about what actually went down before she left the company. Pearl's rejection had been humiliating, and I'd hated how I'd been powerless to convince her to give things between us a chance. Then, after the breakups with Amber and Gabriela and Tala, I avoided the humiliation of failed relationships altogether. "Anyway, I'm seeing someone. I'm not interested in Pearl like that. It just would have been nice to know."

Wes laughed. "I know there's more to that."

"Are we done?" I pushed away from the counter and pulled a bottle of water from the fridge. "Can we dissect my romantic past another time?"

"Sure. Should I bring beer on Friday? I'm buying, since I didn't tell you about Pearl, and you can finally come clean about what happened with you two."

I ignored the second half of his question and just said, "Sure." I should have told him about seeing her in person at the gala, but that would open up questions I didn't want to answer over the phone. Questions I didn't know how to answer, period. I returned to the emails, finally sitting and resting my elbows on the desk, tension coiling in my neck and across my shoulders.

I glanced at the door and remembered the thousands of times I'd imagined Pearl walking through it. I pictured her soft eyes, which had always intrigued me because the rest of her was so sharp—witty, sarcastic, and efficient. When she looked at me, though, I felt like she was touching me with the barest graze of her fingertips. I had to focus on what was in front of me, where things were going in my life, and stop obsessing about when we'd worked together. Because if there was one thing the past had taught me, Pearl was the very last person I should imagine beside me working on a backyard plan.

CHAPTER 7

Pearl

WHEN I WALKED INTO THE OFFICE ON MONDAY, BEA rose from her desk and clapped, the sound echoing in the space until others joined in. "All hail! The hero of the gala!" Across the front of my office door was a banner reading ORATOR OF THE YEAR, decorated with tissue-paper flowers. "Speech. Speech," Bea started chanting, and I smiled despite myself at this over-the-top welcome.

"I think I did enough of that already." I glanced around at my coworkers. Bea still stood, a wide smile on her face. Mara, who had been with OurCode longer than anyone else, grinned indulgently from her desk outside Kendra's office, and Xavier, our social media manager, joined Bea in applause. In some ways it reminded me of being back at FitMi and the way the staff there had fun together, how the office sometimes felt like it could be a living room. The fundamental difference was that no one on the staff here made me want to doodle hearts in the margins of my meeting agenda. "Thank you all. But can we get back to work now?"

Mara joined me as I walked into my office, away from the impromptu party. "You let that go on longer than I thought you would," she commented. "You getting soft?"

"Don't tell anyone." I set my purse next to my desk and shrugged off my coat. The chill of winter was finally ebbing, and I looked forward to storing this thing in the closet for the spring and summer.

"Your secret's safe with me." When she held out two file folders, her purple fingernail polish caught the light. "Sounds like it was an eventful weekend." If Mara knew what had happened with Kendra, she gave nothing away with her cool expression. Her statement hung in the air as I took the folders from her—two agreements to review.

"It was." I assessed her expression. "You heard about Kendra?"

She laughed, a short cross between a snort and a chuckle. "I know everything that happens here," she said. "I'm guessing you'll be needing these."

I glanced down at the folders, one labeled with the name of one of our largest donors and the other with the board's agendas for that year. "Why would I need these?"

She smiled and shrugged. "You can tell me later."

"I don't—"

She held up a hand, interrupting my protest. "I'll be at my desk," Mara said with a wink. "When you're ready to tell me I was right." She'd been out my door only a minute or two when she transferred a call.

"This is Pearl Harris. How can I—"

"Wow."

I tensed at the sound of his voice through the phone. "Cord."

"Sorry, it just threw me to hear you like old times. I heard you answer the phone a thousand times." I pictured him outside Wes's office years ago. They were always in and out of each other's space, but at some point, Cord had started lingering more often, talking to me while perched on the corner of my desk.

"I still answer my phone sometimes with 'FitMi Fitness, this is Pearl' on instinct."

"We'll hire you back anytime."

"You couldn't afford me now." I spun in my chair and watched a group of birds cutting their way across the clear blue sky.

"I know." He laughed, and I remembered a hundred dumb conversations punctuated with his brushing his hair from his forehead and me reminding him that he needed a haircut. "You have someone answering phones for you now anyway. I think my posture improved from the time she picked up the phone. Is it possible someone is more intimidating than you?"

Mara had that effect on people. When I'd first spoken with her, she was as kind and professional as she was in person, but she had this air of confidence that made everyone else feel like they had to get their lives together. "I never intimidated you."

"You always intimidated me." His voice wasn't low or gravelly, but it felt like something changed in his timbre. "In the best possible way, though."

The birds disappeared from view, leaving only the edge of a group of clouds in my line of sight, and not wispy, dreamy, let-me-fantasize cirrus clouds but sturdy, get-your-head-on-straight cumulus clouds. I coughed into my hand and stood from my chair, realizing where my mind wanted to wander. "Well," I said, straightening my shoulders for good measure. "What can I do for you this morning?"

"Oh, yeah," he said through the phone, his voice changing back to normal. "Lunch. Can we set up a time to meet?"

About the board. Of course. Not to catch up—the tech CEO who had been tapped to join the board needed information. He wasn't calling for me. "Certainly." I opened my calendar. "I'm sure you're busy. I can work with your assistant to schedule something for early next month?" An instant message from Mara popped up on my screen.

MARA HERRERA: Kevin's assistant wants to schedule a call with you for early this afternoon.

MARA HERRERA: Just you, not you and Ellie. I know you were going to wonder.

Cord was right, Mara's confidence mixed with her sixth sense for people was intimidating as hell. If Kevin wanted to speak with only me, I wondered if that meant he'd want me to step into Kendra's shoes and take over the leadership role. I did want that, but it was a long-term goal. I'd even signed up to begin an online coding class to learn more about the work our students wanted to do. I'd figured I had time to learn what I needed before Kendra started considering retirement.

"I can schedule it myself," Cord said, and I heard the quick sounds of his noisy keyboard. He'd had a similar one when I worked there, the kind where the keys made that definitive clicking sound. "Are you free today? I had a last-minute cancellation."

"We don't have to meet so soon," I said, closing the message and clicking back to my calendar, where I was free for lunch. I hovered my mouse over the spot to hold it, aware my heart rate had sped up and my fingers were twitchy.

"My schedule is kind of crazy. If not today, it might be a

while, and I'd like to catch up," he said. "It's been a long time." There was that change in his voice, that tone that made me think of the last actual conversation we'd shared.

"It has." And Cord is seeing someone, I reminded myself, pushing aside the cirrus clouds in my head. "Today for lunch is great. I'll send you a location once I get a reservation. Are there questions you have prior to the meeting, or is there other information that would be helpful?"

A silence hung between us for a moment, the real-life version of those text dots appearing and reappearing. "I guess I just want to know everything," he said finally.

"Everything about the board role, I mean," he added, probably picking up on the same conversational uncertainty I was. "And you. I mean, what you've been up to the last five years?"

"I'm not that interesting." Outside my office, Bea was chatting animatedly with Mara, and Ellie walked by with a quick wave before the door in the office next to mine closed.

"Yes, you are."

He's not single. He's not single. I needed to remember that. Oh, and how I broke his heart five years ago.

"I'll compile some information for you on the board," I said, diverting the conversation. "I'm new, but the entire operation runs very smoothly. Knock on wood. It shouldn't be too taxing an experience."

"I'm looking forward to it."

I wanted to ask what favor he owed Kevin that he'd agreed to step in so quickly, because maybe Cord Matthews had changed, but sitting on a board of directors used to be his nightmare. I bit my tongue to hold the question at bay. Outside the glass, Xavier and Bea checked their phones, their expressions changing to something akin to shock at the same time. Ellie stepped out of her office to talk to them, and I couldn't hear their conversation, but she was pointing to her phone as well.

"Cord, I have to step away."

"Oh, of course. I have a meeting, too." The phone rustled on his end, like he'd been holding it too close to his clothes. "But for what it's worth, it's good to see you again. I mean, it was good to see you the other night."

Despite my best intentions, I remembered how his lips felt, how good it was the first time he kissed me, how he kissed with a confidence I hadn't expected. "Same for me."

We hung up, and I took in a slow, measured breath. The kisses we'd shared didn't matter anymore—that had been a long time ago, and he was over it. I was over it. There was nothing left to worry about. His joining the board would be good for the future direction of OurCode. This was going to go well.

I tapped my manicured fingernail on the file folder and glanced back out into the office, where everyone was talking animatedly. I guessed it was something involving a celebrity I hadn't heard of, because my colleagues were very good at reminding me how much younger they were than I was.

"What's going on?" I stepped out of my office and walked toward Bea's desk, where they were crowded around a monitor.

Bea looked up at my approach. "Well, good news and bad news."

"What's the good news?" I slowed my pace, a sixth sense forewarning me that I did not want the bad news.

"The meeting with that lobbyist about STEM education

funding for public schools is confirmed." Bea cast a quick glance back at the screen.

"That is good news—I know a few of those legislators were on the fence about meeting with us." I looked from person to person, all less excited about the meeting than I thought they would be. "What's the bad news?"

"Well," Bea said, turning the monitor toward me. "Bad news is, we may no longer be invited. This dropped today."

I reread the splashy headline three times.

"You've got to be kidding me," I said under my breath, doing a quick scan of the article, which detailed a financial scandal OurCode was now embroiled in, care of our former director.

"Pearl, Kevin is on the phone for you," Mara called from her desk.

CHAPTER 8

Cord

Seven Years Earlier

I SCANNED THE ITINERARY BEFORE HANDING IT back to my FitMi business partner.

Wes shrugged and looked as skeptical as I knew I did about the daylong team-building retreat. "The consultant said it was important for morale and team unity. Too late to back out now. It starts first thing in the morning."

I chuckled and settled back in the chair across from him. "Can we fake a CEO emergency and duck out before the first icebreaker?"

"Way to be a team player." He laughed but looked over my shoulder at the sound of a knock on the open door. "Hey, Pearl."

She'd been with us a little more than a year and still took my breath away. I always thought that was something that only happened in love songs, but sometimes when I saw her, I got so nervous, so in my head about the shape of her eyes and the curve of her hips, that I'd hold my breath.

"Sorry to interrupt, but you'll need these for the meetings you have back-to-back in fifteen minutes." She strode in and handed Wes a stack of messages, along with three file folders. Wes loved having her as his assistant—she was organized and efficient and kept him on his toes. I loved him having her as an assistant because I got to see her every day.

"Thanks, Pearl."

She nodded and stepped back out, closing the door without another word.

"Do you think she enjoys working here?" I asked.

"Pearl?" He looked over my shoulder like she might still be standing there to answer the question herself. "I think so. Why?"

"She's so serious all the time. We try to make this place fun, right?"

Wes flipped through the information she'd handed him. "I'm pretty sure Pearl isn't really the work-should-be-play type. Anyway, she'd tell me if she was unhappy." He glanced over his shoulder again. "I think." Wes shrugged and nodded toward his phone. "You want in on this conference call about the new training protocols?"

"Nope." I pushed back from the desk and stood. "I'll leave that to you."

"I figured." He tried to look annoyed, but I knew he loved that part, the training and coaching part of the job, as much as I liked building the software and tackling programming issues. "And don't worry about Pearl. I think she's just not a very social person."

When I stepped out of his office, Pearl was writing on a pad of paper, the surface of her desk immaculate. I tried my best to never need paper, and I still couldn't come close to the pristine nature of her space. "Excited about tomorrow?"

It was a dumb question. I knew it, and from the micro expression, the quickest hint of *Why are you talking to me about this nonsense?* behind her calm and professional mask, she agreed. "For the team-building retreat," I added, shoving my hands in my pockets. She didn't immediately respond but looked at me in a way that made me feel warm in the light of her attention. "They're going to have us play capture the flag." I said it like I was hyping up my third-grade class for field day. I'd always hated field day, falling from the monkey bars mid-swing so many times, they finally just let me walk across to keep the event moving.

"It should be morale-boosting," she said, setting down her pencil on the notepad and folding her hands on top of it.

"Definitely." I'd never hoped for a bolt of lightning to strike so fervently as in the middle of this awkward conversation of my own making. I'd felt the chemistry between us that first day in the elevator, but since then, our interactions were always like this. Me fumbling to come up with something to say and her politely pretending I didn't sound like a completely clueless dumbass. "Well, see you in the morning," I said with a wave. A wave. *Why am I waving at her?* I finally had the good sense to drop my hand and turn on my heel toward my office down the hall.

"Hey, Cord?"

Sweet Jesus. My name sounded so good when she said it. "Yeah?" I turned, making sure I wasn't holding my breath first. "What's up?"

"Did you guys . . ." She looked between Wes's closed door and me. "Did you assign the teams yet for capture the flag?"

I made the few steps back to her desk. "No. Why?"

"Well," she said, looking around and lowering her voice. "I was working on this," she said, handing me the notebook.

She had a list of everyone from the central office who

would be there tomorrow, plus the coaching supervisors from some key regions. Next to each, she'd highlighted strengths, weaknesses, and special skills. I flipped the pages. When I met her gaze, she was quick to explain, so quick it was more like me fumbling for words than how Pearl normally spoke. "If you're planning to arrange it with central leadership and marketing versus accounting and coaching, I think the numbers would be balanced, but we'd have a slight advantage even though there might be more athletes on the coaching and accounting team." She pointed one delicate finger at the matrix of people on the third page.

"You're right," I said, handing it back. "I can't believe you did all that. It's so . . . devious."

Pearl shrugged and closed the notebook, a hint of a smile on her lips. "Just looking at how we can assure victory," she said, squaring her shoulders. I'd never been a shoulder man until that moment, when I wanted to watch Pearl Harris straighten her shoulders for hours.

"So, you're saying you don't want to be on the losing team, huh?"

Pearl flashed a smile, her professional mask cracking to show a bit of a playful side. "Who wants that?"

"No one, I guess. Show me more. How will we win?" I took one step closer but froze, worried about invading her space, but she opened the notebook again, motioned for me to rest against the clear spot at the corner of her desk, and walked me through the plan.

"I did not know you were so competitive," I said, leaning closer and inhaling the scent of her perfume or lotion—it was like cinnamon.

Pearl shrugged again. "Just a few ideas." As she continued, I saw something else. She knew people—really knew them—and had a sense for how the competition would bring everyone together in the way the consultant had suggested would help. I wondered if Wes was wrong—Pearl wasn't our extrovert, but she was definitely a people person.

"You'll be on my team, right?" I asked, tracing a finger over the notebook like I was following the line of names, but it was an excuse to prolong this conversation.

"Only if you're committed to winning," she said, giving me another of those unguarded smiles. She'd even laughed once or twice. I hated capture the flag and all other games like it, but I knew I was going to stay up all night studying strategy, hoping to get more of those smiles the next day.

"As of this moment, I am very committed."

CHAPTER 9

Cord

Present Day

I LOOKED AROUND THE CROWDED RESTAURANT, ON high alert for Pearl after arriving early. There were a lot of things that should have been holding my attention. The final stages of partnerships with companies in Japan, Italy, and India were in the works for FitMi, and despite the fact that we had hired excellent people to manage them, there still seemed to be a hundred decisions that landed on my desk. I closed the mail app on my phone, unable to concentrate. I'd been to this place a few times. The exposed brick and cast-iron chandeliers, which gave the impression of local-pub-meets-high-end-establishment, made it a good fit for a casual business lunch. Yet I couldn't pretend it was a simple business lunch with Pearl—she was the first woman who ever made me truly understand the meaning of heartbreak.

Mason: Meet us for lunch?

Cord: Can't. Plans.

"What a coincidence," Mason said, walking up to the

table and slipping the phone into his pocket. "In all the gin joints in all the world, you had to walk into mine."

I rolled my eyes. I'd hired him to manage communications for my company years earlier, but I'd come to rely on him as something of a corporate consigliere. Still, he'd have a bunch of questions about me eating with Pearl, and I didn't want to deal with his ribbing. "You couldn't get enough of me in the office?"

Mason clapped my shoulder. "I could never get enough of you and this face. Who—" His smile widened when he glanced over my shoulder. "Well, what a sight for sore eyes."

I snapped my head around, doing something to my neck in the process, but I let the pain fade into the background at the sight of Pearl striding toward us through the crowded restaurant. Her legs seemed to go on forever, up to the hemline of the gray dress that cut across her collarbone.

"Oh, Mason," she said, a smile playing at her own lips. "Your eyes wouldn't be so sore if you stopped being so very punchable."

He laughed and held out an arm to give her a quick hug. After a rocky start, they'd forged an antagonistic friendship before she left. "How's your sister?"

Pearl stepped out of the hug and sat in the seat across from me, giving Mason a side-eye look. "You're a distant memory for Bri," she said.

"I'll never forget her, though." Mason laughed and Pearl's lips twitched. "I'll leave you to it. Welcome home, Pearl. It's good to have you back in the city." He gave a two-finger wave and walked away, disappearing into the crowd and leaving us alone.

"So, Mason hasn't changed," she said, finally looking

across the table at me, and my knee shook at double the speed.

"No, he's the same." I fiddled with the menu, watching her get settled, the way her hands moved. I wasn't sure how to manage it, but I needed to turn off these old habits and stop chronicling everything I noticed about her. "How does it feel to be back? Your parents and sisters must be happy."

"You remember my sisters?"

"Of course. You talked about them all the time." I set the menu aside and leaned forward on the table. "Shea is the youngest and Brianna is in the middle, right?"

Pearl nodded. "Yes. And blessedly moved on from guys like Mason."

"She's in pharmaceuticals and has a kid, right?"

"Tye," she offered, setting her menu aside, too. "They're fifteen now. I can't believe it. They're actually involved with the OurCode program. I've never seen them so excited about anything."

"No way. I remember a little kid. Wild."

"Yeah," she said, settling the napkin in her lap. "Bri has to travel for work, so I'll have a fifteen-year-old roommate for a few months."

"I have a fifteen-year-old roommate, too," I said as a server approached. When we'd both ordered and the server stepped away, I looked back to Pearl.

"Abby's kid?" She didn't seem bothered, just curious, which was a reminder that this wasn't a date, it was a work lunch. Pearl didn't have to remind herself to stop looking at my hands.

"Oh, no. Abby doesn't have any kids." I took a sip of water and then thought through her question. I should have corrected her, making it clear Abby and I weren't committed, but maybe that was the buffer I needed. "And we don't live together. I inherited a cat a couple years ago." I dug my phone from my pocket and opened the app to access my photos on the cloud, which were ninety percent cat photos. I scrolled to one of her lying in a beam of sunlight coming through my front window. "Her name is Peach."

Pearl took my phone, our fingers brushing in a way I convinced myself didn't feel different from any other touch with any other person. Her eyes narrowed slightly, and she zoomed in. "You . . . have a fifteen-year-old hairless cat . . . in a pink sweater . . . and her name is Peach. I'm going to need more information." She handed back my phone as the server returned with our drinks.

"An ex-girlfriend found her wandering in a park and couldn't find an owner, but she wasn't allowed to have pets in her building." When things ended with Tala, I was left with the hot tub and the cat, and looking back, maybe the rocky end of the relationship was worth getting Peach. I scrolled to another photo of us together. The cat's disdainful expression was focused on me, probably because I was taking a selfie and not feeding her. "She didn't want to see her end up in a shelter, and I had space." I handed her the phone again, and she grinned at the screen. "There are several pictures there."

"Why Peach?"

"Short for Peach Fuzz." I watched Pearl scroll through a couple more photos of Peach. "The sweater is only because the breed gets cold easily." I thought my head would explode the first time I Googled cat sweaters, but now Peach's wardrobe was more extensive than mine.

Pearl's lips turned to a small grin as she scrolled until

her expression changed. "What is this?" She held the phone out to me. I scrambled to grab it from her and scroll past the photo.

"Damnit, Wes," I muttered, tucking my phone away. "He taught himself how to do boudoir photos for his wife a few years ago, to surprise her, and he suckered me into helping him practice." He'd sent me one a few weeks earlier to give to Abby for their birthday. I'd been fully clothed, but posing seductively with my chest out and arms over my head, next to a window. The lighting left me in a showy silhouette, and the photo was actually not bad. "He still owes me for that."

"Adopting a cat, boudoir photos, and now joining the board . . . you're a pretty generous guy."

I sat straighter at her comment. It was a joke, and she didn't mean anything by it, but people had told me that my whole life, and despite this particular evidence to the contrary, it wasn't who I was anymore. "Yeah, I guess so," I said, moving my hands to make room for the food. "So, you're going to give me the lowdown on what I actually signed up for?"

I snatched a pickle off my plate to keep from focusing on how her expression shifted from making-fun-of-me Pearl to business Pearl in an instant. "Yes, of course. I should tell you . . ." She glanced around the restaurant, lowering her voice.

I expected her to say she was engaged or married, and she knew that secret could gut me. Of course, I knew she wasn't. Well, I was mostly certain Wes would have told me. I'd instituted a ban on searching online for her years ago. Of course, I still had to kick his ass for not telling me she was in town. And I was seeing Abby, or Pearl thought I was, so it didn't matter if she was engaged. "What's going on?"

"We want you on the board. I want you on the board," she amended, setting her napkin in her lap. "But this morning, some news broke about our former director leaving in the wake of an affair with a board member . . . and some questionable financial decisions." She toyed with her silverware, straightening the fork before picking it up. "It's not the worst scandal, but it's not good. You may want to rethink joining the board right now. It's going to be some work to manage this whole thing."

Mason would be on me as soon as he heard, and I half expected to see him sprinting across the restaurant to stop me from making a PR mistake, but that wasn't why my knee started shaking. In five years, I'd outwardly transformed into a guy who looked like he headed a thriving company. I spoke definitively, I made decisions, and I had a solid poker face during negotiations. That said, in front of this woman, I needed to take a sip from my water while I gathered my thoughts. "What kind of financial decisions?"

She bit the corner of her lip quickly, one tiny break in her perfect composure. "I . . . don't know all the details yet, but I didn't want to bring you into the middle of a crisis, which this might end up being. You're busy and that will take more time, besides the potential for negative press."

"Yeah," I said, thinking mostly that if I wasn't on the board, I might lose my excuse to see Pearl like this. "But what about you? You just started there, right?"

She nodded, sinking her fork into the Tuscan kale salad she'd ordered. "It's my job, though. And I love a challenge."

I knew three things all at once. First, I'd never been this interested in any other woman's mouth when she was speaking to me. Second, I knew nothing would happen with Pearl, that this wasn't a second chance for us, but I wasn't over her. Third, Mason was going to kill me.

"I won't leave you hanging. I'm still on board to join. I want to help."

CHAPTER 10

Pearl

DURING A BUSY AFTERNOON THE NEXT WEEK, I strolled through the OurCode lounge, taking in a group of teens crowded around a table, all focused on one screen, their own devices sitting in silent watch. Five pairs of students and mentors were scattered around the space, and I listened for a few minutes to a group of college computer science majors who'd volunteered to lead a discussion circle at a local college about being people of color in a major dominated by white men. I loved that we had a safe space for students to be, hang, and nerd out together and a place for mentor meetings to occur if needed. More than that, it was a fun environment, and I had a smile on my face when I glanced down at my phone, seeing the text.

Tye: Can you tell my mom I'm old enough stay alone while she's in London?

Tye: Before you say no, remember you, Aunt Shea, and Granny and Grandpa are all right here.

Tye: Think about all the life skills I could gain. You

always say how important it is to gain life skills so I'll be prepared to live independently and never have to rely on someone.

Pearl: That's a well-reasoned argument.

Tye: I know. So, you'll tell her you think I can?

Pearl: No.

Tye: Why not? I'm practically grown.

Pearl: Practically, but not legally.

Tye: Can you at least tell her you think my curfew should be later?

Pearl: Maybe. Write me a proposal why I should.

Pearl: Since you're so interested in life skills.

I settled on the arm of the couch, watching a group of kids Tye's age and two mentors work together on a video game. I wasn't familiar with it, but they all sat rapt, moving their controllers and talking back and forth about flanks, broadswords, and orcs. It looked like a game Tye would enjoy, actually. Around age nine, they decided they wanted to design games, and for years, it was the only topic of conversation that engaged the youngest member of our family. My phone buzzed in my pocket and I pulled it free, taking my eyes off the castle on the screen, now on fire as the players cheered.

Pearl: They're campaigning for a later curfew.

Bri: I know. I told them to create a formal presentation.

I laughed at the similarity between my and my sister's responses, picturing Tye's eye roll at our mirrored answers.

Bri: I can't make it for girls' night. I'm not even close to packed nor is Tye.

The group of gamers cheered loudly and the discussion circle members shot them dirty looks, though both groups returned to their activities, ignoring the others, including the mentors. I let my mind wander, soaking up the energy of the communal space. I hadn't heard Tye talk about game design much in the last several months.

Pearl: Is Tye still doing well with their mentor? I was instructed not to intervene.

Bri: 😂 Did they threaten you?

Pearl: Severely.

Bri: It's good. They seem to like Abby, who has somehow convinced Tye that jobs exist outside gaming.

Abby? I looked around as if someone might witness my revelation. I knew I had recognized the name when Cord introduced us. I had no idea how I hadn't put the pieces together before now. He was dating Tye's mentor. Tye's mentor who was, apparently, amazing.

Pearl: Abby Stiller?

Bri: You know Abby? Tye adores them and has started talking about cybersecurity. I'm honestly just happy to get a break from hearing about parallax and visual scripting.

Pearl: That first one sounds like a band.

Bri: If only, then we might periodically talk about drummers instead of multiplatform integrations.

Bri: Gotta run but I'll message you later.

I tucked my phone away, still processing the news that Tye's mentor and Cord's date were the same person. It wasn't like anything was going to happen with Cord, even if it shook me up to see him in person again after so much time had passed. There were a thousand excellent reasons against us having any sort of friendship, beginning with him being in a relationship and ending with the way we'd parted outside that elevator five years earlier.

I was pulled from my internal psych-up by a finger on my shoulder. "Excuse me. Do you work here?"

I turned, expecting a mentor or one of the older students, but a middle-aged person with a salt-and-pepper goatee and in a polo and jeans stood in front of me alone, and my hackles rose. "Can I help you?"

"I'm David Schooner from the *Times*. Would you like to give a comment on the recent reports that your director took funds to limit diversity in OurCode?" He held up his press badge and held a recording device in my face, and his question landed in a strange moment of collective pause in the room, so the sound of his voice wasn't muted by the gamers or the teens or the mentors. No, it filled the space, and then I felt the eyes in the room shift onto me.

"No comment," I said, standing to my full height. "And this is a private space for children—you cannot be in here without an escort." I searched for the security guard, walking forward to back the reporter out.

"But are the reports true? Did OurCode accept donations from the Smith Corporation in exchange for cutting a proposed program specifically for LGBTQIA-plus kids and youth with other gender-expansive identities and a scholarship program for kids whose families immigrated to the US?" His voice picked up volume and speed as we neared the door, and the security guard finally appeared, stepping in to escort the reporter out. "And do you have a comment about donors abandoning support for the program?" he called out over the guard's shoulder.

My heart pounded, and when I turned away from the door, all eyes were still on me.

"That's not true, is it?" A kid nearby turned to a mentor, but another teen answered first.

"My mom said she saw it online." The two kids nodded together, then looked back to me, as if for confirmation. "Sus."

Well, yes, young scholar. It's true and is sus, but enjoy the free soda and the fruit bowl, probably funded in part by that tainted money. My face heated, and I turned back to the guard, who apologized for the reporter getting in. As we talked, conversations slowly increased in volume behind me, and by the time I hurried for the stairwell to head to my office, no one seemed to pay attention.

After the heavy door clicked shut behind me and I

trudged up the stairs, I took a few deep breaths. The kids in the program knew what was going on, and if they lost faith in us, lost trust in us, the organization was useless. I glanced over my shoulder, catching a flash of a game controller through the door's pane of glass. Part of our plan had been to expand the lounges to include other locations where we could do more programming. I'd even floated the idea by Tye to gauge student interest, and now it seemed like it might never happen.

My phone buzzed in my pocket again, and I tried unsuccessfully to settle my nerves after the encounter with the reporter.

Cord: We're planning our annual FitMi retreat. Can we hire you as a capture the flag strategist?

He'd included a GIF showing a little black bear swinging on a red golf flag. Despite the stress of the encounter, I giggled, the sounds ricocheting off the concrete walls of the stairwell. The little bear made me smile as I watched the clip cycle. I felt my shoulders relax and my mind become less noisy after reading Cord's message—and I tried desperately not to read more into that.

Pearl: Tempting career move. Thank you for the smile.

CHAPTER 11

Cord

I REREAD PEARL'S RESPONSE TO MY TEXT FROM earlier in the day. When I saw I'd made her smile, I'd felt my posture straighten with pride over that. "That's normal, right?" I eyed Peach as I cut through the living room, tucking the phone in my pocket. "Just like asking my cat for approval?"

"Hey," I said, opening my front door.

Abby smiled and rested a palm on my chest, leaning in to kiss me. They'd had a presentation earlier in the day and were in a black dress and heels, making us just about the same height. "And hello, beautiful girl," they said, bending to greet Peach. The cat padded closer, sniffed the outstretched hand, then turned abruptly, her ass in the air as she sauntered away. That she was wearing a yellow sweater with the FitMi logo on it that I had custom ordered made the move look just pretentious enough, but Abby took it in stride. "Your cat hates me," they said with a sigh, setting their purse and bag on the kitchen counter and kicking off their four-inch heels.

"She doesn't hate you, she's just . . ."

Peach meowed to complete my sentence, then scurried off as much as an ancient cat can scurry.

Abby laughed and leaned against the counter. Their blond hair was swept back, and I admired their wide eyes and playful lips, but I didn't feel the butterflies, or the nauseating heart pounding, or the pull to go and stand nearer. I thought I'd wanted that, desired a distinctive lack of butterflies, but standing here, it felt all wrong. I needed to end things, and I dreaded the conversation.

"She's just temperamental." I finished my sentence, defending my cat instead. "She takes a while to warm up to people."

"I'll get over it." Abby scanned my face, assessing. "You look tired. I'm glad that partnership deal is about to go through. You need a break. It's good you're going to that comic book convention with Wes soon."

I nodded, and it was true. Though somehow, I'd gone from fearing making decisions when we started the company to leading major deals, and I liked it. Being in charge was more my thing than I'd thought it would be. I *was* tired, though, and I did still miss getting into the details and coding.

Abby held out a hand for me to take, and I awkwardly slid mine across the counter. "So, I wanted to talk to you about something." They squeezed my fingers and looked down at our joined hands.

"I did, too." I pulled my hand back and turned to the fridge, taking out a bottle of their favorite sparkling water. I couldn't hold hands while I thought about how to end things with them. It made me feel like I needed to move, and I opened the cupboard for a glass. "I meant to tell you. There's some stuff going on with OurCode."

Abby accepted the bottle and the glass and brushed blond hair off their shoulder, flashing a half smile. "It's been everywhere." Abby tipped the glass to their lips. "I feel bad for your friend."

I scratched the back of my neck, feeling guilty even though I hadn't done anything. "My friend?" I pulled Peach's food from its cubby, still eager for something to do with my hands.

"Yeah, the pretty one who was in the gold dress at the gala? She's the new interim director, but I can't remember her name."

"Pearl," I said, glancing up for just a second and then back down at Peach's dish.

"Yeah. I liked her." Abby drummed their short nails on the countertop, making a *tap-tap-tap* sound. "You're not still doing the board thing, are you?"

"I didn't want to leave her hanging." Peach's food clattered into the dish, and I set it back in her spot. "I mean, leave the organization hanging, and I already told Kevin I would accept the position."

"You're such a good guy." Abby grinned and reached for my hand again. "You really are."

I let them take my hand with nothing else to occupy them, but I shrugged. "Just keeping my word."

"I know," they said. "Don't argue. Let me say you're a good guy." They stood and stepped close to me, wrapping their arms around my waist, which gave me that same feeling of wanting to flee. "Let's sit on the couch. I want to talk to you about something."

Abby guided me into the living room, where Peach was seated on the middle cushion, eyeing us both. I thought about moving her, but her position forced us to sit on either side of her, giving me space.

"Is something wrong?"

Abby tried to pet Peach, who rolled toward me and out of their reach. My cat was maybe an asshole. "We've been spending time together for a while," they said, ignoring the cat's rebuff and searching my face.

I wasn't sure what was coming next, but I was certain I needed to do this before Abby got more invested in me. "Ab—"

They squeezed my hand and looked up at me with big blue eyes. "No, please. Let me get it out."

My pulse hammered, begging them in my head not to ask me anything, but I let them go on.

"I got a job offer. It's a promotion and an exciting opportunity . . . and it's in Texas."

"Oh," I said, with nothing else to add. My mind had been going a hundred miles an hour and then hit the brakes. "That's . . . wow. Congratulations. Are you going to take it?"

They nodded, expression solemn. "I really like you, but I don't think I want long distance. And I know you can't leave Chicago. We were never really official anyway, and I don't think either of us wanted to be."

I replayed the words in my head, checking to make sure I was interpreting the meaning right, because it felt like Abby had just given me the gift of ending things before I had to. Yes, at work and in bed, I loved taking charge, yet in terms of relationships and when it came to handling emotions, I was more than happy to be a passenger. "Long distance probably wouldn't be great," I said, squeezing their hand. "But I'm happy for you about the job. Tell me more about it."

It was like I had taken a bowling ball out of the hood of my sweatshirt, and without the heavy weight, I could just care about Abby without complications, which I did.

"Of course. It's such a great opportunity—I'm really excited." They tucked their hair behind their ears. "I was so nervous to . . . you know. No one enjoys being the one to end something."

"No hard feelings." I slid my fingers across my forehead, used to having hair there to sweep out of the way. "Do you have a lot of loose ends to tie up before you leave?"

"It's manageable, but I'm going to hate to leave my OurCode mentee. They're such a great kid, and the program is short on mentors right now. I haven't told them yet." Abby crossed the room and pulled a phone from her bag. "Tye is one of the coolest kids I've ever met, and they're talented. Really talented. I don't want to leave them in the lurch and risk them not getting the opportunities they deserve. They paired us because we had some things in common but they're so short on mentors right now with the scandal."

"Tye?" I straightened, then repeated the name in a normal voice. "Tye. That's your mentee?"

"Yeah, they're fifteen. Sharp as a tack and funny, too."

And, I'm pretty sure, Pearl's new roommate. "I could take over as their mentor," I said before thinking it through. There were about six hundred reasons not to volunteer. I didn't have time to mentor someone, let alone go through the training process for mentors. I didn't know if board members could participate in mentoring, and I was pretty sure it was against some ethical code to have the kind of fantasies about your mentee's aunt that I had about Pearl. But I also remembered Pearl saying what the program meant to Tye, and if Abby was right about the scandal affecting volunteers, recruiting new mentors might be challenging. I glanced over Abby's shoulder at Peach, who was perched in the doorway to my office, tail shifting from side to side and her fuzzy brow wrinkled. The expression conveyed *When is this other human going to leave?*

I added, "I mean, if they needed me. If they didn't have someone else who was a better fit."

"Are you sure? You're so busy, and you'll have to go through training." Abby tipped their head, eyeing me skeptically.

"The house is almost done, and that partnership is almost finalized. I want to do it."

"Like I said, you're such a good guy." Abby wrapped their arms around my neck, and I relaxed, uncertain whether I was making the best possible decision or the worst.

Peach strode into the room, then sat behind Abby and gave a loud meow. "I'm not going to lie," they said into the crook of my neck. "I'll miss you, but I am not disappointed to get away from your cat."

CHAPTER 12

Pearl

"I BROUGHT STUFF FOR NACHOS!" SHEA'S VOICE announced her arrival as she pushed through the front door, her arms weighed down with reusable grocery bags.

"For how many people?" I eyed the haul, already grateful for the distraction from thoughts of work and Cord, both of which had kept me up late all week. Cord volunteering to be Tye's mentor had taken me by surprise when Bea told me about Abby's request for a replacement. I was surprised and kind of touched he would step up in that way.

My sister was sorting containers, unaware of my internal dialogue. "There has to be a variety of toppings." Shea dropped the bags on the counter, one tipping, and a can of refried beans rolled out alongside a box of condoms and a bottle of lube.

I picked up the condoms and looked between Shea and the Trojans. "What exactly do you think we're getting up to tonight when Britta gets here?"

My little sister snatched back the box. "Shut up. I'm heading over to Caleb's place after this. He never remembers to buy them." Before I could respond, she spoke again quickly. "And don't shoot that raised eyebrow at me. It's not a big deal."

I shut my mouth and started unpacking the grocery sacks. Shea's boyfriend was the portrait of inconsiderate.

"Is Bri not coming?"

I set aside three bags of chips, questioning whether Shea knew how much four women would actually eat in one night. I knew she was expecting the raised eyebrow, but I kept my eyes down. "She's still packing and wanted to spend the evening with Tye before leaving."

"Can you imagine two months in London?" Shea looked wistful and pulled two bottles of wine from another bag before setting a package of chocolate chip cookies next to them.

"I already bought snacks," I reminded her, eyeing the growing pile of alcohol and snack food.

"Yeah, but it's probably fruit and vegetables."

"And a cheese tray. It's a charcuterie board."

"Well, now we'll have options."

We unpacked in silence, working together in my small kitchen with the practice of two siblings used to doing this, effortlessly shifting places and circling each other. All that was missing was Bri abandoning us halfway through because she got a brilliant idea for work and had to attend to it immediately.

Shea opened the bag of cookies and grabbed a handful of baby carrots from the board I'd pulled from the fridge. She settled on a barstool at my kitchen island. "Did she tell you her boyfriend decided he didn't want to do long distance for two months? She has had the worst luck with guys. I hope she gets nice and laid in London."

"Or finds love," I said, arranging the cheese Shea had disrupted.

She laughed and shot me a raised eyebrow. "Love? Who are you, and where is my sister?"

There was a knock at the door, and we exchanged a look. I wiped my hands on a dish towel and spoke over my shoulder as I strode to the door. She was right—I wasn't the romantic sister. I was the practical one who reminded Shea to do a criminal record check on her flavor of the month, and Bri to call me when she got home from a date so I knew she was safe. I wanted them to be happy, though, and love would make them both happy, even if it wasn't for me. I'd been down that road before. "I'm full of surprises."

"Girls' night!" Britta exclaimed with a wide smile when I opened the door, holding up a bottle of wine and a brown paper bag.

"I brought stuff for nachos," Shea declared as Britta set the bottle and her bag on the counter.

"Got your text. I brought guacamole from the best place in the city."

I eyed the growing pile of food. "How long do you all plan on being at my house? I told you I'd have snacks." I motioned to my increasingly obscured fruit and cheese tray on the counter.

"We'll eat that, too. What night in doesn't have some junk food, though?" Shea reached for another slice of gouda and popped it into her mouth.

"Hear, hear," Britta said with a smile.

Before I'd moved to California, we'd done this a few times, and this was the first get-together since I'd moved back to Chicago. I needed it after spending the week untangling the messes Kendra had made.

"How is it being back?" Britta settled on a barstool next to Shea. "You guys must have had a wild week."

The news stories hadn't stopped, and the full story had emerged by this point. "'Wild' is one word for it," I said, leaning on the counter and plucking a donut hole from the bag. "The board member involved in the affair was also doing a lot of business with some organizations that are essentially anti-diversity and treat employees with marginalized identities horribly, so profiting on basically everything we're trying to fight." I rubbed my neck, where a tension headache had become a permanent fixture. The only respite from it was when I met with Cord for lunch. I shoved a chip and far too much guacamole into my mouth to distract myself from him, too.

"That's . . . not great, but does that really impact you guys that much if they both left?" Shea slid off her stool and pulled a bottle of white wine from the fridge, pouring a glass for Britta.

"It wouldn't, except he and Kendra took money from them right around the same time some of our latest inclusion programs were canceled or postponed indefinitely. Hard to tell if that was a coincidence or if Kendra and this board member were up to more." Ellie and I had been in meetings with Kevin and the staff all week trying to determine how much wrongdoing Kendra had been responsible for. The board was concerned about the optics, and our donors were skittish, understandably. We'd been putting out the most manageable fires all week.

Britta accepted the glass from Shea. "Mason keeps trying to talk Cord out of getting involved." She'd gone to work for FitMi at the same time that Wes left to pursue teaching.

"Wait, Cord? As in the nerdy white man you were gaga

for but wouldn't date?" Shea leaned forward, and I rolled my eyes, but Britta spoke for me.

"The same," Britta said. "He's joining the board of directors, something he decided to do . . . maybe fifteen seconds after learning Pearl worked there."

I turned away from them to grab plates. "That is not how that happened," I said, handing one to each of them. "And I was not gaga for him, but he is volunteering as a mentor, too."

Shea started piling nacho fixings on her plate and pointed a chip at me. "Does that mean you'll see him even more?"

"Maybe." I wiped a few drops of salsa off the counter, ignoring my sister's assessing gaze. "He's going to be Tye's new mentor." My counter had never been so clean as I searched out any and all sections of the surface I could wipe down instead of looking up. "And we'll be at mentor training together next weekend."

I didn't need to look up as they both began a chorus of "Ooooh" so loud, my neighbors might complain.

"It's not a big deal," I said. "I want to observe our training program, and he'll just happen to be there." Honestly, my heart and stomach were doing a samba at spending two days with him, but I definitely did not want to admit that. It didn't matter, as their excited taunting continued, and I walked into the living room with my plate with a little of everything. "He was my boss then and is dating someone now. Do you need a good K-drama? You're clearly looking for more of a story than exists in this reality."

"Dating? Seriously dating? No!" Shea tapped the buttons on my microwave to melt her mountain of cheese.

Britta waved a hand. "It won't last with Abby."

"That's the person he's dating?" Shea leaned forward, snatching another donut hole.

"Not exactly. I think they're pretty casual." Britta held up air quotes around "casual." "Wes doesn't think he's really that into it."

Her words bounced around in my head, because I'd hoped the same thing but chalked it up to being jealous, not that I'd admit it.

Britta continued. "After you left, he dated a few people kind of seriously, but he's different now. Never commits to anyone. I honestly don't think he ever got over you."

I didn't like how that made me feel simultaneously guilty and excited. "There was nothing to get over." I sipped my wine. That wasn't exactly the full truth.

"Was there something to get . . . under?" Shea pulled the plate from the microwave, and they both walked into the living room to join me. "Did anything ever actually happen with you two?"

"Yes! Spill," Britta said from the armchair. "If Wes knows, he's kept it quiet, but he's not good at keeping secrets from me, so I think he doesn't. Did something happen in San Diego?"

"San Diego?" Shea's mouth was full of nacho, so it came out sounding like *Sammiaho*.

"Right before I took the job in California," I said, leaning back into the couch. The name of the city was an instant time machine to five years earlier.

Shea and Britta looked at me expectantly, and I halted my thoughts before they strayed to those days in San Diego. The wine wasn't as good as the bottle I'd shared with Cord the night everything changed, but the taste of champagne still took me back to wanting something more with him, breaking his heart, and the sobering reminder that it was too late because he was now with someone else. "Not that it matters, but nothing happened in San Diego." That was a lie in and of itself, but one of omission, too. There were so many important moments for Cord and me before San Diego.

CHAPTER 13

Pearl

Seven Years Earlier

MASON WAVED AFTER STEPPING OUT OF A FENCED-off area that was now the holding pen for those captured in this more-intense-than-anticipated team-building bout of capture the flag. He held up the flags he'd taken from my belt and twirled them in the air. "Don't you go anywhere, now, Pearl." His toothy grin grated on my last nerve, and I picked up my phone. I hated losing, especially to Mason.

Pearl: What on earth made you want to date Mason?

Bri: We went out a few times and he scratched some itches.

Shea: Is this the hot one Pearl works with? Is he single still?

Pearl: Don't even think about it.

Shea: Too late. I'm thinking about doing things to that man.

Pearl: Pushing him down stairs? That's usually my fantasy.

Bri: Don't get arrested on my behalf.

Shea: And it's okay if you want him for yourself, Sis.

Just then, Mason's voice rang out again. "Brought you some company," he said, escorting Cord into the pen. "Caught him trying to break you out. Man, am I glad I joined the other team at the last minute." Mason laughed and returned to his post as guard.

I looked up from my spot on the ground and took in Cord's jeans and FitMi hoodie. "You tried to bust me out?"

He shrugged before sitting down on the hay covering the concrete floor. "I saw him catch you and couldn't leave you." He pushed the blue bandanna off his head, our team indicator. The move left his hair a little wild. "Guess my heroism was for nothing, though."

"You didn't have to do that," I said, glancing down at our legs stretched out next to each other, bothered by the way my body reacted to his wanting to save me, even if it was just from Mason's capture-the-flag jail. "But thank you."

"You have that crease between your eyebrows that only shows up when Mason is around." He motioned to my face. "Did he do something besides being an obnoxious winner?"

His gaze zeroed in on the spot, and I mentally ironed out my expression. When his hair was off his face and I could see his eyes, I always felt like fidgeting. For such a laid-back guy—and Cord Matthews was the poster child for laid-back—his gaze was intense and focused. "Why do you dislike Mason? I know you've said no before, but did he do something inappropriate? We don't take that lightly." He bristled, posture straightening.

The change was cute. "Nothing like that. He went out with my sister a few times."

"Ah." He relaxed again, but his gaze was still intent on me, and I noticed how the toe of his shoe tipped toward my foot. "And it didn't end well?"

"Bri said he stood her up, then called later because he'd mixed up the times. Who knows?"

"But . . . cross a Harris once and you're out?"

I nodded. "In my book, anyway. Who needs to learn a lesson twice?"

"Remind me to never cross you." Cord brushed a few strands of hair off his face. "I'll keep you on my team from here on out."

I laughed and settled against the wall, scanning what I could see of the field to look for any of our teammates. The toe of his shoe was still angled toward me, and I tucked my knees to my chest to avoid the temptation to touch our shoes together. "Might not be a great idea. I was captured before I could take anyone down."

"I'm sure you would have been a force." He pointed to my arm. "Is that what your tattoo is? A star for each person you've had to take out?"

"There have been way more than four," I said with a grin. I was surprised he'd noticed that tattoo. "But no. It's not a trophy thing. I'm not tracking my team-building kills." I tugged the sleeve of my sweater up to reveal the three stars in a field of tiny dots. When Cord ghosted his finger along the pattern, an unexpected wave of sensation rolled through me. He hadn't touched me before other than incidental moments of contact, and this was that times a hundred even though it only lasted for a moment. The brief sweep of his finger felt illicit, like it was his lips moving over my skin.

He studied the design closely, his breath tickling my forearm before his eyes met mine again. "Can I know the secret? Does it stand for something?"

I missed the strange sensation of his fingertip as soon as he removed it but tried to blink away that thought. Cord wasn't exactly my boss, but he wasn't someone I needed to be getting stomach-butterfly-inducing touches from, either. "It stands for three things I always want to remember after a time in my life where I was in danger of forgetting." I pointed to the first star closest to my thumb. "Family first." I slid my fingernail across my wrist to the second. "Do work that matters."

"What kind of work?"

I willed the niggling sensation at his touch to stop. "I don't know yet. But something that makes a difference for people. My sister's kid is in elementary school now—I think about the world they'll grow up in. The kinds of opportunities they should have. I started taking classes in nonprofit management and I think I want to do something that can make an impact." My face warmed, and I wasn't sure why I'd said all that to him. I hadn't told anyone besides my sisters, not wanting anyone to know in case it didn't work out, but his grin and the way his eyes met mine made me want to say more.

Cord followed the motion of my finger, and I noticed how long his lashes were with his gaze cast down until his eyes flicked back up to mine. "And the third?"

I outlined the last star with the tip of my nail. Our heads were bent toward each other now, close to touching. "The last star is to remind me to put my head before my heart."

He followed my movement and made a vague outline of the star with his thumb, his palm warm under my wrist. "What made you forget head before heart?"

Ideally, Mason would interrupt this conversation by bringing in another teammate, but there was only the sound of the breeze rustling the leaves of the tree overhead. I still could only barely summon the willpower to pull my hand back into my lap. "A bad relationship that got messy. I should have known better."

"I can't picture you messy," he said, sitting back himself. His gaze swept over me, but not in a creepy or sexual way, more like he was taking in my face and somehow seemed to stop at the top button of my cardigan. "You seem like you have everything together all the time."

I noticed his shoelace was loose and the cuff of his jeans was frayed in the back, and I bit the inside of my cheek. We were very different people. "I am mostly put together now. I learned my lesson well."

"What got so messy?"

There was a shout in the distance and Mason's voice taunting someone, but I was drawn back to Cord and his long eyelashes and frayed jeans.

He followed the sound of Mason's taunts as well. "Unless you don't want to talk about it."

The voices faded into the breeze. "He was a little older and wanted to take care of me," I said, remembering my mother's warnings not to get involved with Jason. "He helped me get a job, and I moved in with him."

The sleeve of Cord's sweatshirt brushed my forearm. "Did you love him?"

I bit my lower lip, remembering the way I'd fallen into that life. "I did. Looking back, I can see I was young and naïve, but I loved him." I stretched out my legs again and swept a hand down my stomach. "You know, that head-over-heels kind of thing where you forget yourself. Ever been there?"

He looked away, studying his shoelaces. "Kind of."

"It felt like a fairy tale, being swept away and taken care of, and I was all in."

"And then?"

"And then he . . . wasn't all in. Wasn't in love with me anymore. And all that support and love and the safety net was gone in an instant." I made an explosion gesture with my fingers and gave him a wry smile.

"Oh." Cord straightened the same way he had when he'd asked about Mason.

"Yeah. I was kind of lost afterward, and it took me a while to find my next steps and to realize he hadn't been a great guy overall."

He nodded, tugging on his hoodie. "So, head before heart."

"Head before heart," I agreed, catching someone walking toward us. "Reminds me to never rely on others too much." I studied my own tennis shoes, which I swore inched closer to his all on their own. "No idea why I told you all that."

"I'm glad you did. And you're onto something," he said. "I grew up with a parent who was very heart before head. It can be a hard way to live."

I opened my mouth to ask what that was like, and I wondered how it affected him, but he glanced at the figure walking toward us.

"Looks like we might be saved."

"I think you're right."

Wes approached with two other staff members in tow,

waving the rival team's red flag. Mason walked behind them, head down, and we both stood, cheering. I took in Cord's crooked grin as he walked toward our team members, returning a high five. I still felt the sensation of his touch on my wrist.

Head before heart, I reminded myself. Head before tingly goose bumps, too. Still, I followed his stride, hoping he might turn and smile once more just to me before we rejoined the group, which he did.

Damn, butterflies.

CHAPTER 14

Present Day

I PULLED THE NOTEBOOK FROM MY BAG AND SETtled in a seat in the back of the meeting room. At the front, Bea and two current mentors chatted animatedly as they prepared for the training to begin.

Shea: Lunch?

Pearl: Can't—in the training all day.

Shea: Oooooh. With your work crush?

Pearl: For my work.

Shea: But he'll be there?

Pearl: Who?

Shea: Don't play.

"Hey. This seat taken?" Cord stood next to the chair to my right, dressed in jeans and a gray hoodie. Everyone was dressed casually for the daylong training, but my heart did an extra *thump-thump* at the sight of him.

"All yours." I motioned to his sweatshirt. "I always liked that one."

Cord looked down at the masked figure on his hoodie, the screen printing cracked and faded. "I can't believe you didn't know who Casey Jones was. Classic *Teenage Mutant Ninja Turtles*." He pulled his laptop and a notebook from his messenger bag and shook his head. "What would your old-school cartoon education look like without me?"

"You spent a lot of time at my desk explaining your clothes to me." He smelled good, like a hint of the cologne I'd caught a whiff of at the gala. When I worked at FitMi, he'd visited Wes's office a lot, passing by my desk all the time, and then he'd found reasons to be there just to see me . . . until it felt like my day was missing something if we didn't get to chat. It had been a long time since I had someone like him to chat with.

"I haven't worn this in forever," he said, tugging on the sweatshirt. "Abby said the masked face on it was creepy."

Abby. His partner and the reason I definitely needed to stop thinking about the Teenage Mutant Ninja Turtles and how good Cord smelled. "It is a little creepy."

Bea walked toward us, holding out a green folder in each hand with the OurCode logo printed on the front. "Good morning. I'm Bea." She held out her hand for Cord. "We're so glad to have you as a mentor. Abby told us she'd talked you into joining us."

I flashed the smile of someone who was quietly swallowing razor blades at the subtle reminder that it was the person he was dating who'd encouraged him to do this. "We're honored you're donating so much of your time," I added, accepting my folder and thumbing through the training materials.

"Happy to." He answered more of Bea's questions, and I tuned out their small talk, pretending to examine the outline for the two-day training session. "What are friends for if not to take over your community service commitments when you leave the state?" Cord laughed with Bea, but I could only tune in to one word. *Friend.*

I sat straighter, trying to contain the flash-bang I felt in my chest at learning he was single. I had so many reasons why that didn't change anything for me. But the flash-bangs continued.

When Bea walked away, Cord flipped through the training manual. "Looks like we'll be busy."

"I remember being impressed with the training when I interviewed." I watched three more people enter the room, and Bea's cofacilitator started the presentation, the logo flashing on the screen.

Friend. I rolled the word around in my head again. It made me feel both better and worse about the stomach-twisting feelings I'd been experiencing around Cord. Nothing had changed—I'd still broken his heart five years ago when I told him I was leaving the state and that the possibility of a relationship with him wasn't enough to stop me from going.

Once Bea began the presentation, I purposefully didn't look over toward Cord again. I didn't want to risk reading into his expression and probing for insight on whether he was relieved or sad about whatever happened with Abby to make them only a friend.

Bea stepped away from the podium and approached the rows of tables and chairs. "And that's how we'll spend the next two days. To begin, please turn to a neighbor and share why you're here."

While everyone else greeted new people around them, Cord and I were the only two in our row. "I guess you already know my story," he said, turning toward me and holding out his hand. "I'm Cord, and I have a hard time saying no when people ask favors of me." Cord's fingertips grazed mine.

"Pearl, and I have no trouble turning people down." I played along and joined the handshake. "I could give you lessons."

He squeezed my hand just enough to remind me that I knew how those same hands felt on the back of my neck and at my waist. "I remember," he said.

The words were like a can of repellent to the butterflies flitting inside me, and Cord's expression twisted almost immediately. "Oh, not because you said no to me, I just meant—"

"Thank you, everyone!" Bea spoke over the din of everyone's conversations, and I turned to face forward, uncomfortable with what my face might have shown Cord. Bea clapped to get everyone's attention a second time. "Okay, next—"

A hand shot up from a woman in the front row. "We had a question."

Bea invited the mentor to introduce themself, and I peeked at Cord from the corner of my eye. He was looking down at his folder, his hand in a fist on the table.

I considered ignoring him and his hand and the nervous way he clenched and unclenched his fist. *Don't worry about it,* I wrote on my notepad, and slid it to him. That was easier than dealing with whatever I was feeling. I didn't need all these feelings while I was in a work setting.

"We were wondering if you could share any steps Our-Code is taking to address everything in the news lately." The woman spun to make eye contact with others in the room. "We're both excited to volunteer, but how is the organization going to address this?"

Bea's eyes widened, just for a moment, before she smiled and hid the mild panic. I should have expected the questions coming up—I'd spent the last week answering that same inquiry from various media outlets, donors, and concerned citizens, containing a variable number of swear words.

"I can field that," I said, standing and smoothing a hand down the front of my silk tank. I was glad I'd ignored Bea's note that the training was casual. "I'm Pearl Harris, and I'm the interim executive director. If you've seen the news, you've likely seen the extent to which former members of the OurCode team violated the trust of our donors and volunteers and the mission of our organization. It's not something we take lightly, and we're working hard to identify solutions, both to make sure this doesn't happen again and to course-correct from the issues in the past." I was proud that my voice remained steady. It did not give away that we had absolutely no idea yet how we were going to do that.

"The staff and the board are committed to making sure nothing dampens the success of this program and the opportunities it provides for our participants. Are there specific questions?" Around the room, heads nodded and people smiled. One man in the back started clapping but stopped when he realized it wasn't that kind of speech. I let out a breath. "Back to you and your team," I said to Bea, striding back to my seat.

Cord leaned closer and whispered, "I really would never guess you were afraid of public speaking." His breath brushed my ear in a way that would have annoyed me from any other person.

"I've had lots of practice lately." I should have leaned away—but I wanted just one more breath against my skin.

"Hey, before, I really didn't mean—"

I did lean away this time. "Don't worry about it." I nodded toward the front, where Bea was beginning an explanation of the mentor expectations. It was a reminder to myself as much as to him that there were other priorities, things more important than the us that never was.

Still, I'd seen this part of the training several times, and I glanced away from Bea and down to my phone.

Shea: C'mon. Wouldn't it be nice to cut loose a little?

Pearl: We work together.

Shea: So? I work with Caleb.

Pearl: And it's messy.

Shea: Be a little messy for once. Messy can be fun!

Pearl: This is a moot point.

Shea: Because you broke his heart five years ago?

Pearl: Because one, we work together. Two, he's Tye's new mentor. And three, he's on the board and we can't handle any more bad press.

Shea: So, don't tell Tye or the press.

Shea: 🔌 in secret.

Shea: It will be a good *outlet* for your stress. Did you see what I did there?

Pearl: . . .

Shea: Are you ignoring me now?

Pearl: Yes.

I scribbled a date on my notepad, mostly to have something to do with my hands. I was ignoring Shea and was going to keep ignoring her, but it didn't mean she was wrong. The phone buzzed again in my hand, but before I glanced down, I felt Cord's breath near my ear. Having him so close both startled and warmed me. "Can we talk after the training?"

Shea: Just think about it. A little messiness won't kill you. Maybe he's good with messy, too.

CHAPTER 15

Cord

THE REST OF THE OURCODE MENTOR TRAINING WAS probably stellar, but all I could focus on was the sensation of Pearl's whisper against my ear. When she replied with a quick "Yes, we should," the brush of heat against my skin felt so delicious, I couldn't stop reliving it. Couldn't stop reliving that and my glib comment that she was good at saying no.

"Let's take a fifteen-minute break," Bea said at the end of a role-playing activity about supporting mentee mental health. "Please be back at the top of the hour."

Everyone scattered, and I found Pearl across the room, talking to her role-playing partner with her back to me. The skirt she wore hugged the curves of her hips, giving just a hint of her figure beneath the conservative fabric. "Pearl," I said, dropping a light touch to her elbow as her training partner stepped back with a wave. "Do you have a minute?"

She hesitated but nodded, and we walked toward the hallway, away from the group. She led us to a corner of the elevator lobby outside the lounge where the training was taking place. I thought I saw her glance toward the elevator, and when her gaze returned to me, she flicked her eyes to my lips for a split second.

Well, I haven't made an apology with a burgeoning erection in a while. I sucked in a breath. "The thing I said at the training, about your saying no." I leaned against the wall, trying to look casual and not like this was the most awkward conversation possible. I cleared my throat. "It was just a joke. I didn't mean to bring up . . . you know, our past."

She visibly stiffened. "Don't give it a second thought. I thought nothing of it."

"You looked upset." I wasn't sure why I pushed the point after she said it was fine, except that I didn't want her walking away yet, especially walking away thinking I'd say something intentionally to hurt her.

"Maybe you just can't read me as well as you think you can," she joked, leaning in a step closer as two people walked by toward the elevator.

I assessed her expression, the shape of her eyes and angle of her smile, still so familiar. "I can read you." I dipped my head lower. "There was a reason we were the standing charades champions."

The laugh erupting from her drew quick looks from the fellow mentors waiting by the elevator, but I forgot all about them when her fingers moved to her lips to cover her laugh. We'd been set to play capture the flag for a second year at FitMi, but the rain kept us inside. I'd resisted, wanting to work while at work and not get involved in games, but when Pearl and I were paired randomly to be on a team for charades, I'd had more fun than I expected. "I forgot about that. We were good."

"We were the best." I held out three fingers and started making a film-camera motion. "It was like we shared a brain. Who else could get me to guess Snuffleupagus?" I remembered her motioning wildly to get me to say the end of the word, waving a hand behind her so I'd guess "gas" to finish the last syllable. "Anyone broken our record for fastest guess?"

When her hand slipped from my arm, I felt the loss. "I think that record will stand the test of time."

"Well, that's the way it should be." A quiet pause fell between us, and her gaze dropped to my hands.

I wanted to fall back into our old patterns, to ask if she missed me, if she missed the deep connection we'd had. The gamble felt worth it, hypothetically, but the elevator dinged behind her, and I was reminded that the odds of that question paying off weren't great. I didn't need her to have missed me. She scratched a spot on her neck absently and I noticed her wrist. "You added to the tattoo," I remarked. "There used to be only three stars."

"Oh." She looked at her wrist as if surprised, and then rested a palm over it. "Yeah. A recent addition." We fell into another moment of silence, and she nodded. "But it's not weird between us, Cord. Don't worry about that." She stepped closer again, raising her hand, but then rethinking it and letting it fall to her side. "I mean, it's not weird for me. I appreciate you checking in, though."

The thing was, it wasn't weird for me. Being madly attracted to Pearl, wanting to talk to her about inane things, to hear her laugh, were the most normal things in the world for me. That was the troubling part. And I could have said that, or I could have lied, or I could have done what I might in a business situation and commit to nothing, but I went with, "It's a little weird. You know I like weird, though."

Her lips parted but curled into a grin. "The shirt was a hint, I guess." Her fingers slid down my arm again.

"And I remember you like a few weird things, too." I

glanced over her shoulder at the elevator, remembering. When I returned my gaze to her face, she was gently biting her lower lip, and I didn't exactly know what I'd say next, but I had to say something. "Maybe—"

"Hey, Pearl," Bea called from the entry to the lounge before I could speak. "There's a situation I need you for."

"No time for maybes." She nodded, not breaking eye contact with me, her fingers finishing their path down my arm, before giving me a small smile and walking backward toward the lounge. "See you back in there."

CHAPTER 16

Cord

Six Years Earlier

THE AREA WHERE PEARL WORKED WAS NORMALLY FILLED with light from the windows throughout our company headquarters. It was only nine in the morning, but now the sky was dark, the sheets of rain and howling wind ominous as the thunderstorm raged.

"Anything?" Pearl met my gaze as I neared her desk from my office across the hall. The internet connectivity had been down for more than an hour.

"Nah," I said with a glance out the window. "Not sure we'll get much done this morning."

A loud crack of thunder sounded, and we both jumped. Pearl clutched a hand over her chest, and I looked elsewhere, because I definitely *wanted* to follow her hand. She was beautiful and quick-witted, kept everyone on their toes, and was still, two years later, completely off-limits to me as one of our employees. The office space was quiet that morning, with everyone out at some meeting or another. We both regained composure after the thunder and shared a nervous laugh.

"Scared of storms?"

She bristled. "I just don't like them. It's all the rain. I prefer to not get wet."

I bit down on my cheek hard to push the thought of Pearl wet from my mind. That was a lost cause. I nodded my head toward the elevator. "Want to get out of here? Go get coffee in the lobby or something until the storm lightens up?"

She glanced between her computer screen and the nearest window, outside which two streaks of lightning traversed the sky. "Okay. Coffee would be nice."

We stood by the elevator in silence. Sometimes Pearl and I would go back and forth with jokes and banter, and it was so easy. When I got it in my head that I needed to impress her, all speech—all coherent speech, anyway—left my brain entirely. When the doors parted, I relaxed. I expected silence in the small space, and I had something to focus on with the flashing lights showing our descent. "Uh, how are classes going?"

"Good, I'm taking—"

The lights flickered, and the elevator jerked to a stop. Our eyes met, hers wide as she reached for the red emergency button on the control panel, but nothing happened. She mashed it another time or two, cursing under her breath. In the meantime, I tried to call the front desk of the building but couldn't get service.

Pearl gave up and leaned against the wall. "Not doing any good."

The lights inside the car flicked again and then shut off.

Trying to get my bearings in the dark, I reached out with one hand, digging in my pocket for my phone with the other. "Are you okay?" In a perfect fantasy, Pearl would have feared the dark and needed me to hold her, but she looked more annoyed than scared.

Her voice was calm. "I just don't like being stuck. I'm fine."

"Sure. Me, too. Hopefully the power will be right back on."

It wasn't.

After a while, I spread my hoodie on the cold floor of the car so we could sit down, with the light from my phone casting a blue glow over us. We sat closer than we would have if there was more light, and because the hoodie only covered a small patch of floor. Being that close to Pearl was equal parts wonder at how she smelled and the warmth she emanated, and terror that I'd say the wrong thing. By that point, my phone showed we'd been in the elevator for forty minutes.

"You're almost done with school, right?" There was no reason to talk quietly, but with our proximity and the darkness, it didn't feel strange to speak so close to her ear.

"Last semester," she said. "I put off my introductory statistics class until the very end, and it's kicking my butt. It's more difficult than I expected."

It felt like we were in some kind of cocoon when she leaned close to me. We weren't touching, save the brush of our forearms, but it still felt intimate, and for a second, I could forget I was essentially her boss. I knew I should pull back and let her sit on the hoodie alone, but I didn't. "I could help. I had to take stats in college."

In the glow of my phone, I followed the lines of her face as she turned, a small grin tipping up the corners of her lips, replacing the panic I'd seen earlier. "You got a C in the class, didn't you?"

I laughed. "C plus. How did you know that?"

She grazed a fingertip at the corner of my eyebrow, and my body reacted immediately, making me adjust my leg. "You squint one eye, just a little, when you're saying something that isn't on the up-and-up. I could make it out even in this light."

I stilled at her touch. "I do?" I wanted her fingers to stay there, but she let them fall back into her lap. I ran a finger over the spot she'd touched. "How did you figure that out?"

The light on my phone cut off, and I missed her expression when she said, "I guess I just pay attention to you."

"Do you want me to take an online stats class so I can suffer with you and maybe do better than the first time?" I liked that her foot had stopped tapping and I could feel her relax against me. I wanted to bottle up this feeling. "I would," I added, nudging my shoulder with hers. "If it would help."

"I know your schedule. You don't have time to take a stats class, but thank you for the offer."

I kept my eyes on her as I swiped the screen on my phone again. "I'd sacrifice sleep for you."

I heard her slow inhale and exhale and worried I'd overstepped. I was seconds away from standing and crossing the small space to give her room when she nudged my shoulder back. "I know you would."

"You're probably not used to struggling with things like this, huh?"

"I've always been good at school—I usually pick things up quickly." She bit her lower lip. "And things my ex would say end up in my head sometimes. I don't like them, but they're there. I never want to believe he's right about what I am capable of."

"I guess this is your chance to slum it with us regular people in periodic fields of B-plus work."

"Wasn't it a C plus?" She chuckled, and her head settled against my shoulder. "Anyway, I'm not sure you get to call yourself regular people. You started a multimillion-dollar company before turning thirty."

My voice was pitched low when I spoke, and even though I knew I shouldn't, I let my arm fall around her shoulders. "I don't think we'd be worth millions if you weren't on the team."

"Want to cut me a check?"

"Sure, just don't leave us when you graduate." The screen on the phone cut out again, throwing us into darkness. "Don't leave me."

She didn't respond immediately, and I searched the dark space for any clues to how she was feeling.

"I'm sorry I snapped at you earlier. I *am* a little scared of storms," she confessed in a hushed voice. "I don't like people seeing me scared of anything."

"It's our secret." She smelled like vanilla and cinnamon, and without thinking too much about it, I brushed my lips across her forehead, feeling her soft skin under my lips.

Every HR manual in existence should have been thrown at me, but she didn't pull away. Instead, Pearl reached across her body and slowly, delicately placed her hand on my chest. We sat like that, her palm over my heart, her body curled into mine, and I could have lived in that elevator for years. I silently prayed for the power to stay out for another hour.

"C'mon. C'mon. C'mon," Pearl mumbled.

"They'll fix it soon," I tried to reassure her. "Let's distract ourselves. Tell me a random fact about you." I cast a quick glance down to her face.

Pearl's soft voice startled me when she spoke, because I didn't think she'd play along. "You first."

"I know all the words to 'Firework' by Katy Perry. It's my shower song."

Pearl knocked her shoulder against mine. "I can totally picture you singing that song."

"Are you saying you can picture me in the shower?"

Her laugh wrapped around me, and she knocked my shoulder again. "Get your mind out of the gutter."

"I'm not the one of us picturing the other naked." Though, of course, I was. "So . . . what's yours?"

She let out a breathy little laugh, and I couldn't take my eyes off her face in that moment, the way it lightened. "It's embarrassing."

"You're drawing this out like a state secret. I'm dying here." It was the furthest thing from the truth, and I didn't know exactly what weather phenomenon caused a thunderstorm or who wasn't responding from the elevator company, but by this point I'd name them in my will.

"I used to make up dances with my sisters to that song. We'd perform it for Tye to make them laugh." Pearl's head dipped, and she was grinning.

I fiddled with my phone, wondering if I could get service. Spotify came to life, and I searched for the song.

"What are you doing?"

"Finding our song," I said, tapping the icon.

"Our song?"

The opening beats filled the elevator car, and I rose to my feet. "Now I know you know the lyrics, too." I held out my palm for her, moving my phone to illuminate where I hoped she'd take my hand.

"No! You'll think I'm so weird. These are the dance

moves of a rhythm-challenged teenager. No way." Pearl folded her arms across her chest and smiled wider, the glow from my phone casting shadows over her features. "What are you doing?"

"Distracting you." I waved my hand in her direction. "I want to see these moves even more now."

"It's dark in here. You couldn't see them anyway." Even though she was protesting, she took my hand so I could pull her to her feet, tucking my phone in my pocket.

"Okay. I'll feel and hear them, then." I held on to her hand, the skin of her palm against mine, her body close to mine as the song surrounded us.

Pearl was laughing, her body shaking when my hand trailed closer to her waist. "You want me to sing along with you?"

"I do." The dip of her waist felt natural under my hand, and her other hand rested against my chest, fingers splayed out. "We can dance together."

We sang along with the song, and I belted the chorus to make her laugh. She felt so damn good in my arms in the dark, even though she wasn't really dancing. "Weak," I said, pulling her closer and spinning us, earning her loud laughter.

"Thank you for distracting me. This has to be one of the weirdest things to ever happen in this office, right?" Her fingertips grazed the base of my neck, and shots of electricity extended from where she'd touched me.

"I like weird. And you're welcome." The song had switched to a song I didn't recognize, one that was slower, and Pearl stayed against me, chest to chest, in the tight space, warm from our closeness. I swayed with her, matching the beat of the new song. "This one isn't as fun."

"I like it," she said, moving with me, sliding the hand joined with mine up my arm in a long, slow stroke. "Do you mind? It's kind of . . . nice." Her breath swept my neck, and I rested my hand at her hip.

"I don't mind." It came out low and quiet, barely audible over the singer's warbling voice and the crescendo of the chorus.

"I don't normally tell people when I'm scared," she said. "It's hard to open up like that."

I was certain she could hear my heart pounding. "You can tell me anything."

The ambient light from my pocket had faded when the screen went to sleep, so when her back hit the wall of the elevator, we were both startled. "Sorry," I murmured, still pressed to her, our thighs touching, her breasts against my chest. My breath was shaky. It took a moment for my brain to reset, but when I began to ease back, she stopped me.

"No." Pearl's fingers worked into the hair at the nape of my neck, her nails gently scratching my scalp. "Stay like this."

"Okay." I dipped my chin and our mouths were close to level, her breath and mine mingling. "I won't move." I lifted my hand from her hip and cupped her neck. Well, I tried to cup her neck. I couldn't see and accidentally palmed her cheek and her nose, earning an exhale that sounded like a cross between a laugh and a groan. "Sorry."

"You found me," she said when my palm caressed her neck, my thumb tracing up the line of her throat. Her sharp inhale when I stroked the base of her throat made me want to trace that spot for hours.

"I did." Our noses brushed, and I dipped my head, my

lips sweeping against her jawline. "Pearl." I wanted to kiss her, keep touching like this, and pull her down on top of me and run my hands up her skirt and over her thighs before begging her to ride me.

"You smell like cinnamon," I said before pressing my mouth to hers, our lips together once, twice, then sliding against each other. I stroked the seam of her mouth with my tongue and she opened for me, her full lips working in tandem with mine, and I pressed against her, wanting to be closer, knowing this was the start of something.

"You—" Her words froze mid-sentence when the lights flashed on and the elevator rattled, then moved. Pearl blinked at the sudden light after such a long time in darkness and then met my eyes. Our bodies were still aligned, her arms around my neck.

"You okay in there?" The voice had us pulling apart as if we were on a spring. It was the building security head calling from the other side of the door.

"Yeah," I called through the door, voice husky. "We're good."

"We'll get you out in a minute," the voice from the other side called.

Pearl flattened her palm against her chest and looked away from me.

I stepped closer, reaching for her again, wanting that moment in the dark back more than anything. "Are you okay?"

"Yep. Great." She straightened her shoulders and adjusted her shirt. "Thank you for distracting me," she said crisply, staring at the door. She was still staring at it a moment later when they slid apart, and I was staring at her, my head spinning over what had happened. The feel of her kiss lingered on my lips, and she gave me just a flash of something in her eyes over her shoulder before stepping into the lobby.

"You're welcome," I said, dazed.

CHAPTER 17

Present Day

BEFORE THE DOOR CLOSED BEHIND ME, I KICKED off my heels and threw my bag onto the kitchen island. I'd lived alone for a couple months, but the quiet seemed louder in this new place. I hit play on my phone to fill my apartment with some music and fell onto my couch, tapping my foot to a Kendrick Lamar song.

The rest of the day had been one crisis after another. As the full scale of my former boss and her board-member paramour's impropriety came to light, there was a shadow cast on OurCode. When I got the notification in the middle of the mentor training, I'd had to run out and deal with the immediate fallout of a news story and several angry donors. This story had included more damning information about the married board member who had been in bed not only with Kendra but also with the Smith Corporation, whose policies around marginalized employees were so problematic, they bordered on illegal. Every day, this job that I had thought was such a dream opportunity was turning into more of a nightmare. The scariest part was this niggling feeling that I wasn't going to be able to fix it. I glanced around my kitchen, trying to summon enough energy to make dinner before attacking work again. I'd just work harder until I could fix things. Resolve in place, I rubbed the arch of my left foot. All of that on top of that strange conversation with Cord at the break, and I was mentally exhausted, and Tye would be moving in later this week.

I hit the call button for Shea while staring into the fridge, deciding what would take the least amount of time to make. Tye needed to finish packing, so Shea was staying at our sister's place for a few days with them before they moved in with me. The phone rolled over to voicemail. "It's Shea. Why not save us both some trouble and text instead?" I rolled my eyes and hung up. With my sister, a missed call was just as good. In the end, I dropped a brown sugar and cinnamon Pop-Tart in the toaster. Cinnamon. Cord didn't know about the Pop-Tarts when he mentioned it; he'd been taking in my perfume before kissing my neck. I hadn't worn the scent since leaving Chicago, since the last time I saw him.

As much as I could put my attention on work all day, his words from earlier stuck with me. It was true, and I supposed I had it coming, but I'd been so shocked when Cord had made that comment about my saying no. He'd explained that it was a joke, and of course it was. It had been years. Before he'd explained, though, I thought that maybe he wasn't over it, the same way I wasn't over it. All those stupid flash-bangs had rushed back uninvited.

My phone buzzed in my hand. I had a slew of messages from Shea, my mom, Tye, Britta. I didn't expect Cord's name to be at the top of the list.

Cord: I grabbed your things when you didn't come back to the training. Can I drop them off?

I gave him my address and sat on a barstool, fingers tapping on the counter. I had left my notebook and training supplies on the table—I'd figured Bea had picked them up, since I'd been fielding calls well into the evening. But of course Cord would have thought to do that. I was always struck by how thoughtful he was in big and small ways, even before anything happened in the elevator at FitMi headquarters. I'd been with other men who weren't, and it was a trait that shined brighter in retrospect.

The beat of the next song on the playlist relaxed me, and I rested my head against the back of the sofa. I'd always thought he was nice, capable, even cute, but in that dark space, we'd sat close together and talked, and maybe it was being in the dark, or being on edge from the power outage, but I'd wanted to be near him in a way I hadn't been drawn to others before, even with Jason. The heat emanating from his body and the smell of him—spicy and subtle—made it feel natural to snuggle against him, rest my head on his shoulder, and wait out the storm. The moment just went too far. We'd both gotten caught up in the closeness and the dark. I'd forgotten my rules.

Cord: Up in a minute.

I straightened my shoes by the door and tried to flatten wrinkles in my skirt with my hands, nervous suddenly, which was very unlike me.

A rapping at the door knocked me fully out of the memory, and Cord stood on the other side holding up a bottle of the iced tea I liked. "Come in."

He handed me the tea bottle and stepped inside.

"How did you know I liked this?" I held up the bottle. "It's my favorite."

"It's what you always used to get when we ordered in for lunch meetings. Just picked it up on the way over." He shrugged like it was no big deal, but it was a reminder of how much he'd still been paying attention to me. Cord ran a hand through his hair and glanced around my apartment, holding up his own bottle of water. "It's a nice place. You've unpacked more than me, and I've lived in my place for years." Cord eyed the framed photos on the wall to his left before dragging his gaze back to me.

"Come in." I motioned him into the apartment, and he followed me to the couch in the small living room after toe-ing off his shoes by the door. "I can't believe you remembered the tea I ordered or that you're drinking water. I remember you being addicted to Mountain Dew," I said, cracking the seal and tipping the glass bottle to my lips.

"Things change, I guess." He opened the bottle, and I noticed the flex in his forearm under the cuff of his sweatshirt sleeve. "I've changed."

I swept my gaze over him—he'd changed physically. Shoulders broader, hair shorter, and posture straighter, but there was something else, something I'd noticed at the gala. He looked more assured, maybe more guarded. "Thank you for bringing this by. You didn't have to make the trip."

"Your place was on the way home."

"You live in the other direction from the office," I said, remembering visiting his place after he first bought it. "Is there another reason?"

He gave a low chuckle, color rising on his cheeks. "Okay, you caught me there. We didn't get to finish our conversation at the break, and it seemed like there was more to say."

"I'll get ice for these," I said. "Well, the last thing you said was 'maybe.' That opens all kinds of conversational doors, right?" To my own ears, that sounded incredibly sexual, and I couldn't keep the temperature in my body from rising as I imagined what kind of weird Cord might like. That last time together, he'd kissed me in a way that made me pretty sure I'd go down any weird trail he suggested.

"I guess so." His gaze made me wonder if he was thinking about going down trails, too.

And now I'm thinking about going down. And him going down.

"So," he said. "Where should we start?"

I pressed too hard on the ice dispenser and the cup overflowed, the shock of the ice on my skin a reminder to reel my imagination back in. "Back then, we had a connection. A . . . flirtation," I said, busying myself filling two glasses with ice. "And thinking back on it is destined to be a little weird since I was working for you at the time, but now I respect your position on the board." I finally met his eyes again as I walked back into the room and handed him the cold glass; our fingers touched for a moment, a beat too long, before he pulled away.

"And I respect your role as the director."

"I guess that's what we needed to discuss, right?"

When we'd worked together, I'd been struck the first time I saw Cord's intense look. Over time, I'd notice flashes of it, and when he took over the company fully, I saw it more and more. His normal expression was open, flexible, and versatile. The intense look focused on me now was something else entirely.

In a flash, Cord scooted forward on the couch and wrapped his fingers around my wrist, stopping me from walking away again. "Pearl." My name on his lips in that kind of desperate way stopped me in my tracks. "Cards on the table. I'm still attracted to you." I stood in front of him, savoring his warm palm inching from my wrist to my hand at a snail's pace. "I can't take my eyes off you. Your voice makes me want to fall to my goddamn knees so I can hear your moan, and when you smile . . ." His sable-colored eyes bore into mine, and he slid the pad of his thumb across my wrist. "I need more of your smiles. I never stopped wanting you."

I swallowed, angling my body to face him, our knees touching.

"So," he said. His expression was earnest and open, and on instinct, I dragged the fingers of my other hand across his forehead, how I used to see him brushing strands of hair back. "That's what I think we still need to talk about." His fingers grazed the underside of my hand, tracing the constellation of tattoos on my wrist, lighting up my nerve endings as his fingers slowly linked with mine. "Do you want me, too?"

I stepped closer, inching between his spread legs, the headiness of the moment wrapping around me like a blanket. "We work together. Again."

"I can't dance around how much I want to kiss you." Cord's gaze flicked to my mouth, and I licked my bottom lip on instinct.

I stepped forward again, and his hand rested at my waist. His eyes moved back to mine, and I slid both hands through his hair, letting my fingers glide through the soft strands. When my fingers brushed his scalp, Cord's eyes fell closed, just for a moment, and I imagined how my touch elsewhere on his body would elicit the same reaction. I was no longer tired. I was no longer worried about work. I was no longer anything else but in that moment with him, in that space so close to his body. "OurCode, though. My job. I am still putting my head first," I said, the lie somewhat revealed by my breathless delivery. "I'm not looking to date."

He laughed with a heavy exhale, his grip at my waist tightening. "I'm not, either. I'm not the same guy I was, but I think about your mouth every time I'm near that damn elevator. And you were right, I was your boss and you had other priorities. So this time . . ." His thumb made a wide sweep over my waist. "We understand each other better."

"Cord," I said with one last slide of my fingers through his hair, enjoying the way he leaned into my touch. I should have reminded him that in addition to our working together, he'd just ended things with someone, or that nothing had changed in terms of my thoughts on relationships. I could have said either of those things, but I felt deliciously warm where he touched me, and Shea's reminder to be messy flashed in my head.

"Yeah?" His brown eyes were hooded and his lips slightly parted, and he kept flicking his gaze between my lips and my eyes. "I know this is a lot to drop on you."

I cupped his cheeks, lowering my face to his. "I take too many chances with you."

"Thank God," he said, and then our lips met softly. He tasted faintly of peppermint, and his tongue swept along the seam of my lips and I opened, our mouths fusing. A shot of want skewered me when he pulled me closer and guided me to his lap. He clasped the back of my neck, keeping us together, the hold unyielding. And we kissed and kissed, the passing of time marked only through the rushes and jolts his lips and tongue and hands sent through me. I gasped when he trailed his lips down my neck, sucking and nipping. His warm hand rubbed insistently at my lower back, and I willed it to move lower, but he continued to tease. "Cord," I murmured again, my body arching against his and the thick bulge of his erection against my thigh.

"God, you're perfect." He spoke against my throat, hand finally, mercifully, sliding lower to cup my ass and pull me closer to him.

"More," I moaned, pulling his lips back to mine, my fingers gripping the back of his head.

Cord growled before kissing me again. I would have giggled at the sound but for the intensity of the bruising, harried way his mouth met mine. We did our best to consume each other, making up for all the kisses we hadn't shared over the last five years while his hands roamed—over my back and hips, up to cup my breast, and then down to my thighs. I wanted to return to my concerns, to the many reminders of why this was a bad idea, but every time my mind attempted to change course, another rush of sensation took over decision-making.

"Why is your skirt so long?" he said into my neck, fingers grazing down to the hem, which fell below my knees even when sitting.

"I look good in this style," I said, following his fingers' slow journey under the fabric and over my kneecap.

"Believe me," he said, nipping at my neck before raising his eyes to mine. A funny half smile graced his lips. "I am well aware of how good you look in these skirts."

I laughed at his expression, to release the tidal wave of emotions and want and need I was feeling.

He stilled his fingers, and they rested motionless on my knee. "I'm serious. I never stopped thinking about you."

"I'm serious, too," I said, drawing his chin toward me

with a finger. "You make me want to take too many chances. That's not like me." Our lips met again with less crazed motion and more slow, intense strokes.

"You're so soft," he murmured against my skin. "You feel like a rose petal." Cord kissed my shoulder, my throat, and up to the corner of my lip. "I like how tough you are, but . . ." He dropped his lips to my throat again. "This soft side undoes me."

"You called me Petal that night," I murmured, the memories coming back to me through the frenzy of my arousal.

Cord's hand resumed its path under my skirt, inching the fabric up. His palm rubbed over my kneecap and higher, grazing the least sensitive part of my thigh, still making me squirm as his fingers rose, grazing the panel of fabric between my legs. I tried to spread my legs, but the fabric was tight, binding me in place, leaving room for only one of his fingers to move back and forth with maddening pressure.

"I'd like to suggest looser skirts," he said against my neck, his breath tickling my ears as I stroked his biceps.

"What about no skirt?"

He looked at me wide-eyed and nodded. It was cute and endearing, and I wanted to tangle my fingers in his hair but also wanted this intense kissing to escalate.

"C'mon," I said, pulling him to his feet and enjoying how his eyes roamed my body. I let my cardigan slide off my arms, and the cool air of my apartment lifted goose bumps on my arms and chest, now bared to the air and to Cord, whose gaze was hooded.

He dragged me to him. His shift from fast to slow made me dizzy, but in the best way. He held my waist, our hips together, and it was like we were dancing. "I've wanted this for so long," he said, voice dipped low. "Wanted you for so long."

"Me, too." I wrapped both arms around his neck, we looked into each other's eyes, and it shook me. He was so focused on me, it was as if he could see inside me. I swallowed, grinding against his arousal, teasing him and taking us back to the safer, physical ground. "Are you going to make me wait much longer?"

"No," he said, walking me backward, a wolfish expression giving his normally relaxed face the best kind of edge. "I'm not going to make you wait at all, Petal."

CHAPTER 18

Cord

I COULDN'T BELIEVE THIS WAS FINALLY HAPPENING. Pearl was in my arms, her lips on mine, and her words rang in my head that she didn't want to wait any longer. I hadn't felt this kind of eager need in five years, and, between kisses, I reminded myself that it was better now because I knew what this was. I could keep my heart out of it.

My dick was almost painfully hard, and I was about to embarrass myself with this woman. I couldn't bring myself to really care, though, when I rubbed a thumb over her hard nipple and she moaned as we made our way down the hall. *Fuck.* That sound. I stroked her again, seeking a repeat moan, and backed her against the wall, our lips melding, tongues clashing. Distantly, I remembered the frenzied way this had happened the first time and how we should have talked about things then just like now, but I couldn't hold on to the thought.

I'd imagined Pearl's breasts were perfect before, but touching her, feeling their weight in my hand, I knew these were the most perfect breasts of all time, and as I teased her pebbled nipples, she bit down on my lip, hard enough to let me know what I was doing to her. Without looking, I fumbled to find the hem of her skirt and pulled it up, gripping her thigh to lift her leg onto me. I needed to touch all of her soft places, to make those moans keep coming.

"I can't wait to touch you again," I said between kisses, already remembering how she felt and wondering how she tasted. My body reacted to everywhere we connected, and Pearl felt right in my arms like she shouldn't ever have left. Like I shouldn't ever have let her go. "I want all night to learn your body," I said against her neck. "I want all the hours I can have."

"No one can know."

"This is just between us," I said, letting my palm skirt higher on her thigh.

"I need—" She stopped talking at a screech behind us.

"Ah! Sorry!"

I dropped her leg and whipped around to see a teenager dressed in gray sweats and a vintage Chicago Bulls T-shirt standing in Pearl's doorway, eyes wide and expression horrified.

Pearl pushed past me, tugging at her skirt. "Tye! What are you doing here?"

My head spun, trying to figure out what was happening with the taste of Pearl's mouth still on my lips.

Tye held their arm over their eyes and turned their back on us. "I'm sorry. You gave me the key, and you didn't answer, and I didn't have anywhere else to go. Shea's boyfriend was freaking out on her."

"What happened? What do you mean?" I heard Pearl's concentration and focus snap back into place at the mention of her sister. Her hair and clothes were askew, but her voice was pointed, concerned, and the one I'd known so well for years.

"Not, like, violent or anything. They're just yelling at each other, but I didn't want to be around it."

I watched from the hall, unsure what to do. The unexpected interruption from the kid and Pearl's shift into concern killed the heat of the moment, and thankfully, my dick was reading the room. I didn't know what was going on, but Pearl's back was to me. She stroked the kid's head. I had the sense I should leave, but it conflicted with not wanting to leave Pearl. She sounded upset, and it felt like my duty to be there for her. Indecision wasn't a place I let myself live very often anymore, but I stayed in the hallway against the wall.

"Cord?" Pearl's voice pulled me out of my head. I'd been staring at the carpet. "Can you get Tye some water? Glasses are to the right of the sink."

I nodded, eager for something to do, and filled the glass. Pearl had moved the kid to the couch, one arm still around their shoulders. When I handed them the glass, Pearl gave me a tight smile of thanks, and I stepped back to lean against her kitchen island. I was a little more certain I was supposed to leave, but I stood there, planted.

Pearl continued to talk in low tones. "Does she know where you are?"

Tye shrugged. "I don't know if she heard when I said I was leaving."

"I'm going to call Aunt Shea, okay?"

Pearl looked at me, her expression a storm of sadness and anger. "I need to call my sister from another room. Can you stay out here?"

I nodded quickly, eager for something to do. "Sure. Of course."

"Cord, you remember Tye is my sister's child. Tye, this is

my . . ." Pearl and I shared a glance. I knew on some level I'd been ignoring for five years that I wanted her to call me her boyfriend, her partner, her soulmate. "My friend Cord. I'll be right back, okay?"

The kid again nodded wordlessly, sipping from the water glass. After Pearl left the room and hurried down the hall, we sat in silence, Tye at one end of the couch, and me in the chair nearby. Pearl's angry muted voice carried from the back bedroom, and I racked my brain for what to say to mask the sound.

"Hey." I was twice Tye's age at least, but I felt my face heat. This certainly wasn't how I planned to meet my mentee, but hopefully Tye hadn't connected the dots yet about who I was.

The kid shot me a withering look that told me exactly what they thought of me. "I'm sorry I interrupted."

"You didn't interrupt anything . . ."

Another derisive look, and I had to remind myself I was an adult. "I saw what you were doing. I'm fifteen. I get it. You don't need to lie."

I nodded. "Okay, I'm sorry. I won't lie to you. But your aunt loves you a lot and wants you here, so don't apologize, okay?"

"Okay," they grumbled, eyeing my rumpled dress shirt.

I'd never been caught making out with a girl as a kid, so here I was, almost thirty and experiencing this for the first time. It was humbling, and I wasn't sure my dad's reproach when I was a teenager would have been more withering than what I was receiving right now.

"Are you, like, her Tinder hookup or something? My aunt Shea says she never dates."

"We're just friends, like she said."

The kid glared, their dark brown eyes shooting another chilling look at me.

I held up my palms. "We worked together. We work together, but now we're just friends. I told you I wouldn't lie."

"Whatever." They returned to their glass, swirling the liquid. The glares and sharp look made them seem older, like an adult; but in repose, their shoulders slumped, and they looked younger than fifteen, like a scared kid. The silence returned, and Pearl's voice again bled through the bathroom door.

"Have you eaten? I'm sure your aunt has something in the fridge."

Tye mumbled, "A little."

When I stood to rummage through Pearl's kitchen, I was surprised that the kid came with me, setting the glass on the counter and slumping against the island. I opened a few cabinets and drawers, finding only utensils and plates. When I glanced up, they looked vaguely amused.

"I've, uh, never been here before."

"She keeps the good snacks in that cupboard there," Tye said, pointing to one at the far end of the kitchen.

Inside were crackers, a box of cookies, and a bag of Gummi Bears, which made me smile. I passed the cookies over and went searching for actual food, finding bread and stuff to make a sandwich in Pearl's fridge. Tye watched me with interest, nibbling at the cookies. Their fingernails were painted black, the polish chipped like they had picked at it, and their hair was cut short, cropped close to the scalp. As I worked—pulling out the meat and cheese—Tye watched me, the derisive look falling off their face. When I turned to search for chips or an apple or something, the small voice took me off guard. "Wait, you work with Pearl? What's your name again?"

I slid the plate across the counter. Busted. "Cord."

The kid looked conflicted and took a bite of the sandwich, then looked back at me. "Like Abby's Cord? They said you were going to be my mentor."

"Uh, yeah. That's me." I wished I'd made a sandwich for myself, because then I'd have something to shove in my mouth to avoid talking. "Nice to meet you." I held out my hand, and Tye eyed it skeptically.

"No way—"

Before they could finish the thought, Pearl walked back into the room. Her body was tense, expression tight, and she clutched the phone. She stopped short, seeing us in the kitchen, and glanced at Tye's sandwich and up to me. I shrugged, meeting her gaze.

She rubbed Tye's back. "We'll get things figured out, but you'll sleep here tonight, okay, bug?"

Tye nodded, taking another bite.

"I'll get going," I said, running my hands through my hair. My gaze flicked to the couch, and I tried to make sense of the turns this night had taken. "It was nice to meet you, Tye."

"It was gross to see you groping my aunt," they called after me.

Pearl led me to the door and dropped her voice, hands wringing in a way I'd never seen. "I need to . . ."

"I get it," I said. I wanted to hug her or cup her cheek to offer some kind of comfort, but she stood rigid in front of me, and I didn't trust myself to know what she wanted. "I'll talk to you later?"

She nodded, and our fingers grazed briefly before she closed the door.

Despite how our evening had fallen apart, standing in the hallway outside her door, I had the overwhelming sense I'd found something inside that felt like coming home, and that scared the hell out of me.

CHAPTER 19

Pearl

Five Years Earlier

June

I STEPPED FROM THE CAR ON THE TREE-LINED stretch of Damen Avenue outside Cord's new house. He walked out onto the stone front steps and waved as I approached. The redbrick Tudor house was beautiful, with tiny overgrown shrubs dotting the yard. "Congratulations," I said, raising the bottle of champagne. Wes, Mason, and I had planned to trek over after work together, but both men got called away at the last minute.

"Thanks." He ushered me inside, where the view was not exactly beautiful.

"Wow" was all I could muster about the gold paisley drapes in perfect shape with sharp creases at the top, likely well maintained over the course of forty years.

"I know what you're thinking," he said with a laugh, leading me through the long living room across scuffed wood floors. "And no, you can't have the curtains. They're the reason I bought the place."

I laughed and followed him through a dining room with a massive wrought-iron chandelier into a spacious kitchen with cabinetry painted olive green, the color beginning to peel. "Sorry I'm the only member of the housewarming party." I strolled around the kitchen. "Wes and Mason had something come up at the last minute."

I hadn't planned to come alone—something about spending time together without the limits of the office was far too appealing to be a good idea.

Instead of addressing that particular elephant in the room, I leaned against the island, where a covered Pyrex dish sat emanating scents of garlic and onion. "How does it feel to be a homeowner?"

Cord laughed unselfconsciously, and I wondered, not for the first time, if I'd really imagined the heat between us. Sure, there'd been that moment in the elevator, but maybe that was just one of those things. I'd gathered every little moment of connection since, keeping them in a special, hidden box in my memory I could come back to while lying in bed alone at night.

"It feels like I'm going to go broke renovating. Though I'm kind of looking forward to a project that isn't work." He motioned to the dish. "Are you hungry? My new neighbor dropped off lasagna along with her displeasure about the state of the front steps and some gossip about the mailman."

"Sounds like an ally to keep on your side. What's up with the mailman?" I peeked under the edge of the Pyrex cover, and the lasagna looked mouthwatering—but I knew I shouldn't stay for dinner. And not just because Cord had no furniture, flatware, or, as far as I could tell, possessions in this house yet.

"He's hot and single, I guess, in case I'm looking for a middle-aged man to join me in this big empty house." Cord laughed again, stepping around the island to look over my shoulder at the lasagna.

"Are you?" The hairs on the back of my neck stood at his

proximity, the warmth and weight of him standing so close swirling my senses with the heady aroma of the pasta and the rumble of his laugh.

"You know, I think I'm good for now regarding hot middle-aged mail carriers." He reached around me and touched the dish. "I wish I had plates or forks. It looks good."

Part of me wanted to step away, but at the same time, taking the risk to be this close felt luxurious, even if it only lasted a moment. "You could eat it with your hands. Or maybe the mail carrier has flatware he could bring over."

When Cord chuckled, his chest brushed my back, and I swallowed the wave of anticipation that incidental contact left sitting low in my body. "He's apparently really quite the looker according to Lou. I'm not sure I could land him."

Cord stepped back around the counter, accepting the dish after I let the lid fall. The fridge hummed in the corner, and he slid the dish inside, a lonely spot of color in the empty appliance. "But I'm oddly picky about men in shorts, and I like women," he said, opening and closing a couple cabinets. I already knew that, or his erection when we were stuck in the elevator would lead me to believe there was some attraction, but my foolish little heart had hoped he'd say he liked me. It was silly. It was beyond silly; it was fanciful, and I had vowed a long time ago to abandon fanciful. Instead, I dug in my purse, where I was pretty sure I had a couple leftover take-out flatware packets.

He stopped his inspection of the cabinets, adding, "But anyone who had a fork handy right now could have my heart, body, and—" He finished his statement just as I held out the packaged utensils. "Oh," he said, and I stifled the urge to throw the plasticware on the counter and either run away or kiss him. Instead, I ignored his proclamation and shrugged.

I thought of the voicemail message waiting to be returned about the job interview across the country as I set the utensils on the counter. "I won't keep you but wanted to stop by to say congratulations. I'm sure you're busy making plans." I'd been happy for him when he'd told me he found a place. His face had lit up in a way it didn't always at work, and he'd shared all his ideas for renovating, for doing the work himself. I'd learned Cord enjoyed building and fixing, but he usually saved it for work and other people. As far as I could tell, the house was just for him. I liked the idea of him making a home he loved, focusing on what he wanted. I crushed the hint of a fantasy that maybe I'd end up in the house with him. I slammed my foot hard on that little idea.

"I'm glad you're here." He leaned forward on the island, with his hands placed just inches from my own. "Do you want the grand tour before you go? The drapes in the master bedroom are leopard print, so . . ." His grin was contagious.

"Sure."

The stairs creaked as we ascended to the second floor, Cord tracing a hand along the gold-filigree wallpaper and commenting about plans to rip it out.

At the top of the creaking stairs, I touched my fingers to the wall. "Fabric softener helps," I said as his hand along the wall approached mine. "There are tools you can buy to poke holes in it, and the fabric softener makes it come down easier." Our fingers brushed for a second, both examining the detail in the paper, but he stepped around me, another reminder that this thing I was sensing might be one-sided.

"I didn't know you were a home improvement expert. Pearl, you've been holding out on me." He smiled over his shoulder and nodded toward the room in the corner, flipping a light switch as he went.

"I'm no expert," I said, giving the wallpaper one last look. My ex and I had talked about buying his grandmother's place and fixing it up, so I did research. I'd researched all kinds of projects, from wallpaper removal to redecorating to accommodate a nursery for the kids we'd talked about wanting. Kids for a home that never materialized in a future that hadn't existed. With that reminder, I followed Cord into the room, determined to cut the tour short and return the message on my phone about the interview.

"This is my favorite room," he said. "The real estate agent called it a sunroom." We were surrounded by windows on three walls, and the hardwood floor under my feet caught the moonlight shining in through the glass—well, moonlight mixed with residual light pollution. "Sorry, the bulb in here is burned out, but look." He motioned to the north-facing window, and I joined him. "I've never had my own yard before."

I stepped to the window overlooking his yard, where the grass was a healthy green, if overgrown, below us. "We had a little one growing up," I said, taking in the space. "But I always wanted a hammock so I could sit outside and look up at the sky."

Cord's body felt closer, too close, but he wasn't touching me. And I wanted him to touch me, which was probably why I kept talking. "I like looking up at the stars. I could get lost and not have to be anything for anyone. It's really the only time I let myself daydream as a kid."

When I looked away from the window, Cord was looking at me, his expression unreadable.

"Sorry," I said with a laugh as my face heated in embarrassment. "I'm babbling. I know that probably doesn't make any sen—" My heel caught on a loose floorboard and I lost my balance mid-sentence, stumbling backward, but I didn't hit the floor. Cord caught me, holding me as if we were doing an elaborate dip at the end of a tango.

"Are you okay?" He hadn't let me go yet; his arms stayed around me as if I might fall again.

I nodded and swallowed. "I'm fine."

"I'm gonna replace this floor." His gaze trailed from me to the offending board. "And what you said made sense to me."

It happened so fast, I didn't remember grabbing hold of him, but while his arms were around my back and waist, my own hands were on his shoulders. It would have been so easy to pull his face to mine, to ease to the floor together and peel off our clothes in the moonlight, taking time to look at the night sky when our bodies were exhausted.

"What do you daydream about now?" Cord's voice was hushed, our faces close, and he shifted to let me stand, but he hadn't let go.

My feet under me again, I tried desperately to quell the urge to confess that I daydreamed about him and me in some kind of domestic bliss I knew would be destined to crumble. I'd had it before, but in Cord's arms, looking out over his new backyard, it was so easy to imagine it being possible again. Almost. That singular wedge of doubt was enough, though.

I'd tell him another time that I'd started job hunting. It was for the best. I released my hold on his shoulders and stepped back, careful to watch my footing this time. "I try to stick with reality now. It's usually the safer bet."

CHAPTER 20

Present Day

Pearl: Caleb is gone?

Shea: Ugh yes. Such a stupid fight. Tye okay?

Pearl: Yes. Not exactly a smooth transition to my place, but it's fine.

Shea: What happened?

Bri: I know what happened and I have questions. You had a guy over!

Shea: WHAT?!

Tye called from the guest room, where they'd be staying. "Warning. I'm stepping into the hall. If any kissing is happening, I'm about to enter the room."

I waited for Tye's self-satisfied grin when they walked in, eyes covered and waving a hand from left to right. "All clear," I said, sipping my coffee and waiting for the toaster to finish. "But thank you for the warning."

Tye grabbed a glass and orange juice from my fridge, and I handed them the box of the cereal they liked.

"Do you want to talk about it?" I ignored Shea's text in the group chat. "Would you like someone else to be your mentor for the program?"

Tye settled on a stool at the counter and dipped a spoon into the bowl. "Nah. Abby said he was good, and they picked him for me."

The sound of Cord's partner's name was like sandpaper on my skin. Ex-partner, I guess, but it didn't matter. "Are you sure?"

"Yeah. I trust Abby, and I guess you trust him, so . . ."

I spread butter and then sprinkled cinnamon and sugar on my toast, avoiding what I knew would be Tye's raised eyebrow. "That was a onetime thing. It won't happen again." I motioned to the backpack hanging on the chair. "Do you have everything from home for school today? We'll get the rest of your things tonight."

Tye nodded and tapped at something on their phone. "I'm good. Meeting with my mentor—I mean, your new *booooooyfriend*—after school at OurCode."

The same gnawing guilt I'd felt since Tye had walked in on us lodged in my chest, but the playful smile Tye gave me without looking away from their phone eased my mind slightly.

Shea: I STG. TELL ME WHAT HAPPENED.

Bri: Tye walked in on Pearl with a guy.

Shea: !!!!!

Bri: And they were . . . how shall I say? On their way to the bedroom at the time.

Shea: I'm deceased. Who is this man?

Pearl: None of your business.

Bri: It was Cord.

Pearl: Where is the loyalty?

Bri: 🤷🏾‍♀️

Shea: Yes! Three cheers for messiness. Three cheers for getting messy with 🔌

Pearl: I have Bri's kid to focus on. No more messiness.

Bri: Don't use Tye as an excuse. They know to respect a closed bedroom door. Just maybe remember to close the door next time.

Bri: Or make it to the bedroom.

I rolled my eyes and set my phone aside. I had to take a slow, deep breath, remembering the feel of Cord's hands on my body, the way he'd felt hard against my stomach, and his lips kissing up my neck. I hadn't stopped thinking about it, hadn't stopped comparing it to five years of fantasies, and knowing reality was so much better. I glanced at the tattoo and ran my finger over the fourth star on my wrist. Cord had kissed me there, his mouth over the design, not knowing how that gesture made my pulse tick up at the soft sweep of his lips and the cognitive dissonance. Without the haze I felt when we were close together, I could see clearly that onetime slip was a mistake.

Shortly after Tye left for school, I logged on to my account for the early virtual meeting with Kevin. Or, I thought the meeting was just with Kevin, but two of the board members I recognized popped into video windows. "Hi, Pearl. You know Amaya and Alison? They're part of a subcommittee I appointed to help the board respond to this mess." We all waved and exchanged pleasantries. Though I'd met them all before, Amaya was the only one who flashed me a smile of recognition.

"Welcome," I said, quickly making notes on the meeting agenda I'd prepared for Kevin alone.

"So, what ideas so we have?" Kevin looked left to right in his window, presumably making meaningful eye contact with everyone's squares.

I expected an awkward silence, but the group was firing on all cylinders right away.

"I wonder if there might be value in a retreat for the board, to do some of this strategic planning," Alison said, reading through the dossier of information updating them on our current standing with donors and partners.

Kevin tipped his head. "That's not a bad idea."

Amaya chimed in. "I don't know if an expensive retreat for the board is the look we need now."

I nodded, glad someone else was here to say that before I had to.

"What if we did something inexpensive?"

"Like a cheap hotel?" Kevin asked, glancing at his phone, his expression conveying his negative reaction to the idea of "cheap" and "hotel" being in proximity.

"What about camping?" Alison waved her hands at the idea. "It doesn't look ostentatious. We could really get out of town to focus on strategizing, and we could promote it as team building to reinforce the team behind OurCode in the scandal's wake."

"That's . . . kind of perfect," Amaya said, grinning at her colleague though the screen.

Camping? I was hoping Kevin would jump in with a reason not to do it. He looked like a pretty solidly indoor guy, and I crossed my fingers off camera.

To my horror, his grin widened. "Love it. Pearl, can your team arrange?"

"Sure," I said, mirroring his grin and wondering who on my staff was going to know anything about camping as I bid farewell to Amaya, Alison, and Kevin and signed off. I held up my phone, swiping to view the new message notification.

Cord: Can we talk about last night?

I'd known it was coming but hadn't figured out exactly how I wanted that talk to go. Part of me wanted it to involve no talking at all and just a return to the heat of Cord's lips and fingers. A part of me wanted so much more. But, as if I needed another reminder that this was complicated, I glanced at the stars on my wrist and thought about how far I'd come ever since I'd put faith in love behind me. I thought about what I'd given up with my ex. I wouldn't lose myself again. Not even for someone who'd helped me find my way in the past.

CHAPTER 21

Pearl

Five Years Earlier

July

CORD PACED BY MY DESK, RAKING HIS FINGERS through his thick hair. "Just now?"

I nodded and held out the notes I'd originally prepared for Wes. Our fingers brushed, and I swallowed the sharp inhale that wanted to escape at the contact. "He would have told you himself, but he had to leave immediately." Wes was supposed to hold the meeting, but his mom had a medical emergency, and he was out the door in a flash.

"Can we reschedule?"

"They'll be here in ten minutes." We'd been working for weeks to arrange meetings with select companies to assist us with dedicated customer-experience-focused data analysis, and if we wanted to implement their suggestions by FitMi's next upgrade, the timeline was tight. The flurry of activity had been a good distraction during the day, an excuse to keep my eyes down and not seek out Cord's across the room after the elevator incident. The toe-curling, fantasy-inducing incident. "You know we're on a deadline." I motioned to the information again. "And everything is here. I've pulled together all the research. We'll hear their pitch, and you can make your decisions after."

He started reading the memo, sitting on the corner of my desk he liked to claim as his spot. "Sorry," he said. "I just hate going into something unprepared." He skimmed my notes, and I caught myself studying the cut of his jaw. He'd dressed nicer than normal today, and the blue button-up shirt was rolled at the sleeves, giving a peek of his surprisingly developed forearms. "This is great prep, though."

"Thanks," I said, shaking off my inspection. "Take a few minutes in your office and I'll stall them."

"You're really a lifesaver. You know that?" He stood and held out a hand like he might stroke my arm, but then let it fall.

"Shoo," I said, taking a step back and motioning toward his office.

He grinned and glanced away. "Oh, do you have their names?"

I checked my desktop, where the meeting details were open. "The company is Analogia, and they're sending Charlotte Hopkins and someone else whose name I didn't get."

He nodded and smiled before closing the door. I gathered my things, trying not to think about how attractive I found those smiles of his. I was never sure why Wes handled so much of the external stuff for the company. Cord was good at it, but he got in his own head. There was something about that I found reassuring, like I could be real with him.

I walked toward the lobby, straightening my skirt. I hadn't been real with anyone since I broke up with Jason, so the feeling was unfamiliar. He hadn't been a wise choice to open up to in the end. The song "Gaslighter" by the Chicks played unbidden in my head. "Sorry to keep you waiting," I said, holding out my hand to Charlotte. "I'm Pearl Harris, and I can show you back to the conference room." She stood alone in the lobby, and I looked around. "Are we expecting someone else?"

"Yes. He'll be—" She glanced behind me. "Oh, here he is now."

I turned to greet the second person and nearly stumbled as recognition hit me like an elbow to the stomach.

"Well, I didn't expect to see you here," he said, looking me up and down. "How are you, Pearlie?"

My voice stuck in my throat for a moment, but I cleared it. "What a surprise to see you, Jason." The words were sand on my tongue. I motioned down the hall because I couldn't think of anything else to say. "This way."

I led them to the conference room, hoping Cord had decided to screw his prep work and come in early, but the room was empty. I hadn't seen Jason in years, not since he'd asked me to leave the keys on the counter on my way out of his place and I hadn't had the words to respond, just stood there embarrassed and hurt and unsure what to do. I tried to push that memory away, but every time he opened his mouth, the conference room and my new life fell away. That was the only point in time I could place myself in.

Charlotte had to step into the hall to take a phone call, and I was left alone with my ex.

"So, you're a receptionist here? I remember you wanted to go back to school, but this is probably a better fit, right? Getting to interact with people without making a lot of decisions." He looked up from his notes but not exactly at me, more in my general direction. "You were always so cute when you couldn't make up your mind."

Cord walked in then, a smile on his face to greet our visitor, saving me from having to respond. "Cord Matthews," he said, giving Jason a firm handshake, and I noticed how

Jason's demeanor changed when Cord walked into the room, the attention he gave him.

"Jason Nostrand," he said with a smile.

Cord's brows jumped at the name, and he cut his eyes to me. It was a common first name, but he guessed immediately, and I couldn't exactly explain the history with Jason watching us, so I nodded, busying myself with the coffeepot.

"Pearl and I go way back, actually. I was just saying she was lucky to get a job at a place like this."

Cord's smile didn't fall, but his tone changed. "We're lucky to have her."

"Oh, sure." Jason leaned back in his chair, still ignoring me. "She makes excellent coffee. I remember that!"

I balled my hands into fists but willed them to loosen before turning to face them both. Cord's shoulders were squared when Jason said, "Actually, sweetheart, could I get a cup while you're over there? You remember how I like it, right?" He somehow spoke to me and down to me without actually acknowledging me. I'd loved this man, fully and completely, at one point, and I had no idea what I'd been thinking. "Full disclosure, we used to date, so I definitely know where her skills lie."

I opened my mouth, but Cord cut me off. "You can help yourself." He motioned to the credenza where the coffee supplies were organized. "Pearl, can I steal you a second while we wait for Charlotte?"

In the hall, I stood straight, worried he'd see me slumping against a wall in the way I wanted to and deduce I wasn't as strong as I tried to appear, but once around the corner, he leaned in close. "That's your ex? The one who . . ."

"Yes, but it's fine."

"It's not fine. He's a dick. I'll kick him out right now. No one should talk to you like that," he said, moving closer. "Are you okay?" Cord's warm hand slid down my bare arm, and my eyes shot to his assessing gaze.

Our bodies were very close together, his face inches from mine as we spoke quietly. His body heat melded with mine, and his hand on my arm was like an embrace. "I'm okay," I said, actually meaning it. With him this close, I felt better. "I was taken aback, and yeah . . . he's a jerk, but Analogia is good. I think you should still hear their pitch. Don't dismiss them because of me."

He searched my face and for a brief second slid a thumb over my cheek. "Are you sure? I could punch him in the nose for you."

I giggled, and his hand fell away from my face. "Have you ever punched someone?"

"No, but I'd want my first time to be special, and this feels like it would be." His hand moved up and down my arm again, the friction platonic, but it felt like more, like the precursor to him wrapping an arm around my waist. "You're important here. And he doesn't have even an inkling of your skills. And you actually make really awful coffee, so that's not why we keep you around."

I swatted him in the shoulder and took a reluctant step back, my head clearer and my heart lighter. "Hey," I said. "Watch it."

Cord brushed some hair from his forehead and searched my face again. "Are you sure you don't want me to punch him in the nose?"

I gently pushed his shoulder and laughed, unsure how I'd gone from wanting to cry to laughing, but I had. "Let's get back in there."

Before we rounded the corner, his expression sobered. "I've known that guy for three minutes and I know he didn't deserve someone as thoughtful and kind and beautiful as you." He opened his mouth to say something else, but Charlotte walked toward us, apologizing and introducing herself. I liked her, but I wanted to know what else Cord was going to say.

When we stepped inside, I noticed Jason hadn't made himself coffee, and I saw his request for what it was—a moment to make me feel small.

"Well, Mr. Matthews," Jason said, standing. "We're excited to talk with you today. It was great to see Pearlie again, but let's get down to the real business, right?"

I squared my shoulders and folded my hands in my lap, determined not to let him get to me again. He wouldn't make me feel small or doubt myself. If I kept my head at the forefront, no one would ever get enough of my heart to have the chance. I dragged a fingertip across my tattoo as if contact with the ink would have magical, confidence-enhancing powers.

"Oh," Cord said, nudging my foot with his under the table and sitting back in his chair. "There's been some miscommunication. I'm just here to listen. Pearl's the lead on this project. It's her you'll need to impress."

Charlotte smiled warmly at me and began their pitch while Jason fumbled with his pen and gave me the open-mouthed, disbelieving stare I was certain I'd given him years earlier. I pressed my foot back against Cord as I pointedly ignored Jason. I wanted to reach under the table and squeeze Cord's hand or shoot him a look saying *What are you doing?* or tell Charlotte I needed a minute, and then kiss the breath out of him for giving me that moment to put Jason in his place.

Instead, I listened intently to the pitch, taking copious notes and asking the critical questions I'd already prepared. And I left my foot near Cord's under the table—the gentle pressure back and forth during the meeting replaced the hurt of remembering Jason. When they took a brief pause to find a report, I leaned over, my lips inadvertently brushing his ear. "Thank you."

He nudged my foot with his in response, and I wondered, momentarily, if maybe my heart could come first for the right person.

CHAPTER 22

Present Day

I ADJUSTED THE BLUETOOTH DEVICE IN MY EAR AS I strode toward the OurCode building for my meeting with Tye. Wes was taking far too much joy in my embarrassment when I gave him the high points of the night before. "No way. Your mentee walked in on you and Pearl making out?"

My face heated. We'd been on our way to doing a lot more than that. Her body under my hands had been better, more supple yet firm, than I had remembered, than I'd fantasized. "So now I'm heading to meet with my mentee and it's going to be awkward as hell."

He chuckled. "Yeah. No way around that. You talk to Pearl about it?"

"Texted this morning, but she said we should probably keep things professional."

I could picture my best friend's wince from the sound he made. "That's rough. Because of the kid and the board thing?"

"Yeah. And it's a little more complicated than that."

"Because of whatever happened in San Diego that you've still never explained?"

I pressed against the wall of a building to avoid a group of tourists. "What do you mean," I asked.

"Buddy. Every time I brought up her name, you got this hangdog expression and then changed the subject."

"It's embarrassing," I muttered.

"Well, I stood by you when that girlfriend of yours in college insisted you bring back puka shell necklaces, so I think embarrassment isn't exactly unfamiliar territory in our friendship."

I laughed at the memory of that unfortunate phase. That girlfriend, it turned out, was wrong, and I was not getting in on a trend early. I was getting made fun of, mostly by my best friend. "That's true, but I'm getting close to OurCode." I scanned the building's windows, wondering if I might catch a glimpse of Pearl. "You can interrogate me some other time."

The OurCode lounge was paradise, or at least, as a proud adult nerd, I thought so. There were screens and terminals everywhere, and a group in the corner appeared to be practicing problems from the Advent of Code, a competition to complete programming puzzles offered every December, and it reminded me that I hadn't had time to participate the last few years.

I pressed the sticky name tag all mentors were asked to wear to my chest and wandered to the table near the vending machine, where Tye and I had agreed to meet for the first time. The training had gotten me excited about mentoring, and not just because it meant being close to Pearl. The facilitators talked about the need to support these kids and the ways mentors could make a difference, but the thing that had resonated most was that being a mentor didn't have to mean having all the answers or saving the day, that it could just mean having a relationship where you help someone step toward their goals. That felt like a weight being lifted, and I was praying I hadn't ruined the possibility of that with Tye already.

I glanced down at the name tag to avoid the embarrassment I still felt at being caught making out with Pearl. I was trying to convince myself that after all the years of growth as a leader in my company, I wasn't bothered by awkward situations, but when Tye tossed their backpack on the floor and slid into the seat across from me, I realized I was kidding myself.

"Hey," I said, tucking my phone into my pocket. "How's it going?"

Tye fiddled with something on their own phone. "Okay."

It was possible I'd gotten worse at dealing with awkward situations and not better. I tried to determine if it was possible to sink through my chair and into the floor.

"But," Tye continued, "I haven't walked in on any of my relatives about to smash today, so I guess it's a good day." A new wave of embarrassment crashed over me, but Tye smiled, a wide, teasing grin followed by a chuckle. "Will you always be this easy to mess with? I'm good."

"Fair enough," I said, turning my tablet over. There was a list of things we were supposed to cover in this first meeting, none of them having anything to do with smashing. "For the record, though, I'm sorry we met like that. If you want someone else as a mentor, now or later, I won't be offended."

Tye nodded. "We're good. Can we talk about something else, though?"

"Yes!" I nearly knocked my tablet off the table in my excitement to move on. "Of course."

"I know they paired us up because Abby suggested it, but I hope we have some things in common." Tye glanced at a notification that popped up on their phone and then set it back down. "Are you in cybersecurity like Abby? They were going to help me look into camps or trainings for kids my age."

I shook my head. "I used to be, but several years ago, a friend and I built a fitness app that's taken off, and now I run that company. We can still look into camps, though. Tell me about you. Why are you in the program? What do you want to accomplish?" The words felt stiff on my tongue as I read them off the guide Bea had shared. I couldn't imagine having those kinds of answers when I was fifteen, but Tye started in immediately.

"I wanted to be a game designer or work in gaming forever, but when they paired me up with Abby, I started learning more about cybersecurity, and there's so much going on there. I guess I want to know as much as I can about my field before I go into it—that, and knowing people already doing it. I know I'm going to be good—but I want to be great. And I still love gaming, but it's kind of dope to know what else is out there, so you can help me explore that stuff."

I was floored by their answer. This kid had all the confidence it had taken me decades to figure out. "What's your favorite game?"

"*Knights of Armageddon*. No question." Tye's face lit up.

"The graphics are amazing," I jumped in, already forgetting about the scripted conversation. "The designer is supposed to be at a con I'm going to next month."

"Their games are always on top. Next meeting we gotta play. Are you any good?" Tye pointed across the room.

"They have a gaming setup over there. Loser does my computer science homework for a week?"

"Nice try," I said, laughing, before returning to the list of decisions we were supposed to talk through together about how we'd spend our time.

About forty minutes later, we wrapped up, and Tye joined a group of kids they knew at the gaming station while I packed up to head back to the office.

Cord: Had my first meeting with Tye.

Pearl: How'd it go?

Cord: They have their life plans together more than I do. Excited to get to know them better.

Pearl: They already texted to tell me you're not too bad, which is high praise from a fifteen-year-old.

CHAPTER 23

Pearl

I SLAPPED AT MY ARM, UNSURE IF THERE WAS RE-ally a bug crawling there or I was just hallucinating.

"I take it you're not the outdoorsy type?" Bea reached into the pocket of her vest and handed me a bottle of mosquito repellent.

"Not even remotely." I spritzed my arms, spreading the repellent like a luxurious moisturizer. "You?"

Bea motioned to her plain T-shirt and khaki shorts. "Stereotype checks out. The Montanan is at home in the woods. Well, some of the stereotypes. The Chicago transplant and melanated goddess you know and love still does it in full eye makeup."

I laughed while admiring Bea's winged eyeliner and red lip. "A true Renaissance woman." Bea and Xavier had taken charge of making the arrangements for the board's camping trip / strategic planning session, and our site was dotted with tents and stocked with coolers, some of which were full of beer. When I'd raised my eyebrow, Bea assured me it wasn't camping without beer, and Xavier suggested some of our board members might be a little looser with brainstorming after a few. After only a couple hours, I was ready to go digging for the secret cooler containing the hard stuff.

"Everyone should be back from fishing at the lake soon, and then we can get into our first session before dinner." Bea checked her watch, which matched the cargo shorts more than the green eye shadow. "How are you feeling about this?"

I let out a slow breath and brushed off the seat of a red mesh-back camping chair. "About camping? I miss my air conditioner."

"City girls," Bea said, squatting down on the edge of the firepit. "I mean, do you think we can come back from everything Kendra left us with?" Bea motioned around the empty campsite, where the seven members of the board plus our staff were staying, and my gaze drifted to the dark blue tent on the northeast corner.

After that weird night, I'd shut the attraction down, telling Cord we couldn't let that happen again, that it wasn't worth the messiness that could follow. Cord and I hadn't talked since he'd replied with a thumbs-up emoji, and it had been two weeks. I hadn't worked it out in my head yet, and Shea and Bri were very little help. Bri reminded me that the man couldn't read my mind, and Shea added that if he wasn't ready to take charge now, what hope was there for the bedroom?

I looked back at Bea, hoping she couldn't read the conflict on my face that had nothing to do with our organization. "I hope so."

"I really liked Kendra. I still can't believe she'd be in bed with people who would push such hateful agendas and then cut programs based on it. Technicolor was going to be so great for kids. It's something I wish I'd had back then. It's a little better now, but I can't imagine how my path might have been different if I had the chance to see more people of color, especially trans and queer people of color, in different professional roles when I was young." One program that was stalled was the pilot program Technicolor, geared to supporting LGBTQIA+ and other gender-expansive kids of color interested in tech. Bea had proposed it and built the infrastructure, including lining up a series of incredible speakers and professionals from different areas of tech. It was ready to launch when Kendra said funding had to be diverted. That was all before I arrived, but it made sense now, and the diversion lined up with the tainted infusion of money.

"It's first on my list when we get our funding sources shored up again, I promise."

Bea smiled and looked over my shoulder. "The troops have returned." She stood and brushed off the dirt from her shorts, calling out to the group, "How did it go?"

I turned to greet the team, plastering on a smile I didn't think reached my eyes. *God, I miss air-conditioning.*

Kevin shrugged and turned to a few others all holding fishing poles. "At least we tried."

"Good thing we weren't counting on this for dinner," Alison said, setting the fishing poles aside where the rental place had left them. The group gathered near the firepit, and Bea motioned to the cooler for water and the one with beer.

"The only one who caught anything was Cord," Kevin said. He accepted a bottle opener from Bea and motioned to a group of board members, where Cord brought up the rear. He was in jeans and a T-shirt that fit him tighter than I remembered his T-shirts did in the past, the gray fabric taut across his shoulders, shoulders I remembered holding on to when he had me against the wall in my apartment.

"The fishing award goes to Cord," Bea said, offering him the choice of a beer or a water bottle.

"Don't celebrate me too much yet," he said, avoiding my gaze and taking the water from Bea. He held up something glittering in his other hand, the light catching on where he held it next to me.

"Is that a diamond necklace?" The light ricocheted off the necklace in the afternoon sun, and Cord's eyes swept over me. It only lasted a second, and no one else would have noticed the way his eyes met mine, dipped to my lips, and then were moving away in a flash. No one but me. "I'm ninety-nine percent sure it's a toy," he said, tucking it back into his pocket.

"But there's a chance. What did I tell you about bringing this guy on?" Kevin slapped a hand on his shoulder. "He's already bringing in valuable finds."

The group members all began taking seats around the empty firepit, chatting and laughing as we settled in. I was about to snag my same chair again, the one across the way but not directly in Cord's sight line, when Kevin pulled me aside. It made sense to touch base on how we wanted to frame some of our discussion items, but out of the corner of my eye, all I could see was seat after seat being taken. By the time Kevin said "Great!" and walked toward the circle, the only open seat left was right next to Cord.

I adopted a cheery tone. "This spot taken?"

"No, of course not," Ellie said from the other side of Cord. She'd been looking at the necklace and handed it back to him. "Too bad it's not real." Ellie had been a really valuable member of the team as we dealt with all the public fallout, something I both appreciated and worried about.

"Still better than a catfish," I said, trying to join the conversation without obsessing over how the man between us kissed. My joke fell flat, but the awkward silence only lasted a moment.

"Let's get started, everyone!" Bea and Xavier stood at the front of the group. They'd asked me if I wanted to kick things off, and the "no" was out of my mouth before they finished. We needed hype, which was not my speed. I was relieved to sit back and watch my team shine, though. "We've already shared the agenda for the next two days. We'll be focusing on new ideas, big ideas, and communication opportunities. In conversation with Pearl, we also thought it a good time for everyone to get reacquainted with our mission and goals."

"Teamwork makes the dream work!" Xavier chimed in, his swoopy hair and boisterous expression giving him the energy of a high school cheerleader. "To kick us off, form four groups of three with the people near you and share why you're here."

"I love this," Amaya exclaimed. "Such a great way to kick off." She had been on level ten since we arrived, and while I appreciated that kind of commitment to the organization, it was clear she was the odd one out with Cord and me, who both nodded along. I thought I caught the corner of his lip in a grin when our gazes connected, but I might have just been imagining.

"Cord, how about you? You're the newest member. You start us off." She scooted her chair around so we sat in a tight circle.

"Well," he said, pushing his hand through his hair. "I honestly joined as a favor to Kevin, and a friend talked me into it. They were a mentor for a long time. But I'm glad I'm here, and I just started mentoring."

"Great," she said. "Kudos to your friend."

Cord's gaze skated over me to look at his hands and then back to Amaya. "What about you?"

Amaya smiled a toothy grin. "I love to talk about this. Well—" Her phone rang from the cupholder where she'd dropped it, and her smile turned down at the caller ID. "Excuse me. It's the office." She stood and walked away, her tone immediately shifting from the joyful, light one we'd just been engaging with to one you'd expect from the head of a company regularly in negotiations with the DoD. "Go for Adkins . . . No. No. That's unacceptable. Get Charles on the line."

"That sounds like it might take a while." I looked back at Cord.

"Yeah. I have nightmares about those kinds of calls," he said.

"Well, to be fair, Charles is an intimidating guy with the mullet and the exposed chest hair." I grinned at his laugh.

"You're right. It's like he forgot the second half of the buttons to his shirt." The imaginary and powerful stranger was giving us a perfect break in the tension. "You know my Charles?"

"We dated briefly," I said, crossing one leg over the other and leaning forward. "Didn't work out, though."

Cord leaned forward, too, his forearms resting on his knees. "He's intense. All that CIA training probably left him a bit too controlling?"

"Not near controlling enough." The words spilled out

before I could catch them, and I checked Cord's reaction for surprise, but he didn't react beyond laughing. I supposed he had no reason to guess the double entendre, or that I'd learned I liked not having to be in control in intimate settings. *What is wrong with me?* This line of thought was wildly inappropriate around a campsite with a board of directors and the man I'd already swore nothing could happen with. "I can share my answer."

"Yes. Why are you back, Pearl?"

He was mirroring Bea's and Xavier's tones, asking a straightforward question, but I got those same damn butterflies as before.

"I believe in the mission. I've seen firsthand what it means when people, especially women of color, get support in STEM early. My middle sister had a baby at sixteen, and when she was struggling to finish high school, a community member who knew my parents looked out for her, encouraged her, helped her connect with resources, scholarships, and college advisers. But she also helped Bri explore all the options in front of her. She went into biochemistry and pharmaceuticals, not anything with coding or software, but that mentoring was key for her." I glanced at Cord to find his attention rapt on me, and I looked away, giving Amaya a grin as she motioned that she was almost done with her call. "We do that here—help make those connections—and I loved the work that was happening. I wanted to be part of it."

"Family first. Do important work," he said, quoting what I'd said about my tattoo. He didn't add the third one.

"Yes," I said. "And it's good to be home, to be close to . . . everyone I left when I moved to California." *To you, even though I can't ever admit that.*

"Sorry about that," Amaya said, breezing back into the

conversation and breaking the eye contact we'd been holding. "You talk with one senate aide, you've talked with a thousand. What did I miss?"

Cord's eyes met mine for a flash, but I looked away. "Nothing, just me sharing how I believe in OurCode. How it aligns with what I want to do."

"Perfect. What's next?" She looked between us, and then the three of us sat back to await instruction on our next activity from Xavier and Bea.

CHAPTER 24

Cord

AMAYA HAD GOTTEN THREE MORE URGENT PHONE calls and was possibly now on hold for the joint chiefs of staff. She mouthed "Sorry" and motioned for us to go ahead. Pearl's team had given each group an hour to go for a walk and brainstorm ways to embrace and embody our mission. "Looks like we're on our own." I nodded toward the woods, doing my best not to make eye contact with Pearl for longer than needed.

"I have to admit, I'm feeling a little inadequate that not a single government official has needed me on the phone this entire time," I said, grabbing my hoodie from the back of my chair as the temperature dipped. "Am I second string, here?"

"Probably closer to third," she joked, tucking her little notebook into her back pocket. "I think Kevin was on with the EU earlier when we were unpacking s'mores stuff."

I chuckled. "Wow. Okay." I let her walk ahead of me, and I told myself I was just checking that her notebook hadn't fallen out of her pocket. That was why my gaze swept down across the back of her jeans. "I need to step up my game."

Pearl and I walked along the path leading into the woods. We'd been waiting for Amaya for about ten minutes, so everyone else had already scattered for their own brainstorming. "If a giant mosquito gets me, I'm holding you responsible for suggesting a walk in the woods."

"Heavy is the crown." The wooded area held its own sounds—birds, sticks and dirt shifting under our feet—but there was otherwise silence. There were also a lot of things I wanted to say, like "Can we talk about how my hand was up your skirt?" or "Elephant in the room, it's taking every inch of self-control to not stare at your lips right now." I shoved my hands into my pockets. "Where should we start?"

Pearl didn't seem bothered by the tension I felt, so maybe it was one-sided. After all, Pearl always had it together. She was the picture of resolute, and she'd said to cool it. And she was right. I'd stared at her message a long time to figure out the right response, because my first instinct was to make my case for taking things further. But after going so far as drafting the response, I deleted it. The thumbs-up emoji was decisive, simple, and even though it was a lie—*And are there worse lies than those we tell ourselves in emoji form?*—it was a lie that made me feel like I was holding on to some control.

"I've promised the staff one of my first priorities is relaunching the Technicolor program that Bea was about to pilot. I don't want to lose that, but it's not a no- or low-cost option." She shook her head, brow creasing. "I still cannot believe Kendra let someone with those kinds of priorities and that much hate do so much damage." Pearl kicked a rock with the toe of her sneaker, a bit of her normally contained personality escaping. "It matters, you know?" She shook her head. "Anyway, I'm really glad the board is all in for getting back on track with our PR and donors so we can get back to doing all the things that matter for the kids."

I bit my tongue, because my instinct was to ask what the program would cost, call my bank, and wire the money first thing Monday. I knew that wasn't my role, that she wouldn't want someone to swoop in and save the day, or at least she wouldn't want me to. I'd gotten that message loud and clear five years earlier after we left San Diego. "We'll do it." I looked ahead on the path, seeing no one. The campground and park area wasn't huge, but it was midweek and the crowds were gone. It was like we were the only two people around. "I was being interviewed a few weeks ago, and the reporter asked me how I know when to push for what I want at work and when not to. I gave my answer, but I realized it's maybe less complicated for me than others. I mean, I'm a cisgender white guy, and one with money on top of that."

Pearl nodded. "Oh, yeah. Being assertive looks different when people have preconceived notions about the angry Black person or the hotheaded Latina in the room. Lots of aspects of being and being seen as professional look different."

"I had never really thought about it in those terms before," I said, remembering how I'd admitted that to Tye. They'd seemed surprised that I admitted it, and even more surprised when I asked questions. "What if OurCode hosted a training or a seminar on some things like that?"

"On how to play the game and how to change the game in corporate settings," she suggested, rephrasing the idea.

"Yeah, that sounds better," I said, nudging her with my elbow. "What if it was a short-term workshop, a day or two?"

"Yes . . . yes." Pearl pulled the small notebook from her

back pocket and scrawled down our idea. "Might be a way to pull in new professionals with a low-commitment activity while still bringing them into the organization, too. Plus, it would be good for teens." She looked up from her notes, her lips turned up in a grin. "I like this."

This was like old times, with us bouncing ideas off each other, and I felt my smile grow at the sight of her and the way the streak of light through the trees fell across her expression. The light caught in her eyes, and I was helpless not to stare. "Me, too."

She searched my face, eyes skating across my brow and flicking down. All my resolve to be cool flew out the window and my cock stirred. I leaned toward her, needing her lips on mine. In an instant where I was confident she'd kiss me back, where I anticipated the soft give of her mouth, where I was ready for what was next, she smacked my cheek hard, the sting leaving me slack-jawed.

"Sorry!" She pressed her fingers to her mouth. "There was a mosquito," she said, motioning to my face. "I didn't think. I just went on the offense."

I laughed at her reaction and brushed the spot she'd smacked. "Did you get it?"

She nodded. "Here, let me." She stepped into my space, sliding her thumb over my cheek. I understood she was scraping a dead bug off my face, but the touch still sent a rush of heat down my spine.

"I got it," she said, still standing close, her chest almost touching mine. "Sorry again for slapping you."

"You've got a pretty good arm." I spoke quietly, like using a normal volume would remind her to step back. "Hold on." I brushed the backs of my fingers along her cheek.

"Did I have one on me?"

She didn't, but I swept my hand again before letting it fall. "Just practicing."

Pearl coughed and stepped back. "Us: one; mosquitoes: nothing." She nodded toward the path. "We were efficient. We still have, like, thirty minutes and we have our idea all set."

"Did you want to head back?"

"Let's walk a little. I have bloodlust now . . . ready to kill some more bugs."

"Hopefully not on my face."

"Be a team player, Matthews," she said, smiling over her shoulder again. "I'm excited about this idea. No one ever exactly taught me how to play the game when asking for what I want."

"I've gotten better at asking for what I want," I admitted. Though Tye had reminded me that as a white, cisgender man, I didn't always have to. They were right. "You always seemed so good at it, though."

Pearl swept a hand down the front of her T-shirt, smoothing the fabric. "I never trust others to give me what I want or need, so I always ask first. But sometimes people don't respond well to that."

I turned her words over in my head. "That must weigh a lot sometimes."

Pearl shrugged. "I've figured it out at work. And Kendra's mess aside, OurCode is a good place for me."

"And personally?" My body tensed as I asked, even as we still ambled along the path. I both wanted to know and knew it wasn't my place to ask. I was taking a very real risk of getting slapped again.

"Personally . . ." She looked toward the break in the trees ahead, where there was a clearing. I wasn't sure she was going to answer. "Personally, it would be nice to trust someone to give me what I needed without me always feeling I have to ask."

A hundred ideas of what Pearl might want ran, unbidden, through my head. "Can I tell you something without you getting mad?"

She glanced at me, her head cocked and a look of confusion replacing the somewhat whimsical look in her eyes from before. "Probably not. Who starts a sentence like that?"

"Okay, you're right. Can I tell you something, even though it might make you mad?"

"What is it?"

The sticks and dirt beneath our feet ground and cracked, birds above us chirping and red and gold leaves falling around us. "I know all the reasons I can't be, but I want to be the guy you trust to give you what you need without you asking. Truth is . . ."

"Cord."

"I want you." I shoved a hand in my pocket and took a deep breath before speaking again.

She stopped walking and looked at me, mouth open and eyes wide. I wasn't sure what the expression meant, so I interrupted before she could speak.

"I know you're not dating, and I'm not either. I know we work together and it's unprofessional and we have a past." I reached for her hand, wondering if she'd let me touch her. Her hand was warm and soft in mine. I led her off the path to a clearing where the ground was blanketed by soft leaves, trees surrounding us. "And I know I sent a thumbs-up, but that wasn't honest. The other night wasn't a fluke."

She still hadn't spoken. Pearl looked down, her hand unmoving in mine. "You're so different from how you used to be." She laughed, her face cracking into a warm expression, her perfect lips turning up. "You were never so direct."

I took a risk and twined my fingers with hers, taking a half step closer to her.

She shook her head, stepping back, pulling our fingers apart. "I have to focus on work and family. I have to make time for that, and everything at OurCode is so up in the air now."

"I don't need to be your focus, Pearl. Put your head first—that's the smart thing to do. I see that now. I'm doing that, too." I slid a hand down her hip. "But let me put you first, your body first, for a while."

She paced in the small clearing, hands on hips. "Cord. This is a bad idea."

I copied her tone. "It was a bad idea the first time. It didn't change the fact that I haven't stopped thinking about it since. Have you?"

She hadn't met my eyes again. "What if this blows up in our faces?"

I closed the distance between us, my palms sliding up her biceps and willing her to lift her chin. "It wouldn't be the first time. We'd figure things out." We stood there, leaves rustling around us in the still woods.

Her brown eyes searched mine, and I didn't speak, afraid to interrupt while she was thinking about what I'd said, hopeful she was talking herself into believing me. She finally spoke, licking her lips and drawing my gaze there momentarily. "I can't give you everything you want."

"I want different things than I used to." It was true, or at least I wanted it to be true.

Pearl glanced over my shoulder, her teeth nipping at the corner of her lip. Her wheels were turning, and I dropped my hand from her arm, resting it at her waist. We were mere inches apart now, the tips of our shoes grazing. In an instant, we were moving together and Pearl had gripped my neck, pulling my face to hers as her other hand held my shirt. Her tongue slid along mine, the soft velvet of her kiss gentle and then deepening. I placed my hand on the small of her back and pulled her against me, our mouths slanting against each other. "It has to be casual," she panted when we pulled apart.

I dragged my lips down her throat, tasting and nipping toward her collarbone and pulling her curves against me. "Casual. Definitely," I said into her neck, my hands dipping lower to cup her ass, letting my fingers sink into her flesh through the jeans. "As long as it's with you." I returned to her lips, walking her backward to a tree, our kisses intensifying, heat rising with her back against the bark and our bodies melding. "God, I missed this," I said, working a thigh between hers.

"Me, too." She ran her fingers through my hair, nails grazing my skin. "Cord." She said my name on a pant, grinding down against my leg. The pressure and heat of her body against mine made my head spin, and when her breath quickened, I slid my thigh back and forth.

"Are you going to come, Pearl? Do you want to?"

She pulled my hair, bringing my lips to hers again, her body needy and hungry against me. I dragged a hand from behind her to slide between us, and I wriggled my fingers to the button of her jeans, fumbling with the clasp. Only I couldn't get a good angle and finally broke the kiss, though it killed me to do it.

"What are you . . ." Pearl, breathless, looked confused, her body still arching into me.

"Sorry. I need to see while I do this. Do you trust me to give you what you want?" I sank to my knees in front of her, pulling at the closure of her jeans. She nodded and helped me push them down, eager. "Are you in a hurry?"

She glared, and I smirked as her belly became visible, her pubic bone and the spot I longed for. I dragged a finger over her slick folds and she shuddered.

"Oh, Pearl."

"Please," she said on a breath, thighs spreading.

"What do you want? My mouth? My fingers?" I dragged a knuckle slowly along her slit, up and around her sensitive bundle of nerves, before sliding a finger in teasing circles.

Pearl bucked against my hand, breath quickening. Her face contorted in the sweetest expression of want and need and breathless anticipation.

I felt like a superhero when I brought my mouth to her mound before she answered, my fingers already gliding into her. Sliding my tongue across her wet flesh, brushing over her swollen clit once, then again. It wasn't tender, but neither of us wanted that. The debris on the ground dug into my knees, but it seemed beyond inconsequential as she gasped and pushed against me, fingers gliding into my hair. When she whimpered, I wrapped my lips around her flesh, sucking, learning what pressure she liked, what made her quiver. *God damn, her quiver.*

She moaned my name, gripping my hair and grinding against my face. That moment was the single sexiest of my life, the hottest moment I might ever experience, and I could have died happy there on the ground in the woods with this incredible woman coming apart under my touch. I continued my tongue's swirl around her flesh, alternating licking and sucking in a way that seemed to work. Her thighs shook, and I crooked my finger, taking one last swipe over her slick, sweet skin, when she convulsed inside and out, panting. I risked a look up to her, still lapping my tongue along her sensitive flesh. She'd pulled her forearm across her mouth, maybe to stifle her cries.

I dragged my fingers from her, licking them as she watched me. She tasted like the best decision I ever made, and I wanted more. She gazed down, eyes hooded, biting that plump lower lip that made my cock harder, if that was possible. I rested my hands on her hips, rubbing small circles at her hip bone.

"Cord. My God." She ran her fingers through my hair once again, not in the gripping, frantic way she had when coming, but sweetly, stroking it off my forehead. "Get up off the ground."

"I kind of like it here." I kissed her hip bone and met her eyes again, the taste of her on my lips. Lamenting the obstruction of my new favorite view, I pulled her panties and jeans up, knowing her beautiful ass must be rubbing against the bark.

"I can't kiss you if you're down there."

I stood and wrapped her in my arms. "Good point." This kiss was tender, slow, and seeking, not the frenzied, breathless kind from before.

Pearl stroked my arm. "Do you have a condom?"

Fuck my life.

"No. I didn't think I'd need any while camping." I patted my pockets. It was a fool's errand—I didn't even have my wallet with me. It was back in the tent. "But if I did. That can be part of casual, too?"

She laughed, the low rumble of a laugh. "I'd like that."

I kissed her wrist like I'd done all those years before. She'd been moving her hand down my stomach, and I wanted her to touch me more than anything, but I knew we needed to get back to the group. "Take care of me next time. It will give me practice asking for what I want. We have to get back." I dropped a kiss on her cheek and took a step back so she could button her pants.

"I know." She reached up to finger comb my hair. "I made a mess of you." Her palm was so warm against my head, and when she slid it down, I leaned into her grip. "First the bug and now this."

"I prefer this to the bug, just for future reference." We joined hands, fingers linking, and strolled toward the campsite. "So, how does this work?"

"I don't know. I've never had casual sex in the woods with a colleague before."

"Do we tell anyone?" It wasn't like I had that many people I'd tell. Wes would never press for details, but he was also the only person I ever really talked about things with.

"I don't want Tye to know anything has changed. They have too much going on and it might be confusing. And of course no one with OurCode can know."

"Okay, I can see that. And will we see other people?" *God, I hope not.*

Pearl glanced away. "You should see whoever you want to."

"I don't want to see anyone else."

"Cord."

"Pearl."

"Well, if you want to see someone else, you can. Like, dating, not . . . another casual thing."

"It's just you." I squeezed her fingers. "And is it okay to

text you and tell you how much I can't get the taste of you out of my head? Because I think that will happen."

She smiled, pausing her steps. "I could get behind that. Can I text you back?"

"Only with photos."

She kissed me, her fists curled in my shirt. "Deal."

"Can I text you to tell you that you're beautiful and I love your laugh, too?" I wrapped my arms around her waist, holding her in a hug. "That I've been thinking about you all day?"

"Cord."

"Pearl."

"Let's go." She started back down the path. "I'm sure you'll have a call from the head of Google soon and you'll want good cell service."

I watched her walk for a moment, my head spinning. This was real. I'd had Pearl in my arms and against my lips, and I would again. We were going to give this a shot. And it was better this time. It was casual and no one would get hurt, and I wouldn't end up becoming my dad or changing my backyard again. I grinned and followed her down the path, and the only word that came to mind was "perfect."

CHAPTER 25

Pearl

WHEN WE ARRIVED BACK AT THE CAMPSITE, NO ONE else had returned, and it seemed unreal that everything that had just happened had been within our one-hour window for returning. I'd kissed Cord. He'd gone down on me in the middle of the woods. I'd committed to something despite years of vowing to put my head first, and now we were alone as I remembered all the reasons why what I'd let happen in the woods was a horrible idea.

"I need to check in with Tye," I said, holding up my phone. "I'll be back."

"No problem." Cord settled into the camping chair again. "Waiting for a call from the International Space Station anyway."

Pearl: SOS

Shea: Same. Tye was admiring the tattoo on my shoulder and wants one. Is that allowed? I was thinking for their birthday in a few months . . .

Bri: No.

Shea: Are you sure?

Bri: Do not let my fifteen-year-old child get a tattoo, Shea.

Shea: Okay. But I'll tell them you'll think about it.

Bri: Please don't.

Shea: Too late. Also, they've been hanging out with a kid named Peter. Do we like him?

Pearl: Hello? HELP.

Bri: ??

Shea: Did you accidentally have sex with 🔌 in the middle of your work trip and now don't know how to process breaking your own rules?

I glanced over my shoulder at Cord, who was doing something on his phone, a tiny grin on his face, a ghost of the smile he'd flashed me in the woods from his vantage on the ground.

Pearl: . . .

Bri: NO.

Shea: NO!

Pearl: It just . . . happened. We were talking and . . .

Shea: Details?

Pearl: No.

Bri: C'mon. I am living in a hotel with the world's hottest neighbor and getting none. I need details.

Shea: And I'm just nosy.

Pearl: Can you two be horny later? Advice, please. How do I keep it from being awkward the rest of the night with everyone around?

Shea: Well, try to stay out of his pants during discussions of synergy.

Bri: And climax quietly if you're analyzing financial statements.

Shea: And definitely don't accidentally talk about his length and girth when you mean to talk about donor longevity and giving patterns.

Pearl: I hate you both.

Bea's group returned a minute before I could disown my unhelpful siblings. As we shared our ideas, Amaya was elated with the workshop concept we had brainstormed, and everyone else around the circle was, too. I took pages of notes about the ideas from the other groups, ranging from programming to social media campaigns to targeted personal outreach. Everyone around the campsite was buzzing with energy, and I momentarily forgot my nerves about hooking up with Cord, because I hadn't felt this confident about being able to bring OurCode back from the brink since before the news about Kendra. Now I had a cautious hope that maybe this would end up being fine. During a brief break in the conversation, I'd glanced at my phone to see that my sisters had kept going without me.

Shea: We were just kidding.

Bri: Talk to him, but take Shea's lead. It's okay to be a little messy.

Shea: I'm not messy.

Shea: I'm not *that* messy.

Bri: Your roommate, James.

Shea: His betta fish died . . . He needed cheering up.

Bri: Your professor.

Shea: Ex professor . . . I dropped his class a few hours before we hooked up.

Bri: Chad, Bhodi, and Thien of Beta Eta Mu?

Shea: I have no explanation for that weekend other than it was a hoe phase.

Bri: Anyway, P, don't stress. Roll with it and see what happens.

Shea: And don't, under any circumstances, ride him like a pony in the middle of a PowerPoint presentation.

Bri: Or if you do, switch it to kiosk mode first.

Kevin cleared his throat, standing and holding out a beer. "I'm excited about all of this," he said, surveying the group. "Before we get going with dinner, I wanted to say something else." He sipped from the bottle, and I tucked my phone into my pocket. Annoyance tickled up my spine, because I'd worked closely on the agenda with Bea and Xavier, and Kevin giving a speech was not on it. Still, I leaned forward attentively. "By now, we've all gotten very familiar with the fallout from the scandal. It goes without saying, but I'll say it anyway. We all have to be above reproach, both on the board and off."

From the corner of my eye, I saw Cord's gaze swing to me, but I fought the urge to meet his eyes.

"That's financially and, of course, to make sure there isn't a whiff of impropriety among us."

My face flushed hot, and I worried he'd be looking straight to me, that someone had overheard us or seen us in the woods, but Kevin continued to casually address the entire group, most of whom probably didn't need to squirm in their chairs at the memory of the lips of someone else in the circle on their body. I nodded along with everyone else.

"Not that I'm worried. I mean . . . I think we've all had front-row seats to what can happen with a sex scandal on the board." He chuckled and raised his beer, and I looked at my notes to have something to do. "Anyway, enough of that. Let's eat!" Everyone shuffled forward, and Xavier called from the grill that the burgers were about ready, but I busied myself with my notebook.

"You okay?" Cord was looking at the fire, arms resting on his knees casually. I imagined we looked like everyone else making conversation, but his chair was still next to mine and our bodies were close.

"What? I'm fine." I tucked my notes away.

"Do you want to talk about what happened in the woods?" His low voice was too quiet for anyone else to hear, but it felt like it wrapped around me like a blanket. "Did what Kevin said bother you?"

"We can't talk about this here," I said, standing and brushing my palms down my jeans. "Someone might hear us."

"Okay." He straightened and glanced to the line by the grill, his face a shadow of a look I'd seen before, the look of someone with something to say who wouldn't say it. For a moment I both wanted him to drop it and wanted him to put the words out there, have them between us—he never used to say what he wanted. But when he didn't say anything, I took a step back, looking from side to side to make sure we weren't overheard.

"But, Pearl?" He was shoving his hand in his pocket, his posture casual, but his expression was intense in a way that reminded me of the woods and his insistent touches. In a way, I hadn't seen him like this before, and I really liked that this was new. "We'll talk later. That wasn't a onetime thing."

CHAPTER 26

Cord

"HEY, MATTHEWS," KEVIN GREETED ME AS HE APproached the spot I'd staked out on the far side of the firepit, a little away from everyone else chatting and laughing. "I gotta tell you, man. I owe you big for taking this board spot." He fell into the chair next to me, clinking his bottle with mine. "That idea you and Pearl came up with—great."

"Yeah," I said, taking a drink. "I'm glad you talked me into it. I'm mentoring, too."

"Really?" Kevin took another drink before adding, "Don't know where you find the time."

I glanced at the screen of my phone, where I'd lost track of how many emails sat unread, the to-do list my assistant had compiled on our shared cloud space growing to something I couldn't scroll to the end of quickly. "I don't think I do, but you make it work when it matters, right?"

"Course." We both scanned the gathered group. Four people were playing dominoes at a card table lit by a lantern, and Pearl and a few members of her team were making s'mores. Her head tipped back in a laugh at something one of the staff members said, her face lit by the light from the campfire. "Did Pearl talk you into mentoring when you had lunch? I like her, but she's a force."

Force was an understatement. "No, my ex." I'd given up on trying to think of a socially acceptable way to refer to Abby as the person I had on hold as a plus-one and with whom I was having sex.

"Ex? Not the knockout from the gala?"

"Abby. I took over mentoring their mentee."

"Sorry, Matthews. Can't imagine you'd get lucky with someone that hot again." He grinned and I joined him in laughing at the joke, though my gaze flicked back to Pearl. "That's a hell of a thing to do for an ex, though."

I shrugged. "It wasn't for them. Just wanted to try it out."

"I always remember that about you. You'd do a favor for anyone, anytime."

I wanted to argue the point, but the photo of Peach on my lock screen reminded me that he was right. It was easier to say yes than risk letting someone down. I'd never seen it as a problem until recently. Pearl stood, using her hands to tell a story, her expression animated. I thought about our conversation and asking for what I wanted. "I'm not doing you any sexual favors. Don't get any ideas in your head," I said to Kevin, dragging my gaze from Pearl.

"Damn. I'll live with the disappointment, then." Our laughs faded and we both looked into the fire, but he must have caught my gaze straying to Pearl, who was talking to Bea and Amaya. "Was she like that when she worked for you? Having it all together all the time? Kendra was ecstatic about getting her, said she'd run a tight ship."

"At FitMi?" It was a stupid question, but I was trying to think of a way to frame the answer. "Yeah. I mean, she was still finishing her degree and was our executive assistant, but tight ship is right."

"I had my reservations, but Kendra got one thing right, I guess."

Pearl had returned to her seat and was checking her phone, the blue light casting a glow on her face.

"Reservations?" I took a swig from the beer, my attention catching on that word.

"Between you, me, and the fire?"

"Sure," I said, nodding and turning to him.

"She'd dated her boss at the last nonprofit she worked at, some green-energy guy who started a foundation when he sold his software company."

My stomach dropped. I'd never heard anything about it. "How did you find out?"

"She disclosed it to Kendra in the interview, said it lasted a few years. Nothing exactly scandalous, but you never know about that kind of situation."

"Yeah," I said, gaze wandering back to Pearl. She'd dated her boss. She'd dated her boss and it got serious. A combination of embarrassment and frustration and regret swirled in my head, remembering her insistence that we couldn't do anything because she worked for me, that she had to focus on work and family. Her tattoo lived rent-free in my brain. "I guess you never do."

"Worked out in this case, though. And whoever got you roped in, I'm glad you're here." He slapped my shoulder twice and stood. "I'm gonna get in on that s'more action. Want one?"

I waved him off. "Nah. I'm good."

When I was alone again and Kevin had joined Pearl and the others, I let myself process everything Kevin had said.

From his assessment about me doing favors to the shock that Pearl had once dated her boss, I was calling into question everything from that day. Across the way, Pearl looked at her phone again, and I shot off a quick text, immediately regretting it.

Cord: You dated your boss in California?

Her expression changed and her eyes lifted, meeting mine across the clearing.

Pearl: Yes.

Cord: Can we talk later tonight?

Pearl: I think we should wait until we get home. Less risky.

She met my gaze again after her new message came through. She was right, of course, and if Kevin knew she'd dated a colleague, I got how the thing between us might look even worse for her. Still, I felt unbalanced for the rest of the night.

CHAPTER 27

Pearl

LATER THAT NIGHT, I LAY AWAKE, STARING AT the roof of my tent. I had no idea how Cord had heard about Richard, but I'd hated seeing that look on his face, the hurt he was trying to mask with a cool expression. I knew his cool expressions and I could see through them. There hadn't been time to tell him my former boss was a safe choice for me. We'd gotten serious, but I wouldn't ever fully fall for him like I'd fallen for Cord. I wouldn't have let myself fall like that again.

He hadn't come back over to me the rest of the night, and I hadn't seen him before I turned in. I curled my toes, enjoying the stretch in my legs as I let my mind wander to how it felt when he'd dragged my pants down over my hips, how he'd gripped my waist. That whole time, he'd been supporting me, holding me up. He was good at that. Too good.

I rolled over again, feeling so claustrophobic in my tent, I let out an audible heavy sigh. I ventured outside, where everything was quiet. Everyone was settled into their own tents—only the chirps of crickets and the brush of rustling leaves filled the quiet night. I took a deep breath, looking for the cooler that had held the water bottles earlier, and a blue light from Cord's tent caught my eye. I bit my lower lip, waiting for it to flash off, for him to go to sleep, but it stayed on. I walked quietly to the outer corner of the campground, glancing at all the tents as I passed, checking for lights or movement, but it was still save the rustling of the leaves.

It's hard to knock on a tent, so I whispered instead. "Cord, are you up?"

Inside, there was the sound of shuffling before the zipper opened and he knelt at the entrance. His sleep pants hung low on his hips, even while kneeling, and the white T-shirt stretched across his chest. "Is something wrong?"

"Can I come in?"

Cord cocked his head. "To my tent? Are you sure?"

I shifted from foot to foot, the cool air chilling my bare arms. I hadn't planned on being outside long in my tank top, and I wrapped my arms across my chest, covering my nipples, which had puckered from the cool breeze along with the memories from earlier in the day. "No one is awake."

"Sure," he said, seeming uncertain, but he moved out of the way to let me in. "It's a little risky to come to my tent in the middle of the night, though."

His tent was identical to mine, and his sleeping bag was spread out on an air mattress. After rezipping the tent, he settled back on one end of the air mattress, forearms resting on his knees, with enough moonlight filtering in that I could see him clearly.

"I know. I couldn't sleep," I offered by way of explanation, tucking my legs under me and skirting his comment.

His gaze traveled to the bare skin above my chest for a moment, and my nipples tingled. "I thought you wanted to wait until we were back in town to talk."

"I . . . uh . . . I wanted to say . . ." I glanced all around. In the clearing alone, I'd been certain I knew what I wanted to say, but being near him, it felt wrong.

"Wait. Before you do, let me say something." He leaned forward, cupping my cheek in one hand and letting the other slide to my waist. In the small space, our knees touched, and I let my eyes fall closed. He didn't kiss me, though. "I'm sorry I asked you about California." He looked into my eyes, shadows playing on his face in the dark, with only the glow from his lantern lighting the space. "It took me by surprise, but it's none of my business and you don't owe me explanations for anything. There's nothing between us that gives me the right to ask for explanations."

"I was thinking I should explain *because* you deserve that from me. Whatever we're doing now, we still have a history." I slid a palm slowly up his stomach to his chest, enjoying the way his breath quickened. "And I still care about you."

Cord didn't pull away, and his fingers stilled on my skin like warm pebbles.

"We started dating about a year after I got to California, and it lasted a couple of years. It was serious." I skated over the rest—how we'd moved in together, how he'd been kind if inattentive, how when Shea talked about moving in with me after she graduated, he'd balked. How he'd never been Cord, and that was one of the reasons why it ended. "I thought a lot about head before heart and tried it, honestly."

"And it changed your mind about putting your head first?" His fingers made small circles at my side. "He was the guy you took a chance on?"

"No." I shook my head. "In the end, it cemented the importance of not taking chances."

"But you're here," he said, tracing the shell of my ear. "With me."

"I still want my head to speak first." I heard the waver in my resolve. "But it's like I lose all sense of caution around you." Outside, crickets chirruped, and a breeze blew through the tent. "And you do, too. In San Diego . . ."

"That was a long time ago. I'm really not the same person I was then." Cord searched my gaze and then slid his hand down from my face along the line of my arm, bringing my wrist to his lips. "The fourth one," he said.

"That's a story for another time," I said, not moving my arm when his lips brushed over my skin. "I was also thinking . . ."

"About what?" He pulled me toward him, our bodies pressed together in the tight space. The warmth of his arms surrounded me.

I slid my thigh across his lap, straddling him. "About finishing what we started in the woods." I studied his expression, the look of relief and arousal, and that was all I needed to confirm the decision. I kissed him, needing more, wanting everything. No matter my resolve to put the brakes on things, his touch, his voice, his . . . everything pushed me in the other direction.

He responded immediately, dropping his hands lower to pull me forward against his growing erection. "I like that idea." His lips trailed down my neck and over my collarbone, one hand firmly planted on my backside, but the other exploring, massaging, and thumbing over my nipple, that movement making me grind against him, my center aching and wet.

"I still don't have a condom," he said into my neck.

"I'm on birth control and I've tested clear," I said as he lifted his eyes to meet mine. I wedged my hand between us, stroking him through his pants.

"Me, too." We spoke in hushed whispers, and I kissed him again.

I worked my hand into his pants, gripping his hot, hard length in the palm of my hand, and his head fell back. "I want you, but Cord?"

He nipped, then slid his lips across, my earlobe. "Petal?"

He'd called me that the night in my apartment, and it took me back onto that beach with him, imagining a different outcome; a different way our future could have unfolded. In that whispered, gravelly voice, I rolled the name around in my head. The one I could have heard repeatedly for the last five years.

"We'll have to be quiet," I said, giving an experimental stroke up and down his length.

Cord growled into the hollow of my neck, and I gripped him more firmly. "Can you?"

The way his voice vibrated against my skin sent a shot of pleasure down through my core. "I can be quiet," I whispered.

He slid a hand down the back of my sleep pants, massaging and squeezing before pushing them down my hips. Without any hesitation, he guided two fingers between my legs, where I was pulsing and wet. I welcomed the way his fingers curled inside me and bit my lip hard to stop from crying out.

Cord kissed me, sucking gently where my teeth had been while pushing my sleep pants all the way down. "I don't believe you."

It wasn't graceful in the small space of the tent, but we'd maneuvered, and now we both kneeled on the air mattress, my back to his front as he worked his hands up my shirt and down to stroke between my legs. The dual sensations partnered with him pressing hard and ready against my back were too much to handle. Before I could cry out again, he angled his lips to mine, stealing my cries.

"Do you like it this way?" He gently pushed my shoulders down with one hand, his pelvis still holding my hips in place. When I rested on my forearms, I felt exposed—he was still fully dressed and I was before him, his hand still on my back, but I loved it. Shea had encouraged me to let my life get messy, and this was the textbook definition of it.

"God, yes."

"Do you trust me to give you what you want?" He trailed his fingertips down my spine, making me shiver with anticipation. He was slow and deliberate. I was learning Cord in the bedroom differed from elsewhere—Cord in the bedroom was controlled and kind of dominant. When his fingers met the lowest part of my back, he swept them around my waist and stroked my clit again. "You can use the pillow if you need to block any noises," he whispered as he dragged his thumb achingly slowly over my clit with just a brush of pressure. He arched over me, his chest to my back. "I really hope you need to," he said, pulling his fingers away, their glide moving back up my waist and down between my cheeks.

He continued stroking my folds, this time from behind. "Are you sure?" His other hand held my breast, gently squeezing and pinching the nipple, and it was as if Cord had six hands. I couldn't catch my bearings between caresses and squeezes. I couldn't get a hold of myself and I didn't want to. I rolled my hips, waiting, wanting, and when his finger grazed over the spot no one had ever stroked before, I tensed, but it was a good tense as he circled and teased.

"Yes," I whispered, or maybe I cried out. "Yes. Why are your pants still on?"

"My hands were busy," he said with a chuckle, and I heard the rustling of his sweats as he pushed them down.

I spread my thighs wider, dipping my head in anticipation. "Well, get started, and your hands will be free again."

Cord chuckled again, but I felt the press of the wide head of his cock against my opening. "You're so bossy." He slid into me slowly, my body stretching to accommodate his length as he filled me. The sensation was overwhelming, painful for just a moment and then so, so good as he seated himself in me. He paused, his breath erratic, before pulling out slowly, then inching back in, the pace slow and controlled as he reached around my body, stroking my clit again with that same feathered touch. When I kissed him, I thought we'd end up in a romantic embrace, missionary with long, intense eye contact, but this was so much better.

"I know what I like," I whispered before a moan escaped my lips.

"Shh . . . use the pillow, Petal." He thrust harder the next time, his speed picking up and his thumb worked over my clit in tight circles.

"You're bossy yourself," I whispered, but the shift in sensations in both places left me backing against him and grinding my hips. I buried my face in his pillow, breathing in his scent and moaning, then crying out into the fabric as Cord thrust deeper and harder, nudging at my G-spot while my swollen clit pulsed under his touch. His other hand, warm and wide, rested on my back, somehow calming at the same time as he held me in place.

"I know what you like, too," he said, thrusting again,

his breath labored as his pace quickened. "Or I'm quickly learning."

He pressed his thumb down harder against my clit and I cried out into the pillow, moving a hand over his, pressing him against me. That intense burst of pressure sent me so close to the edge, my head spun. "Don't stop," I said before returning my mouth to the pillow as his thrusts grew more powerful, the backs of his thighs hitting mine, his hand in place on my back.

He panted. "I won't, not until you come, Pearl." His thumb continued in tight, firm circles and my thighs quivered, my hips moving with their own rhythm as I fell into oblivion, his thick length nudging my G-spot the entire time, the sensations dually fanning out my thighs and up my core, my body a tighter and tighter coil.

"Cord," I whimpered into the soft cotton of the pillow.

"Pearl," he panted, continuing the same insistent press on my clit, but his hand on my back pushed my shoulders down, and his thrusts moved deeper, the angle shifting.

I cracked, my arms almost giving out at the explosion of pleasure, the jolt of the release, and my entire body convulsed. My arms shook, my thighs quivered, and my center pulsed around Cord's erection. He pressed his hand between my shoulder blades and slowly, so slowly, moved his other hand to my waist, pulling me against him, his thrusts shallower, slowing as my body rocked.

When I pressed backward against him, he gripped my waist and thrust once more in that slow shallow way before taking me deep, fast, and hard. The pressure of him against my G-spot, where it felt like he'd been nudging for hours, sent me over the edge again, and I came hard, suddenly, pressing my mouth to the pillow once more. This time I shook, my arms giving out, and Cord crashed down behind me, his whispers frantic.

"Fuck. Oh, God, Pearl. I'm gonna come." His last thrust sent aftershocks through me, and he dug his fingers into my hips as he climaxed, his body covering mine, buried deep inside me.

We both lay there, connected, our bodies reeling. My *mind* reeling with how the air around me felt electric. After heaving a breath, Cord kissed my shoulder. It was the sweetest, softest kiss of my life and, alight with adrenaline, I felt it through my whole body. I leaned and he slid, and we ended up side by side, him still inside me, softening, my body still shaking from the impact of the dual release, the two strongest orgasms of my entire life. He pulled me to him, wrapping me in his arms, his warmth surrounding me. I let him hold me, and he kissed my shoulder again, that peck conveying everything I knew he felt, and everything I knew I couldn't.

"Cord," I said in a murmured whisper. I didn't have the right words to say I needed more of what just happened, but I couldn't give more than my body. I didn't know how to phrase that I was afraid he could be someone I would want to rely on, and I couldn't risk getting hurt again, couldn't risk sacrificing everything again. My mind wouldn't pull the words together, but maybe my body did because I needed him to hold me more in that moment than I'd ever needed anything. Naked and limp in his arms, I wanted nothing more than to let him take care of me and throw every iota of caution to the wind.

He squeezed me more tightly and kissed my shoulder again, his lips lingering against my skin. "I know," he murmured. "It won't be like five years ago."

We slumped down together, wrapped in each other while I inhaled his scent, soaking up his touches. "We'll be more careful. We won't let this become something it can't be."

I thought we'd lie there together in some kind of peaceful euphoric haze, but the air mattress groaned beneath us and we both giggled at the sound. Cord squeezed me tighter. "Now, how are we going to get you back to your tent without getting caught, seeing as you'll have trouble walking?"

"Oh, c'mon, we had this whole moment happening," I said, sinking against him. "Now it's over."

"We're still having a moment," he said, squeezing me again.

And of course he was right. When I finally pulled away from him and gathered my clothes, I stole a glance and studied Cord stretched on the mattress, body loose and his expression contented. I wondered if we'd ever really stopped having meaningful moments together.

CHAPTER 28

Cord

Five Years Earlier

August

PEARL KNOCKED ON MY OPEN DOOR AND GAVE ME A slow and assessing once-over.

I'd gotten a haircut the day before in preparation to feel more professional on my first day as the boss, but I swiped my hand over my forehead out of habit. I sat at my desk, staring at my screen—Wes had left the company we created together, and I was now the lone man in charge.

"Hey," Pearl said, handing me a plastic cup from the break room. Our logo printed on the side with the phrase THIS CUP CONTAINS TEARS OF THOSE WHO DOUBTED ME. "I thought you might need this." Her fingers were wet from the condensation when they brushed mine.

"Is it whiskey?"

"Mountain Dew." She sat in the chair next to my desk, resting one forearm on the wood.

I took it from her and grinned at the contents. "You brought me my favorite."

Pearl shrugged one shoulder in a move that had the bare skin of her arm catching the light. She wore a dress that had distracted me all day, even as I silently panicked about it being Wes's last day with the company. I'd wanted to touch her.

"Thank you," I repeated.

Pearl crossed her long legs, the toe of her black heel nudging my leg. "You got a haircut."

"I thought it made me look more . . . in charge." I ran my fingers through my hair, unused to the short length. "Still no vest, though."

"Well," she said, grazing a finger over her collarbone the way she did when she was distracted. "Baby steps. It looks nice, though." I followed the motion of that finger, wishing it were my own. Wishing it were intentional and not just an absent gesture.

I was circling the question I always circled. What would happen if I told her how I felt? If I admitted I was head over heels in love with her, what would she say? I glanced toward my computer, where the slide deck for the next day's investor meeting was open, and let the question keep circling silently. I'd crossed the line too much already, and as her supervisor, I couldn't. "I am terrified of public speaking," I admitted. "Think I should have brought that up sometime between starting a business and running one solo?"

Pearl chuckled. "I'm afraid of it, too, honestly."

"No way. You're not afraid of anything." Of course, I knew that wasn't true because she'd let me see her fear during the thunderstorm and let me hold her in the dark, but we'd never talked about it afterward.

She stretched her leg out and playfully kicked me, but it was a soft kick I could almost pretend was her sliding her foot up my leg. "It's a front."

Her foot lingered for a moment before it fell back to the floor. "I never would have guessed," I said, looking down at our shoes only a few inches apart. "So, I guess asking you to do this for me tomorrow is out of the question, huh?"

"Absolutely."

"Too bad."

"But I'll be there, in the room. If you get nervous, just look for me." Pearl tilted her head to the side. "I'll flash the code for 'You can do it.'"

I grinned, turning my chair so our legs were closer. "What's the code?"

Pearl sat up, placing her arms in her lap. "I'll go like this." She tilted her head again, this time biting her lower lip. It was subtle, but her teeth sinking into that lower lip was something I'd spent hours considering and imagining. So her sitting so close to me and doing it was either torture or kismet.

"That's kind of a cute secret code." I crossed one leg over the other, begging my cock to chill out and stop reacting to Pearl biting her lower lip while sitting in my office.

"I wasn't going for cute," she said, standing and tracing her hand along my bookshelf. "Maybe I should come up with something else."

"No," I said, watching her. "It's a good code. It's just that anything you do will be . . . cute. I mean, not in a dismissive way, but cute like adorable. Or maybe like—"

"Cord, is there a point somewhere in all that?" She didn't sound annoyed, and when I met her eyes, she was smiling at me, a little smile I knew was genuine. A real Pearl smile as she walked back, sitting on the edge of my desk like I normally sat on hers.

"Just that any code you come up with will be great," I said, chickening out. "Because you're great."

"Well, you're great, too. You'll do well tomorrow," she

said, her palm resting over my hand on the desk, the heat and weight of it making my skin feel like it was on fire. "I'll just hold up a sign since my secret code left a bit to be desired."

It left everything to be desired, but not in the way she thought. "Do it again, so I remember what it is."

This time she did the same movement but puffed her cheeks and crossed her eyes.

"Oh yeah, that's better. Do that tomorrow."

Her hand was back on mine, and I should have pulled back, but instead of doing that, I shifted my pinky finger just an inch, over her skin. "What sign should I give you?" I kept moving my finger slightly, so slightly she probably didn't notice.

Pearl glanced at our fingers and then back to me, her voice soft. "Why would I need a sign?"

"Well, in case you ever have to do something hard and you need to look at me." I moved my finger in a wider arc, but Pearl didn't pull away. "Like when you leave us for a great new job and have to give a speech in front of hundreds of people." The thought was like razor blades, but she'd finished her degree and I knew she was qualified for so many jobs.

Pearl's lashes lowered. "I saw one posted, but I don't think I'll apply. It's a big-deal job. They'd never hire me."

"No," I said without thinking. "Anyone worth their company charter would be out of their mind not to hire you. You're amazing."

"It's going to be competitive." She waved the words away. "I'm sure I don't have the skills or experience to even be considered. But maybe something at a lower level."

I shook my head. "That sounds like your dipshit ex in

your head. He is a jerk and he was wrong about you. I knew that within thirty seconds of meeting him. Promise me you'll apply if you want the job." I forecast what it would be like to not see Pearl every day but also what it would mean to Pearl to land this amazing job. She'd be so happy getting to do the work she cared about. A brief fantasy of meeting after we both left work, being able to go back to my place or hers, to be together. I held up my thumb. "How about this sign? I could just give you a thumbs-up?"

"Not very subtle. What else do you have?"

I had nothing. No ideas, no thoughts, and no hope of thoughts in the future, because Pearl had shifted her fingers and they were slowly toying with mine. "Um, maybe I could brush my hair off my forehead."

Pearl's fingers were linked with mine, her thumb sliding over my palm and leaving a trail of nerve endings on fire. "You do that all the time. How would I know it was for me?"

"You'd be the only person in the room I'd see," I admitted, dragging my thumb along the side of hers.

"I don't know. I think your eyesight is pretty good."

The joke fell flat, but I didn't care. "You're usually the person in the room I pay the most attention to."

"I am?" She glanced down at our hands, our fingers touching, the soft brushes of her thumb driving me wild.

I followed her gaze to our hands, and I wished I was the guy who'd just make a move, consequences be damned, but I'd never been that guy. "You are."

"I didn't know you noticed me like that." She inched nearer to me on the desk, and I did the same, pushing my chair closer.

"I thought it was painfully obvious." I thought back to the steady stream of awkward moments I'd had in front of her.

"Not to me," she said. "If you brush your hair off your face, I'll know you're thinking of me and cheering me on." She lifted our joined hands, and I guided them toward my heart. "And then I'll tell you to go get another haircut."

I laughed and she grinned, and her hand was over my heart, which was beating wildly as I figured out what to do next. "You're going to do well tomorrow. I know you can do this."

"I don't really have a choice." The playful tone I'd hoped for didn't reach my lips, and she slid her fingertips across my forehead. We hadn't been this close to each other since that day we were stuck in the elevator and my heart raced.

"You're ready to lead."

I closed my eyes at the onslaught of rising emotion her words and that touch left me with. It surprised me, but I turned into her hand, feeling her fingers against my face. "I don't know if I am," I admitted, giving voice to the worry that had been plaguing me for weeks.

"You know what this company needs. And I think you know what you want."

I met her gaze, drank in her dark irises. I wanted her. I wanted these touches and so much more as I took in her expression. And then, slowly, she bit her lower lip, tilting her head to the side.

"That's the signal." Her hand fell to my chest again, and she pressed more firmly over my heart. "So, tell me what you want for the company."

If this were a comic, her palm would have sparked something inside me and we'd be surrounded by energy and light. That's what it felt like, and after a beat, I answered her. "Globalization. I want FitMi in other countries and customized for those cultures."

"What else?"

"AI coaching as an added option on top of our human coaches. For those who want it, it would ease the pinch points we find with staffing and be a new technological challenge."

She grinned and nodded, her palm still against me. "What else?"

I leaned forward in my seat, excited that these ideas that had always felt muddled in my head were out there and they sounded good. "Partnerships with in-person gyms."

"See?" Pearl smiled at me, and I placed my hand over hers, holding her to my heart, holding on to that feeling.

"How do you do that?"

"Do what?"

"Make me feel like I can do anything." Our gazes were still locked, and I waited for what felt like the inevitable next step between us, but then her hand fell from my chest and she glanced away.

"I'm a good assistant," she said, as if stepping away from something dangerous. "And you're a good boss." Her gaze was cautious. "But you're . . . my boss."

I nodded, understanding crashing down. At least before, I'd been able to tell myself there was a layer between us, that I wasn't her direct supervisor. I nodded again with my body protesting the words. "Sure. You're right."

She gave a small smile, walking toward the door. "For what it's worth, I forgot for a few minutes, too."

After she walked out, I let my head fall to my desk. Nothing good would come from this, and maybe it was okay that she was considering another job.

CHAPTER 29

Cord

Present Day

I WOKE WITH A SMILE ON MY FACE, JUST LIKE I had every day since returning from the camping retreat. Today, it was also to soft skin brushing my chin. Unfortunately, it didn't belong to Pearl, who in my dream had been touching me and kissing me and dressed as Okoye from *Black Panther*. No, the nudge was from Peach, and the soft skin was one of her back legs as she settled on my chest, reminding me that I was a disappointment as a food distributor.

"Hey, old girl," I said, stroking behind her ears. The bright blue *Doctor Who* TARDIS sweater was another one I'd found online. She purred under my touch and stretched on top of me, the thoughts of food momentarily abandoned for comfort.

Outside my window, the sun cracked through the clouds, giving the light a muted energy, but there was nothing muted about the way I felt. My mind and body were sharp with the realization that Pearl and I were together. Well, sort of. Enough. The decision to be casual, to leave old feelings and old . . . everything behind was freeing. My bedroom looked out over my yard, and I grinned at the weed patch and doghouse, deciding that this would be the week I took care of them and started making the space what I wanted it to be. Things with Pearl were working, and it felt like I'd turned a corner. I could spend time with this incredible woman, keep it casual, and not get hurt. "New me, girl," I said to the cat, who eyed my verve skeptically.

I slid out from under Peach, scrunching up the blankets near her so she had a cocoon. She glanced at me before tucking in for a nap.

Pearl: Good morning.

I could imagine her going back and forth on sending that text. It was usually my line, and I knew she was wary of this feeling too much like being a couple. That she still sent it gave me hope.

Cord: Good morning. Can I see you soon?

Pearl: You leave for your trip on Friday, right?

That she remembered, knew that about me, made my lips tip into a broader smile.

Cord: Yep. I can make any night work, though. Just tell me what's good for you.

I reached into my shower to start the water, enjoying the way the bathroom filled with steam. Waking up dreaming of Pearl wasn't new, but waking up from the dream, even with Peach's ass in my face, and getting to talk to Pearl every morning had made me a morning person.

Cord: I'll be slow to respond. I'm just about to hop in the shower.

Pearl: Just about to? As in, you're texting me naked?

Cord: You texted me first . . .

Pearl: You didn't have to reply without pants on.

Cord: Or underwear. Want proof?

The dots bounced, disappeared, and then bounced again.

Pearl: Okay.

I hadn't expected that, and my dick twitched at starting something over the phone with her. Better sense prevailed, but much to the chagrin of my body. I snapped a photo of my bare feet on the bath mat.

Cord: Dirty girl. Here you go. Note the length.

Pearl: I was admiring the width.

I laughed, the sound bouncing off the tiled walls.

Cord: I'm sorry to disappoint. Do I get a photo in return?

Pearl: I'm already out of the shower.

Cord: Even better—no danger of the phone getting wet.

Pearl: Dirty boy. I'll talk to you later.

I held my breath when the dots started bouncing. The photo of her feet inside fuzzy pink slippers came through. Her legs were crossed at what looked to be her kitchen table, and I laughed again before stepping into the shower, whistling to myself. This was going to be the best of all worlds.

THE CHAT WINDOW from my assistant popped up on my screen.

Tye Harris is here for your 3:30.

I'd had a busy day with one meeting after another, and I dropped a message in the chat of my fourth video call of the day to slip out. At some point, I would need to drop Abby a note and thank them for talking me into mentoring. In the beginning, I would have described it as suckering me in, but meeting with Tye every two weeks had become a highlight. Abby'd been right—we clicked well, and the hour we had scheduled always flew by.

Tye pushed through my door as if we were mid-conversation. "See episode three yet?"

"Are you kidding? As soon as it dropped." I motioned toward the table near the window in my office, and Tye threw down their backpack and rifled through it.

Tye tossed a worn and dog-eared notebook on the table between us. "That's at like two in the morning. You need to get more sleep."

I waved off their chastisement. "It's *Starfighter*. Who can sleep when the best superheroes join together in a big-budget series? I actually scored VIP tickets to a meet and greet with the actors at a con in a few weeks."

"Whoa! Really?" Tye's face lit up, and it gave me a certain sense of pride to have maybe impressed them. That was immediately dashed when their smile faded. "That's no excuse. You still need sleep."

"How old are you?" I asked.

Tye rolled their eyes. "Old enough to know better. How are you going to be the best you can be on no sleep?"

"Fine. Fine. I'll get more sleep." I pointed to the page in the notebook Tye had opened to. "What's this?"

"Oh, yeah." Tye looked at their notes as if reminding themself. "I'm supposed to interview someone for my class, like, someone who is a professional who we're not related to. Can I use you?"

"Sure. When is it due?"

"Um." Tye gave me a sheepish grin. "Tomorrow morning."

"I get to lecture you about planning if you get to lecture me about sleep."

"Yeah, but I'm a kid. I'm supposed to mess up. You're old. You should know better."

I sat back in my chair. "Weren't you asking me for a favor?"

Tye laughed and poised their pen over the paper and began asking questions about my title and my role with the company. "Why do you like your job?"

I thought about it, looking around as if for an answer. "Every day is a little different. I get to solve problems, and I work with great people. I used to get bullied in school," I said, realizing mid-sentence that I hadn't shared that with anyone in years.

Tye nodded, their pen paused.

"Well, coding was an escape. I got into the games and I wanted to know how they worked. Add to that, this kind of career means you're surrounded by people who are enthralled with making things work, building things, creating things. It's why I think programs like this are so important, because we need all kinds of minds creating and building."

"Did you take that from the OurCode website?" Even as Tye teased me, I saw the warmth in their expression, and they looked a little like Pearl for a moment, the same smile.

"Sarcastic teenagers aside, I get to work with pretty amazing people."

"Like my aunt Pearl?" Tye didn't look up from their notebook, where they were scribbling my answers.

"Sure." I didn't elaborate, remembering Pearl's warning. "Oh, and I get to talk to cool kids about their procrastination on school assignments."

"No one says 'cool' anymore." Tye gave me a rueful smile. "And what do you not like about your job?"

I leaned back in my chair and crossed my leg over my other knee. "I have to talk to uncool kids about their procrastination on school assignments."

Tye started writing for a second before they caught my joke and looked up, annoyed.

"Okay. Okay. Um . . ." The room still provided no answers. "I miss writing code. That's the part I love, and I don't get to do it as much anymore. For the record, that's part of what is awesome about hanging out with you. I get to talk about it and do it again. And I get to see your skills get stronger and stronger." I tapped the table, watching Tye's scrawled handwriting fill the page. "Is 'awesome' still allowable as a word?"

"You could say 'hits different,'" Tye said, pen poised. "But thanks. Um. Next question . . . are you single?"

"You have to ask me that for class?"

"It's a thorough interview."

I narrowed my eyes, fairly certain I was being played. "Yes. I'm single."

"And if you ask someone out, do you treat them well?"

"There is no way this is part of your assignment." I made a grab for the notebook, but Tye swiped it away. "Don't you want to talk about schooling or professional development?"

"I'll get to that. I'm following the story." Tye pulled the notebook close to their chest. "So . . . ?"

"Yes. I do my best, anyway," I said, leaning forward on the table. It was time to figure out how to divert Tye to something else. "How is that project for your programming class going? You two were working on your friend's mom's website, right?" Tye perked up, and I thought I'd found the code, but then they returned to their notebook.

"Nice try. So, in summary, you're single and you treat your partners well. Last question. Did you know my aunt Pearl loves *Starfighter*?"

I saw through their little game, but I still replied with the first question that came to mind. "She does?" I'd had no idea Pearl was a fan. I'd been reading the comics since I was a kid and watching the web cartoon since college. "I mean, wait. Did you even have an interview you had to do for class, or was this just some trick to get information from me?"

Tye laughed and tucked the notebook away. "The first questions were real, and it's due tomorrow. I'm just saying that if I never have to see you make out, you should maybe ask her out or invite her to watch episode four with you if you do it at a decent hour."

"Noted. Are you ready to talk about your class project now?"

Tye beamed and pulled their laptop from their bag. "Yeah, check it out. Here's what we've been working on for Peter's mom's flower shop website. She is going to let us do some work on a page for the project."

We hunched over the screen together and talked about how Tye and their classmate Peter had been employing what they'd learned. I tried to play it cool, but seeing them get so excited about putting the information to work was amazing. It made my chest swell with something like pride, and we spent the rest of the hour with Tye explaining things to me and me offering ideas or suggestions. They only brought up Pearl one more time, then quickly added that they'd text me if they had more questions about the interview.

Cord: A little bird told me you like Starfighter.

Pearl: Stayed up way too late to watch episode three.

I grinned and strode back to my desk. Maybe Tye was onto something.

CHAPTER 30

Pearl

"WORKING ALL NIGHT?" TYE PULLED THEIR KNEES to their chest and nodded toward my notebook.

"It's what I do." I scooted back on the bed, tapping at the keyboard on my laptop. By the end of the retreat, the board had loved the idea of the identity-conscious professional development workshops but had also wanted us to focus on more technical training and workshops for the students to harness the interests of our donors. It was a great idea, but I had no background in that area, whereas Ellie started out as a software developer. From my vantage point, it was looking like this would be the bigger priority, and maybe she should have been promoted. It was why I opted to start the online coding classes sooner than I'd planned.

"It's Saturday." Tye stood, glancing at their phone with a smirk. "You should take a break."

"What are you smiling at? Peter?"

Tye's face flushed, and I noticed the way their lips turned up. "Yeah. We're meeting up later with some friends." Tye handed me their phone, where a chat window was open. "But also this."

TyeForTheWin: You busy?

Cord.Matthews: No. Everything ok?

TyeForTheWin: You should ask out Aunt Pearl.

TyeForTheWin: She's just going to work all night and I'm going to hang out with a friend later.

Cord.Matthews: It's weird that you're trying to set us up. Go be a kid. I can get my own dates.

TyeForTheWin: Clearly not. Plus, you said you're not busy.

Cord.Matthews: Bye, Tye.

I looked up, confused.

"He's not doing anything tonight."

"That's not what he said. He just said he wasn't busy at the moment." I glanced back at the message exchange before handing Tye the phone back. "And stop bothering him with stuff like that. You're supposed to look to him for professional guidance."

"I'm getting guidance." Tye rolled their eyes, slipping the phone back into their pocket. "Anyway, I'm not bothering him. Cord loves me." A chime sounded from Tye's pocket and they pulled their phone back out, smiling at the screen and tapping out a message. "And . . ."

A silence hung in the air for a moment, and then my phone rang, Cord's name flashing across the screen.

Tye laughed and walked out, calling over their shoulder, "He loves you, too!" Tye pulled my door closed.

I leaned back against my headboard with a sigh but tapped the accept icon. "Do you always let fifteen-year-olds manipulate you like this?"

"Damnit," Cord muttered into the phone, and his frustration—the kind with no real teeth—made me chuckle.

"Yep. Told me everything."

"Even the last message?" His voice was back to playful.

"No. What was it?"

"Nothing." I imagined him shrugging his shoulder, that small, almost undetectable smirk crossing his lips when he was sure he was pulling something off.

"You're not going to tell me?"

"Nah."

"C'mon."

"Let a man have a few secrets."

"Fine. Bye, Cord."

"No, no, no. Don't hang up." Noise on the phone hinted he was shifting, and I imagined him sitting like I was on his bed. Swallowing, I tried to tamp down the low coil of heat that imagining him inspired. He continued, his voice over the phone doing nothing to quell that low simmer of arousal. "I just asked if you were home now and they said yes. No big conspiracy."

"I was expecting some great secret. Some highly sought information. Disappointing, Matthews."

"Well," he said, phone shifting again. "It's not like I would tell Tye my secrets regarding you."

I settled back against the pillows. "What are your secrets regarding me?"

"Hmm," he said, voice rumbling through the phone. I

could almost imagine the feel of his lips on my collarbone doing that humming thing, the vibrations traveling up my neck. "Well, for starters, I can't get the taste of you out of my head."

My thighs clenched, my body shifting as a full body tingle wound through me at those words.

"And I've been thinking about kissing you all week."

I licked my lips. "Kissing me where?"

"Do you want specifics? First on your lips, then down your neck." His voice had grown deeper, and I knew he was getting turned on.

As he described brushing his lips over my stomach, his breath hitched, and I wondered if he was hard thinking about it. When he described parting my thighs to kiss there, I let out a small whimper. My body whipped into a frenzy of memory after the last week not seeing each other.

"Pearl," he said.

"Keep going," I whispered.

"You like hearing me describe how I'd touch you?" His voice was still low and sexy, but he sounded genuinely surprised.

"You're good at it. Yes."

He swallowed thickly on the other end of the phone. "Let me see you tonight. I know you're squirming right now but won't take care of yourself properly while Tye's in the apartment."

"I should get work done. We have a strategy meeting on Tuesday."

"You've been working nonstop all week. Do you know the data?"

I nodded. "I do."

"Backward and forward, I bet. Why not take a break? I can bring you dinner or we could go out."

"What about the rest of the kissing?"

He laughed, a low throaty sound. "You mean, will I ever get to the part where I run my tongue over your sweet, soft, wet . . ." He trailed off into silence, and I squirmed again, thighs rubbing together.

"Are you going to finish?"

"It will be better in person. Can I come over?"

My body was frustratingly on the edge of pleasure. "Dick," I muttered.

"That will be better in person, too." His words came out in a sputtered laugh, and I imagined his smile and the way his eyes lit up.

"Get here at seven and we'll see if I forgive you for leaving me hanging."

I DRIED OFF after stepping out of the hot shower. Once Cord said he was coming over, I'd scrambled into the shower, eager to see him. I opened my drawers to get dressed, and my hands hovered over my underwear collection. It was nighttime and I was staying in. I was positive nothing would happen with Cord, not with Tye at home, but I still reached for a pretty pair, just in case, and pulled on a matching bra.

When I rounded the corner into my kitchen, Tye and Cord were on either side of the counter, Tye with Diet Coke and Cord holding a bottle of Mountain Dew. They were hunched over Cord's phone, watching something. My heart tugged seeing them together in the kitchen, where smells of dinner cooking surrounded us. I met Cord's eye and hoped what I was feeling didn't show on my face, because I didn't know exactly what it was, but it didn't feel casual.

"Hey," he said, standing straighter. "How was your shower?"

"It was good. Thanks." I pointed to the phone. "What are you watching?"

"Tye was showing me this comedian's stuff on YouTube. Pretty funny." Cord handed his phone to Tye, who chuckled at the screen. When Cord took a step closer to me, my mind swirled with thoughts I shouldn't be having.

Hug me.

Touch me.

Kiss me.

I thought better of it, and maybe he did, too, since he just put his hand in his pocket.

"It smells good in here," I said, glancing over Cord's shoulder.

"Food is almost ready. Tye helped me, so it went a little faster."

I rubbed Tye's back. "You never help me."

"You never cook. What help do you need with ordering takeout?"

I swatted at their arm, enjoying the smirk on their face, the playful expression again. "Listen, kid."

Tye jumped out of the way with a laugh and set the phone down. "I'll check on the chicken. It needs to be a hundred sixty-five degrees, right?"

I gave Cord a wide-eyed stare as Tye fiddled with the meat thermometer I'd forgotten I owned and had never seen Tye use. He shrugged. Was it possible for a shrug to be cute? If so, he had done it.

"Wine? Tea? I picked up that kind you like," he said over his shoulder with a grin.

"I think I'm supposed to be the hostess."

"Nah. You've got a lot going on. I can handle pouring drinks." His words were innocuous, but I couldn't quite silence the reminder that this was another tiny way I was letting him take care of me.

"Tea is good. I could use the caffeine."

"Still working tonight?"

"All the time," Tye said, setting the timer for another two minutes after checking the chicken. "She never sleeps. Kind of like you."

Cord's expression turned on me at Tye's words. "That right?"

"Stop ganging up on me. I sleep; I just have things that have to get done. Sometimes you have to sacrifice for your goals."

Tye's eye roll was sweeping. "I know. I know. You've been telling me that since I was a kid."

"It's true." I sipped from the tea, the chilled liquid cooling my heated face.

"Your aunt is a hard worker," Cord said, looking away to check the rice on the stove.

"I know," Tye said. The two of them moved around each other in my kitchen like it was choreographed, alternating between giving me a hard time and talking to each other about some anime show they were both into.

Tye finally nodded toward the table. "Let's eat. I'm starving."

The three of us sat, Cord's hand brushing my arm as he reached for the salt or passed the rice. It was nice, almost like a family.

Girl, step back.

After dinner, Tye asked to be excused to FaceTime with Peter and left Cord and me to finish the dishes. Their plans had fallen through, so I imagined most of the evening would be spent on the phone or gaming, their interest in our company having expired. Standing side by side at the sink with Cord, I had that feeling of family at the familiar way he handed me a plate. I shut off the water and stepped to the left, even though it felt wrong to break the connection between us. "Thank you for cooking dinner." I handed Cord a bottle of the soda from the fridge. "Where did you learn to cook like that?"

He shrugged his broad shoulders. "It's nothing too complex—I picked things up here and there. It was that, subsist on takeout, or starve, and after spending all that time renovating my kitchen, I wanted to use it."

I remembered the kitchen when he bought the place and the kid-in-a-candy-store look he'd had on his face discussing renovations. At that point, I'd never seen him get excited about something that was just for him. It had been nice to see that side. "Well, you impressed Tye. I'll tell you that."

"They're a really good kid, if kind of nosy."

I closed the dishwasher and nodded toward the living room. "It's a Harris trait, I'm afraid. They learned from the best."

"Oh yeah?" He tugged my hand and pulled me down next to him on the couch, where I sank against his side. "Does that mean you've spent time playing matchmaker?"

My phone buzzed on the coffee table, and I laughed. "I'm usually the one trying to make sure everyone keeps their eyes on their goals."

"I get it." His arm was draped across the back of the couch, and he squeezed my shoulder. "Head before heart."

"Yeah," I said, dragging my thumb across my wrist. "Exactly."

We both sipped our drinks, the faint sound of music coming from behind Tye's closed door.

"What would you like to do tonight?"

"What are my options?"

I touched my lips on instinct, remembering what it felt like when his lips melded with mine, frenzied. I couldn't help but notice how his eyes followed my finger. I glanced again at Tye's closed door. "There are lots of options."

Cord quirked an eyebrow and inched closer to me. "Oh yeah?"

"Yeah." I slid my fingers to his, and he leaned toward me, our breaths mingling, eyes locked. This felt familiar, too, but the heat between us was safe and not complicated by the creeping sense of falling for this man again. "Options are good."

"I agree." His lips brushed my jaw. "I missed you the last few days."

I wanted to protest the comment, the sentiment, but across the room, my alarm beeped, the intermittent ringer growing louder with every third ring and interrupting the moment.

"Shit," I muttered, jumping up to turn it off.

He followed me, a confused look on his face. "You have an alarm set for eight fifteen p.m.? Is that your setup to get me out of here?"

"No, no," I said, fumbling with the phone. I never swiped the correct direction the first time, so I'd set it to snooze by accident. "It's my reminder to check on some account things for work. I set it before I invited you over." All I wanted was to be back on the couch, back to being moments away from a kiss and more, but, like always, real life interrupted.

"I should go, so you can work."

"No," I said, panic seeping into my voice. "I can do it later. It won't take me long."

"You're a terrible liar." He grabbed his keys from the counter and slid them into his pocket. "It's okay. I know your work is important." Cord stepped closer, taking the phone from my hands and setting it on the counter. "I understand." He leaned in, a hand wrapping the back of my neck.

The kiss was slow and sweet, building up like my alarm until I was backed against the counter, breathless.

"Go work," he said, a puff of breath near my ear, his fingertips grazing the nape of my neck. "I'll see you tomorrow. Maybe we can watch episode four of *Starfighter* together."

"You haven't watched it yet? It came out days ago."

Cord grabbed his keys from the counter. "I told you." He pressed another gentle kiss to my lips. "I'll wait for you."

CHAPTER 31

Cord

I SIGNED THE LAST DOCUMENT MY ASSISTANT handed me, tucking it back into the folder. "Anything else?"

He shook his head, taking up the piles of signed documents and discarded meeting information. "Nothing else from me. You're a free man."

I was flying out a day ahead of Wes for a VIP event I'd scored tickets to at the con and couldn't wait to get on the plane in the morning. I was reaching for my laptop when my phone rang, and my assistant glanced at the caller ID over my desk.

"Kevin Corbin calling. Want me to take a message?"

I sighed and fell back into my seat. "Nah. I'll take it." I hadn't spoken with Kevin since the retreat, and our last conversation came back to me in pieces through the onslaught of new Pearl memories—like the way she kissed and the methodical way she loaded the dishwasher, bending to fill the back row first. I grinned to myself at the thought of her and remembered all the times I'd teased Wes for acting googly-eyed over Britta's idiosyncrasies. Here I was now, googly-eyed AF.

"Hey. Glad I caught you," Kevin said. "Got a few minutes?"

I drummed my fingers on the desk. "Just a few—about to head out for a few days of vacation."

"Nice. I sometimes worry you're gonna work yourself into an early grave, man. Though aren't we all?" He wasn't wrong, exactly. The last vacation I'd taken had been with a woman I'd been seeing for a while, and she'd wanted to go to Orlando for a week at Disney. She'd had a great time; I'd wanted to lock myself in the airplane bathroom to get two minutes away from crowds, people, and faking enthusiasm for the relationship.

"Anyway," Kevin said, "I wanted to check in. I know I roped you into this board thing, and I'm glad to have you, but you're doing a lot. Figured I'd make sure you knew you didn't have to be so involved."

"Appreciate it." I drummed my fingers on the desk again. Two other board members had offered to create a subcommittee to support the new initiative, so it wasn't only me. Though the two of them probably hadn't signed up because it would be an excuse to spend more time with Pearl. "I'm good, though. Wasn't planning to get involved, but I liked that idea we brainstormed at the camp. I want to help."

"I know you and Pearl first came up with the idea, and you know I think she's great, but between you, me, and the wall, she might be in over her head. This new project might be a lot more work on you than you think."

Hairs rose on the back of my neck, and I bit back the urge to come to her rescue like a boyfriend, because I wasn't one. "She seems to do fine."

"Yeah, but we might have jumped the gun promoting her. It was a toss-up between her and Ellie. They were evenly matched—we honestly thought it would look better to have Pearl at the helm."

I saw red and stood behind my desk. The phone pressed to my ear, fists clenched at my sides because I needed to do something. "Look better?" I knew what he meant, but I really wanted him to backtrack and give a better reason. I imagined the side-eye look Tye would give me at his words.

"It doesn't matter," Kevin said, and I imagined him waving away the question. "At our next meeting, I'm going to suggest she and Ellie colead the organization for now. I don't want to see you and the other board members getting burned out."

"I'm fine," I said, thinking of Pearl the night before, planning to work into the night on top of taking a coding class to be even more prepared. She'd be hurt by this, bothered in that way where she didn't show it except for a twitch in her brow. "I don't think us stepping in has anything to do with her not doing a good job. I disagree with what you're saying."

"I know you worked together before. Just something I'm thinking about. It might be better if she and Ellie shared the role. Ellie has more technical knowledge, and then you and the other board members wouldn't feel the need to be so involved."

I glanced at my cell, debating whether I needed to give Pearl a heads-up.

"Anyway, I'll let you go on your vacation. We'll talk about it more soon."

I cursed my brain for taking so much time to process and to decide how best to respond, because we'd disconnected before I figured out what else to say.

Cord: Just talked to Kevin . . . you have any time to talk? I want to give you a heads-up on something.

Pearl: He mentioned he had something to tell me. We probably shouldn't talk about board things with the thing between us. Better to keep those worlds separate. Don't you think?

I examined the text and was drafting a reply that it might be important when I was interrupted.

"What's that face?"

I looked up from my phone to see Wes standing in my doorway, fist poised on the frame and his backpack slung over his shoulder. "You look like a gym teacher," I said, motioning to the track pants and the T-shirt with the school's logo on the breast.

"We prefer physical education educator." He walked in and fell into my chair, letting his bag fall to the floor. "You look like you were doing calculus on your phone or your mom just accidentally sent you nudes."

My gaze had drifted back to my phone but snapped to him at his words. "What the hell?" I dropped my phone. "What are you even doing here?"

He laughed, shoulders shaking. "I was just getting you to pay attention. I'm waiting for Britta to finish up a call. What's going on?"

"I got some weird news about OurCode. Wanted to tell Pearl, but she sent back this." I slid the phone across the desk and watched Wes scan the message.

"What things are between you?" He handed my phone back to me, and I knew my best friend well enough to know he wouldn't scroll up to investigate himself. "And do I need to kick your ass this time?"

"Maybe." I nodded toward the door, and he swung an arm back to close it. "We've been doing a . . . casual thing."

He arched an eyebrow. "A casual thing with the woman you've been in love with for almost a decade?"

"She has a lot going on right now and didn't want to get too serious. And you know I gave up on serious a long time ago."

Wes nodded, looking like he was weighing his words. "Ah yes, the whole avoiding your dad's life thing?"

"It's more complicated than that."

Wes leaned forward, the playful and chiding look on his face replaced with something closer to concern. "I'm just wondering if casual is enough for you. I know it was with other women, but this is Pearl. Are you happy with that arrangement?"

I was happy with her when we were together, but I felt the need to pace at his question, because I hated feeling uncertain after reading her text, and I knew there were other moments where I'd been reminded that Pearl and I weren't a real thing. Wes let me stew on his question, eventually rapping his knuckles on the desk at the sound of Britta's voice in the hall. "We'll be at the con all weekend. We can talk more."

"Yeah," I said, still thinking over his question. "I fly out in the morning. I'll see you when you get there on Saturday."

"It'll be good to get away," he said, opening the door. Britta was waiting there, chatting with my assistant, and Wes's expression shifted when their eyes met. Publicly and mutually adoring each other. I felt an all-too-familiar pang in my chest. I glanced back at my unfinished text to Pearl but decided to tell her in person.

I grabbed my messenger bag and followed him toward the door. At this rate, I wasn't ever going to get out of the office, but still I halted when my phone buzzed in my hand and a notification from Tye popped up.

TyeForTheWin: Hey, best mentor in the world.

Cord.Matthews: Hey, mentee who clearly wants something.

TyeForTheWin: I need your help.

CHAPTER 32

Pearl

"WELL, WELL, WELL." SHEA SIPPED HER COFFEE as I walked into my mother's kitchen. "Surprised you're here this morning."

I rolled my eyes, filling a glass of water before joining her at the kitchen table. "Like we're not all here every Sunday?"

"Yes, but you've been occupied lately. Thought you might be . . . busy this morning." Shea leaned in, lowering her voice. "So?"

"So, what?"

Shea glanced in the direction of the living room, where we heard our mother's voice from her side of a phone call. "So, what's going on? I can tell you're getting laid."

"You want the details?"

"Obviously." She smirked. Though we were five years apart, she and I had always been close. She knew everything about me, so it was odd for her not to know what was going on with Cord. I also knew she'd have a lot of thoughts.

"I'm not giving you a play-by-play when Mom might walk in at any moment."

"So, you two are still hooking up?"

I pursed my lips but nodded. Really, I was busting to talk about Cord.

"And?" Shea's smile was wide and her big brown eyes almost twinkled. Her well-shaped eyebrows rose. "How is it?"

"Why do you want to know?"

"Because I'm nosy!" She kept her voice low, reaching her hand across the table. "That you're not answering tells me it's either very good or very bad."

"It isn't very bad," I said under my breath, the memories rising up from how his kisses heated my skin in the woods, or from the shower when he'd dropped to his knees the week before, the water cascading down his back as he buried his face between my legs.

"Girl," Shea said, drawing out the word. "Are you together, then?"

Her question hit me in that always present bruise of guilt. We weren't together—I'd been insistent, but hooking up felt like a deeply insufficient term, and I wasn't so resolute that I didn't realize how I felt around him.

Instead of answering Shea, I glanced left and right. "He's supposed to be going out of town this weekend for some comic con thing. You know I don't have time for something serious anyway. I need to focus on work and family."

The smile fell off Shea's face, and she rolled her eyes. "It's been years. I think it's time to let go of how awful Jason was." Shea had been too young to know everything from that relationship, and I'd kept most of my relationship in California from my sisters. It was unlike me, but it was safer, so I never had to fully let Richard into my life. Still, the head before heart lesson was something I had needed. "What?"

"There was also Richard in California."

Shea's voice filled every corner of the kitchen. "Is that what that fourth star tattoo is about? You dated a billionaire you almost never talked about. C'mon. Details!"

"What's going on in here?" Our mother swept into the room, and Shea and I pulled back as if caught.

"Pearl was telling me about her new job and all the things her predecessor got up to," she said, shifting her expression.

I was always a little troubled by how fast and how easily Shea could shift into a believable lie, especially with our mother. I shouldn't have been. If I was the quintessential oldest child, Shea was the embodiment of the youngest, learning from Bri and me early in life. She was skilled at winning people over, especially our parents.

"Mess. Mess. Mess." Mom spoke over her shoulder as she headed for the stove, stirring and checking on lunch. "That woman caused a whole mess." As always, the kitchen smelled amazing, and I knew enough to not touch anything until she asked or told me to. No matter how many decades I'd spent watching her make macaroni and cheese or any of her other specialties, in her mind, anyone but her was likely to add too much paprika or not enough salt and ruin everything. I supposed I'd inherited her tendencies toward control and perfectionism. "Pearl, are you enjoying it so far other than that? The work is interesting?"

"It is. It keeps me busy."

"Any nice single men working there?"

"Mom," I said with a long and drawn-out vowel sound.

Across the table, Shea smirked, and I threw a balled-up napkin at her.

"Don't even. You don't go to church with me anymore and all you do is work. Where else are you going to meet someone?"

"She doesn't need to meet someone," Shea said, standing to refill her glass. "She's busy." Shea shot me a look, then added, "I mean, maybe not right now, but she'll be . . . getting busy soon."

Mom didn't notice the double entendre, but I narrowed my eyes, my death glare saying everything. I didn't break eye contact with my sister.

"You're grown women and it's the twenty-first century. Date who you want." She rubbed her hands on her apron, and Shea and I exchanged a curious look. She held up her hands. "I have no more lectures to give."

We both snorted at the obvious lie.

Mom waved her hands at us, dismissing our laughter with one word: "Hush." Shifting gears, her expression turned more serious. "Tye didn't want to come today?"

I shook my head. "They put off some assignment and are working on it at the OurCode lounge with their partner." Tye had looked guilty when they'd asked if it would be okay if they and Peter spent the morning working together to get the assignment done before Monday. It took a little coaxing to get out of them that they'd asked Cord to help.

He agreed to help a lot, and Tye was getting used to it. I was, too, and I didn't like how easy it felt. "Tye's OurCode mentor is helping them. They've gotten close."

"You've gotten pretty close with him, too, haven't you?" Shea looked over her shoulder from her spot at the counter, where she was chopping celery. "I mean, all those late nights for work, and what with you both being single."

I was going to murder my sister. And in that moment, who could blame me?

"Oh?" Mom's expression was alight. "A potential boyfriend? How well do you know this person?"

I had to smile. "I know him very well, and Tye adores him."

Mom's and Shea's expressions shifted, and they both focused on me with a laser-like precision. "They spend a lot of time together?" Mom asked.

My face heated. "Yeah. I mean, he's a wonderful mentor, and we're old friends."

"This sounds kind of serious for you," Mom said, standing again and returning to the stove. Her voice was uncharacteristically unsteady. "You're being careful?"

"Yes, Mom." I softened. She'd taken care of me after Jason kicked me out, like she always had her girls. My parents had seen me broken and lost, and I never wanted them to see that side of me again. "He's not my boyfriend, but he is special, and I'm being careful."

She wanted to say more—I could tell by the square of her shoulders and how she paused her stirring. She would probably have said something to remind me how secretive I was about things with Richard and about how she should have known something was off, but voices from the front room interrupted our conversation and my dad walked in along with my uncle John. Dad went straight to Mom, dropping a kiss on her cheek. They were so affectionate after all these years. I was used to it—we all were—but it set a bar few of our own relationships ever lived up to. Mine never had. Except with Cord. I remembered the way Cord called me Petal in a soft murmur and dug my fingernails into my palm to remind myself that that wasn't a relationship, not like the one in front of me. I'd once thought we'd all have that kind of love someday, but now I knew some people were just extremely lucky.

My dad pulled away and glanced over Mom's shoulder at the stove. "Smells great in here."

I listened to them talk about the meal and grinned, checking my phone absently. I'd hoped to see a message from Cord, a hope I squished. Instead, I had a series of emails from Ellie. Another major donor was planning to pull their funding and wasn't happy with the progress we'd made. I scrolled to the message from the day before, where Kevin had replied with a suggestion that two people in the interim role might be better than one to keep arms around everything.

"What's wrong, sweetheart?" My dad settled at the table next to me.

"Just work," I said, tucking my phone into my pocket.

"You're still working too much. I can tell." He sipped from his glass of lemonade and studied my face in the way only my dad could. "Makes it hard to have any fun."

"I'm finding time for fun, Dad. I promise."

"She is, Daddy." Shea leaned over and dropped a kiss on our dad's cheek while shooting me a sly look.

"I don't even want to know," he said, glancing between us. "How's Tye?"

Shea started telling him about the role Peter had in our daily conversations, and I glanced down at my phone after it buzzed, seeing a message from Tye. I stepped out the back door, breathing in the cool air.

Tye: Check it out.

Tye included a screenshot from the FitMi page, and I zoomed in on the website that had once been as familiar to me as the back of my hand. It looked like a screen grab from the registration page.

Pearl: What am I looking at?

Tye: We added this.

I scrolled through the demographics section, still unsure of what I was looking at, when my gaze snagged on the section where we used to ask for the user's sex, giving them the option to select male or female. Now the box asked for gender and provided a list of options, along with a text box labeled "I identify as (please specify)" where users could enter their own option. There was an additional question related to gender pronouns. It was much more thorough than I'd remembered.

Tye: We were supposed to add some elements to Peter's mom's website, but it crashed or something so we needed a new project. Cord helped us add this and work on how all data is fed out in their system. It's going live next week after their team tests it! Like, live across the app!

I bit my lower lip, tears pricking at the back of my eyes.

Pearl: Really?

Tye: Wild, right? This is going to be the biggest thing anyone in the class got to do and he said on Monday they'll figure out how to pay us a fee as consultants!

"Lunch is ready." Shea stepped onto the porch. "What's going on?"

I didn't look up from my phone right away, and Shea spoke again. "Hello?"

"Sorry," I said. "Was texting with Tye. Cord gave them and Peter a chance to adjust the FitMi website for an important assignment for their programming class."

"Saved the day?"

"Yeah." I glanced back at the text, scrolling past the screenshot and rereading Tye's posts. "Yeah. He kind of did."

She pressed her index finger to my wrist. "Sounds like he put your family first to do work that matters." She tapped her finger with the subtlety of a rhino. Shea finished in a singsong voice before sauntering away. "I'm just saying, maybe it's time to give him another chance and start putting your heart first."

She was right, and I scrolled back through the text thread with Cord, full of jokes and innuendos and heart-eye emojis. It wasn't just *my* heart I had to think about this time.

CHAPTER 33

Cord

Five Years Earlier

August

"LATER!" MASON FLASHED A QUICK GRIN AND WAVED to us, following the redhead toward the exit of the hotel bar after we'd closed a deal with a national chain of gyms to partner with FitMi.

Pearl sipped from her cocktail and shook her head, her earrings tinkling. "What do these women see in him?"

"I don't know," I said, finishing my drink and enjoying the hazy feeling surrounding me after three too many celebratory drinks. "He's charming?"

She reached for her purse, pulling out her wallet. "Is he, though?"

"I got it," I said, tugging my wallet from my back pocket and almost tipping off my stool in the process, until Pearl's hand steadied me. "Sorry." My face flashed warm from the alcohol and embarrassment, but also with Pearl's hand touch. I set my credit card on the bar for the server, wondering what it would be like for Pearl's hand to keep going up my arm and over my shoulder, around my neck. I remembered what it felt like in the dark, and I'd fantasized how much better it would be if I could see her face.

I shook off the thought. "Um, is he good-looking? I'd say so."

Pearl's hand had returned to her side of the table, her fingers toying with the stem of her champagne glass. "I guess. Not what I go for, though." Her lids lowered and she looked into her glass, and, God, I wanted to get close enough to count her eyelashes before kissing her and not coming up for air.

The question was out of my mouth before I could pull it back. "What do you go for? Or, who, I mean—what in who."

Pearl's lips parted, and then she smiled at my fumbling. "It's amazing you were so articulate this afternoon with the pitch."

"Mason insisted on shots to celebrate the deal when we first arrived. I would have asked that much more smoothly without tequila."

"It was kind of smooth," she said, meeting my eyes with a grin. "What do I go for?" She touched a fingertip to her chin. Her fingernails were a light tan color, and I followed the path of her finger to her full lower lip. "Well, I don't know. I haven't let myself go for anyone in a long time."

The server picked up my card, but I barely looked away from Pearl, the image of her letting herself go wild with someone playing on a loop in my head.

"I guess someone who cares about people, who is comfortable in their own skin." She sipped from her glass. "Someone who makes me feel cherished."

"You should always feel cherished," I said, taking in the lines of her face, the stretch of her neck, and the delicate rose gold necklace sitting across her collarbone. "Who could be with you and not cherish everything about you? If that guy exists, I want to fight him."

"Maybe I need to get you some water?" She slid her fingertips over the back of my hand again.

"Why?"

"Because you're threatening to get in a fight with an imaginary boyfriend who doesn't love everything about me." She asked the server for a glass of water when he returned my card. "And I don't want you to feel sick tomorrow."

"I would fight him if you needed me to, though."

She laughed. "Noted, but I don't think I'll need you fighting anyone for me." Pearl touched a finger to her lip again and held my gaze. "I've always kind of liked that you're a lover and not a fighter anyway."

I took a long sip from the water glass the server set in front of me to give me time to process Pearl saying she thought of me as a lover and also being a little too drunk to work through the particulars of that phrase.

"Come to think of it, I'd go for that, too. A good lover."

I choked on my water, sputtering. "A good lover?"

"Sure." She waved a hand in the air as if she hadn't just upended my brain. "Someone who knows what they're doing, or who is a quick study."

"You mean . . ."

"Yeah," she said, finishing her champagne—the sight of her lips on the rim of the glass was a straight shot of energy to my cock. "That. Like I said, it's been a long time since I felt cherished."

I debated dropping to my knees in the middle of the crowded bar and offering to cherish her right there, but public exposure, sexual harassment, and basic common sense held me in place . . . but only barely, and I let out a shaky breath.

"Sorry. I don't know why I said that." Pearl slid off her stool, standing so her face was a little above mine. "Too much information. Too many sips of champagne."

"No." I stood, too. "Not too much. Just the right amount. That is important. I haven't . . . cherished someone like that in a while, either."

She nodded toward the beach beyond the hotel without responding to my confession. "Do you want to take a walk? I want to soak up some of this San Diego weather before we go back to Chicago." The evening was still warm with a cool breeze as we walked from the bar's patio down the stairs to the sand. Our hands brushed a few times as we walked, more because I wasn't walking a completely straight line than because of anything intentional, but I still buzzed with anticipation with every graze.

Pearl's voice was soft, barely audible over the waves as we neared the shoreline and settled in the sand. "I bet you're good at cherishing."

"I try to be," I said, sitting without even the illusion of coordination. "I mean actually cherishing. Well, the other cherishing, too. I like the other kind a lot. You should be with someone who likes to . . . cherish you." My mouth and brain were having one of those childhood, draw-a-line-down-the-middle-of-the-room kinds of fights because I knew I needed to stop talking. Meanwhile the rest of my body was taking sides, because my dick was very interested in talking more about cherishing her, and my heart was pounding at both the embarrassment of admitting it and the anticipation of doing it. My mouth took charge again. "Why has it been so long?"

She tilted her head, clearly not following my jump in conversation. "For me? Well, school keeps me busy, and I don't do casual, so I haven't had time to really get to know someone. I spend all my time at work. What about you?"

"I can't have the person I want. Anyone else would be a distant second place."

"Did you try fighting for them?"

"I'm a lover, not a fighter, remember?"

"I think you're more of a fighter than you give yourself credit for. You fight for FitMi. Look at the deal from today."

My neck warmed at the unexpected compliment. My whole life, I'd never pushed for what I wanted—it made more sense for me to let things happen and let people who enjoyed leading lead. She was right, though. I had fought for this deal. And it had felt good.

"You inspired me." The sand was cool beneath me, and my head spun with the lingering effects of the shots Mason had talked me into. Pearl stretched out next to me, watching the waves, the moonlight playing off her skin.

"You did it," she said, patting my knee. Her hand was warm, soothing, and I let my eyes fall closed against the sensation, my reaction time too dulled to play off how good it felt.

"We did it." I fell back onto the sand and enjoyed how the stars swirled with the rhythmic crashing waves as a soundtrack. "What would I do without you?"

Pearl laughed in this wistful, quiet kind of way and patted my knee again. "You're drunk."

"Just a little." I dragged my fingers through the sand at my side. "And you're touching my knee."

I worried she'd pull away, so I didn't look down from the stars. She didn't, though. She squeezed my knee, leaving her hand on me. "I guess I am."

"I like it when you touch me."

Her hand lingered for another moment, and then the weight of it was gone, and I eventually peeked at her. She was in the same white tank top and black pants, one arm resting on her bent knee and the other in the sand. Her hair was swept up in some kind of bun. "I know you do," she said, her voice barely audible over the crash of the waves. "I like it when you touch me, too. But we shouldn't do it."

I thought the slide through the sand to brush her hand would be smooth, but my coordination was off and I accidentally smacked my hand against her, knocking her off balance. Pearl tipped toward me, surprised by my knocking her hand away. Then she fell against me, her hand on the side of my stomach, and I settled a hand on her back on instinct. The instinct to hold her to me. "Sorry, I just meant to touch your hand."

With Pearl's upper body aligned against me, her soft curves and the faint smell of her perfume took over my senses. "I don't know . . ."

"I told you I'm not that smooth," I said, my hand still at her back, afraid to move.

Pearl lowered her head to my shoulder, her hand remaining on my stomach, which I didn't know was an erogenous zone until that precise moment. "I like that about you."

I moved my hand up her back, then down, feeling the silky fabric of her sleeveless shirt. "We're going to have sand all over us."

She nodded against my chest, and I wanted to analyze everything that was happening, but I was too drunk and overwhelmed to put the pieces together outside of knowing Pearl's body was against mine.

"I like it when you touch me," I repeated, staring up at the stars. "And when you talk to me. And when you look at me." I inhaled the scent of her hair. "And when you're nearby. And when you're far away but I know you're coming back."

I stroked her shoulder, each pass over her soft skin leaving me more enamored. "Do you know your skin is like a flower? Like a rose petal. Pearl the petal. Pearl petal."

"You're drunk," she repeated. "And talking in circles."

My mind moved in slow motion, and I inhaled the scent of her again and traced my fingers over the silky, smooth fabric of her shirt. I murmured, "Petal," and I listened to the water, thinking that if I could make it until the next wave crashed down, I'd know what to do. But then Pearl moved her hand a few inches and the line of fire that ignited in my nerve endings left me opening my mouth.

"You smell like cinnamon sometimes." I let my head fall back, inhaling the night air and the woman beside me. "It's my favorite smell."

"I need to tell you something," she said. "I, well . . ." Pearl's voice stuttered, and I flattened my palm at her back. Everything in this moment felt so right.

I knew I was a little drunk but also knew I'd remember every moment of this night. This felt like the start for us. "You can tell me anything, Petal."

Pearl relaxed against me and then stiffened, her palm over my heart. "I got the job."

I sat up immediately, wrapping her in my arms. "That's amazing! I'm so happy for you!" I thought about how nervous she'd been to apply, how her normally unflappable posture had faltered, and what it meant to get the job and prove to herself she deserved it. I squeezed her to me. "I knew you would," I said near her ear.

"There's something else," she said, pulling back from me. "Something I didn't tell you about before."

"I want to know everything, but I have something I need to tell you first." I focused on the feel of her body rising with each breath under my hand, and the rightness of it, and even though I'd heard her, I had to say it right at that moment. The words were banging on the door in my brain. "I know I'm drunk, but I'd say this sober. I'll fight for you and cherish you. I want my house to smell like cinnamon." I linked my fingers with hers. Jumping in with both feet and then getting burned was something I'd seen my dad do time and time again, but this was different. This was Pearl. "I know I'm talking in circles, but I'm in love with you. I've been in love with you for years, and now you won't work for me. It solves everything."

I searched her face and I thought she'd be happy. I was sure she felt the thing between us, too, but her eyes looked sad.

"Cord . . ." She touched my face, her fingertips near the edge of my lip, and shook her head. "The job is in California. I'm moving to LA in two weeks."

She stilled her hand. She stilled her entire body, and we sat there in silence until the next wave crashed down, her words taking over and blocking out anything I could see around us.

CHAPTER 34

Cord

Present Day

AFTER LEAVING TYE AND PETER AND RETURNING TO my place, I fell onto my couch, tipping a beer to my lips. I glanced at my phone after a notification pinged on the account Tye had had me make. I smiled. The kid was hilarious. Not kid hilarious, but genuinely funny. The work the two teens had done today to make the changes we hadn't implemented yet was great, and their curiosity reminded me why I loved this. More and more, I wanted to be someone who mattered to Tye, independent of wanting to be someone who mattered to Pearl.

Pearl. I sat back and remembered how she'd felt against me the last time, how she'd tasted. Closing my eyes, I pictured her perfectly full breasts and their weight in my hands. I couldn't wait to see her again, to hold her and touch her. I groaned, sliding my palm down my stomach. I'd spent more time in this aroused state since the camping trip than I had since I was a teenager, and it took just the hint of thinking about Pearl's smile for my dick to wake up. Even Peach's disdainful stare from across the room wasn't enough to curb my thoughts, but a knock at the door interrupted.

Fuck. I thought about ignoring it but stood reluctantly,

adjusting myself and trudging across the room. I looked through the peephole, not quite believing my eyes.

"Hey," I said, opening the door to Pearl.

She stepped into the foyer and immediately wrapped her arms around my neck. "Hi." Pearl's kiss took me by surprise, and I fumbled to push the door closed behind her, wrapping my arms around her, my hands taking in her body. Pearl pushed me into my living room, and we dropped onto the couch together, almost falling. When she straddled my lap, burying her fingers in my hair, her kiss was deep and hungry.

I wondered if I'd fallen asleep and was dreaming, but I didn't care, because Pearl was pulling my T-shirt over my head and my hands were sliding into the waistband of her jeans, cupping her ass and deciding to ask questions later. Our lips parted for a moment to pull my shirt over my head, and we were kissing again as I worked the buttons on her shirt open. Pearl's body was in motion, her hips gyrating against me, and hands sliding down my chest. "Hey," I murmured. "What's gotten into you?"

Her hand slipped into my sweatpants and my head fell back at the feel of her palm and fingers wrapping around my length as her tongue swept against my neck. "You," she said, sliding back on my legs and kissing across my chest, her hands stroking up and down at a maddening pace. My head fell back again, her kisses sending my body into overdrive. I missed the heat of her center against me, but Pearl lowered to her knees in front of me, smiling up as she urged me to help get my sweatpants down, her hand going back to my shaft.

"Let me take care of you first," I said, brushing a finger down her cheek, that perfect cheek where her skin was so smooth. It was like she was painted by a master artist.

"Cord?" She stroked up and down my length, her grip firm, speed increasing, and I moaned.

"Yeah?" I spoke on an unsteady breath.

"Sometimes I get to put you first."

I barely had time to make sense of her words when she swept her tongue over the head before gliding her plump lips down my shaft, and my vision went hazy. Her fingers continued to work me, cupping my balls and gripping the base of my cock. Her mouth was heaven. My body pinged with anticipation, and her hot mouth took me in, sucking and licking like she knew exactly what was in my head. I gripped the couch cushion. She'd styled her hair and I didn't want to mess it up, but damn, her mouth. My breath quickened, and my hips longed to pump into her mouth.

"Pearl, I'm going to come," I said, my body tense, the warmth at the base of my spine building.

She stroked me firmly, her lips coming off me with a pop. "That's kind of the point," she said, taking me into her mouth again, her fingers caressing my balls.

I'd never felt this all-encompassing pressure on all the right places. "Pearl," I said, gripping the cushion again, unable to stop my hips from pumping into her hand, her hot mouth. "Petal," I groaned as the orgasm barreled through me, leaving me unable to breathe for a moment, my release spilling down the back of Pearl's throat. I shuddered again and she slowly eased her lips off me. I panted, staring down at this beautiful woman, who took in deep breaths of her own. I stretched out my arms, pulling her onto the couch and wrapping her in them, meeting her gaze. "You're incredible."

She closed her eyes for a few moments without responding, then kissed me softly, almost tenderly, and rested her head on my shoulder, sinking into me.

We snuggled on the couch in silence for a few minutes, my fingers stroking up and down her back, her steady breaths against my chest and a sinking feeling in my heart that maybe I was making a mistake with keeping this casual. That maybe Pearl was worth the risk of everything that could go wrong. I inhaled the scent of her cinnamon perfume, letting the idea make a home in my head. Pearl was worth the risks.

"Tye showed me the coding you three did."

"Yeah?"

"I think it's safe to say you have a fan." Her hand settled on my stomach, and I admired her long fingers and dark painted nails against my skin. "And I guess a new employee?"

I chuckled. "You might be right. Our youngest consultants to date. I wanted to make sure they were compensated, even though it was for their class."

"And you changed the website." She spoke against my chest, and it felt like the most natural thing in the world to be sitting there, her in her bra, me almost naked, talking about coding.

"It wasn't a big deal," I said, tracing a finger along the back of her neck. "It's something we should have updated years ago. I'm ashamed Tye and Peter had to point it out."

Pearl raised her head, meeting my eyes. "But when they did, you listened. It means a lot to Tye that you listen." She glanced down at her own hand, which she'd trailed up my chest. It rested over my heart and I covered it with mine. "It means a lot to me, too."

"You both mean a lot to me," I said, dipping my head to catch her eye. I cupped her neck, letting my fingers caress her sensitive skin. "You mean the world to me, actually."

"Cord . . ." She trailed off, but I kissed her, stopping the rest of the sentence, a slow press of my lips.

"I know. Casual." I met her eyes again. I knew. I'd listened and I would wait, and if I wasn't fully happy with that, I'd swallow it. Getting to hold Pearl like this meant too much. The moment was too serious, though, too wrought with emotion we weren't going to do anything about, so I changed the subject. "You know, that thing I wanted to tell you about what Kevin said . . ."

"Yeah. I really do think it's inappropriate for me to get inside information." Pearl scratched her nails gently over my chest. "I just don't want to mix worlds, but I appreciate you trying to look out for me."

"You sure?"

"Yeah." Pearl snuggled close to me again, her body pliant against mine, and I rested my head next to hers, or I tried to. Our foreheads collided when she sat up suddenly. "Wait! What time is your flight?"

I rubbed my head where we'd crashed together. "It was supposed to be at eleven this morning, but I changed it to tomorrow."

"You changed your flight?" Her eyes were wide, and she'd scooted from my lap.

"Yeah. I mean, Tye and Peter needed help, and once we got into it, I wanted to walk them through everything. And it was kind of fun."

"Cord." She placed her hand on my chest, where the weight felt so natural. "You can't rearrange your plans for us. You've been looking forward to that trip for months."

"Sure I can." I ran my hand down Pearl's arm to her waist, pulling her close again. I knew what she was saying, and it was probably several layers of a bad idea, but I was all in for Pearl and I wasn't good at pretending not to be, even when the only person who knew that was me.

"It's . . ."

Without warning, I shifted, rolling her back onto the couch, her unbuttoned shirt spilling open. I pressed my finger to her lips, needing to quiet her objections. I hovered over her before lowering my lips to her chin, her neck, and down to her collarbone. "I believe it's your turn to stop talking and let me take care of you."

"You love it when I talk," she said, her breath hitching when I pulled a nipple into my mouth over the satin of her bra.

"You're right." I pulled the cup down and ran my tongue across her now peaked, dark nipple, loving the way she whimpered when I did that. "We can practice asking for what we want. Tell me all the filthy things you'd like me to do to you." I took her other nipple in my mouth. "Be specific." I trailed my lips lower until I reached the only place I'd wanted to be since Friday night. "I'm an excellent listener."

I wanted to rearrange all my plans for this woman. And I was beginning to realize that would never change.

CHAPTER 35

Pearl

I READ THE INTRODUCTION SENTENCE FOR THE third time, words like source code and identifiers running together. I had fifteen minutes left on my lunch break, and I reread the text, willing it to make sense. The buzzing of my phone pulled me from near tears when it still didn't coalesce into something I could decipher.

Cord: How's the studying going?

Pearl: Slow.

The dots bounced as he typed his reply. We'd worked into a kind of rhythm since I visited his place. I felt like casual was working for us, and it was starting to feel easy between us. Almost. Except that I thought about him more than I should. He came over a lot of nights—I didn't want that to change, especially since Tye had gotten used to him being around and the two of them seemed to click. They even dragged me into their gaming sometimes and then laughed at me when I crashed the car or got stuck in a corner or whatever the game was. We were careful not to sit too close or act like we couldn't wait to touch each other when Tye was around, but when they left for a friend's or to go to their room, it was like our hands couldn't be on each other fast enough. The night before, he'd worked late, and I'd gone to sleep feeling like I was missing something. Even on the nights when we could only steal a quick kiss, I was growing attached to the dependability of those kisses, those touches, which were the opposite of casual and definitely the opposite of my philosophy of putting head before heart.

Cord: Can I help?

Cord: I know a little about this computer programming stuff.

I bit my lower lip and glanced between the phone and my studying. His thoughtfulness always twisted me in knots.

He meant it. I knew he did. The familiar guilt at keeping him at arm's length emotionally while I took care of myself weighed on me when he said things like that.

Pearl: No, it's still work-related . . . I should tackle it on my own.

Pearl: Thank you, though.

Cord: Anything for you :) I'll still see you tonight for Starfighter!

Really, I felt it when we interacted at all. I closed the window, unwilling to work myself into a deeper hole until later that night, when I could spread things out at home. Instead, I swiped to a new chat window.

Pearl: Please remind me why I want this job.

Shea: Why?

Pearl: Because I want to toss this programming crash course out a window and devote all that studying time to other things.

Shea: Don't you mean other people?

Shea: Like maybe nerdy white guys who look at you like you're Beyoncé?

Pearl: He does not.

Shea: Zendaya? He's fallen under the Harris women spell. It happens. Have you seen our asses?

Pearl: I don't think we need to compare.

Shea: Don't need to. Genetics for the win.

Bri: She's not wrong. Same is true across the pond. We're irresistible.

Shea: And, for the record, Cord is not the only one who looks like a fool in love.

Pearl: I'm muting you now.

I sighed, ignoring the niggling ache between my legs at the memory of Cord's touch, and started back to my office, only to find Ellie waiting for me. "This is awkward," she said, taking the seat across from my desk.

"Okay . . ." I set my things on the corner of my desk and attempted to slide into a power pose, though I had no context on what to expect from this conversation.

"The board wants more integration between the leadership and the content our programs focus on. I'm more qualified for that. I just wanted to be straight up with you. I want this job and I think I'm qualified for it." Ellie sat back in her chair, and I admired her confident body language. It was possible Ellie's I-got-this persona was even more honed than mine, which made me wonder if the behind-the-scenes doubts were the same, too.

"Okay." While I'd had countless mentors and teachers in my nonprofit management training and I'd worked with some shrewd leaders, the best advice I'd ever received was from my father, whose approach to discipline always started with "say less and let them confess." It always worked on me and Bri. Shea figured out that if she also remained silent, Dad would eventually cave. The silence hung between Ellie and me for only moments.

"You're the interim director and I respect that, but I wanted to be candid about the fact that, given the opportunity, I will take advantage of a chance to move up."

I nodded and turned to my mother's strategy, a small smile on my face that I knew didn't reach my eyes. A smile still let them know you were kind and hid all manner of other thoughts and intentions. "I appreciate you telling me." I stretched my arm across my desk to take her hand. "And I want it, too, and since it's mine now, I'm going to keep doing it." We shook, and I waited for her nod of acknowledgment. "We'll see what happens."

"We will." She leaned forward. "May the best woman win."

A FEW HOURS later, when I arrived home, mind still slogging over what Ellie had said, Cord stood in the kitchen talking to Tye about a coding camp.

"Hey," I said, smiling at Tye's rapt attention. The scent wafting from the box of pizza sitting next to Cord filled the kitchen, making my mouth water.

"Hey, Aunt Pearl. Is it okay if I go out with Peter? We won't be out too late, but there's a concert we want to see." Tye adopted the puppy-dog expression they thought always won me over. They were right—it usually worked, but still. "I know we were going to watch *Starfighter,* but I already watched it."

I glanced at Cord, who shrugged and looked a little sheepish. "Sure. I guess so. Text me the details so I know where you are."

Tye wrapped their arms around me and ran to their room. "I gotta change!"

"I'm sorry we got ditched right after you got here." I set my bags on the counter, stepping into the kitchen and closer to Cord. "Where is the little baby I used to know, and who is this almost adult?"

He laughed, leaning against the counter. His sleeves were rolled up over his forearms, the smattering of light-colored hair covering the firm muscle. "I think the ship has sailed on Tye as a little kid."

Cord reached for my hands, pulling me closer, and I let him, casting a glance at Tye's closed door. "Are you going to be okay being the aunt of an almost-adult?" His arms slid to my waist, and I stretched to rest my hands on his shoulders. The heat from his body relaxed me to my core, and I leaned into him as his face drew nearer to mine.

"I guess I don't have a choice. Bri is in denial that they're going to college in just a few years." I lowered my head to his shoulder. "So if you can tell them how much you loved your local university . . ."

We both laughed, and his lips met mine in a soft kiss, his tongue sweeping my lower lip. "Hi. I missed you the last couple of days."

My cheeks heated, and instead of answering and revealing too much, I kissed him again. Tye's door opening, their voice carrying down the hall, made us spring apart like some kind of mechanism had been deployed.

"Okay! I sent you the details. It's not a school night. Can I stay out late?"

"How late?"

Tye's voice raised, and their face twisted into a hopeful expression. "Midnight?" Tye listed off a few friends of theirs I knew who would be with them, and I agreed.

"Do you need to study?" Cord reached for my hand again.

"Yes," I said, returning to my position against him, sliding a hand down the side of his stomach.

His sharp inhale when I touched him was kind of sexy, and his lips turned up in a smile. "Should I leave you to it?" he asked, dropping his lips to the hollow of my throat.

A little whimper escaped me when his teeth brushed my skin. "Probably," I murmured, my fingers sliding over his abs and up his chest, the soft material of his shirt like butter beneath my fingers.

"Maybe you changed your mind on letting me help." He stepped back, and I missed his heat immediately. "This is your study guide?" He picked up the course packet and flipped through it to where I'd bookmarked a practice quiz.

"I think it might be a little basic for you," I said, leaning against the counter, so that the edge of the granite pressed against my back. "It's kicking my butt, though."

He scanned the pages and nodded. "Maybe you just need better motivation." Cord stepped back toward me and pulled me to him, his lips near my ear. "What if I kiss somewhere new for every correct answer you get?"

We swayed like a slow dance, and my pulse sped. "A kiss per answer?"

His lips trailed down my neck, kisses tracing my throat. "You ready?"

I released a raspy breath in the way I seemed to always do at the feel of his soft kisses. "Okay."

"What's the only language that a computer can make sense of?" The pad of his index finger touched a spot on my collarbone, making a tight, tickling circle. "High level?" He tapped another spot. "Application?" The next two touches made me tingle down to my core. "Machine, or assembly?"

His eyes met mine as he toyed with the buttons on my cardigan—popping open the top two.

"Machine," I said with a grin.

Cord pressed his lips to the hollow of my throat, his tongue swirling as he slid the fabric off my shoulders to reveal the black camisole I wore underneath. "Correct."

"I don't think this is going to help me learn," I groaned

as he nudged up the bottom of my thin camisole and traced his fingers along my stomach.

"Are you saying I'm not a good teacher?" Cord tapped and then circled a spot near my belly button. "Which is not a programming language? Java?" That same finger slid achingly slowly up my ribs but stopped short of my breast. "Python?" He glanced behind him and over his shoulder at the study guide, his fingers still moving, grazing over one nipple before tapping my sternum. "Ruby?" He touched my sternum again, stroking up and down. "Or C++?"

I let out a raspy breath, his teasing touches leaving me on edge. "You touched me there already."

Cord shrugged and tugged on the camisole, working it over my head. "If you get it right, I'll kiss you there twice." He stood waiting for my answer, but the heat in his gaze was unmistakable.

"I think that's a trick question," I said, trying to ignore the way his eyes trailed over my body.

"You think or it is?" Cord stepped into my space, his eyes meeting mine again.

"It is." I reached behind me, unhooking my bra. "Those are all programming languages."

Cord grinned and dipped his head to kiss the spot between my breasts where he'd pressed his fingers, his lips and tongue insistent, teeth grazing the sensitive skin. "See, you're more prepared than you thought." He bent to kiss a trail from my sternum to the spot on my ribs. "Are you ready for a hard one?"

The groan that escaped my lips when he fell to his knees and kissed the spot on my stomach turned to a giggle. "Is that a euphemism?"

He looked up and grinned again. "Get your mind out of the gutter. This is computer science, woman." He kissed the spot on my stomach again as the coolness of the air in the room made my nipples ache for his touch. "In coding, we use reserved words." He toyed with the waist of my pants before tugging on the zipper. "Name three common ones." His fingers brushed along the line of my panties, making goose bumps rise on my skin.

"Um . . . 'if,'" I said, closing my eyes against the anticipation and trying to remember what I'd studied.

"Yep." Cord pulled my pants down and tugged my panties lower, dropping kisses along my abdomen as his finger brushed just above where I ached for him.

"'While.'"

He nudged my pants to the floor and dropped soft kisses over my mound through the fabric of my underwear, his fingers teasing the edges of my entrance.

"Cord," I groaned, nudging forward, trying to guide his fingers or mouth to where I wanted them.

"Give me one more, Petal," he said before kissing me again, his fingers circling closer through the cotton fabric.

"I . . ." I racked my brain as his fingers teased through the fabric, his lips shifting ever closer to my clit. "I can't think when you do that," I said, running my fingers through his hair.

He dropped a kiss at my hip but sat back on his heels, fingers brushing up and down my thigh.

"Why are you stopping?"

"You think I'm some kind of pushover? No right answer, no reward." His grin was playful, and he clearly knew what he was doing to me.

"I think we're done studying." I cupped his face in my

palms as he stood, my eyes meeting his and the humor in his expression doing little to calm the electricity between us.

He took a step forward, backing me against the fridge. "I guess I'll get going, then." Cord sucked at the sensitive skin where my neck met my collarbone, one thigh wedging between my legs the way it had the night he'd first kissed me. The kisses migrated to my lips, deepening, and I stepped out of the pants puddled at my ankles. I was bare against him, enclosed in his arms.

"You're not leaving yet," I said on an exhalation, the press of his erection through his pants an irresistible temptation.

He shifted his thigh against me. "Doesn't exactly feel like you want me to."

I pulled his face back to mine, all my big talk of willpower and good decision-making dissipating. *Like it does with something casual.* "I don't." I dragged his zipper down, freeing his hard length, stroking him firmly and enjoying the way his head tipped back at my touch.

"'For,'" I said. "That's a third reserved word."

"Good job." His words were a growl. "Answer one more question," he said, grinding into my hand. "And I'll do so much more than kiss you."

I bit my lip and gave him a long stroke. "Okay."

He shifted, sliding a finger down between my breasts to my belly button and lower to between my thighs, stroking me, his finger making perfect figure eights. "This is easy," he said, making an extra circle around my clit, enjoying the teasing.

"I'm ready."

"I can tell." He slid his lips up my neck and whispered in my ear. "When you get the right answer, I'm going to take you against this wall, Petal. Do you want that?"

I squirmed under his touch. "You know I do."

"What was the first programming language commonly used?" He pressed his middle finger into me, curling it and stroking at the same time as my head circled the sensation, trying to grasp the ends of my memory through the haze of pleasure.

"I don't . . ."

"Shh," he said near my ear. "I know you studied this." He pressed a second finger into me, pressing against the spot that had me tipping closer to the edge, already so turned on from our study session. His thumbs moved around my clit in tight circles and my legs shook.

"It's . . . it's . . ." The answer was right there. I'd studied it. I didn't think he'd stop, not now, but I still wanted to get it right, to prove to myself I could. The building pressure was maddening as my body sought friction, and I desperately tried to remember the section on history. I tried to grasp the thoughts as my core rocked in anticipation, and I had no idea why Cord was the only person who could overwhelm my body and jumble my thoughts like this. My head lolled back as the pleasure built, but the answer flashed in my mind.

"FORTRAN!" I was in his arms, my back against the wall in an instant, with Cord's cock pressing at my entrance. I shifted against him, bringing him inside me. "Is that right?" I panted.

"I don't care." His muscular arms engulfed me, and I wrapped my legs around his waist. "I got you." Cord kissed me, a hungry deep kiss, and I knew he meant it. He had me in every sense of the word, even if I told him I didn't need it. He had me, and I craved it. Craved the support and control and care.

"More," I gasped as he slowly sank into me, and then he thrust, our bodies colliding so forcefully, all I could do was hold on to him, digging my fingers into his shoulders.

"Everything," he grunted, slamming into me as an orgasm crashed around me, my walls convulsing and every nerve ending electrified. "I'll give you everything," he repeated, his features shifting as I saw his own release barrel through him.

Eventually, he slowly lowered me to the floor, never letting me go, and dropped a sweet kiss to my lips. "For what it's worth, my next question was about the Big O notation," he said between kisses.

I pulled him closer. "That is not a real programming thing."

"It is, actually." His lips fell to my neck, a warm palm covering one hard nipple. "I'm not interested in talking algorithm efficiency right now, but we can study that one later."

I groaned, seeking friction against his thigh. "Maybe sooner than later."

CHAPTER 36

Cord

I SLID TWO PERFECTLY GOLDEN GRILLED CHEESE sandwiches onto a plate before setting the pan in the sink. The untouched pizza still sat on the counter, but after two hours with Pearl against the wall, in bed, and in the shower, I'd never felt happier to be so hungry. Yet I was whistling to myself because I'd also never made grilled cheese on the heels of an orgasm four-peat for my partner, either. Balancing the plate with two bottles of water and some baby carrots from her fridge, I headed back to the bedroom.

Inside, Pearl sat on the edge of her bed smearing lotion over her long, perfect legs, her hair pulled up into a pink scarf. Watching her hands move up and down her calves and then slowly over her knees and thighs, I had half a mind to drop the food, kneel at her feet, and worship those legs and what was between them. She looked up at me, a smile on her face.

"How did you know I loved grilled cheese?"

I shrugged, setting the food on the bed and stroking a finger up her arm. "I know your body."

Pearl set the lotion aside and climbed onto the bed, motioning for me to join her. "Stop being charming. If I don't get food, I may pass out from too much sex."

I handed her the plate and snuggled into the bed next to her, glancing at the clock. We still had a few hours until Tye came home. "We earned this comfort food."

Pearl was already digging into her sandwich and making yummy noises. She held out her palm for me to smack.

"Good, huh? Maybe you'll keep me around."

She smiled but didn't respond right away, taking her time chewing.

I didn't mean to say things like that—or maybe I did. She'd told me in no uncertain terms she wanted casual, she wanted space, and she didn't want commitment. Every day, it was harder to keep to our terms—Wes's question about whether this was enough for me kept circling around my head. "Can I ask you something?" I took a sip from my water bottle and leaned back against the headboard, crossing one leg over the other.

"Sure." She leaned against me, resting her head on my shoulder. I smelled the lotion she'd rubbed on her body and inhaled the now familiar scent of the product she used in her hair—it was sweet and nutty at the same time, and I always wanted to bury my face against her.

"I know this is casual." I hurried forward when she stiffened against me. "Which is what we both wanted." I spoke fast, worried she'd try to interrupt or stop me. "I'm just wondering if it's still what you want. Like, once you get through this rough patch at work, or when I'm no longer on the board, or when Tye's mom is back in town, would you want to be more . . . formal?"

She was quiet, and I waited, but after a full minute, I

glanced down to make sure she hadn't fallen asleep. Stroking her arm, I checked in. "Petal?"

"I don't know," she said very quietly.

I nodded, even though she couldn't see me. That wasn't the worst answer. "Okay." I tried to squelch the disappointment in my voice, the gnawing sense that I knew the full answer was coming. We sat in relative silence for a few minutes, both finishing our food. I was afraid I'd say something that would push her too far, and I wasn't sure what had left her silent.

"It's not you, you know," she said into my chest.

I smiled despite myself, though I doubted it reached my eyes. That didn't matter. She wasn't looking at my face. "That's an old line."

I felt her cheeks pull, maybe in her own smile. "I know, but it's . . . There's a reason."

"I know. You're busy and work is important to you. I'm a—" I paused, because saying the word left an unexpected lump in my stomach. "I can be a distraction, and you have to focus."

Pearl sat up, examining my face, biting that plump lower lip I loved sucking on. Her expression was pensive, like she was weighing the best options for how to proceed. And I hoped none of the options involved kicking me out.

"What is it?"

"It's more than that." She dipped her head, averting her eyes in a move that might be cute were it not for the worry lines on her face.

"Pearl, it's fine. I didn't mean to upset you." She let me take her hand, and I moved the plates out of the way before taking her other one. "I'm sorry I brought it up."

She lifted her head. I expected to see tears, but her eyes

were dry. "I told you how I was with Jason before I worked at FitMi?"

I nodded. "Sure. I remember that guy. It's what made you get your tattoo."

"I didn't like who I was in that relationship. I didn't like what I settled for." She took a slow breath in, her chest filling with air. "I let myself believe it would work, that I could rely on him, and I couldn't."

I still held her hands in mine.

"I had to live with my parents when he kicked me out of his place. I hated being someone else they had to worry about." She glanced away. "Shea was a teenager, and Bri had Tye, and I always worried that the stress was too much on them. More than that, I hated feeling out of control. I hated that I'd let myself fall so hard for someone who could leave me so easily." Pearl straightened her spine and rolled her shoulders back. "It was hard. Beyond hard, but I made it."

I swallowed, the tune I'd been whistling earlier forgotten. "And I remind you of him?"

"Not in the slightest." Pearl leaned against my chest, letting my arms come around her. "You're nothing like him."

For the first time in my life, I was eager to say something, but I didn't have the words.

"I never wanted to feel that way again—like I was trapped—and after I left Chicago for California . . ." She squeezed my hand, because I knew the subtext there—*after I left you*. "I met someone reliable, dedicated to public service . . . someone I thought was a safe choice."

I wrapped an arm around her shoulder, kissing her forehead. I saw how things connected, remembering Kevin's words from the retreat. It didn't lessen the acrid taste in my mouth at the mention of that guy.

"He was my boss, but we were all about the work, all about doing things that mattered, but in the end, he didn't want me to advance or grow in that organization. It was the opposite of my first relationship, but it still wasn't good." Her warm skin against mine felt so right, and I dropped a kiss to her jaw.

"I owe it to myself to make the most of this chance, if that makes sense. I don't think I can do work, family, and a relationship at the same time, so I promised myself if I got the chance again, I wouldn't let anything steal my focus."

I pulled her close, kissing the top of her head again. "Head before heart." I held up her arm. "What does the fourth star mean?"

"I've never told anyone." She examined her own skin. "And as much as I want you," she said, pulling back and looking up until our eyes met. "And I do want you, Cord. Make no mistake. I want you. I have to do this first, and I have to do it right. And I don't have an end date, especially with taking on this course and everything with work and keeping ahead of Ellie."

Telling her I loved her, that I'd loved her for years, was on the tip of my tongue, but I knew that wasn't what she needed to hear or even what she wanted to hear. It occurred to me that as much as I didn't want to be like my dad, changing course with each new woman, Pearl didn't want that, either. Maybe in that way we were the same, and it wasn't fair for me to change the plan. Instead, I cupped her cheeks and planted a slow, soft kiss on her lips. I climbed off the bed and pulled my clothes off the floor.

"Are you leaving?" Pearl watched me intently as I pulled up my pants.

"Nope." I glanced around and plucked her sweatshirt

up from where it was draped on a chair, tossing it to her. "Get dressed."

I headed out to the kitchen and looked through the bag she'd set on the counter hours before, finding what I was looking for almost immediately. There were so many things I couldn't fix for her, that she wouldn't let me fix, but I could do this.

When Pearl emerged from the bedroom a moment later, in the sweatshirt and the shorts she'd been wearing in bed, I motioned to her table and carried over her laptop, notebook, and statistics book. "What are you doing?"

"Helping you actually study. No funny business." I pulled a chair around next to her. "Do you want to start with reserved words and how they appear in different programming languages?"

Pearl smiled at me, a genuine smile, even after the tough conversation we'd just exchanged. A little part of me started to hope maybe she knew I was trying to tell her I loved her without using the words.

CHAPTER 37

Pearl

"ATTENTION! ATTENTION!" XAVIER STOOD AT HIS cubicle and clapped as Bea summoned everyone in the small office suite to gather. This kind of fanfare was usually reserved for birthday cake in the break room.

"What's this about?" Mara arrived at the tiny gathered crowd the same time as me.

"No idea," I said, glancing around, monitoring where Ellie stood opposite me. She'd been honest with me, not actively working against me or in a way that would challenge my leadership, but it hadn't mattered. Kevin had given me the option to make the change myself or wait for the board to vote on the shift to Ellie and me sharing leadership. I was supposed to get back to him by the end of the day.

"The board members will be here for your committee meeting in twenty minutes," Mara said. "Do you want to be in your office or the conference room?"

"Conference room is good," I said, scanning the gathering group of my coworkers.

"I was about to beat my personal best in *Knights of Armageddon*, so this better be worth it," Mara said, tucking her phone into her pocket.

"Is that a sign we don't keep you busy enough?"

"It's a sign I'm efficient. And good with a broadsword."

I laughed softly, waiting for the last two people to shuffle forward. "Noted. I'm appropriately warned."

"We jointly wanted to share some great news," Xavier said, pointing to the computer screen. "Tomorrow a story will run in the *Tribune* about the program's effectiveness, the new initiatives, and how trust is being restored among donors."

I clapped along with everyone else, celebrating the good news even though I knew about the article already. Two donors who had initially pulled out had been interviewed about why they had begun donating again. They'd specifically cited our new initiatives. I'd worked closely with one of them and Ellie with the other, which I was sure looked like a point in the column of us sharing leadership for the time being.

"And we have to tip our collective hats to our fabulous leader," Bea said, starting another round of applause and pointing to me. "Another speech!"

"Why are you always calling for speeches?" I waved the applause away with a smile. Across the room, I saw Cord standing in the entryway to our office suite. He was on the subcommittee and I knew I'd see him, but his figure in my space was still jarring. Jarring in the best way, because I fought the instinct to flash a smile at him, but in the worst way, because that should not have been top of mind; around him, I should be focusing on things between us staying under the radar.

My gaze flicked back to the group, and even though it felt like I was conceding, I motioned to Ellie. "Give some of that applause to Ellie, who has been working double time to get us back on track." The group cheered again, and when we split, I felt spirits around me high. It was a good feeling, or it would have been if the anxiety of the call I had to make to Kevin wasn't eating at me.

"Mr. Matthews, you're early. Can I get you water or coffee?" Mara greeted him, saving me the awkward moment of shaking his hand when I wanted to press my lips to his.

Cord's eyes flicked to me. "No. Thank you. And please call me Cord."

Mara nodded, and I suspected there was a grudging approval for him—she wasn't a fan of people who were overly formal when there was a power differential. His eyes flicked to mine again.

"Does Pearl have a few minutes?"

"I'm sure she could squeeze you in." She motioned for him to follow and walked him to where I was finishing up with Xavier outside my office. "Your schedule is open until the meeting," she said, giving me a quick smile before turning on her heels. Not her, too.

I closed the door behind us, but instead of taking a seat, Cord sat on the edge of my desk.

"What's up?" I walked toward him, noticing the way his slacks fit across his thighs and how the skin on his forearms looked against the white of his shirt. I planned to walk around him and sit at my desk, but his hand snagged mine as I neared, pulling me forward.

"Hi." His thighs bracketed my legs, and his fingers linked with mine were so warm, like the counterpoint to the chill of the air conditioner in my office, like my personal source of heat.

"Hi," I said, giving in to the moment, just for a minute. "You're early."

"I know." His hand fell to my waist and slid down my hip. "I have kind of a thing for the person in charge here."

"You need a haircut." I slid a fingertip along his hairline, enjoying the way his eyelids fell at my touch. "And if you have a thing for the person in charge, you might have to go visit Ellie next."

Cord stiffened, his hand stilling at my waist. "The board didn't vote on that yet."

His hold on me felt protective, and I wanted to lean into it—which was exactly why I shouldn't. "We shouldn't do this here." I stepped back, putting distance between my body and his, his skin and his hands. "Nothing official yet, but Kevin said the board can decide or I can decide to share leadership."

Cord's brow furrowed and he opened his mouth, but I held up a hand.

"It makes sense, and she's good at what she does, it's just . . ." An unfamiliar prick behind my eyes made my breath hitch. I didn't like failing. I didn't like not rising to a task in front of me, and that's how Kevin's suggestion had made me feel. I warred with myself, though, because even as I felt it, as my stomach turned with anxiety, I knew I was being unreasonable.

"Hey," Cord said, reaching for my hand again and tugging me forward but allowing more space between us than last time. "It's okay."

"I need to work harder, maybe put in more hours. I don't know." I rested my free palm on my stomach, taking in a deep breath.

"Petal, you work harder than anyone I know." His fingers flexed against mine until I met his eye, and his thumb traced over my wrist. Without looking, I could imagine the look of his thumbnail against my tattoo. "Let me talk to Kevin. He can't just decide—the board has to vote. I can . . ."

"No." I rested my hand on his chest. "You're right. They get the final say, but the organization is in such a precarious place right now . . ." I brushed his hairline again, wanting something to do with my hand, because the feel of his chest under my palm was too inviting. "And if you stand up for me like that, they'll know. It will be a thing."

"What can I do?" He nodded and tugged me incrementally closer. "Do you need me to step back? From you? From us?" He searched my face, his brown eyes skating between mine. "I don't want this to be over, but if you need more time or space to take care of things, I can."

He meant it—I could tell by the set of his jaw and the way his features were flexed. He didn't want to step back from me, from us, but if I said yes, he would. It was the opposite of what any of my exes would have done, giving me space to take care of things that mattered to me instead of stepping in to show their own control.

"I know our situation is strange." His hand fell to my waist and tightened, bringing me against his body with a slow pull. "And I know OurCode means a lot to you. It means a lot to Tye. So it means a lot to me, too. I'll fight for you to keep this job. I'll call in favors from Kevin. I'll quit if I need to, but only if you want me to."

Cord pressed his lips together as if weighing something out and thinking through the outcomes in his head. And I circled back to his offer to step away from us.

"You don't have to—"

Cord never talked over me, so when he interrupted me, the hairs on the back of my neck stood up. He tugged me closer. "It's not what we agreed on. I know we said no reliving San Diego, but I just want you to know I am waiting. Waiting for our situation to change, waiting to kiss you in public, waiting for . . . you, whatever you'll share with me. I didn't want to date, but I changed my mind. I'm waiting for you."

"You're waiting?"

"Yes."

I met his eyes, searching the sable irises and long lashes. "But you wanted casual."

"I did." He raised his shoulders. "I thought I did, but I don't anymore. Casual isn't what I'm looking for with you. So I'm waiting."

"It's not fair to you to wait for me, though." I shook my head, stepping back, pulling our fingers apart. "I have to focus. I have to make time for work and my family, and I don't have any time for a relationship. It might be a long time, Cord."

"I'm fine. I'm not rushing you, I just don't want you to think I've given up, that I'm looking for another woman. I'm not. I'm on the shelf for you. If I'm taking you away from doing this work that matters, I'll wait for as long as it takes."

My chest was close to his, our faces only inches apart while his thighs bracketed my legs. I was safe in his arms even as he reassured me he'd step back and let me do it alone, and I felt small and protected and overwhelmingly powerful at the same time. I felt it all, and I suddenly wanted more. I wanted to ignore my code and take a chance. "Go on a date with me. A real one."

His eyes snapped from their perusal to meet mine. "What?"

"Not dinner at my place or sneaking off to your place and making out in front of your cat. An actual date."

"I thought you wanted to keep it casual. A secret."

I leaned in to him, enjoying the way his arms closed around me. "I do. I mean, we still have to keep it kind of secret, but it's a big city, and I don't want you to step back here, and I don't want casual anymore, either."

"You want to date me?" There was a smile in his voice.

"I want to figure this out, and I want to be around you while I do." It wasn't a big declaration, but it felt big to me, and the way his smile widened, I wondered if it felt big to him, too.

"Okay." His fingers skirted over my lower back, and he pulled me in for a hug, his breath against my ear. "But can I still bring Peach? She's gotten used to watching us."

"Don't push your luck," I said into his ear.

"She's got some business savvy. Britta bought her a sweater with 'Business Bitch' embroidered on it. Maybe I could just bring her into the office."

I laughed, covering my mouth too late, and the sound bounced around my office. All this felt so right, being in his arms and laughing. Even trusting him with what I was feeling about Ellie. "I—"

"Hey, Pearl. Before we—" I leaped back from Cord's embrace at the sound of Ellie's knock and voice on the other side of the door, and the two if us sprang apart like a snapped rubber band.

Ellie's eyes darted between us quickly. "I didn't mean to interrupt. Sorry. Just wanted to run this by you before the meeting." Her expression looked skeptical, but she stepped forward, saying hi to Cord and handing me the agenda for the meeting along with some relevant data I'd asked her to gather. Her expression looked normal when I thanked her, and while I reviewed the document, she made small talk with Cord.

It must have been in my head. She didn't see anything inappropriate between us.

"I'll be down in a minute," I said as she walked out, and I gathered paperwork from my desk.

"Do you think she saw?" Cord's voice was pitched low, and I shook my head.

"I don't think so." Our hands were close on the top of my desk, and I pulled mine back, clutching a notebook to my chest. "We need to be more careful."

"Yeah," he agreed, motioning for me to lead the way, but speaking again in that low, almost-whisper-quiet voice before we got out of my office. "I'll keep my hands to myself until our date. Then all bets are off."

I straightened my dress and took a deep breath to get my game face on, but before we left the office, I spoke over my shoulder. "Promise?"

CHAPTER 38

Pearl

Five Years Earlier

September

I RAN A HAND OVER THE SMOOTH, EMPTY SURFACE of my desk, free of anything except a folder labeled "Transition Information," and I straightened it. There was nothing else to do, pack, or prepare; all that was left was to say goodbye.

My phone pinged with a reminder. *ORD to LAX: Flight 2039 to Los Angeles departing in three hours.*

Cord's door was closed, but the light was on despite everyone else having left for the day. We hadn't talked much since San Diego, and the last two weeks had been awkward and lonely, no one perched on the corner of my desk, no memes sent in the middle of meetings. We'd spoken, but it was perfunctory. It was professional.

I drew in a deep breath before taking the first steps toward Cord's office. Despite my best efforts, the sound of his voice from the beach played in my head on a loop. *I'm in love with you.* And then there had been the questions. Why LA? What was the job? Was I sure? And then there were my answers, in a voice I wanted to sound more certain than I really was. And then there had been silence, with only the sounds of the ocean between us. Shea asked me later if there was anything he could have said to change my mind; if he had fought for me to stay, would it have changed my decision? I still didn't know the answer. As I wrapped my fingers around the cool metal of his door handle, I reminded myself that he hadn't fought for me to stay. He'd finally said congratulations, and we'd parted ways, heading back to our hotel rooms.

I took in another deep breath before knocking.

"Hey," he said from behind his desk. He looked tired, glancing down at his keyboard before looking up at me and plastering on a fake smile. "Last day."

I nodded and stepped into the room. "I prepared some notes for your next assistant," I said, stepping forward and handing him the binder of resources and information.

"Thank you." He thumbed through the binder and didn't look up. The way he schooled his expression said everything. I felt guilty and also kind of annoyed. Yes, I'd broken his heart a little in San Diego, maybe. Definitely. But we were adults.

I squared my shoulders. "Well, then. I'm off. Good luck with . . . everything." I hoped to make it out the door before the tears threatening to well began to fall. I had a sinking feeling I was making a mistake, anxiety roiling in the way it did when something felt so wrong, my body revolted.

"Stay."

I stopped at his words, my back to him and an open door in my path.

"Pearl." His voice wasn't loud, but the words landed with impact, making me turn as he walked around his desk. "Stay."

"I have a flight to catch."

"Don't go to LA." He motioned from him to me. "There's something here between us and it's special. And I know I'm asking a lot, but stay here with me." He pressed his palms to his chest, and I remembered the feel of those hands.

"My job," I said. "It's the opportunity I've been waiting for."

"Then long distance." Cord stepped forward, reaching for my hand. "I'm saying don't leave this behind, this thing between us. I meant what I said. I'm in love with you and I want to build something with you."

"You know that I can't." I battled with wanting to step back and wanting to step straight into his arms. I ended up doing neither and stayed rooted in place. "I need the job. I need to take this opportunity, and everything is set for LA. I've moved out. I can't just decide to stay in Chicago."

"You could find a job here. And until then . . ." He looked around as if searching for an answer before his gaze snapped back to me. "Until then, live with me. I bought this big house." Cord studied my face, and I knew he saw the doubt, but he kept going. "And I know that's too fast, but I can't just let you walk away, Pearl. Stay." He held both of my hands in his. "Please."

"Live with you?" I could see it, all of it. I could picture waking up in his arms. I could picture sitting under the night sky in the backyard. I could picture a life with him. But I could also picture the end and the hopelessness and helplessness that could bring.

"For now, until you find a place and . . ." He ran a hand through his hair. "I know I'm asking a lot. I know I am. But let me take care of you while you find the dream job that lets you stay here."

I could picture how it would all end, and I still wanted to say yes. I wanted to stay in Chicago and be close to my family and see what happened with Cord. I stepped forward, catching his hopeful expression, but I forced myself to remember what it felt like to lose everything, and I shook my head. "I have to put my head before my heart. If I don't, I could lose *everything*. I could put everything I've worked for at risk. I'm sorry, Cord."

I was waiting for the elevator when I heard his footsteps jogging behind me, and I closed my eyes, trying desperately to remind myself what I was working toward. "Wait. Pearl. Wait!"

CHAPTER 39

Cord

Present Day

I TAPPED THE BUTTON ON MY CONTROLLER, AND MY character on the screen jumped over Tye's. "Aren't we supposed to be talking about school or your coding work?"

"I went to school today," Tye said, executing a spin move I'd been trying to figure out. The OurCode lounge was a large open room on the first floor of the main office filled with computer terminals, comfortable couches, and a gaming console collection donated by some generous and smart soul. There were only a few other kids and one mentor and mentee pairing in there, which meant Tye and I had the couch and massive screen TV to ourselves.

"Did you learn something interesting?"

"Avoid the tater tots on Thursdays," Tye said, jerking their controller to the left and attacking me, my character falling to the ground. "Yes! That's two. Why do you even show up to compete with me?"

I laughed and set the controller aside. "Who is mentoring who?"

Tye set their own controller aside and settled back into the couch. "I don't know. I mean, I'm clearly schooling you on this game, helping you with your love life—"

"Something you should stop doing, since it's creepy and I don't need your help."

Bea walked through, chatting with some kids, and waved at us. She was one of Pearl's favorites, though I admired how Pearl showed care for everyone on her staff, even Ellie, who I knew she saw as her competition.

"Yeah, right." Tye stood and spoke over their shoulder, walking toward the small kitchenette in the lounge's corner. "I'm getting a Coke, you want anything?" They held up a hand and laughed. "Never mind. I didn't need to ask. I'll bring you a Mountain Dew." They laughed again at their own joke and ambled toward the fridge, giving me time to check my phone.

"Hey, Matthews," Kevin said, walking through the lobby. "What're you doing here?"

I motioned to Tye, who'd stopped to talk to a few other kids. "Shaping young minds." I glanced around the space and noticed Bea had tensed and was following his movements. "What about you? Want to join us for a conquest?"

Kevin laughed and sat on the edge of the couch. "Wish I could. Need to talk to Pearl about the figures she shared a few days ago. Between you and me, I don't normally like to be this involved in the day-to-day, but after the issues with Kendra and now the shortfall . . ." He ran a hand through his hair. "I'm getting worried."

My hackles rose when he brought up Pearl, and I flashed back to the look on her face when she'd told me he wanted her and Ellie to share leadership. The budget shortfall might only give him more reason to push for action from the board. "How much?"

"Thirty grand. They'd need at least fifteen or twenty more to move forward with the plan we laid out. I'm really not sure we put the right person in charge to steer the organization out of this mess," Kevin said in a low voice, picking up the controller, fiddling with the buttons, and eyeing the screen wistfully. "Man, I wish I could join you, though. I love this game."

"He's a good person to play with," Tye said, joining us and handing me the green bottle, condensation sweating on the plastic. "It's like playing against a toddler."

"Rude." I shifted to make room for Tye, still thinking about Kevin's comments, as he laughed and handed over the controller.

"Rain check?"

"Sure," I said absently as he strode away.

"He not sticking around to play?"

"No. Why? Sick of me already?" I tried to shake off what Kevin had said, wanting to give Tye my full attention.

"Obviously." They tapped the buttons to start the new level and cut their eyes toward me, an expression that meant they were about to make fun of me. "Nah. You're kind of growing on me."

"Thanks," I said, acknowledging player two was ready. "Did you get a chance to look at that stuff about the summer coding camp at Thurmond University?"

"Yeah," Tye said as the game started. "Looks good. I'm gonna talk to my mom about it."

"How is your mom? Are you excited about having her home soon?"

"Yeah, I guess." Almost immediately after entering the game, Tye was scoring points left and right, leaving me to trail behind. "I miss her, but I know she's gotta do her own thing, you know? Her and my aunts talk about that all the time. *No man is going to take care of us like Daddy takes care of*

Mom, so we have to do it ourselves." Tye hurled three rocks at a passing villain and transformed into another level of armor. I really needed to practice before playing with them again.

"Blah, blah, blah," Tye added. "They've been saying that forever. Who wants someone to take care of them, anyway?"

"Yeah," I said, narrowly missing an arrow from one side of the screen and Tye's dagger from the other. "It's nice sometimes, though."

"I guess." Tye leaped over me in the game and ran toward me with a sword.

We played. Well, Tye played. I mostly got slaughtered for another fifteen minutes until I had to get back to the office. All the while, I thought about what Tye had said, and wondered if being taken care of, even a little, was something Pearl wanted but wasn't asking for.

CHAPTER 40

Pearl

A RAY OF SUNLIGHT CUT ACROSS MY OFFICE AND fell on my face—the warmth and light like a reward for getting to the reports I'd been setting aside for weeks. Months earlier, Kendra had worked with a professor doing research on communities of color and STEM outreach and had been interviewing our alums out in the industry. The results were inspiring, and I'd taken pages of notes from their findings as I'd pored over the preliminary report. There were a hundred great ideas in those pages if we could only keep the organization afloat. I closed the browser window. The world outside was bright, a wide-open blue sky above and the city stretched out below. I grinned at the idea of taking a walk at lunch.

"You look so joyful," Mara commented, stepping into my office after knocking on the doorframe. "What inspired that kind of smile?"

Cord. Cord's voice. The memory of Cord's arms around me. "Nothing," I said, straightening. "Just admiring the nice day."

Mara's smile was indulgent, showing she knew I was thinking something else, but she let me and my sad lie off the hook this once. "Knew you'd want to see this. Ellie brought it in." She handed me a stack of papers and a manila folder. "Anonymous donor," she said as I thumbed through the documents, landing on the page that outlined the donation as a flat thirty thousand dollars. I read and reread the number three times before looking up at Mara, wide-eyed. "Anonymous?"

Mara shrugged. "That's what Ellie said. Someone who reached out to her directly."

"Can you have her come by when she's free?" I stared at the number again. It was more than what we needed—it put us back on track to moving forward after returning the tainted funds from the Smith Corporation. I scoured the documents for some clues, but my head swam with everything we could do with this money.

"She's out until two—I'll let her know to find you after that." Mara left me in my office to wonder at the donation.

I pulled my purse from the drawer in my desk and tucked away the donation paperwork—Shea, Britta, and I had a lunch reservation soon and I needed to get across town. Sitting in the back of an Uber, I made a checklist of priorities we could tackle with the infusion of cash, and the ideas came faster than I could write them down until my phone buzzed in my lap as we approached the restaurant.

Shea: I'm running late, but I'll be there.

Britta: Can't wait to see you guys!

Shea: Tye told me someone has had a regular gentleman caller lately.

Britta: I'm so excited.

Shea: She's been tight-lipped with details.

Pearl: Apparently you don't need me for this conversation.

Shea: Ahem. Details.

Pearl: You're nosy. I'm walking in now to get the table.

Britta: We had to watch this thing slowly build for years. Think of us as interested parties.

Shea: Be prepared for questions.

That annoying grin was still on my face as I rolled my eyes. I couldn't shake it, especially at the thought of the man in question. I hadn't hung out with the girls in almost two months and I missed it. Shea and I talked all the time, but it was usually over text or with Tye.

My phone buzzed on the table, and I grinned.

Cord: Does your girls' night have a slumber party component, or do I get to enjoy an empty apartment with you tonight?

Pearl: You're in luck—we had to move dinner to lunch, so no slumber party.

Pearl: I have some great news to tell you, too.

He sent a GIF of a maniacal-looking raccoon rubbing its

paws together, and I laughed, drawing stares from a few nearby tables.

"Just as I thought."

My head snapped up at Britta's voice. I hadn't noticed her walking toward me, and she took the seat to my left. "Cheesy grin and total absorption in a text. I can't wait to hear this."

I rolled my eyes and turned my phone over. "You've spent too much time with my sister. How are you?"

Britta waved a hand in my direction. "Life is good. Work is good. Wes rocks my world and I rock his right back, but that's old news. You're not changing the subject."

"You started without me?" Shea slid onto the other stool.

"There's really nothing to tell," I insisted, earning a brief reprieve when the server arrived to deliver my iced tea and get Britta's and Shea's drink orders.

When she walked away, both women gave me expectant stares, and I sipped from my glass.

"Are you two together now? Officially?" Britta asked.

"We are dating." I loved him, even if I wasn't willing to admit it out loud yet, even if it scared the hell out of me. He'd spent almost every night at my place, sometimes for sex but often just to be there. I was used to sleeping with him now. His body heat and the way he sometimes snored had become comforting.

He'd asked Tye's permission, he told me later, making sure they were okay with him in the house at night. That small gesture—both his asking and really listening—left unexpected tears welling in my eyes.

"Finally!" Shea said. "You'll be more fun now that you're getting sex on the regular."

"Shea."

"She's not wrong," Britta chimed in. "I mean, everyone is more fun when they're getting serviced properly. I was a bear when Wes did that study-abroad trip and was gone for three weeks."

"Unless . . ." Shea eyed me critically, her brow scrunching.

"What?"

"Unless you're not getting serviced properly. Is he not . . . everything you'd hoped in the bedroom? Because sometimes chemistry takes time."

My cheeks heated. "C'mon."

"No! Seriously?" Britta's chipper smile fell, and she looked at me with almost a pitying look.

"No," I said in a whisper-hiss. "He's . . . fantastic."

Both of their eyebrows rose. "Fantastic as in . . . skill, equipment, or creativity?"

I sipped my drink, wishing I could blame alcohol for loosening my tongue. "Hat trick," I mumbled, smiling despite myself at their joint whistles of approval. "It's good." It was beyond good. Cord oscillated widely between generous and cuddly to dominant and demanding, taking and giving control in the most erotic ways. I hadn't expected that. Hell, I never knew I wanted that until him.

"Hot damn," Shea said, smacking the table. "Caleb is on my list right now. Since we got back together, he refuses to be in the same bed when I'm on my period, like he'll catch menstruation or something. As if I wouldn't have given it to him already if I could."

"This IUD. I'm telling you," Britta began. "Magic. I don't even get them anymore."

Shea and Britta went back and forth about the merits of IUDs, but I stopped listening, setting down my glass after the last sip. I hadn't gotten my period since Cord and I had been together, so we hadn't ever had the conversation again after that first time. I counted backward in my head, chiming into the conversation absently. I pushed the worry from my mind—missing a month wasn't uncommon, especially under stress. I sniffed the air subtly. When Bri was pregnant with Tye, her sense of smell was off the charts—she could detect everything. I didn't trust my brain—I smelled the nearby appetizer tray and someone's perfume, but maybe that was normal. I lifted the glass to my lips, sipping, but set it down again, unsure.

"Right, Pearl?" Britta's voice cut into my head, and I nodded.

"Sure."

The discussion continued, and I ordered a glass of water, unable to shake the worry about being late, even though I knew it was next to impossible. I was diligent in taking my birth control and we'd used condoms almost every time except that night in the tent. I did the math. Shit. Not possible. Did my boobs hurt? Not possible. The internal monologue swirled in my head, and after an hour, I told Shea and Britta I wasn't feeling well and requested an Uber to get back to the office.

I REASSURED MYSELF that I was overreacting and it wasn't possible, even as I thought back over the last couple of months. I walked past the student lounge, empty for the moment, and up the stairs to our office. I didn't want the reminder of elevators while my head was in this place. My phone buzzed twice in my hand.

Shea: You took off so fast. You okay?

Cord: When should I get to your place?

I collided with someone as I flung open the door to the third floor and stumbled backward onto my butt.

"Oh!" Ellie jumped back but held out a hand for me. "Sorry. I was just looking for you."

I rose to my feet, brushing my palms down my skirt and trying to get my mind back on the game. "Yes, sorry. I just wanted to ask you about that donation."

She smiled and motioned toward her office, which was next to the stairwell. "Amazing, right? I'd love to take credit, but they just called me with that amount to donate."

"Completely anonymous?"

Ellie looked away and then back at me. "I know who they are, but they didn't want their identity shared. I did due diligence, though. Nothing untoward, no caveats on the money, nothing like the funds Kendra was funneling in."

Ellie's office was homey, and I realized I had spent almost no time inside it. She had a throw pillow on the little chair in the corner with the OurCode logo, and photos of family and friends covered her desk and ledges. My office was spartan, with only two photos—one of my parents and one of my sisters and me with a five-year-old Tye after I'd gotten my tattoo. "Excellent," I said. "And nice work, even though they approached you. This is exactly what we needed."

"Are you okay? You look a little dazed. You didn't hit your head when you fell or anything, did you?" She searched my gaze, and I willed the muscles in my face to get it together.

"Just tired. Thanks, Ellie." I walked toward my office. There was a CVS near my apartment and I could pick up a test on my way home, though I had no idea how I was going to focus the rest of the day. Only the thought of finding out turned my stomach. When I set my things down on my desk, a few message notifications waited for me.

Cord: Episodes 8 and 9 of Starfighter and some pizza sound good?

Shea: Are you sick? You left so soon. Should I bring you something?

I tapped on Shea's message.

Pearl: I'm late.

Shea: For what?

Pearl: Late. Late.

A notification from Cord popped up and I tapped it away without looking.

Pearl: My period is late and I'm never late. I'm scared.

I sucked in a break and waited for a reply, letting my vision go out of focus after typing my reply to Shea, waiting for her to say something funny or irreverent to pull me out of this headspace. I'd set the phone aside immediately, opening my inbox to dive into work, but her reply came only a moment later.

Except it wasn't from Shea. In my haste to reply to Shea, I hadn't dismissed the text from Cord, I'd opened it, and of all the things to accidentally send him, there was no backtracking that one.

Cord: You're pregnant?

The sun had shifted positions, and now it was only the shadow of the windowpane over my hand as the dots on the text thread bounced, disappeared, then bounced again.

CHAPTER 41

Cord

PREGNANT. PEARL MIGHT BE PREGNANT.

I'd shoved my wallet, keys, and phone in my pocket but was still standing in my doorway. Oddly, her saying she was late, that she might be pregnant, didn't send my head spinning. Her admitting she was scared, though—that wasn't like Pearl, so I shook myself out of it and stepped out the door.

I'd planned to stop at the drugstore near my office to buy more condoms before going to her place that night, so the irony of standing in front of rows of pregnancy tests wasn't lost on me. I stared at the labels: early detection, digital readout, a single test, a three-pack. The options seemed to go on and on, and another customer a few feet away was staring at me curiously and I considered asking her advice. I quickly grabbed a bunch of the most expensive boxes and hurried out of the aisle. Near the checkout, I grabbed a bottle of the tea Pearl liked so much and waited as impatiently as I ever had for anything for the man in front of me to finish checking out.

The teenager at the checkout counter eyed my multiple boxes. "Bruh, that's a lot of pregnancy tests," he said, eyeing me.

"Yeah." I mumbled, focusing on swiping my credit card more than I needed to.

"These are all multipacks in different brands." He held one up. "This is like twenty tests."

"Yeah. It's fine."

"I'm not supposed to tell customers this, but if you need to buy in bulk, just order online. It's way cheaper. Did you get, like, a bunch of people pregnant or something?"

He must have picked up on my expression, because the commentary ceased and my purchases were quickly stuffed into a bag.

I made it to Pearl's office fifteen minutes later, still clutching the bag in one hand and her bottle of tea in the other.

"Hey," she said when she answered the door. "I didn't mean to freak you out."

She was in a pencil skirt and this soft pink sweater that looked like it was almost as nice to touch as her skin. I gave her outfit only a passing glance, though, because I pulled her into a hug as soon as the door was closed behind me.

"It'll be okay," I said into her ear. When I pulled back, I held up the bag before emptying the contents onto her desk. "I didn't know if you had one already, so I brought a few kinds."

She laughed—it wasn't joyful, but I was glad she'd relaxed enough for that. "Did you buy all they had?"

"Give me a break—the kid at the checkout counter already made fun of me." I rubbed my hand over her back. "I wanted you to have options."

"It's sweet. Thank you."

"Do you, um, feel okay?" We stood in her office like we had fifty times before, but I felt like it was our first conversation, like I had to be careful. The voices and sounds of phones ringing outside her door were a reminder we did need to take care.

"Yeah. I'm fine."

I didn't mention that she was clearly lying, instead picking up one of the boxes. "How do these work?"

She took the box from my hand. "Well, I pee on it and then wait. Not too hard." She studied the instructions on the box, and I read over her shoulder, enjoying how she let me wrap my arms around her.

"Do you want me to pee on one, too? Like, as a control?"

She gave me one of her raised eyebrows over her shoulder before returning to read another box. *Okay, not funny.*

I stroked my hands down her arms. "It will be okay."

Pearl nodded once and replaced the boxes in the plastic bag. "I'll test when I get home. I can't do this here." She motioned to the office outside her door and let out a slow, measured breath. I worried she might pull away to handle her emotions on her own like she handled most things, but she stepped toward where I sat against the edge of her desk and leaned into me, her back to my chest and my arms falling around her waist.

The pink sweater was soft under my hands, and I rested my chin on her shoulder, inhaling the scent of her.

When she spoke, her voice was low. "There were a few times we didn't use a condom."

"I'm sorry," I said, pushing her braids away from her neck.

She gave me another arched eyebrow over her shoulder, this time with a touch of affection. "I think that first one in the tent was on me."

"You jumped me."

"You didn't seem to mind."

"Eh. I guess it was fine." I shrugged before dropping a kiss on her shoulder. "One of the best nights of my life, Pearl."

She eyed the door and then glanced at her watch. "I can't believe this is happening. With Tye, with the job, I'm barely balancing things as is. I let myself take so many chances when it comes to you. It's like I forget to be rational."

"We—I mean, you—have options, no matter what." I continued to hold her, waiting for her. "I'll support whatever you want to do, and we'll be okay."

She didn't respond but rested her weight against me. My entire life, I've never known when to leave well enough alone, so I kept talking. "And if it's positive, I'll take care of you."

She stiffened and spoke slowly, so slowly I knew I had said the worst possible thing, but I didn't know how to change course.

"I don't want to be taken care of."

"I know. I didn't mean it like that. I just meant I *would* take care of you. You and the baby. And Tye!" I stumbled over my words, desperately trying to get the moment back where she was letting me offer comfort. "I just mean financially, and otherwise, so work and family wouldn't have to be roadblocks."

Her eyes narrowed.

Shut up, dumbass!

"They're not roadblocks. My family and my career are what I've been working for—they're what I value most."

"I know." I angled to face her, reaching for her hand. "I know that. I just meant it wouldn't be the end of the world, right? I'd be here, so we could do it together, like a family."

Pearl's eyes widened and her breath hitched. Standing, she rubbed the back of her neck, then began pacing the small space. "What the hell? It's like you've planned out an entire life for us without consulting me. We just started actually dating."

"No," I said, standing and stepping to where she stood. "This is coming out all wrong. I'm just trying to say I'll be here for you."

"No, you're saying you'll provide for me. I don't want that." She stepped toward me, backing me up. "You're waxing poetic about the family we'd create while I put all my plans on hold."

I looked into her eyes, desperately searching for the right thing to say. "I'm not upset. That's all I'm saying. I'm not worried, and yeah, it's not planned, but maybe it's fate. It doesn't have to be a big, scary thing."

She parroted my words back, tone cool. "It doesn't have to be a big, scary thing."

"I mean . . ." I trailed off, seeing her expression morph from cool to angry to panicked.

"Oh, God," she mumbled to herself, pushing her hands over her hair. "What am I doing?"

"Pearl, I get I'm saying the wrong things. Please tell me what you want here." I glanced at the office door. "Can we just wait to find out and go from there?"

She shook her head, and her expression was resolute. It wasn't the open and warm smile I'd gotten used to, or even the wry grin I knew from when we'd worked together. She dipped her head to her chest. "This is a lot. This is a lot." I couldn't read her mind, but I didn't need to in order to know being out of control of this situation had messed with Pearl's equilibrium. "I think . . . I think you need to leave."

I reached for her, cupping my hand under her elbow. "I don't want to leave you."

"It's best if I handle this alone. I just need to . . ." She stepped away from me, pacing and pressing her palms to her skirt. "To think."

Tension and anxiety rolled off her in waves, and I did the only thing I could think of—I stepped toward her, and, in a quiet voice, far from the right key, sang the chorus to "Firework" by Katy Perry. The lyrics had been burned in my brain since we'd been stuck in the elevator, and it had become the soundtrack to a secret I knew about the woman I loved. Pearl stared at me blankly for a moment before she registered the song and a tiny, quick-as-a-flash, but impossible-to-miss smile tipped the side of her lips. She didn't pull away, so I risked dropping my hands to her waist and tugging her back toward the desk with me, all the while singing.

Her palm rested on my chest. "You remembered."

"You needed distraction."

Her body relaxed, the tension in her muscles giving way. "I'm sorry I snapped at you."

"I'm sorry I knocked you up."

"Potentially knocked me up."

"I'm sorry for the potential." I kissed her forehead. "And for saying the wrong thing. I don't want to take care of you at all. I want you to take care of me, so get back to work to bring home some bacon so you can keep me in the luxury to which I've become accustomed."

Her soft laugh against me was all I ever needed to hear.

"We'll figure it out together. I promise."

Pearl nodded and stepped back, meeting my eyes. "I know I freaked out on you, but is this really something you'd want?"

"It doesn't matter what I want right now."

She traced a fingertip over my eyebrow. "What do you want? From me?"

I was about to wave off her question again but spoke up. "What I want?"

"Yeah." Pearl's voice was low.

"A chance."

"A chance?"

"A real chance to make it work. I like dating you." Our eyes met again, my hand still working in circles over her back. "I'll date you for as long as you need, and I don't necessarily want kids or a big, formal commitment. I think we'd have to decide those things together, but if you're asking what I want, that's it. A chance to be your person. A chance to be yours. And this," I said, motioning to the bag on her desk, "this maybe forced our hands, but I'm here."

She rested her palm against my face, looking at me intently. "Then I'm asking you to come over after work to be with me when I take the test. Let's take a chance."

I kissed her, holding her close to me again. "Do you want me to stick around for a while?"

"No," she said, stepping away, her hand still in mine. "I have some meetings this afternoon. Thank you, though." She pointed at the bag overflowing with tests and the bottle of tea sweating on her desk.

I kissed her wrist, my lips falling over the star I knew meant family first. "Okay. Text me when you leave and I'll head to your place." I followed her toward her office door, the sounds of the office outside growing louder as I neared it. Opening the door meant putting on the facade of the professional relationship, but I didn't care. I'd fake it forever in public knowing she was giving me a real chance outside the office. Risk of a broken heart be damned. I had my girl. She had her career. Things were going to work out.

"We'll discuss it later," I said with a small smile after she'd opened the door.

"Definitely."

Ellie walked toward us, clutching a laptop. "Hi, Cord," she said, glancing between us as she reached Pearl's door. "Pearl, you ready for me?"

"Yeah," she said, a lightness returning to her voice. "C'mon in."

I fought the urge to reach for her but held my hand still. "Thanks for meeting with me."

We were in a little bubble of love and affection, and both realized a second too late. She'd invited Ellie into her office, where a large bag of pregnancy tests sat on her desk.

CHAPTER 42

Pearl

SHEA WAS WAITING ON MY COUCH WHEN I WALKED into my apartment. "Hold on," she said into her phone. "She just walked in."

"What the hell, Pearl?" Bri's voice erupted from the screen before I saw her face on it.

I tossed my bag on the counter and toed off my shoes, gingerly setting the canvas bag I'd borrowed to store the pregnancy tests for transport home. "Isn't it past midnight in London?"

"You're right—my sister is in trouble, but I should get my beauty sleep." Bri was usually the calm to Shea's eruptive.

"What's going on?" "Are you pregnant?" Their questions toppled out on top of each other, making it impossible to separate who was asking what despite Shea standing in front of me and Bri with us on FaceTime.

"I haven't taken the test yet," I said with a sigh, motioning to the bag on the counter.

Shea's brows pinched after she held up the bag. "Why do you have an Iowa State University Department of Computer Science Alumni tote bag?"

"I need a drink before I tell this story."

"No!" Both sisters yelled again when I pushed past Shea for the fridge.

"Water. I'm getting a drink of water."

The impatience rolled off them in waves as I filled the glass.

"Shea, why is your sister taking her sweet-ass time filling a glass of water instead of telling us what happened?"

Shea's voice was soft as she walked back into the living room, taking Bri with her. I wasn't sure what was in the water, with her being the calm one and Bri being impatient. Well, and me being the messy one. "C'mon, Pearl. Talk to us. Bri will calm down. I promise."

I set down the glass. "He showed up at my office with these." I pointed to the bag. "We kind of fought. My head was all over the place."

"Understandable," Bri said, trying to read me through the screen, which froze momentarily, her fingers poised at her hairline, grazing the satin edge of the cap covering her hair. "Was he upset?"

"No," I said. "He said he wanted to take care of me, financially and otherwise, so work wouldn't be in the way of me making my decision."

Shea winced, and my heart melted in a puddle of appreciation as Bri spoke up. "Why would he think you'd want that?"

"I think he was just trying to say the right things at that point, but it made it so clear . . . he wasn't upset about the possibility of a pregnancy. He seemed almost excited about it."

"He wants it all," Shea said.

"Yeah."

"And you're not ready."

I shook my head. "No. Not for it all, but after we talked, I thought I was maybe ready to give him a chance."

"Okay, so . . ." Bri was holding back what she wanted to say. I could tell from four thousand miles away. "So, leaning into the idea of being with Cord, and you're calmer than I would expect about the possibility of a baby. Why do you look like you're ready to flee?"

"Before he left, Ellie walked in and saw the pregnancy tests and the two of us together."

"Oh, shit," both sisters said at the same time.

"That's the woman who wants your job?" Bri asked.

I nodded. "I just told the chairperson of the board I wouldn't voluntarily make that move. That I'd make them force my hand."

"So, the exact person you don't want to know there might be something with you and Cord."

"Exactly." I sipped from my glass again and glanced at my phone, which I'd set down on the table.

"Did she threaten to tell them?"

I had to hand it to Ellie. "No. She didn't. She actually lent me the bag so people didn't see the tests. God, assuming no one noticed when Cord walked in." I looked at the tote sitting ominously. She hadn't threatened me, not about the tests. "She asked if I was feeling okay, and if I needed anything. She was . . . kind. About that."

"What was she not kind about?" Bri's voice sharpened through the screen.

"I'd sent Cord away before I talked to her, but she told me she would disclose that she suspected a board member and I were in a relationship if I remained the sole director." She made good points—the potential for scandal or intragroup interference was real.

Shea sucked in a breath through her nose, her expression twisting in a way that mirrored Bri's.

Bri asked, "Would it really matter, though? I mean, okay, I get the last manager was in bed with a board member, so it's not great, but that had a financial component, right? This looks bad but is different. There's no money moving around."

My phone buzzed on the table.

Cord: I'll be up in a minute. Waiting for the elevator.

My sisters waited for me to respond. It turned out the situation wasn't that different, but I didn't know how to explain it quickly. "It's a little more complicated than that, but he'll be up in a minute and I can't process any more complications right now."

"Sure," Shea said, standing.

"Let us know as soon as you know, though?" Bri kissed the phone before ending with, "Tell Tye I'll talk to them in the morning."

Shea walked with me toward the door. "Do you want me to stay?"

There were three raps on the door, and I shook my head, reaching for the doorknob. I was still trying to decide how to bring up to Cord what Ellie had said. "Hey," Cord said, his hand poised to knock again. "Hi, Shea."

"Don't make me kick your ass," Shea said, patting his shoulder before giving me a hug. "Let me know. And don't stress about Ellie. Well, don't stress yet."

After Shea closed the door behind her, Cord glanced around my apartment, hands shoved in his pockets like he was afraid to touch me. We'd clearly gotten in some trouble with the touching lately, so it wasn't the worst instinct. "Tye's at a friend's," I said, finally catching on.

"Oh, good." He stepped forward and pulled me into a hug, his biceps boxing me in and his hands spread across my back.

Even as my thoughts whirred, worry, anxiety, and anger playing tug-of-war with my focus, his hug felt safe and warm, and I sank against him.

"What happened with Ellie?" He spoke near my ear, words gentle and curious.

"Let's do this first," I said, pointing to the bag. After stepping out of his embrace, I picked the top box from the pile. I'd done some Google searching, and it was a good one. I opened it to look at the instructions again, and I walked toward my bedroom and en suite.

"I'm going to sit quietly until you tell me not to," he said, sitting on the edge of my bed, mimicking zipping his lips. "That might be safer."

I gave him a small smile, and when I emerged a couple of minutes later, he hadn't moved. "Takes a few minutes."

Cord motioned to the spot on the bed next to him, and I considered taking the seat, letting him wrap his arm around me, and leaning on him, literally and figuratively. I knew he wouldn't say it again, wouldn't make promises to take care of me or to jump in to save the day on my behalf. He wouldn't say it again because I'd told him not to, but it didn't change that he wanted to. It didn't change what he'd done. I paced instead, ignoring his invitation.

"Petal?" He hadn't moved from the bed, though I could see from the way he held himself that he wanted to. To jump in again. To put me first again, like always. That was a good thing until it wasn't, and I suddenly had to know.

The carpet was soft under my bare feet, and I stopped pacing and faced him. "Why did you do it anonymously?"

He looked confused for a second, and then his eyes widened. I'd hoped there was an explanation, that he'd meant to tell me or some communication had been lost, but he had the unmistakable look of someone who was caught.

"Because instead of telling me what you were thinking of doing, you went through Ellie to donate thirty thousand dollars to the program I run, so I seemed like a stronger leader to the board." If there was one upside to this turn of events, it was that I was getting mad all over again, which left my anxiety about the little plastic stick in my bathroom to take a back seat. "Do you realize how that looks?"

"I . . . yeah. I guess I do. I just wanted to help, and if I went through you, you wouldn't accept it."

"Of course I wouldn't," I hissed. "The man I'm sleeping with gives money to push programs he believes in. How is that different from what Kendra did?"

His body language tensed, but he remained seated, letting me hold the dominant position. "It isn't the same. I gave the money to save the programs, not cut them."

"You gave the money to save me, Cord. I know you care about OurCode, but you gave the money to save me."

"I—"

"No." I cut my hand through the air. "I don't need saving. I don't need a protector. I don't want that. And then to go behind my back?"

Cord didn't respond, but he didn't look away. His hands were pressed firmly against the bed, clutching the edge of the duvet. When he spoke, it was through gritted teeth. "I'm sorry I went behind your back, but I didn't see another way to s—"

"I don't need saving. I don't know how to make that any clearer to you."

Cord was on his feet in a flash, his body close to mine and his features set in a way I hadn't seen before. "I was going to say *support* you." He didn't touch me, but our bodies were inches apart. "I was trying to support you." He threw his hands in the air, taking a step back. He wasn't yelling, exactly, but his voice had hardened and felt like it filled the room. "And you know what? If I was trying to save you, then so be it. What is so fucking wrong with me trying to save your job, a job you love, when I have the means and access to do it? What is so fucking wrong with me trying to take care of you sometimes?" Now he was the one pacing, brushing his hand across his hairline like he used to, brushing away hair that was already in place. "I want to adore you, okay? That's my big secret that's no fucking secret. I want you to let me love you and you just fucking won't, and I don't know what to do with that."

I felt the shakiness in my voice before I opened my mouth, so I stood resolute and silent. I wasn't scared of Cord, despite the outburst. I was almost proud to see him standing up and pushing back. But in another way, I saw how everything could go wrong, and I looked down at my wrist. I pulled in a deep breath. "I told Ellie to return the money."

"What?"

"Not like this." I shook my head. "We can't take it like this. Do you know how she looked at me when she connected the dots? Take it back."

"No."

"I'm not asking."

Cord's definitive, loud "Not happening" bounced off the walls, and a moment later there was a knock at the door.

"Aunt P, I just got home. You okay?" Tye's voice was tight and worried, and I schooled my expression before responding, hoping the calm came through in my voice.

"We're fine, bug. I'll be out soon." I stepped closer to Cord, lowering my voice. "You don't have a choice."

Cord returned to his pacing. "What else is new?" His tone was sarcastic. He'd never been sarcastic with me—not like that. And I saw from his posture, heard it in his voice that he didn't understand what I was saying, and maybe that was all the sign I needed.

"You should leave," I said,

"We don't have the test result yet." His voice sounded on edge, and he glanced toward the bathroom door. He could have taken three steps and looked himself, but he remained planted where he was. "Even if you're mad, I'm not leaving you to deal with that alone."

I brushed past him and looked down at the test without pausing. One line. I barely took time to collect my reaction. "It's negative."

His features softened, and he stepped toward me. Or he started to.

"You should go. Tye is home."

He looked at the test in my hand and then up at my face. "Do you want to talk about this?"

"Are you going to take the money back?"

He straightened. "No. And I will not apologize for helping the woman I love."

He'd said "love" twice. We weren't on the beach, and there was no alcohol in sight. We both had clear heads, but the words hit me the same way. They made me not trust myself, because I *wanted* to hear him say it again. Those words from Cord made me want to reconsider my stance on men who save the day. And that was exactly why they were dangerous. "Then leave." I tossed the test in the trash and crossed the room to open my door.

"Fine." He grabbed his phone from where he'd dropped it on my bed and shoved it in his pocket. "I give up. I can't play this game with you anymore. It has to be a secret, it has to be casual, it has to be one-sided but not too one-sided. I have to be in love with you without showing any care for you. Call me when you figure out what the hell you want." He stormed through the door and down the hall, and I heard him say a quick goodbye to Tye, his harsh voice softening with them before the front door closed with a definitive click.

CHAPTER 43

Cord

UNCHARACTERISTICALLY, I WAS TWO BEERS IN WHEN Wes arrived at my place. Even more out of character, I was out back sitting in the hot tub alone with the water swirling around me. "Hey," I said with a nod.

He motioned to my two empty bottles and raised his eyebrows. "Another?"

I nodded. I rarely liked the numb feeling from alcohol, but the beer in concert with the hot water was working for me.

"Didn't know this was on the agenda. I didn't bring my suit," he said, motioning to the water. Wes set a bottle on the wood surface of the shelf near me along with a bottle of water and took the seat on the other side of the table, tipping his own beer to his lips.

"You want to borrow one? You can come in naked, but you should know my neighbor Lou is observant and the fence isn't that tall."

Wes climbed to the side, sitting on the edge with his legs dangling in, jeans rolled up. Like normal, we sat in comfortable silence. I pointed the bottom of my bottle at his left hand, where his ring caught the light. "How long did it take you to get used to wearing that?"

"Dunno. It actually feels weird when I don't have it on now."

"Guess you get used to things." I'd been spending most of my time with Pearl and Tye, and he'd been busy with teaching and Britta, so we hadn't hung out since the con had ended.

"How's Pearl?" He knew. He had to know something was wrong, but he asked anyway. I simultaneously loved and was annoyed by the question.

"Fine." I took another pull from the bottle, stretching out in the water. "Probably."

"I thought things were going well. What happened?"

"One minute we were fine, then she didn't want me around her. She kicked me out of her apartment and hasn't responded to any messages since."

"That doesn't sound like Pearl. Did you do something?"

"I don't think I did anything wrong. She . . ." I hadn't told anyone and questioned for a minute if I was supposed to keep things private, but damnit, he was my best friend and she wasn't talking to me, so I wasn't sure where my worry about loyalty came from. "She was worried she might be pregnant."

"Oh, shit," Wes said, setting his bottle aside and kicking water at me. "You knocked her up? Of course she was pissed. You weren't using protection?"

I narrowed my eyes at him, not sure why the phrasing bothered me. "Yes, we did. Well, except for a few times." I felt defensive for her, like he was impugning her honor or responsibility or something, even though he was getting on my case. "She's not, though. Test was negative."

Wes shook his head but bit back whatever smart-ass thing he was going to say. "So, if she wasn't pregnant, why did she kick you out?"

"It's complicated. I told her I'd support her no matter what." I took a swig from my bottle. "I would have, financially, but I would have gone with whatever she wanted to do and stayed by her side." I would have held her hand and rubbed her back, no matter the waiting room. Maybe that was why her kicking me out, shutting me out, hurt so much.

"Well, what else could you do? Who knows what to say in that situation?"

I shrugged. "Apparently not me."

We let the silence surround us again, and behind Wes, I watched Lou settle at her patio table with friends. She waved but thankfully was too busy for a lecture. I battled with telling Wes the other part, about the money. Pearl had been so worried about Kevin and the board and being replaced, and with the shortfall taken care of, she could keep doing the work she cared about. I'd thought I was doing a good thing. That's why I'd said what I'd said, but it had just kept making her more and more mad. "And I donated money to OurCode."

"Back up. Why is she mad you donated money to her organization?"

I could see her face clearly from the other night when she'd morphed from anxious and worried to furious. She'd stood straighter. The softness in her face had disappeared, and she'd looked like she didn't even know me. "They were still short on reaching some goals and needed a certain amount to save a program she was excited about. I didn't want the board to see her in a negative light, so I donated the difference anonymously."

"I don't get why she'd be mad about that." Wes leaned forward on his knees. "What was the shortfall? A few thousand?"

I sipped my beer, the taste unmemorable. "Thirty," I said under my breath.

"Thirty grand?"

"I know," I said, sinking deeper into the water and wondering how long I could stay like that, with the water at eye level. "But I figured if I could intervene anonymously, she wouldn't know it was me and the board wouldn't have a reason to question her leadership. She's so good. She just got dealt a raw deal with the way the last director left. I couldn't donate that much anonymously online, so I went through her number two."

Wes nodded, contemplating the bubbling surface of the water. "But she found out and didn't see it that way?"

"Aren't we supposed to step up to help the people we love? Isn't that part of being in a relationship? It's not like I'm going to use that donation as leverage or something."

"Does she know that?" Wes must have read my face, because he held up his hand before I could speak again. "I mean, does she think someone would?"

"I'm not her exes. Shouldn't she know that?" I took a long pull from the bottle, realizing too late it was over half-empty already.

He shrugged. "I don't know. Exes can do a number on you." He tapped his bottle to mine. "You still can't wear puka shell necklaces," he said with a smirk.

I didn't want to be pulled from my dismal mood, but I still laughed. "Fuck off," I said, putting the beer bottle to the side, appreciating the temporary levity.

Wes spoke up. "Did you try just apologizing? I mean,

sometimes I have no idea what I've done to make Britt mad or I think she's being unreasonable, but I still apologize. It's just easier, you know?"

I smirked, despite my mood. "You're so pussy whipped."

"Damn straight." He smiled, wearing the jab like a badge of honor. "And in the end, I usually understand better why she was mad in the first place."

"I tried to apologize. I left voicemails and texted saying I was sorry. She wants me to take the money back and I don't want to, but I offered to talk about it. I even sent her flowers. Nothing." A tinge of embarrassment worked its way into my mind over how long I'd spent deciding on the right flowers to send, lingering alone in my bed, clicking through the florist's website. It felt pathetic to be this uncertain, and I didn't like it. Besides feeling empty and embarrassed, I was angry she could ignore me so easily. It made the departure from my keep-it-casual approach feel like a mistake.

"Shit," Wes said, tipping his bottle to his lips. "Talk to the kid at all?"

I nodded. "Tye texted me a few times, mostly to ask about school or talk about games. They're a good kid, you know? It's been fun hanging out with them."

"You kinda had a little family with them both, huh?"

I didn't respond, but I didn't need to. I was sure he saw it on my face. I had thought of it that way—a little family, even though Pearl and I were only dating and barely even dating, and Tye wasn't her kid. It still felt real. It felt right. The memory of her words telling me to leave stung like she'd just said them, and I tipped the bottle up, drinking the rest all at once because she didn't want me to be part of her family.

"Do you want me to ask Britta to check in with her?"

I shook my head. "I don't think it will do any good. Besides, if she'll talk to your wife and not me, what does that say?"

Wes shrugged again. "Maybe there's something else going on you don't know about. How's the fallout from the scandal with last director going?"

"Not great. Her number two—that's who the board is thinking of promoting—I went through her to make the donation and she'd promised anonymity, but then she walked in on us." I grabbed the beer again. "With a bag of pregnancy tests."

Wes winced. "Oh, shit."

"Yeah." I lifted the bottle again before realizing it was empty. "Anyway, Pearl said I was trying to save her and she didn't want that. But you'd do anything to save Britta, wouldn't you? What did I do wrong?"

"Hm," Wes said without expanding. "I don't know, man." He stood, leaving his bottle on the ledge. "Where's your extra suit? You're pathetic in there all alone and I don't want you to be intimidated by my naked body in the water." He set out toward the house, and I let it go unsaid that I appreciated him knowing I didn't want to be alone.

I dried my hand on a nearby towel and reached for my phone, the screen dark. I debated texting Pearl again, knowing at this point it might be fruitless at best and harassment at worst. *Fuck it.* She'll tell me to stop if she wants me to.

Cord: I'm sorry. Will you please talk to me?

Like all the messages above, row after row of only my words when I scrolled up, this text went unanswered. The beer filled my empty stomach, my head light, and I felt a little nauseated. Excellent. I opened the bottle of water and had finished most of it by the time Wes returned.

"How's work been?" Wes deftly changed the subject and sank into the water across from me, having earned a cheer from Lou and her friends when he walked shirtless across the short stretch of patio.

I'd been going through the motions all week. "The deals in Japan and Italy are all but finalized, and we're announcing a new marketing campaign next week."

He smirked. "How many conversations will you have to have with Mason about the hotness of the models?"

I laughed. "Too many."

"I don't miss that shit."

"I—" My phone buzzing on the table interrupted my retort. Pearl's name flashed on my screen with an incoming text. I fumbled, almost dropping my phone in the hot tub in my hurry to unlock it.

Pearl: I've gotten your messages. I'm sorry I didn't respond.

Cord: Can I see you?

I stared at my phone as if prolonged eye contact with the screen would make her response appear faster.

"What did she say?" Wes asked.

"Just that she got my messages." I looked up. "That's a good sign, right?"

"Has to be."

Pearl: No. I need more time to figure this out.

Cord: Okay. I can do that. Maybe next week?

The dots showing she was composing a reply bounced on my screen. I could wait a week—it would be hell to spend another week without her, but if I knew what was going on, I could make it work. I was already planning how I'd distract myself when her reply came in and my stomach dropped.

Pearl: I think it's best to wait until after the board meeting next month.

"She wants time," I said without looking up, seeking counsel from Wes.

"Time? Like to figure stuff out? How long?"

I swallowed the rising bile. "Next month."

"Why so long?"

"I don't know." I looked back at my phone. I felt the beers, the alcohol coursing through my system, and the water suddenly didn't feel hot enough.

Cord: I don't want to wait that long to talk to you.

Pearl: I'm not giving you a choice. It's not up for discussion.

I stared at my phone.

"What did she say?" Wes asked before I handed him my phone. He read quickly, his expression pulled back when he read her last line.

"That's a shitty thing to say, right? That's not just me?" I took my phone back.

"Not just you," Wes said.

Cord: That sounds a lot like you breaking up with me.

Pearl: We can't be together when my job is potentially on the line and you're on the board.

Pearl: I don't want to hurt you, but I don't trust you to not step in.

I let my phone fall the short distance to the shelf, wanting to swipe the empty bottles to the patio to stop myself from sinking my head into my hands. I slid my phone to Wes again. "What the hell?"

"Something has to be going on with her. This isn't like Pearl." Wes read through the messages again.

"That seems pretty fucking clear." My leg bounced under the table, nervous and angry energy vibrating together.

Wes nodded, his brow pinched. "Yeah, I guess it does. What are you going to say? What if you just took the donation back?"

"No," I said, picking up my phone. My palms were damp against the phone, and a flush of embarrassment ran up my neck, followed by a wave of anger. "I donated the money to save her, but I believe in what they're doing. I'm not going to take it back, and I'm tempted to tell her she can give it back when she's ready to explain to the kids why they can't be helped."

"Don't say that," he said, grabbing the phone from my hand. "You'll regret it."

He was right, but I didn't like it. I stood up, wanting to

feel more powerful than I did at that moment. "I know." I blew out a slow breath and held out my hand for my phone.

"Don't do it," Wes said, eyeing the phone.

I didn't. I also stifled the urge to write a message telling her she was ripping my damn heart out again, only this time via text message. I set my phone down. "What the hell do I do?"

"I don't know, man." Wes shook his head. "I don't know."

CHAPTER 44

Pearl

TYE FOCUSED ON MY HANDS, SLOWLY APPLYING THE dark red polish. "Will you stop fidgeting?"

"Sorry," I mumbled. "I have some things to get done tonight, though. Are you almost done?"

"Beauty takes time," Tye said, echoing my mom.

"Uh-huh." I eyed my laptop sitting a few feet away, knowing that opening it would reveal a long list of to-do items for work, plus my assignments for the online course. The course hardly seemed relevant anymore with everything that had happened. There was no way my beginner-level technical knowledge would matter now. I wanted to open it less than I wanted a root canal, and yet I wanted to stay on the trend of excellent grades in the class. It was something I could be good at. My phone buzzed next to me and my eyes shot to it immediately, hoping and dreading I would see Cord's name, but Tye still held my hand in place. I was good at school. Relationships, on the other hand . . . "We don't all have this kind of time."

Tye clucked their tongue, another mom move. "It's not like you've got somewhere to be."

"Smart-ass." They'd asked me several times over the last week about Cord, and I'd skirted it. It hadn't occurred to me until that moment that Tye might have reached out to him directly. They talked all the time. I tried to make my voice sound casual, like it was a flippant question. "Did you talk to Cord this week?"

Tye didn't look up from my nails, but I saw a very familiar raised eyebrow when they answered. "Yep."

I had no idea what Cord would have told Tye. Surely not everything; he wouldn't do that. I hoped he wouldn't do that.

"Want to know what he said about you?" Tye finished the pinky finger on my right hand before meeting my eyes.

"What? No, of course not. I was just curious if the mentoring was still going well."

Tye pursed their lips. "Yeah. Right."

Shea opened the door to my apartment and strode in, depositing her purse on the counter. With no preamble, she dropped into the chair next to me at my small table and set her palms on the surface. "What did you do?"

"What are you talking about?" I shifted in my seat, but Tye grabbed my wrist.

"Your nails are wet. Sit still."

"Yeah, sit still and start talking," Shea said.

I glared at my sister. "There's nothing to talk about."

"Aunt Pearl. I don't know what happened, but Cord hasn't been around, and he's asked me a couple times if you're okay." Tye sat back in their chair, and I saw their manipulation in the full light. "And I heard you two fighting."

"Did you paint my nails so I'd have to sit here and talk to you?"

"You're a perfectionist. You hate smudges." Tye shrugged

and smiled. The evil little observant genius. "Shea gave me the idea."

"Narc," Shea said, pushing their shoulder. "Why is Cord asking if you're okay?" she asked me.

"We just haven't seen each other in a few days," I lied, blowing on my nails.

Two faces with arched eyebrows matching my own met mine.

"We had a fight, okay? It's not anything mysterious. Tye, what did you tell Cord when he asked?"

"I told him you seemed sad, and I asked why you were mad at him," Tye said, capping the bottle of nail polish. "He didn't tell me." Tye's expression was solemn when they looked up. "I'll stop talking to him if you want me to, Aunt P."

"No, bug. It's nothing like that." I reached for Tye, but they pushed my arm gently down.

"Your nails are still wet. Don't mess them up trying to hug me or something." Tye stood, stepped around the table, and wrapped their arms around my neck. "I hope you stop being sad soon."

I pressed my lips together, meeting Shea's eyes across the table. With Tye's arms around me, voice muffled against me, it was easy to remember little Tye doing the same thing. "I'll be fine," I said gently. I met Shea's eye again, debating how much to tell her, knowing I'd tell her everything eventually. "Do you mind leaving me and Aunt Shea alone to talk for a bit?"

Tye stretched, standing to their full height—almost as tall as me now—and nodded. "Sure. I'm going to go talk to Peter." Tye gave Shea a quick side hug and disappeared into their room.

"Okay. Out with it." She walked toward the fridge, pulled out a bottle of white wine, and grabbed two glasses from my cupboard. "What's going on? You told us the test was negative. What the hell happened?"

"I don't even know where to begin," I said, pressing a palm to my forehead, careful to hold my nails out. Tye was right. I hated when one of them had a smudge—it would drive me nuts.

She handed me a glass of wine. "Take a drink, then start at the beginning."

"You know how I told you we were short a lot of money with our fundraising goals?"

"Sure. I donated a couple hundred bucks after you told me."

"Thanks," I said, surprised, with the glass paused halfway to my lips. "I didn't know you did that."

Shea shrugged. "Like I was going to not help? C'mon. It's your organization and it's Tye's thing. As far as I'm concerned, it's part of the family now. And it's a good cause, so I gave what I could."

I weighed out Shea's argument, which was a lot like Cord's. In fact, it was basically the same, but with a few extra zeroes. I dismissed the thought. Of course it wasn't the same. *This is my sister.*

"So, what happened? Cord had something to do with the shortfall?"

I held up my hands for inspection, unable to tell if they were dry or not. "No. He approached Ellie to make a donation."

"Okay. What's the problem?"

"He donated thirty thousand dollars."

Shea pressed her hand to her mouth to stop from spraying her drink of wine all over me. "Excuse me?"

"He donated thirty thousand dollars on the condition that the gift was kept anonymous." I pressed my fingers to the table. "He knew I would tell him not to donate just to make me look like a stronger director to the board, and he did it anyway."

Shea nodded and took a sip from her glass. "Okay. I wish it wasn't the middle of the night for Bri, because I'm not used to being the voice of reason."

"I don't need a voice of reason," I grumbled, dragging my fingertip along the edge of my nail to test how tacky the polish still was. Tye had added a few layers of a slow-drying topcoat, apparently.

"I think ya do." Shea angled to face me. "First, your guy has thirty grand to donate at the drop of a hat?"

"I don't know his net worth, but I'm sure it didn't bankrupt him." I pictured Cord's old jeans and the T-shirts he loved best. The most extravagant things in his place were the cat's wardrobe and her closet full of toys.

"So, a rich man who could afford it donated thirty grand to your charity to help kids and to make you look good?"

"It's more complicated than that," I insisted, but Shea held up a hand.

"I'm sure. So, a rich man who could afford it donated thirty grand to your charity to help kids and to make you look good?" she said, emphasizing each word as if I had a listening comprehension problem. "And this man is in love with you."

"He's not—"

"Pearl." Shea gave me a firm stare. "And he lied. I get it. That's a fuckup. I'll give you that. But what could be so complicated that cutting him out of your life is the most logical response?"

I let out a heavy sigh. "I forget to be careful around him, Shea. I forget to be cautious, like I've always been." I'd almost turned around five years earlier after walking out on him at the FitMi offices. I'd been a heartbeat away from walking back in and telling him I was staying, when the car pulled up. I'd been a heartbeat away from giving up on my goals again, and that uncertainty had bothered me for years. "And Ellie saw the pregnancy tests. She connected the dots. It's too close to what happened with Kendra. It's not professional."

"Didn't that man go down on you in the middle of the woods during a board retreat before breaking your back later that night in a tent twelve feet from your colleagues?"

"It was like forty feet," I mumbled, regretting spilling the details to her and Bri. It was a weak defense, but still.

"You blew past unprofessional a while ago. What's really going on? Because, sorry, sis. I don't get it yet."

On some level, she was right. The lack of professionalism was something I'd been flirting with this whole time, even if it had all been a secret until the donation. I leaned into the idea of admitting she was right, of loosening the metaphorical fist I had around this decision. "No," I said, standing, still careful to hold my hands up to avoid incidental fingernail contact. "That's the problem. I set aside my professionalism and my priorities, and that's what opened the door to this—here I am making all the same mistakes again." I pointed at my wrist and the four stars. "Family first. Do work that matters. Head before heart."

"What about the fourth one?" She pointed. "You've never told us what the fourth one means."

I dropped my hand, flinching when it smacked into the back of the chair I'd pulled out of. Glancing down at my nail, I saw the smooth red surface marred with wrinkled nail polish. "The fourth one is just one more reminder that I haven't learned my lesson well enough."

CHAPTER 45

Pearl

Six Months Earlier

"SWEET CAROLINE" BY NEIL DIAMOND WAS PLAYING low on the overhead speakers in the well-lit space, the white floor and gleaming lights above giving the impression of walking into a bare canvas. It was a far cry from the first tattoo parlor I'd visited near my parents' home in Chicago. This was new, though I was returning for the same reason as the first time. Back then, I'd had my sisters and Tye to help me choose. Now I was alone, and I didn't need help to decide what I wanted.

As I settled in the chair, waiting for the coolness of the alcohol and press of the tiny transfer, I closed my eyes and let out a slow breath and tapped the fingers of my left hand on the arm of the chair as the tattoo artist prepped my right wrist. Despite having worn the diamond only a few hours, I still noticed the lightness of my ring finger and kept replaying my last conversation with Richard.

He'd taken me out on his boat to watch the sunset and share noodles from our favorite local place, a tiny restaurant tucked away on a now pricey stretch of real estate that had escaped the gentrification that had pushed so many businesses owned by people of color to the margins. Richard had intervened. He'd helped them stay. He was a good man. It was something I reminded myself of often when I worried about the lack of butterflies and the way I always felt in control of my emotions around him.

"It's so good," I'd said, taking one last bite and enjoying the subtle movement of the boat under us as a breeze tempered the last rays of sunlight. Dating a billionaire was strange, and I'd been uncomfortable with being near so much wealth, but I didn't hate casual dinner dates on a yacht at Marina del Rey.

"The best." He'd kissed the side of my head in the way he did. These moments on the boat were nice, but those kisses always gave me pause somewhere in the back of my mind. He was a generous and kind man, but those kisses felt perfunctory, and I never knew why. "For my best."

I rolled my eyes at the cheesy line. Those weren't the people we were. No pet names, no silliness. He was a serious man who had goals and priorities that he never got distracted from. It was nice. It was safe. There'd been no drama, no dark corners and secret kisses. There'd been forms with HR and clearly defined expectations.

"Pearl," he said, holding my hand and looking into the distance. "Marry me." The words hung in the air as if waiting for a breeze to carry them out over the ocean, and I waited for my body to react. It wasn't until later that I thought back on the lack of a question mark. The ocean air hurled me back in time, and I remembered how my breath had caught in my throat when Cord had told me he loved me on the beach down the coastline from where we now floated. I remembered how, even though my mind had paused back then, my body had felt as drawn to him as my heart. A cool breeze cut through the moment, but my breath was steady and my body was waiting for instruction. "I know you'll love it." Richard let go of my hand and pulled a box from his pocket, opening it to reveal a massive diamond surrounded by smaller ones.

I met his eyes. I shouldn't have expected him to look nervous—it wasn't a setting he had. He looked calm and patient and certain, and I reminded myself that was what I wanted. Butterflies and drama led to confusion. I didn't answer, but he slid the ring on my finger, the weight of it surprising me. The glitter of the setting sun reflecting on hundreds of flawless angles was captivating.

"We'll be good together," he said, holding my hand and meeting my eyes. "My first wife didn't get it. She needed to be the center of my world, which just doesn't work with my life." He touched my chin, a soft touch, and I, again, hoped for the smallest, tiniest butterfly. "You never expect that from me. You know saving the world is more important."

"Sometimes," I said, taking in his expression. He did important things. He fought against companies polluting poor communities; he worked toward infrastructure funding in developing nations. I admired him, but as I looked down at the ring, I still felt nothing close to what I had on the beach that night with Cord beside me.

"And I know that sometimes saving you is important, too." He winked and squeezed my hand. "Saving you from that dead-end job in Chicago was the best thing I've ever done, Pearl. You're so much bigger than that work. And I know you love your family, but it's so clear you were taking on too much of their issues. Now we can travel the world and do whatever we want together."

I bristled at the implication he'd rescued me when hiring me. "Well, I still have a job and my family."

He waved a hand. "Your family will be okay without you in the country part of the year. And you don't need to work in the office anymore. You can work as my partner. I need someone by my side to come home to." He stroked my cheek, his thumb smooth but cool. "And it should be you."

The hairs on the back of my neck stood. We'd been dating a couple years—this proposal wasn't a surprise, exactly, but he'd never talked about leaving the area or me not working. I didn't like the implication that I could just wait for him. As I decided how to frame my thoughts, because Richard wasn't someone I spoke to without thinking, I caught the logo from the take-out bag and traced the curve of the lettering, the simple logo on the otherwise plain brown bag. "Why did you help this place? Like, out of all the restaurants?"

I'd never asked, but the rest of that neighborhood's businesses had closed when rents went up and had been replaced by trendy boutiques and artisanal cheese shops.

Richard laughed. "They make the best kor moo yang." He shrugged, standing to clear the food. "Didn't want to risk losing my favorite meal." He bent and kissed my head, leaving me to take the trash and uneaten food into the galley as the sun continued to set over the horizon. He called over his shoulder. "It's the same reason I was so adamant about infrastructure work in Botswana." He pointed to my ring. "Can't have the countries that mine my favorite diamonds unable to support the industry." He smiled, an easy smile, and my chest felt funny, only it wasn't butterflies: it was the full weight of how wrong this all felt to me.

THE TATTOO ARTIST waited for me to approve the placement of the star, and I nodded. "Got it." She adjusted her supplies and nodded toward my wrist. "Looks like you're adding to a set. It means something?"

I glanced at my empty ring finger and down at the stars—and the feeling of Cord's lips against them rushed back, the feel of his breath and the simultaneously insistent and gentle way his hands held me in place. I shut my eyes, knowing how close I'd been to turning back, to risking it all to be with him. I nodded to the artist. Richard had shown me that motives weren't always abundantly clear, and I knew I needed to remember that while I pushed old what-ifs from my mind. "This is to remind me to beware of white knights."

CHAPTER 46

Cord

Present Day

I SCROLLED UP THROUGH MY TEXT THREAD WITH Pearl. It wasn't healthy and I knew I should just delete it, but I read the jokes and sexy exchanges and the simple thumbs-up emoji she'd send when I let her know I was getting close to her place. It felt like all I had left. A notification popped up across the screen.

TyeForTheWin: Best grade in the class!

They sent a photo of an online grading system where an A and effusive praise from the teacher were next to the write-up of the project they'd done with Peter on the FitMi website.

Cord.Matthews: Amazing! You two did great work. What's next?

TyeForTheWin: I think I'm ready to take your job.

Cord.Matthews: All yours.

TyeForTheWin: I think I'll keep you on with the company. Maybe in the mailroom. Are you qualified for that?

Cord.Matthews: So funny. Congrats on the A. Anything else going on?

TyeForTheWin: Maybe you should say you're sorry to Aunt Pearl.

I glanced at the ceiling, wondering how I'd let all of this get so out of hand. Tye wasn't supposed to be worried about me and Pearl. I was pretty certain the training I attended would have directed me that Tye shouldn't know anything about anyone I was seeing.

Cord.Matthews: Don't worry about us. You've got a company to run now.

Cord.Matthews: Are we still on for Tuesday? Want to prepare for that summer coding camp application?

Tye was composing a message for a minute but then just sent the thumbs-up emoji, and I set my phone down. The Post-it pad next to my laptop was mostly for doodling and the odd note I had to leave myself during calls, but I tapped the edges with a nearby pen. Peach let out a loud meow from my feet and pulled me from my thoughts of how else I could say I was sorry. Her green sweater had little superheroes on it, and across her back it read PUSSY POWER. I hadn't been paying attention when I put her in it—that one had been a Britta purchase.

"Hey, girl," I said, reaching down to scratch behind her ears. "Where were you hiding?"

That I wished she could respond was enough justification that I was going stir-crazy. I gave Peach another few strokes, because it wasn't her fault. I was in a sour mood, and her wrinkled head felt good under my fingers. "I'm not making a mistake, am I?"

Peach tilted her head, nudged my hand with it as if to say, *Of course you are, dumbass, now focus on me until I'm done with you.*

My phone flashed with an incoming call from Mason, and I reluctantly tapped the accept button.

"Matthews!" Mason spoke over the background noise that sounded like a bar. "What are you doing tonight?" There was rustling, and then the background noise lessened. "You're at home with your cat, aren't you? Come out with me!"

I strode to the sliding glass door leading out to my backyard. "Why do you assume I'm home alone?"

"I could detail all the reasons, like that you've been moody and sad lately, and tell you that Britta has a big mouth and I know you and Pearl are splitsville, or you could just get down here and have some fun."

I followed the line of fencing surrounding my sad patch of weeds posing as a garden. "Nah. I'm good."

"Yeah. Right." He rattled off an address close to my place. "Get here in twenty. Your cat will be fine."

I groaned and looked back to Peach, who rubbed her head against my hand again. I didn't feel like going out, but he was right—I had been in a bad mood all week. I had an email waiting from Ellie asking whether, given the circumstances, I still wanted to make the donation. I'd left it sitting at the top of my inbox for four days. I let my gaze wander to the doghouse before turning back toward my living room.

When I left Pearl's, I'd been certain I was right to not take it back. "I'm still certain," I said to Peach, who eyed me skeptically and then jumped to the other end of the couch, circling twice before settling into a nap.

I wanted the programs to continue and I wanted Our-Code to succeed. And, yeah, I wanted to be the one to save the day for Pearl. I paced my living room, Peach ignoring my cognitive dissonance in favor of her preferred couch cushion. I understood the conflict of interest, but I hadn't put any stipulations on the money other than anonymity, and I thought Pearl was blowing it out of proportion. The thing she seemed most mad about was me wanting to do it for her. I just didn't get what her issue was with that part.

Still, the text thread with nothing from her in the last several days made my chest feel tight. It made me feel like I needed to act, and I vowed to at the very least put Pearl and the other women I'd dated behind me and make that yard my own. I could do that, and I could do more.

I retrieved my phone from the couch and replied to Mason. He was right. I needed to get out of the house.

Cord: I'll join you next weekend. I need to do a few things.

I snatched my laptop from its place on the coffee table and opened a new email. Taking some action had to be better than doing nothing.

CHAPTER 47

Pearl

MARA KNOCKED ON MY DOOR. "KEVIN IS HERE. YOU ready?" She cocked an eyebrow.

I nodded and stood, sliding my palms down the front of my dress. "Thanks for coming down," I said, welcoming him into my office after Mara closed the door.

"Not a problem. I have a meeting down here at ten anyway. You wanted to talk about the director role?"

"Yes," I said, straightening a pen on my desk so it lined up with the one next to it. "I've given it more thought, and I think the board should lift Ellie to the director role instead of me."

Kevin sat up in his seat. "What? Why? That was never what I hoped for in asking the two of you to share leadership." He leaned forward in his seat. "I think we need both of your skill sets, and we don't want to lose you. You've done tremendous work since everything happened with Kendra."

It would have been easy to take it back and leave things there, but I pressed forward. "We could share leadership, but there's something else."

"What on earth could be in the way? We're so close to getting back on track."

I adjusted the pen again before meeting his eyes and reminding myself I valued honesty and transparency even when I really didn't want to. "I've been involved in a romantic relationship with a board member."

Kevin sat back in his seat and dragged his hand over his face, and his voice was resigned. "Who? For how long?"

"It's been a few months, and now there's been a financial donation from this board member. It's complicated, but I haven't acted in a way that keeps the organization's best interests in mind, especially with the fallout from Kendra's actions. I think I should step back as director." I thought if I said it one word at a time, barely taking a break to breathe, it wouldn't sound so bad, but the words were acrid in my mouth. The admitting I'd done wrong part—that always made my anxiety rise—but also the suggestions that I step back from a job I loved.

"This is a lot to process," Kevin said after a moment of tense silence between us. "Which board member?" he asked again.

I'd hoped he wouldn't need to know, but of course he would. "Cord Matthews." While the rest of what I'd had to say was sour on my tongue, saying his name just made me feel an ache in my chest. "He donated thirty thousand dollars to the program—our shortfall—and with that amount of money, I thought you and the board needed to know the circumstances before OurCode accepted."

"Matthews." He let out a slow breath. "Well, that makes a little more sense now," he said to himself.

"Excuse me?"

Kevin shook his head to himself and met my gaze again. "If you want to quit, I can't stop you, but I think the board needs to discuss this. And the affair isn't great, but I meant what I said. We need you."

"But the conflict of interest with the money," I started, unsure why I was having to fight this man to acknowledge the ethical screwup. I had spent a lot of my adult life trying to never be in this kind of position, but I hadn't thought it would be such a challenge to get someone else to be upset with the issue.

"Cord resigned from the board last night. He said he no longer had the time." Kevin checked his watch and grimaced. "Did he not tell you?"

I hadn't expected that. "No. We . . . haven't spoken recently."

"Well," Kevin said, sitting back in his chair and letting out another slow breath. "If the board reviews the donation with all the information, I don't think there will be a problem. I have to run, but I'll be in touch. Can you stay in the role as director for now?"

I nodded, standing to show him out. "Yes. I can." I followed Kevin to the door. This conversation had not gone like I'd thought it would, and I felt unsure about my decisions. I'd been prepared for him to make Ellie the director or even fire me immediately, though he couldn't technically do that without a board vote. A board that no longer included Cord. "He just quit?" I hadn't meant to ask it out loud, but Kevin turned to face me before opening the door.

"If I had to guess, that was to protect you, and it's better that he's off the board with this revelation. That said, yeah. He just quit." Kevin glanced at his watch again. "I'll be in touch. Keep doing what you're doing." He opened the door and motioned to the people bouncing between offices and cubicles. "I think this team doesn't need another big shake-up."

I watched him walk toward the exit, waving to Mara,

who shot me a look across the office that I knew translated to mean that she'd be in to see me soon to get details about what had just happened. I stepped back to my desk in anticipation of speaking with her, but all I kept coming back to was Cord quitting the board and Kevin's guess it was to save me.

Pearl: Cord quit the board.

Shea: And you've called him to tell him you were wrong?

Pearl: I wasn't wrong.

Shea: . . .

I dropped my head to my desk. I'd been so certain this time, certain I was doing the best thing, and now it was all up in the air and I'd walked away from Cord *again*. But from what Kevin had said, OurCode wasn't between us anymore, and all that was left was a man who loved me. A man who made me forget to be cautious but made me feel cherished. A man I loved, and from whom being apart for these past weeks had felt completely wrong. If I could have Cord and have my career, I could have it all.

Pearl: I was somewhat wrong.

Shea: It's nice to be the sister who gets to hear that from someone else for once.

Pearl: He still lied to me.

Through the glass, I saw Mara approaching, and there was a slate of meetings on my calendar the rest of the day. I cared about the lie, but it felt less significant now, and I tried to balance out the justice of sticking to my guns with the possibility of never feeling his kisses on my neck or his hands at my back ever again.

Shea: Want me to bring over Britta and nacho fixings tonight?

Pearl: And wine.

I traced a fingernail over the fourth star on my wrist, around the thin, dark outline of the shape. I had to do something.

CHAPTER 48

Cord

"IT'S COOL YOUR COMPANY IS DOING AXE THROWing for a corporate retreat." The server set down a pitcher and a stack of glasses on the table.

I spoke under my breath. "Way better idea than capture the flag."

"We're celebrating. Who knew this man would be such an animal in the boss's seat?" Mason clapped me on the back and flashed the server a wide grin. Her response of a giggle was all it took for Mason to abandon us.

I had to admit it was fun, or it would have been fun if I wasn't in a perpetual bad mood. Still, I sat back and sipped my beer and looked around for the coach, the woman who was going to show us how to hurl axes across the room and not decapitate one another.

My phone was notificationless, which I'd assumed it would be, but it was still a tiny yet not ineffectual punch to the gut to hear nothing from Pearl. I'd stepped down from the board a week earlier and hadn't heard a word from her. My normal meeting with Tye that week was uneventful, and they hadn't brought her up.

"It's not too late to add a strip club to the night's agenda,"

Mason said, sliding back into the empty spot next to me. "A friend owns one up the street and she'd get us the VIP treatment."

"I can't believe I have to say this, but no strip club at the corporate retreat," I said, taking another drink of beer and motioning to Wes.

"Well, I meant for after. Some of us are still searching for the loves of our lives." He laughed and poured himself a glass.

"You're planning to meet the love of your life at a strip club?"

Mason clinked his glass to mine. "I rule nothing out. There are so many women in this city that I'm destined to meet." He looked around, surveying the crowd. "Or meet again, like Pearl's sister."

I knew he was waiting for a reaction at his mention of Pearl, but I didn't respond, checking my phone again before shoving it in my pocket. "Well, good luck at the club. And Bri is in London."

"Ah," he said, leaning against the table. "All good. Pearl might actually murder me if I dated her sister again. Your girl is scary when she wants to be."

I bit the inside of my cheek, then took another drink.

"But she's not your girl anymore?" He raised an eyebrow, but his expression sobered. "I'm just giving you a hard time," he said, his voice more serious. "You guys still aren't back together? What happened?"

"I don't really want to talk about it," I said.

True to form, Mason ignored me. "She is scary, but she's also pretty awesome, and you're marginally awesome when you leave your cat at home. I thought you two were good together."

"Yeah, well . . . I guess not."

Mason flashed a smile at a group of women on the other side of the axe-throwing facility but returned his attention to me. "What did you do?"

"I donated thirty grand to her charity and stepped down from the board of directors so she wouldn't have to deal with a conflict of interest. Damning offenses, right?"

Mason looked into his beer thoughtfully. "I don't know what all that means, but can I give you some advice?"

"Advice you picked up at the strip club?"

Mason laughed. "Advice I got once from my dad."

"I doubt I could stop you from telling me." I knew I sounded like a dick, a dick under a storm cloud. "What's the advice?"

"He always said to speak to your partner like you're speaking to your mechanic—talk about everything on the front end or you'll pay for it later." Mason tipped his glass to his lips, this time winking at the server who brought another pitcher and more glasses.

"Okay," I said, mulling the advice in my head. I'd talked and talked to Pearl, though—she knew how I felt. I'd told her, but I'd also shown her time and time again. "Good advice, but it's not applicable here."

Mason shrugged. "I just mean, maybe these grand gestures—the money, leaving the board—maybe you'd save yourself some trouble just having a straight conversation with her instead of trying to continually prove you're the guy she needs. Just be the guy. At the very least, you'd know you shot your shot, said what you needed to say, and she didn't end up being the one." He set his glass down and waved to the coach, a tall redhead in a tight-fitting flannel shirt. "I'm just saying, if you don't tell them your brakes are acting weird when you go in for your oil change, you'll have a clean engine when you wrap yourself around a tree."

I'd only finished half my beer, but Mason's advice was making sense, so I'd officially entered the Bizarro phase of my breakup. "I understand," I said. "Thanks."

I sat back as Mason greeted the coach, and rolled his advice around in my head. It was true I had been trying to prove something to Pearl, maybe to myself, the whole time we were dating. I set my glass aside and joined the group for the coach's instructions. Pearl didn't want to be saved by anyone in her life, and she'd thought that's what I'd been trying to do. I didn't want to lose myself in her, but I couldn't seem to help falling more and more into the quicksand of loving her. Question was if I knew how to show love any other way, and if I'd even get the chance to try with her.

My phone buzzed in my pocket and I jumped, pulling it out and stepping away from the group to glance at the screen.

Dad: Long time no see 🤡

I smiled at the unexpected text from my dad. Emojis and punctuation were always kind of a crapshoot in terms of what he'd pick. That, or he was just roasting me via text.

Cord: Sorry, work has been busy. What's up?

Dad: Hoping you'll be my best man again.

Dad: And I know you think I'm rushing in and maybe I am but I'm happy.

Cord: You are happy, though? You're sure she loves you for the real you?

Dad: I decided a long time ago to just be with the person who makes me happy. Can't predict the future, but yes, she does.

I'd spent such a long time trying to not be my dad, trying to avoid falling into the traps he had, that I hadn't stopped to look at how happy he was with each of them at some point. Maybe there was a middle ground.

Cord: I'll be your best man again. I'll have my tux ready.

Dad: Bring a date this time. I need at least one wedding photo where you're not standing alone.

Dad: 🤡

He was roasting me. I was about to flip the phone over when a notification pinged.

Britta: I just talked to Shea. What are you doing at four tomorrow?

CHAPTER 49

Pearl

I WRAPPED MY ARMS AROUND BRI'S NECK. I DIDN'T realize how much I'd missed having her close. "It's so good to have you back!"

Tye strolled in behind her. "She's been hugging me nonstop since she got off the plane. I'm glad for the break."

"You're so full of it," Shea said, shoving Tye's shoulder lightly and pulling Bri from me into her own hug. "Your kid is full of it," she said into my sister's shoulder.

"I know. They take after their youngest aunt." Bri tugged Shea to her side anyway, and the Harris sisters were back in the same country. "So, here we are again," she said, motioning around the tattoo parlor.

I thought back to ten years earlier, when they'd all been with me for the first tattoo. Tye, then five, had picked the stars. "We should call Granny," Tye said, pulling out their phone. We'd never let Tye forget the reaction my mom had had when, at five, they'd asked about the secret ass tattoo Shea had convinced them their granny was hiding. It was now a running family joke, and Mom threatened all the time to actually get one and make us all come along.

"I want to hear all about London," I said to Bri, noticing how good she looked—not different but relaxed.

"When I'm not jet-lagged, I'll tell you everything."

Tye was staring at their phone, and Shea leaned in close. "Everything? Because you mentioned a certain British gentleman a few times, and I want those details."

"Shush," Bri said, and I noticed the way the corners of her eyes crinkled even as her face grew a little redder. "Not in front of Tye." Bri turned her attention to me. "Anyway, we're here for this one," she said, motioning to me. "I'm having trouble keeping up. What's this star for? Keeping Cord? Forgetting Cord?"

I opened my mouth to respond, but Bri's eyes widened, and behind her, Tye looked up from their phone and smiled.

"I'd like to know that, too."

I whipped around to find him standing behind me, just inside the door with his hands in the pockets of his jeans. Cord wore a T-shirt, one about the *Oregon Trail* game, and he looked like he had the day I met him. Only this time, I knew what was behind the silly shirt and the casual attire.

"What are you doing here?"

"The Harris grapevine."

I glanced over my shoulder at Shea, who was sharing an unsubtle high five with Tye.

Cord pulled my attention back from my traitorous family members. "Can we talk for a minute?"

I motioned to the woman at the reception desk that I was stepping outside and joined Cord on the sidewalk just as a cloud passed in front of the sun, casting us in a temporary shadow. "What did they tell you?"

"Just that you were going to be here, and if I wanted to

talk to you, this was a time to do it." He brushed his hair off his forehead.

"And you wanted to talk to me?"

"There's never been a time I didn't." His eyes met mine, the same intense color that I'd been mesmerized by since the first day I met him. "There's actually a lot I want to say, and I want to just say it all at once. Is that okay?"

I nodded.

"I'm sorry I went behind your back about the money. I shouldn't have done that, and if you need to turn it down, I understand, but I hope you don't."

"You left the board."

He glanced down at the sidewalk. "Yeah, and I should have talked to you about that, too." When he looked up, his eyes meeting mine, a tightness in my chest I hadn't known I'd been feeling relaxed. "You asked me what I wanted. I told you I don't want casual. I told you I'm in love with you. I told you I'll wait. It's all true. But I let you off the hook for saying it back, and that's what I really want. It's what I deserve, and you deserve to trust yourself enough to say those things if you feel them."

A couple arguing about walking versus taking an Uber strolled past us, and Cord stepped closer to me, letting them pass, the warmth of his body noticeable even in the sunshine. "I've been trying to show you I'm the guy for you to make sure you know you're the woman for me. I think somewhere along the way I lost track of needing us both to figure out how to be together."

I searched his face, and I kept coming back to this relaxed feeling in my chest, like I was breathing easier with him nearby.

"That's a lot, and I'm paraphrasing something Mason, of

all people, said, but . . ." He touched his fingertips to the back of my hand. "When I heard you'd be here, there wasn't anywhere else I wanted to be. So, I don't know what this tattoo is for, but if it's reminding you to forget me, can we talk about it first?"

I rotated my hand to catch his fingers and stepped closer. The clouds shifted, and I watched his skin brighten in the sunlight as more people passed us by. It was one of those magical romantic moments in the city, until the bump against the glass behind me startled me and I looked over my shoulder to see Shea, Bri, and Tye pressed to the window.

Cord chuckled. "Quite the audience we have."

"Always," I mumbled, ignoring my nosy family and turning to him again. "And the tattoo isn't to remind me to forget you."

"No?" He held up my wrist, sliding the pad of his thumb over the stars like he had on the beach, like he had so many times that it felt like an extension of my code that he was the one touching me.

"No." I followed his movements with my eyes. "You've made a lot of big gestures. I wanted to make one, too. I thought it was time."

"Are you getting my face across your lower back?"

I laughed, and his thumb continued the slow path back and forth across my wrist. "Just a long extension cord up my spine," I said.

"That sounds like a Shea suggestion." He gave my wrist one last stroke and let it fall gently back to my side as we laughed.

"I got this to remind me what matters," I said, pointing at the original stars. "It's been my code. The thing is, I think some of my code is wrong." I pointed to the third star. "I think if I was smart, I'd want my head and my heart to work together."

"Yeah?" His expression was hopeful but guarded, which I deserved.

"But the rest of my code was solid. Do work that matters. Do you know how much working with you has meant to Tye?" I motioned over my shoulder, where I knew my family practically had their noses pressed to the glass. "And family first is a given, but the thing is . . ." I let my wrist fall so my palm settled over his heart. "I don't want casual. The opposite of casual is what I want. I want you as part of my family."

His expression shifted, his mouth moving into a wide grin. "You do?"

"Yeah, as long as you stop trying to swoop in to save me," I said, stepping in to him, enjoying the feel of his hand at my waist.

"I can do that." His breath mingled with mine. "Pearl . . ." He lowered his chin, our mouths close together, but I interrupted him.

"This tattoo will be to remind me how this feels and to never settle for anything less than this, to never be with someone unless I feel like I do when I'm with you. And I know now I can have my goals *and* you. I think we can stand by each other while we both do great things. I didn't trust myself to have it all before. But I do now. I wanted to get it before I told you that." I stroked my fingers along his cheek.

"I love you." We said it at the same time, both smiling, a light between us that was only partially the sun reflecting off the tattoo parlor's front window.

"Hey," I said. "It was my turn to say it back."

"Sorry." His hand tightened at my waist. "Can I kiss you now?"

I lifted onto my toes to press our lips together. When our lips met, his were the perfect mix of soft and unyielding, and I heard a cheer from behind the glass, reminding me we had an audience.

"I need to get in there," I said, not stepping away from him. "Do you want to stay?"

"Yeah." Cord nodded and kissed me again, taking my hand when we finally pulled apart. "I'm not going anywhere." I tugged him toward the entrance, and his lips brushed near my ear when he held the door for me. "You think they have any last-minute openings?"

"You're getting a tattoo, too?" Tye blurted out when we stepped inside.

"I've been thinking about my own code," he said, resting a hand on my lower back. "Got any design ideas for me?"

Tye laughed and scrolled on their phone. "When it comes to style, you can use all the help you can get."

"Well," Bri said, turning from Tye and Cord. "I guess the new star *is* to keep him."

"If only someone had suggested that months ago," Shea interjected, pressing a manicured finger to her chin. "Someone who would sure love to hear how right she was."

I rolled my eyes at her teasing but let my gaze drag over her shoulder, taking in Cord's laugh as Tye pointed something out on their phone. "You were right," I reassured my sister. "And no, the new star isn't to keep him."

In the last few days, I couldn't stop thinking about going back to the beach in San Diego and looking up at the night sky with Cord. Back then, I'd still felt like magic was possible, like on some level it would work out. "It's to remind me to look up at the sky. That sometimes there are possibilities I haven't imagined."

They called me back for my appointment, and I left Cord sitting with Tye and my sisters, scrolling through tattoo suggestions like nothing had changed.

"You ready?" The artist greeted me and motioned to the seat.

"Yep," I said, glancing again at my people. "Completely."

EPILOGUE

Three Years Later

Shea: Send a selfie. Show me the dress.

Pearl: I'm not taking a selfie.

Shea: Bangable?

Cord spoke over my shoulder, handing me a glass of champagne. "Definitely bangable." His breath brushed my ear, and I grinned.

Pearl: I'll send you a photo later.

"How is Shea enjoying New York?"

I sipped from the glass of champagne and scanned the banquet hall. After three years, it was as if OurCode had never been touched by scandal. We'd sold out of tickets faster than ever before and were heading into a second year of exceeding our fundraising goals. "She said she met a hot guy at the Rockefeller Center Christmas tree lighting on Wednesday, but she's annoyed she had to miss this for work."

"I promised I'd record it for her," he said. "Like the excellent brother-in-law I will be."

"We're not engaged," I said, pushing back his shoulder, then brushing the sleeve of his tux. I still liked his hoodies best, but he looked so good in a tux.

"That reminds me. Will you marry me?"

"Not yet," I said with a laugh.

"Proposing again?" Bri joined us, wearing a pink gown that matched Tye's bow tie.

"She turned me down again." Cord handed Bri his glass. "I'm wearing her down, though."

I watched him walk back to the bar, stopping to chat with Kevin and another board member who'd just arrived.

Bri followed my gaze. "When are you going to put that man out of his misery? He asks you like once a week."

"Twice a week now," I said, waving to Ellie. In the end, the board kept me on as director and promoted Ellie to a corporate liaison position we created. She was perfect for it and had brought in more collaborators than we could keep up with. "It's almost like a running joke with us now, but soon. Tye ready?"

"That child was born ready." Bri nudged my shoulder as the lights flashed.

"That's my cue," I said, walking toward the stage. "I'll see you after the presentation." It was easier to step up to the microphone now versus that first time, but I still looked out into the crowd for Cord as I spoke. He was always there looking back, right until my last portion, where I introduced our student speaker for the night.

"Thank you. Wow! There's a lot of people here." Tye straightened their bow tie and brushed their shoulder. "It's a good thing I look so great in formal wear." The room erupted in laughter, and Tye grinned. "I'm Tye Harris, I'm a senior, and I've been in OurCode since my first year of high school. Other than looking good onstage . . ." Tye struck a model pose with a steely gaze into the distance and earned another laugh. They were a natural out there, and I was ready to hand them the entire script.

"Other than looking good onstage, I'm supposed to use my time up here to tell you what I got out of participating in the OurCode program. But my teachers tell me I follow directions *creatively*, so instead, I'm going to talk about family.

"This is my mom," Tye said, pointing to a photo on the screen of an eighteen-year-old Bri holding Tye in a pumpkin Halloween costume next to a photo of the two of them at her college graduation. "She's always been my rock, and she's incredible. She had me at sixteen and is a single mom, but we were never alone. I always had my aunts and my grandparents." Tye flipped through a few photos of the family, and I glanced at our family table, where, true to his word, Cord held his phone up, catching the presentation for Shea, and cut his gaze to me with a wink.

Tye advanced the slides to a photo of them with my parents at a Pride event where they sported shirts that read FREE GRANDMA HUGS and FREE GRANDPA HUGS. "My grandad helped me with my tie tonight, and my aunt helped me get this cat eye perfect. They've always seen the best in me and made sure I saw it in myself." My mom was openly bawling, and Daddy put an arm around her shoulder.

"So, three years ago when my first OurCode mentor moved and I was assigned a new one, I wasn't stressed. I already had a team behind me. What difference could a stranger make?"

The photo switched to one I'd snapped of Cord and Tye

hunched over a laptop together in the OurCode lounge, trying to solve some coding problem. "That's my mentor, Cord. I didn't think I needed anyone else in my corner, but I was wrong." The photos of the two of them shifted on the screen, and I watched Cord smile and then laugh at the photos. "He did more than help me understand coding. This is when I talked him into co-coaching my school's robotics team, and that's me defeating him in *Knights of Armageddon* for the fiftieth time." Tye paused for a short laugh before continuing. "This man needs help on that front.

"There are lots of moments without photos, though. Like when he helped me look for tech internships and then prepare for the interviews, or when he helped me with the app design project that helped me get early admission and a full scholarship to Thurmond University to study computer science." The hall erupted in applause, and Tye beamed from the stage. "And when he agreed to accompany the robotics team to a competition at Disneyland in May. He doesn't know about that one yet, so everyone pressure him to say yes."

Tye soaked up another bout of laughter from the crowd. "And he's not my family by blood, but he's my family in all the ways that count. Along with the rest of my family, he's helped me see what my future could be and envision my career not as a hypothetical but as a reality I can control. He's always seen the best in me and made sure I saw the best in myself."

The photo switched to Cord and Tye in matching OurCode hoodies at an event we'd held in the fall, and I watched Cord swipe a hand at his face. "That's what this organization does. It gives kids like me more people to have in our corner. A mentor to turn to, staff to advocate for us and teach us." The photo changed to Tye and several other kids at the kickoff for Bea's Technicolor program. "And a program that makes sure we see all the options we have in front of us and that they're within our reach." Tye held on to the podium and scanned the crowd.

"If you're a volunteer, I hope you'll keep giving your time and your talent to OurCode, because every kid deserves to picture themselves on this stage with a thousand things to look forward to and an entire family behind them, making sure the path is as clear as possible. And, if you get a chance, remind Cord how much he loves me and how great Anaheim will be. Thank you."

Tye stepped back as the audience rose to their feet, no one cheering as loudly as the Harris table, with Cord in the middle. I was pretty sure he'd be on that trip to California.

One Month Later

"Five! Four! Three!"

Cord grabbed me by the waist, pulling me flush against him. "Two," he said, lips a breath away from my own.

"One," I said in return, the smile spreading across my face just before his lips met mine. The TV playing the countdown blared, the music and festivities flashing in quick bursts between shots of the crowd.

"Happy New Year, Petal," Cord said when we pulled apart, his arms still wrapped around me. His hair was mussed, his smile crooked after the champagne.

I slid my fingers through his hair and enjoyed the press of his body as we swayed to a slow song that wasn't playing. After I'd given in to how much I felt for Cord, things were perfect. He'd been asking me to marry him since the month after we moved in together, and I kept telling him I wanted to wait. I wanted to make sure I was in the right headspace to be a great partner, and I wanted to make sure we were really good at communicating what we wanted. And we really were. "Happy New Year."

He was solid, warm, and wrapped around me in a way I knew wasn't temporary. "Do you wish we'd gone out?"

I shook my head. We stayed like that for a minute or hours, eyes meeting, lips brushing, bodies entwined. We'd originally planned to go out, but something about staying in, just him and me, felt better. It was perfect. "Nope. Not even a little."

"If we were out, I couldn't do this," he said, dropping his lips to my neck.

"Well," I murmured. "You could. Kissing my neck isn't so salacious."

"No?" He squeezed my ass, pulling me against his growing erection. "How about this?"

The friction left me tipping my head back. "Wouldn't get us arrested."

"True." His hand migrated, fingertips dancing slowly up my side to cup my breast through the thin material. We'd spent the evening in pajama bottoms and T-shirts, completely casual, but it felt like my sexiest outfit. He rolled a pert nipple between his thumb and forefinger. "Would this?"

"Probably not on New Year's Eve," I said on shortened breaths. I rolled my hips against him, eager for the friction, eager for more.

"You're right. It's a lenient holiday," he said, pinching my nipple again as he nibbled on my earlobe.

I ground against his thigh, which had worked its way between my legs. "Why are you so invested in what we could get away with in public?"

"I want to keep it exciting for you."

I pulled back, taking his hands and leading him to our bedroom. "I'm excited."

"I can tell." He cradled my face and kissed me again, this time deepening it, leaving him gasping for a breath in the doorway of our bedroom. "I love you."

"I love you, too." I pulled the tank top over my head and stepped back, pulling him onto the bed, his body settling against me, hands already at the waistband of my sleep pants and inching them down. Cord's lips at my neck were familiar—familiar and exciting as the slow and maddening way he sometimes teased me, brushing his fingers over my hip bones until I was ready to scream. "Any New Year's resolutions?" I squirmed, trying to maneuver his hand where I wanted it as he trailed his lips down my body.

He avoided my shifting, moving his hand around to grip my ass, rubbing in small circles as he released one of my nipples from between his lips. "Only to do this as much as possible."

"That's a good resolution," I said, punctuating it with a moan as he pushed down my pants and underwear before his fingers drifted between my legs and slipped between my wet folds. "I want more."

"Don't I get to know your resolution?" He smiled, a devilish expression, pausing his movements.

"I'll tell you after you make love to me." I pushed down his pants as far as I could, stroking him. For a moment, though, he just looked at me with a wide grin. He always got that kind of dopey expression when I said "make love"—when I said "love," period—like he couldn't quite believe it.

We liked to experiment, try new positions and angles, but that night, he settled over me and moved in and out of me slowly, our breaths mingling as his body pressed into mine. Our eyes locked as the sensations built—I was full, the friction delicious—his thumbs stroking me perfectly, and his eyes told me everything I needed to know about trust and safety and how much this was right. Our tension built for what felt like hours, him alternating between shallow and deep thrusts, our kisses moving from soft to bruising and back. When we finally crescendoed, we collapsed together, chests heaving. "Happy New Year," he panted.

"Happy New Year." I curled into him, resting my head and hand on his chest, one leg thrown over his.

Cord's breaths tickled my ear. "So, what's your resolution?"

I bit my bottom lip and traced a heart on his chest with my fingertip. "To say yes."

He stiffened under me, maneuvering so our eyes met. "Seriously?"

"I told you not until this year," I said, stroking my fingers through his tousled hair. "I don't want to wait any longer. Tye was right. You're family in every way that matters. Let's make it official."

Cord kissed me, our lips and tongues sliding together. When we pulled apart, he brought my left hand to his lips. "Really?"

I nodded.

He kissed the fourth finger on my left hand and then the stars on my wrist before climbing out of bed and pulling on his sleep pants and tossing me one of his hoodies.

I pulled it over my head. "Where are we going?"

"C'mon," he said, tugging me out of the bedroom and downstairs, putting shoes on. I slid into fur-lined Crocs that were hideous but perfect for quick moments outside in the winter. In our hastily bundled state, he tugged my hand and we stepped into the backyard.

"It's freezing," I said, bouncing on my feet.

"I know," he said, dropping to one knee. "But this is my favorite place." Behind him, the wide lawn was covered in snow. We'd worked together to replant grass after he tore out his garden and trashed the old doghouse. The hot tub was drained for winter but remained. He'd wanted to get rid of it initially but decided it might be worth keeping after a few adventurous evenings when we were thankful for the barrier shielding us from his neighbor Lou. "It's my favorite place to look up at the stars, but only because I get to look up with you." Behind him were the posts he'd installed to hold the two-person hammock. It was the perfect fit for the two of us. "And it took me a while to figure out that what made this space perfect was the right woman to share it with."

Cord kissed my fingers, the softness of his kiss lingering when he asked, "Will you watch the stars with me until we're no longer able to make it into that hammock?"

"No," I said, squeezing his hand, the tears threatening to freeze against my cheek. "We'll keep watching them long after that." I bit my lip and nodded. "Of course I'll marry you. Yes! I can't imagine a better way to spend forever."

ACKNOWLEDGMENTS

Thank you to every person who sees the Goliath-sized obstacles ahead, those who stare injustice in the face and say no. Thank you to those who show up to what can feel like a losing battle, because the fight always matters.

```
While (true) {
I.love(you) :
}
```

Translation: I love you infinitely forever. Thank you always to my husband and tiny (but no longer so tiny) human. You're my home, my heart, and my happiness.

My heart is a stack,
and you make it overflow.

There's a photo of me as a baby on my dad's lap playing on a computer keyboard in the early 1980s. Thank you to my parents, who always showed me how technology could keep me connected to the people I love and the world I hadn't seen yet. Thank you to Jay, Amanda, Mike, Melissa, Bruce, Jean, Barb, Tim, Allison, Kaitlin, Crystal, the absolute best two nephews and niece, and the army of aunts, uncles, and cousins.

The Big O notation describes the performance or complexity of an algorithm. (In romance, it of course means something else!)

Thank you to my agent, Sharon Pelletier, who is a consummate guide through the complexity algorithm that is bringing a book to life. Thank you for your candor, humor, care, and general amazingness. Thank you also to Lauren Abramo, Andrew Dugan, Nataly Gruender, and Gracie Freeman Lifschutz at Dystel, Goderich & Bourret and Kristina Moore at UTA.

Why are programmers so good at dancing? They have great algorithm.

Thank you to Kerry Donovan, who makes my words dance. I am eternally grateful to work with such a wonderful editor who shows such love for my stories. Thank you to the Berkley team, who are always dancing backward and in heels to make everything coalesce for our books. Thank you especially to Mary Baker, Dache' Rogers, and Hannah Engler, along with the Berkley creative team. There's a special space in the world for copy editors who do magic and make me realize I've never once in my life known the correct way to use commas. I appreciate you, Janine Barlow. Thank you to Addie Tsai for your thoughtful contributions. Finally, thank you to Ellie Russell and the Piatkus team in the UK.

0101011101101111011101110010000100001010
(Translation: Wow!)

Thank you to Monika Roe, who designed this exquisite cover. I never thought I'd be enamored with binary code, but you've captured this book perfectly, and I'm so grateful.

Spiders are excellent programmers.
They're just so great at debugging.

Thank you to Janine Amesta, Allison Ashley, and Rachel Mans McKenny, who helped me find this story and these characters. On top of the book being better after your feedback, the tent scene stayed in the book, and Cord stopped drinking so much Mountain Dew! Thank you for sharing your feedback and talents with me! Thank you to NTL for sharing your technical and gaming insight with me (and for being a dope human—I'm so excited to see how high you fly).

You're the stop condition
to my heart's search algorithm.

Great mentors make you feel like your concerns are valid, your victories are earned, and you can do anything. Thank you to Jen DeLuca, Priscilla Oliveras, and Ann G-T. There aren't really words that capture the 😍😍😍 feelings I have for Emily (aka Jill Patriarchy), Bethany, Tera, Kelly, and Ashley and all the Cardinal Women*, Jen, Matt, Jasmine, Aiden, Jacki, Amanda, Sahira, Kenyatta, Suzi, Libby, Regina, Brenda, and Brian. Whether or not you know it, you have kept me going, writing, and believing I can do it.

Without you, my world is null.

What would I do without the RFC and Better Than Brunch group chats? Luckily I don't have to find out. Thank you to Beth, Janel, Allie, and Tova. You're my turtles. I'm so lucky to have Charish Reid, Cass Newbould, and Taj McCoy—you're like mimosas times 1,000.

What kind of dogs do programmers have?
Computer Labs.

Thank you to the bloggers, BookTokers, Bookstagrammers, and everyone out there shouting about books, especially books by authors of color. Thank you for reading my books, but more importantly, thank you for making sure my TBR pile is hundreds of books deep. I appreciate your creativity, your energy, and your love of love stories. Thank you especially to the queens of Read It or List It, Phoebe (@readandwright) and Ashley (@_shelflove_); Mel Gill (@bookrecsbymel), the powerhouse behind Steamy Lit Con and Steamy Lit; Brit (@britreadsbooks), who will always make sure my TikTok feed is sprinkled with the very best teasers for romance novels; Marisol (@marisolreadsbooks), whose TikTok videos about my books have made me cry and given me life; and Gallane (@travelingloveReads), who may not know how much their Insta posts give me joy. If you love books, give these folks a follow—you'll be so happy you did.

A wonderful local bookstore is a blessing, and I am quadruple-blessed. Thank you to Dog-Eared Books in Ames, IA, and Storyhouse Bookpub, Beaverdale Books, and Reading in Public, all in Des Moines, IA. You do so much more than sell books—you advocate, you bring people together to find community, you help people escape into all kinds of adventures—and we Iowa authors are lucky to have you. And to anyone else reading this, they also sell books, and you can usually find signed copies of mine inside:

- Dog-Eared Books: dogearedbooksames.com
- Storyhouse Bookpub: storyhousebookpub.com
- Beaverdale Books: beaverdalebooks.com
- Reading in Public: readinginpublic.com

How many software developers does it take a screw in a light bulb? Zero. That's a hardware problem.

As always, thank you to my readers. This is my ninth book, and it's still wild to me that you are excited about spending time with my words—it's something that I will never stop appreciating. Thank you for falling in love with my characters and making them part of your day. Thank you to the Juicy Readers Group—you're a powerhouse group of bookish wizards and always make me smile.

Technically Yours

Denise Williams

READERS GUIDE

Discussion Questions

1. Pearl's tattoo is to remind her of important lessons she doesn't want to forget: do work that matters, put family first, and head before heart. If you were to get the same star tattoo, what lessons would your tattoo symbolize?

2. Cord is afraid of repeating his dad's mistakes and falling so in love he loses himself or gets hurt again. Pearl is afraid of falling in love after a relationship left her feeling unmoored and lost. How are their emotional wounds similar? How are they different?

3. The relationship between Cord and Tye was one of the author's favorite parts of writing the book, in part because Cord, as the mentor, benefited just as much as Tye, the mentee. Have you had a formal or informal mentoring relationship? What did you gain from the experience, and did it help you move toward your goals?

4. Pearl finds herself increasingly unable to resist the physical connection she feels for Cord. Have you

ever been in a situation where your physical and/or emotional pull to someone made you act out of character?

5. When they first meet, Pearl works for Cord's company, and the power imbalance of boss and employee is part of what keeps them at arm's length. In romance, do you enjoy reading about boss and employee affairs? What is the appeal or deterrent for you in reading about them?

6. Do you think Pearl overreacted to Cord's donating the money to OurCode behind her back? How would you have reacted in that situation?

7. Pearl sees herself as the sensible sibling. While younger sister Shea is free-spirited and often comic relief, middle sister Bri is characterized as adventurous and laid-back. How do you think the siblings complement one another? Do you see these dynamics in your own family?

8. OurCode's mission is to empower underrepresented kids to pursue careers in tech. What impact do real-world organizations like this (e.g., Girls Who Code) have on our workplaces, communities, and children?

9. Mason ends up being the person to give the best advice to Cord when he tells him, "Speak to your partner like you're speaking to your mechanic—talk about everything on the front end or you'll pay

for it later." Why is it sometimes difficult to take this advice in relationships?

10. What do you think happens to Pearl and Cord after the epilogue? How do you picture their lives looking ten years from the end of the book?

Keep reading for a special preview of

Just Our Luck

the next romance
from Denise Williams!

Sybil

YOU HAVE A MESSAGE FROM CARL K.

My sister eyed me from her spot across the table. "What are you doing?" Around us, the buzz of conversations grew. We were at a trendy bar where the energy of an increasingly drunk crowd was palpable.

"I'm just checking messages. There's a guy I've been talking to." I held up my phone as proof, and the screen glowed, showing the inbox for Hooked, the dating app. Well, dating wasn't what most people were on it for, but I was hopeful I could find love and a satisfying time. I clicked on Carl K's profile and motioned for Grace to look.

"Maybe save virtual guys for when you're alone and can't interact with actual people." She motioned around the bustling space. She didn't get it, though. Grace had met her fiancé in an old-fashioned, non-digital, inappropriate work flirtation kind of way. Since I lacked a workplace, that would be hard for me.

"This is a real person. He's not an android or something." I admired the cut of his jaw and his soulful eyes under thick, well-maintained brows. We'd been talking for a few days, and I was hoping we'd meet up soon. "I mean, I'm ninety percent sure I'm not being catfished. Plus, he has the most amazing eyebrows." He also had a real, grown-up job in finance; liked dogs; and didn't make me cringe politically. As far as I was concerned, he ticked all the necessary boxes.

She rolled her eyes again, looking away from me to scan the room, probably for Warren, her besotted former colleague. "I'm sure he's a dreamboat," she said dryly.

"I don't think you realize how judgmental you sound."

"Oh, no." She gazed at me over the top of her wineglass with a wry grin. "I do."

"Well, hate if you want to, but he seems to really get me. I think this guy is like me and looking for something real. Something deep . . . I don't know . . . this could really be . . . something, he's—" I'd started talking when I'd clicked on the notification about the incoming message from Carl K and now stopped mid-sentence.

Filling my screen was an out-of-focus, erect, and badly framed penis. The THUG LIFE tattoo on the pale white skin of his thigh highlighted his less-than-impressive and poorly groomed package. The text included only a question mark and a winking emoji.

"Oh."

"What?" Grace set her wineglass down on the table and stretched to look at my screen. "You're right. That really *could* be something. I guess the grooming stopped with his eyebrows."

Warren chose that moment to return to the table with a plate of food he handed to my sister. When she'd told me she was going out with a fellow dentist named Warren, I'd envisioned thick glasses, ugly sweaters, and a personality the flavor of plain oatmeal. What I hadn't expected was the smooth-skinned, deep-voiced, damn-he-works-out sweetheart who was going to be my brother-in-law.

Taking a seat next to Grace, he asked, "What could be something?" He followed Grace's gaze to my phone and paused. "Um, context? Whose dick am I looking at?"

"Sybil's soulmate," Grace said, popping a piece of cheese in her mouth.

I dropped my head to the table. "He seemed like a good guy. We talked about books and politics."

"I think if social media has taught us anything, it's that guys who send unsolicited dick pics can still care about politics." Warren's voice was as even as ever. With my head down, I didn't have to see him and Grace to know they were touching, being adorable, and each in no danger of receiving an unwanted genitalia photo from the other. Unless that was a new thing they were into. *Ew! Delete! I do not want to think about Warren's junk.* Sure, he was hot, but now he was basically my brother, so nope, nope, nope.

Grace reached across the table and flicked my arm. The grown-up, adult, sisterly way of comforting me, I guess. "We're just kidding. Sit up. Turn off your phone. We're out having fun."

I groaned but lifted my head. "I'm going to be alone forever."

Warren, his arm behind Grace's back, motioned to my phone. "I think if you want company, that guy seems available."

I groaned again and dropped my head back down.

This time, Grace patted my arm but then did a much more sisterly thing: she asked Warren to get me a drink.

I LEANED AGAINST my sister as we stumbled away from the bar. "All I want is a nice, normal guy. Is that too much to ask? Are there any guys left who don't send dick pics?"

"I don't," Warren offered, nuzzling my sister's neck. "Unless . . . do you want me to?"

I didn't wait for her response, reading enough of her reaction from her dewy expression. "Yech. Stop it. I hate you and your . . ." The word I wanted escaped me, so I finished with "love." I stumbled and regained my balance as we approached a Kum & Go gas station. In Des Moines, I grew up with them, so I never got the joke until I started college and my roommate from out of state thought it was hilarious. Years later, I could always buy her a birthday present on the cheap, since something from the gas station would make her day.

"Let's get you some water," Warren said, holding open the door. "And we need some more, um . . ." He and Grace shared a cute silent exchange before he walked to the aisle with condoms as we surveyed the water options.

"Aren't you on the pill?"

Grace plucked three water bottles out of the case. "I don't want a baby. Not yet, anyway, and birth control's not foolproof." She eyed Warren thoughtfully over a neat row of Cheetos bags, the level of affection in her expression far too significant for a gas station snack aisle.

"You'll make pretty babies," I slurred. "You will have a pulchritudinous stack of nerdy babies." I slurred the word almost beyond recognition, but even a little drunk, I wouldn't abandon my reputation as the family wordsmith and Scrabble champion. It was the only thing in my family I seemed to be best at. The only thing they acknowledged, anyway. No one appreciated my ability to sweet-talk my way into extensions on rent payments and sweet-talk my way out of speeding tickets. "A bevy of babies," I added for my own amusement.

"Not tonight we won't." We strode to the counter and met Warren, who was tucking something in his pocket—no doubt the aforementioned preventatives.

"That," I said, abandoning my image of their children and pointing to the illuminated sign advertising the current jackpot. "Forget men. That's what I need."

"You need seventy-five million dollars?" Warren raised his eyebrow.

"Yes. That's all I need! Seventy-five million dollars doesn't send you a picture of its dick instead of asking you on a date. Seventy-five million dollars never lies about being married or living in its mother's basement." I reached for my wallet. "I need seventy-five million dollars. And maybe a donut, too. Do you sell donuts that replace genuine human affection?"

The cashier shook his head slowly. He pointed to what could dubiously be called a bakery case where four sad, dry donuts rested, and I leaned my head on Grace's shoulder. "Nothing is going my way. I can't even get seventy-five million dollars and a donut."

With a shrug, the cashier added, "There's a place down the street open late that makes fresh ones, though."

I fished a few bucks from my pocket, and the cashier handed me the ticket, saying as he did so, "Maybe you'll get lucky."

AUTHOR PHOTO BY D&ORFS PHOTOGRAPHY

DENISE WILLIAMS wrote her first book in the second grade. *I Hate You* and its sequel, *I Still Hate You*, featured a tough, funny heroine; a quirky hero; witty banter; and a dragon. Minus the dragons, these are still the books she likes to write. After penning those early works, she finished second grade and eventually earned a PhD in education, going on to work in higher education. After growing up as a military brat around the world and across the country, Denise now lives in Iowa with her husband, son, and two ornery shih tzus who think they own the house.

CONNECT ONLINE

DeniseWilliamsWrites.com

NicWillWrites

NicWillWrites

AuthorDeniseWilliams

NicWillWrites